Great Britain

United States

r

a
Mission at Waiilatpu
Walla Walla River
Camp on Walla Walla River

a Mountains

✹ CAMPSITES

╋ MOUNTAINS

● TOWNS

ation

Snake River

THE
Brightwood
Expedition

THE
Brightwood
Expedition

KAY L. McDONALD

Kay L. McDonald

LIVERIGHT

NEW YORK

FIRST EDITION

THE TEXT *of this book is set in RCA Videocomp Times Roman. Composition, printing, and binding are by Kingsport Press, Inc.*

Library of Congress Cataloging in Publication Data
McDonald, Kay L
   The Brightwood expedition.
   I. Title.
PZ4.M13483Br [PS3563.A285]   813'.5'4   75–25793
                ISBN 0–87140–605–5

          1 2 3 4 5 6 7 8 9

To the memory of my
mother
who had a special kind of courage
and to Donna
who used to pretend with me

The Columbia River—
September 1842

MARLETTE was awakened by the shouts of the seamen and instantly caught the urgency in their voices. The barque gave a shudder, then surged mightily upward. From habit she gripped the bunk rails and knew by the violent pitching and agonized creak of timbers they were entering the mouth of the Columbia River. Her mind savored the knowledge that their sea journey was almost over, but the relief was short-lived. The real journey was yet to begin. The challenge to her physical and mental existence during the interminable eight months at sea had been merely a training ground for the challenges that lay ahead in the wilderness of the vast Oregon Country.

Unable to remain passively in her bunk, Marlette rolled out and, keeping a steadying hand on the rail, opened the salt-crusted porthole. The sun, already well up, reflected off tremendous jade green waves, almost blinding her unprepared eyes. Squinting against the glare, she could soon see a jagged spit of black, sea-scoured rocks curving out from the north shore and running parallel with the ship's course. Behind the rocks and across the roiled, sandy, gray-tinged water, so near the color of her unbound hair, she saw a grim, densely forested range of hills.

She came away from the porthole and dressed with difficulty as the ship plunged in the vicious cross-currents. Her dress hung pathetically on her tall, painfully thin frame. The tense slash of her mouth, once generous and full, twitched with weary annoyance.

Bracing herself before her small mirror, Marlette pulled her limp hair into its usual neat bun, lengthening her already long neck. The reflection showed how the months on ship had aged her. Large blue eyes, heavily shadowed with anxiety, looked grotesque in her gaunt face with its sharp, thin nose. She turned quickly away.

Slipping a shawl over her shoulders she left the cabin and mounted the stairway to the deck. A cool, damp breeze assailed her. It smelled of salt and sea, mingled with the odor of decaying sea life. Most of the men of the expedition were on deck, except for the frail Isaac Thompson. Rough seas left him green and shaken. The two strongest members of the party, Major Holliway, a retired veteran of frontier forts, and the brutish, arbitrary blacksmith, Evan Long, stood at the port rail. A few steps away from them lounged their would-be companion, Gaylord Taylor, young and obnoxious.

The ship sailed into quieter water, and Marlette released her grip on the door casing and moved to join two of the more likable members of the expedition. Herman von Hout, a rotund Pennsylvania dairy farmer and Andrew Proctor, a longtime friend of the Brightwood family, turned to greet her. Von Hout's round, pink face broke into a happy smile, his blue eyes crinkling merrily at the corners. He had insisted she call him Papa Hout.

"Goot morning, my girl. At last ve are here, ja? Vat you tink of Herr Lee's paradise?"

"Good morning, Papa Hout; Andrew." She won a shy smile from Andrew. "Just now I feel mostly relief at leaving the ocean at last."

Von Hout chuckled. "Just like a voman. See here vat a nice place it is."

He swept an arm southward across the rolling water toward a narrow, grassy plain lying between the golden sandbanks of the ocean and the high, timbered hills rising rugged on the east.

"You see dat grass? Vat a place for my cows! With green grass the whole year vat cheese and milk I could make. Now you tell her vat you tink of the trees, Andrew."

Andrew cleared his throat nervously. Giving opinions was something he was not used to, but lumber was his business and he knew it well.

"It looks very good from what I've seen. Of course the extensiveness of the forests and the quality of the lumber will have to be considered before I can really judge."

Marlette looked again toward the rugged hills, her eyes following the point of land that reached into the river. Her feelings in a turmoil, she watched as the ship sailed near the westernmost post of the Hudson Bay Company—the old Astor fort. This ill-fated attempt by John Jacob Astor to establish American dominance in this rich fur-bearing territory, although short-lived, nevertheless added substance to America's claim to the Oregon Country.

There were a few canoes drawn up below the post and people moved around the stockade. However, since the expedition was already long overdue because of unforeseen delays, they had decided not to stop here but sail as quickly as possible upriver to Fort Vancouver. Her first look at life in the West depressed her. The fort looked forlorn, as if rejected by the wilderness from which it had been carved.

Marlette turned away as she heard her father's voice. He was coming toward her with the ship's captain. She despaired at how old he looked. His face had sagged and his coat flapped ridiculously. Though his hair grew whiter and thinner daily, his spirit never failed. No matter what happened he remained calm and smiling, encouraging or pacifying his companions with unfailing good humor. Seeing the glow on his face and his confident step only made her more aware of their differences.

"Ah, my dear, here you are. Breakfast is ready."

"Good morning, Father; Captain. I'm afraid the sight of land is much more appealing right now than the cook's breakfast."

Her father chuckled as von Hout said, "Ja. But you come eat anyvay. A strong vind vould blow you avay."

The captain nodded in agreement. "Aye, lass. Ye should eat. Ye'll nae be able to walk the good earth if ye do nae keep up your strength."

She nodded and took her father's arm, following the others toward the steps. Her eye rested on the captain's solid figure. Her only regret on leaving the ship was that she would not see this flinty-eyed Scotsman again.

They found their places in the cramped dining quarters which smelled strongly of coffee and salt pork. Even Isaac Thompson joined them, looking pale, but well enough to complain. They had long since learned to talk over and around him. Marlette often felt sorry for him. He was a failure both as a person and a lawyer, but the partners in his firm were not. They had money and influence, and he was their emissary.

Today the excitement was evident in the men's voices as they neared their destination. Marlette didn't share their enthusiasm. Instead her mind drifted back to the beginning.

It had really begun when she and her father attended a lecture by Jason Lee of the Methodist mission in the Oregon Country. Lee had spoken glowingly of the richness and beauty of Oregon and the great things that could be accomplished if he had more money, more settlers, and United States protection for the Americans already in Oregon.

Jason Lee's fervent concern for the Oregon Country infected Joshua Brightwood. No amount of reasoning had sufficed to persuade him it was folly for a man in his fifties to become an explorer. He was convinced the ultimate destiny of the Oregon Country rested on the results of his expedition.

He recruited the unlikely members of the party through advertisements in the large eastern papers, hoping for men of considerable substance to finance the exploration. Although the response had not come in the quantity he had hoped for, at least each man had paid his way, and all had something valuable to contribute to the success of the journey.

During the voyage, the plans and ideas for the exploration of the Oregon Country became an obsession with all but Marlette and Gaylord Taylor. Gay was an unwilling volunteer. His father was a wealthy banker and often a financial friend in the early years of her father's struggling wagon-building business. Joshua could hardly refuse when George Taylor had asked them to take Gay along.

At first it had been beyond her understanding why any man would willingly suffer hardship, and possible death for no more reward than just having done it. But as she listened to them, week upon month, repeating their philanthropic and political motivations, she began to perceive the real humanity they wished to serve—themselves. Without exception, their incentives were selfish ones including her own. From the hero's glory that was Holliway's dream, to her own need to be indispensable to her father, they risked their lives in hopes of personal fulfillment.

She knew she should not be with them, and her insistence upon coming had almost dissolved the expedition. But in convincing them, she also convinced herself that she could be useful to the expedition. Her very presence would help convince the Indians and the British of their peaceful intent. She also shrewdly suggested that after a white woman saw the wild country and experienced the inevitable hardships, the Indians and British could be even surer that nothing would come of the expedition. A woman would surely discourage other women from coming to such a wilderness.

She had broken down their resistance, fully realizing that if she showed any sign of interfering or weakening they would send her back at the first opportunity. It took every bit of her self-discipline to remain outwardly calm and strong. Once, the captain told her she was a courageous woman. Marlette had laughed bitterly, glad for the darkness that hid the tears of frustration that came with the realization of the lie she was living. She had turned away from him with a shiver, afraid he would see her anguished face.

She remembered the feel of his hand on her shoulder and his voice, trying not to sound gruff, saying, "Courage comes in many forms, lass."

She had turned back to him, a powerful ache in her heart. "Thank you, Captain. I don't feel I deserve such a grand compliment, but it is nice to hear."

He had cleared his throat disconcertedly, resisting her unexpectedly feminine response to his praise, and retreated with, "Well, good night to ye now. I must check our course."

She had watched him walk away and she remembered the sudden wave of loss that had engulfed her. She had been so close to letting herself go into his arms, needing to cry and be comforted. With tears still brimming in her eyes, she had realized then what he must have known all along; she could not allow herself the indulgence of self-pity. Subsequently, she had pulled her guard even tighter.

Possibly understanding her better than she understood herself, he had not withdrawn from her, although he never spoke another word that could be mistaken for an invitation. Often he would stand on deck beside her in the darkness of night, sometimes never speaking, just offering the comfort of his presence. Somehow, that was enough.

After breakfast Marlette felt it was a good time to begin the log she was to keep during the journey. In her cabin she unbolted the small shelf which served as a writing table. In her neat, precise hand she wrote the date and "Entered the Columbia River this morning." Beyond that brief statement she was unable to find anything worth mentioning. She stared at the page, annoyed with herself. Surely there was something more noteworthy than the simple line she had written. After the better part of a year at sea there should be. She remembered some of the passages she had read from the Lewis and Clark journals. They had not been unable to find words to capture the mood of this wild land. Their descriptions had been written with worshipping hands, and she wondered if a woman saw only the harshness that would face any woman coming to live here and lost the beauty. She wondered what it was she lacked that she could not see the beauty as well as the challenge of this land as a man did. Or for that matter, what did any woman have that enabled her to follow her men to this wilderness. Was it love? Was this the awakening she needed? For years she thought she knew love and now realized that she hadn't known love at all. Her love had been bound in duty and in loyalty and how cruelly they had ruled her life. With swift perceptiveness she saw the emotionless vacuum that had been her life so far. Just hours ago she had been thankful for the encompassing numbness she had drawn around herself early on the voyage. It had helped her to endure the long, tedious days. But now she could see this shield had existed long before the start of their trip.

Her brother had died at an early age and her mother had lived only a few years more. Her once warm and loving father had buried himself in his work to relieve the double pain of his loss. With that warmth and love withdrawn from her, Marlette had tried to bring it back by replacing her brother and mother and by becoming indispensable to her father. She had nearly succeeded. She felt that he respected her and was proud of her, but his love remained unexpressed and she hungered for a moment of real warmth between them.

Until now she had allowed herself no regrets and only now was she aware that she had indeed missed something. She thought of the captain and tears sprang to her eyes. She despaired to think that she might very well die unloved and unfulfilled in a wilderness lurking with unknown terrors. If this journal were to be her only remains, she found it unthinkable that she could not find words to describe her burial ground.

She returned to the deck with new determination and paused, momentarily blinded by the blaze of brilliant sun after the dimness of the passageway. The healthy sea wind whipped her skirts and loosened a pale tendril of hair, as she made her way to the seat the seamen had built for her in the prow of the ship. Kneeling on the bench, she leaned far over until the wind-caught spray prickled her face, and looked upriver where a high, black rock promontory crowded the river toward the north shore. Her eyes followed the hills marching eastward from the shore to a white-mantled, cone-shaped mountain. That she found it serenely beautiful pleased her and she stayed in her seat, watching with increasing anticipation for what lay around the promontory that loomed closer and closer. The captain joined her as the ship rounded the cliff, changing direction. He removed the pipe from his mouth to say, "Yon is the Indian village your father wishes to visit."

Her forehead creased. "I wish we could be sure it was safe."

He chuckled at her worry. "These people are traders. They would rather bargain than fight. Something the white man has nae learned yet."

She shrugged the dread away and said, "Whatever, I'll want to go with them. Will you let me come with you?"

"Ye know I would, lass." Then was a gayer twinkle in his gray eyes he added, "But I must warn ye, they do nae wear much more than earrings and necklaces."

She felt the color rise in her cheeks as she replied, "Thank you for preparing me. Perhaps, we can set an example for these poor Indians."

The captain chuckled and shook his head. "The likes of us should be so poor."

"Why, Captain? Surely they don't have money as we have."

"No. But they are by nae means to be considered poor. Of all the ports in the world, the natives here are among the richest. Few of us so-called civilized humans can get by, working only a third of the year for our food, and take the rest of the year off to enjoy ourselves as these people do. Ah, look now! Yon are their houses."

She followed his pointed pipe stem upriver. They were approaching a large grassy island that choked the broad river into two narrow channels. Across from the head of the island, stood four large buildings of reddish brown wood. Except for some men working on a large canoe on the riverbank, there was little life in the village. But up a smaller tributary river, screened by thick groves of trees, billows of smoke rose into the air. It was hard to believe any uncivilized people could have built these large, sturdy, wooden structures. Before she could ask about them, Indians suddenly appeared from the woods. Several of them ran for the canoes pulled up on the bank and launched two.

The uncertainty she felt must have shown, for the captain asked, "I'll take ye below if ye wish."

Repressing her panic as the canoes surged through the water toward them, she answered, "No. I'll be all right."

He took her arm and they walked to where her father and the rest of the men were gathering to watch the oncoming canoes. Marlette turned her head away as they drew near. Gaylord Taylor was watching her with an amused smile. She squared her chin and looked back to the rail.

The first Indian was swinging over rail wearing little more than a broad smile of recognition as he greeted the captain. He was shorter than she, with a stocky body, wiry legs, and a forehead sloped like a pyramid.

After a brief exchange the captain interpreted, "Ye are invited to to the village."

Joshua smiled warmly. "Good!" he said. "Tell him we accept."

The captain turned back to the Indian with the answer. The Indian smiled and with surefooted agility, swung over the side and disappeared. The captain ordered the longboat lowered and in a few minutes they were in the water, escorted by the canoes to the village. Marlette sat primly, eyes fastened on the village ahead and the people gathering on the riverbank.

Andrew Proctor, next to her, breathed in awe, "Just look at their canoes, and those buildings!"

Evan Long snorted sarcastically, "Who's lookin' at logs. Look at their women!"

The captain cautioned, "Hold your tongue, mon."

They reached the village and the captain supervised the distribu-

tion of gifts they had brought from the ship. The Indians accepted
the brightly colored beads, fine steel knives and other tools, and gay
calico cottons with childish enthusiasm. It helped Marlette to feel less
uncomfortable and she began to observe the people with blushing
interest, finding a gruesome fascination in their oddly-shaped heads,
and noting the glass beads strung with shells that adorned their necks
and the complete outer rim of their ears. She didn't observe them long
for their head man soon sent them back to the woods behind the
village.

The Indian was talking to the captain and the captain advised,
"We've been invited to eat."

Her father quickly replied, "Let's not offend them by refusing."

Marlette reluctantly took the captain's arm and followed their
Indian host toward one of the dwellings. The doorway of the house
was a round hole about three feet above the ground. Gathering her
skirt awkwardly around her, Marlette stooped and stepped through
into the dim interior. Her sensitive nose picked up a medley of unpleasant smells.

They were seated on woven cattail mats on the hard-packed, dirt
floor. Their host ordered the women of the house to prepare food for
them. As Marlette grew accustomed to the dim interior, it was easy
to see the structure was not built by white men. It was as big or bigger
than her home in Philadelphia, which was not considered a modest
home, but this house was not partitioned although it housed more
than one family. It was built on a frame of massive cedar logs, sided
with upright cedar planks, and roofed with more planks. The open
ceiling of cross-rafters was hung with whole dried fish and other dried
food. Other household goods were stored surprisingly neatly on
shelves built around the walls of the building. The Indians did not
sleep on the ground as she had supposed, but had sleeping shelves
piled deep with robes of fur and feathers. Lower still around the room
were sitting shelves.

A wayward thought crossed Marlette's mind and she paled,
shocked that a lady could wonder how it would feel to lay naked in
a bed of feathers and fur.

The captain was saying, "These people have different eating customs. They rinse their mouths before eating and wash their hands.
They do nae drink water while eating, so 'twould be wise to drink

when they pass the water bucket."

The women came with water in wooden bowls and towels of fringed cedar bark. They rinsed their mouths and washed their hands, the men's eyes not missing the bronzed nakedness moving around them.

Gaylord Taylor eyed the women boldly and asked, "Say, Captain, do they ever sell any of their women?"

The captain replied, with a warning look, "No, Mr. Taylor."

Long laughingly commented, "It sure is hell when money don't buy everything, ain't it?" The sweat glistened on his forehead.

Marlette was glad the dimness of the room hid the warmth flushing her cheeks. In silence they waited until the women brought them small mats of food and small wooden bowls filled with a repulsive, fish-smelling liquid.

The captain, seeing her hesitate, whispered to her, " 'Tis just dried fish. They dip it in the oil like we would in gravy. 'Tis both sauce and frosting to them."

Gingerly she tasted the fish. It wasn't altogether disagreeable, though it needed salt. She dipped one small piece in the oil, but found the taste too medicinal.

As she ate she watched the men. Isaac Thompson picked suspiciously at the fish, but, surprisingly, said nothing. Major Holliway ate stolidly, but Marlette guessed he found it as distasteful as he did all things Indian. Gaylord ate like a gourmet, relishing his experience, while Andrew, von Hout, her father, and the captain ate politely, admiring the craftsmanship of the bowls and baskets more than the food. Evan Long, as usual, ate all there was and belched contentedly.

When they had finished, the water was brought around and they washed again. While they paused, the Indian questioned the nature of their journey and Joshua adroitly avoided a direct answer, not wanting to upset him. Then the captain explained that they did not intend to stay in the country, which seemed to satisfy their questioner.

Again the women came, this time carrying long wooden platters fashioned like their canoes, filled with sizzling salmon steaks which had been broiled on a fire outside. On the same platters were flat cakes of a bread-like substance and more fish oil.

Marlette asked the captain, "What is the bread made of?"

" 'Tis made of roots they dig. Could be thistle root or a bulb they call camas. 'Tis nae bad."

She took a small bite. Though the flavor was different and somewhat bland, it wasn't bad. The broiled salmon was much better than the dried fish, but also needed salt.

Once more they washed before the last course of their meal was served. The dessert was various dried berries served with fish oil. It would never take the place of Martha's homemade pie. The thought of their housekeeper, Martha, brought on an ache of homesickness and Marlette swallowed hard. When they had finished the women brought water for washing and drinking.

Joshua expressed sincere thanks through the captain and asked if they might see where the fish were caught. The Indian agreed and led them outside and along a trail through alder groves up the smaller river, until they came to a narrow place in the river. Here the men of the village had built a walkway across the river on sturdy poles driven into the river bottom. Underneath the water the poles were strung with netting made from the tough cattail reeds, forming a barricade. From the banks, canoes, and the walkway, the men speared salmon milling behind the net.

The smoke Marlette had noticed earlier was from fires of alderwood built under rows of wooden arbors where the salmon, split and wedged open, hung drying. A number of women were working the fish with their hands and rearranging them over the fires.

The visitors walked back to the village and stopped on the riverbank where a few of the older men were working on the large canoe they had seen when they first arrived. It was much larger than the other canoes and hewn from a huge cedar log. With an air of pride the Indian explained the work to the captain, who interpreted for the others.

He explained, among other details, that this was a whaling canoe, and like all their canoes was shaped by being filled with water. Hot stones were dropped into the water, heating it, so that the log could be wedged apart into the shape the Indians desired. The water was then dipped out and the canoe left to dry. The chief showed them a bow left in a nearby canoe and explained that the unique Cupid's curve was obtained in the same manner, by softening the wood in boiling water, bending it to shape, and letting the wood dry.

Andrew, taking it all in, examined the wood with an expert's eyes.

"Captain, ask him if he'll show me how they split this wood?"

Captain McNeal made the request and the Indian was soon driving several wooden and iron wedges into a nearby log with a stone hammer until the log split nearly full length. With little effort he pulled the slab away.

Andrew took the slab and exclaimed, "Just look at that! Straight as any board run through my mill." The Indian smiled at Andrew's admiring grin.

Marlette understood now why the captain considered these people among the wealthiest in the world. Their wealth lay in their environment.

The captain signaled for the long boat, and the Indian called to his women who brought gifts of brightly-colored, woven baskets; carved wooden platters and ladles; the Cupid's bow and arrows tipped with slender, barbed bone heads, and some beautiful shell necklaces. They loaded their gifts into the longboat, shook hands with the Indian, and returned to the ship.

The captain ordered them underway as there was still an hour or more of daylight left and enough wind to move them upriver. Marlette remained on deck and watched the village until the barque rounded a bend in the river. Slowly the tension in her dissipated and she sank onto her seat to watch the sun disappear behind the timbered hills. The captain joined her and she smiled at him.

"Good evening, lass."

"Good evening, Captain."

"Yon deer is a creature worth seeing, is he nae?" He nodded to the deer drinking at the water's edge, the impenetrable gloom of the forest behind them.

"Yes, they are beautiful. I don't think I could ever shoot one."

He smiled reassuringly. "Ye could, if it needed doin'."

His words reminded her of the life and death struggle that was a part of this wilderness and her smile fled. She asked, "How long before we reach Vancouver?"

The captain raised his head as if he could read the answer in the air and replied, "With any kind o' wind at all, we should nae be more then a day an' a half away."

"Will there be any more Indians to visit?"

"No. There's nae the Indians there used to be. The white man's diseases have thinned them out between Vancouver and the sea. At Vancouver there'll be Indians, mostly from east o' the mountains." With a chuckle he added, "They wear more clothes."

She said, "Thank heaven for that," her cheeks hot. Then she added, "They weren't half as frightening as I imagined. Do they really catch whales in those canoes?"

He smiled. "Aye. I would nae doubt the oil they served ye today was whale oil." If he was going to say more, it was forgotten in a sudden shout of warning that startled them both. The captain wheeled away from the rail, exclaiming, "Indians!"

Panic filled Marlette as she ran to follow him. He yanked the bell rope as he passed and the clanging was more shattering than shots in the night. He stopped near the stern and called out in the dialect he had used in the Indian village. The seamen were scrambling from below as Marlette peered over his shoulder and saw dark shapes gliding noiselessly around the ship.

The captain, remembering her, snapped over his shoulder. " 'Tis nae place for ye. Get below."

As she stepped back to leave a voice in the darkness shouted an order and there was an immediate ring of fire around the ship. Marlette stood transfixed as the voice shouted to the ship.

The captain swore under his breath, then answered the voice. One of the torches moved closer. The captain stepped back from the rail and told his second in command, "Tell the men not to let any more of the Indians on deck but what's in the first canoe."

The seaman hurried away as Joshua rushed up. "What's wrong, Captain?"

"Get your people up here, Mr. Brightwood. One of them's taken something from the village."

Joshua looked dismayed and turned away. The captain looked at Marlette intently a long moment, then asked, "Ye did nae take anything did ye, lass?"

"No. Of course not."

"I thought as much. Why aren't ye below?" He took her arm as if to lead her away. She resisted. "Please, Captain. I'd better stay."

He looked at her again, admiration in his eyes. The Indians were on deck now. They stood silent, their faces filled with suspicion and anger. She hardly recognized the leader as their friendly host of the afternoon. The captain was speaking to the Indians in a quiet, firm voice, trying to pacify them.

Joshua came up with the members of the expedition and the captain advised them, "The Indians are missing a medicine object from the village. If any of ye have it, ye'd better return it now." He eyed each man in the flickering light and all denied having taken anything.

The captain repeated their denials to the Indian leader. The Indian's mouth twisted downward, refusing to accept the denial. They talked heatedly for a few minutes. At last the captain agreed to the Indian's demands. He turned back to them.

"Ye leave me no choice but to let him search ye."

Major Holliway immediately balked. "This is highly irregular, Captain. We will not submit to a search by these savages. If *you* want to search, you have my permission."

"This isn't the Army, Major. He doesn't trust me any more than he does ye."

Gaylord Taylor smirked, "Captain, don't forget we are your passengers. You're supposed to protect us from all harm."

The captain snapped, "Mr. Taylor, I'm more concerned about my ship and my crew than your obnoxious hide. And since ye volunteered, ye can be the first to start stripping down to your skivvies."

Still enjoying the whole ordeal, Gaylord Taylor sat down on the deck and started removing his clothes. Reluctantly, they all submitted to the search, except for Major Holliway.

The captain turned to him when the rest had been searched. "Well, Major?"

Drawing himself up stiffly, Holliway coldly retorted, "You have my word, Captain. That should be good enough for any fellow officer."

The captain pulled a small pistol from under his coat and pointed it at Holliway. " 'Tis nae me that's doubtin' your word, Major. Now strip."

Holliway undressed, his eyes blazing with anger. Marlette wondered, anxiously, if she could escape the search, until the Indians, finishing with Holliway, pointed at her.

The captain tried to intercede but the leader stubbornly shook his head. Turning to her, he said gruffly, "I'm sorry, lass."

Aghast, she choked, "Surely, you don't expect me to undress here?"

"I have nae other choice."

She heard Gaylord Taylor snicker and turned on him furiously. "Gaylord Taylor, you're despicable. If this wasn't so serious, I'd think you planned this." With equal vehemence she faced the captain. "Can't you make these men go below?"

"I'm sorry, lass, I can't, but I can make them turn their backs."

Joshua protested. "Really, sir! This has gone far enough."

The captain turned to him. "Mr. Brightwood, we both know your daughter did nae take the thing, but they won't be satisfied unless they know it too."

Marlette controlled her indignation. "Father, it's all right. If this is what I must do, I'll do it." She started unbuttoning her dress.

With each garment the captain pleaded with the Indians. When she finally stood in her thin undergarments, the Indians were satisfied she hid nothing.

The captain turned to them after another discussion with the Indians and asked, "Before we search any farther, do any of ye want to give up the thing?"

There was a long silence while the men eyed each other suspiciously. Finally Gay stepped forward, looking amused. "Captain, I believe I have the object they're looking for. You'll find it in my cabin."

As Marlette stood frozen with anger, the captain, with a solid, smashing right, sent Gaylord crashing to the deck. Rubbing bruised knuckles with a smile of satisfaction, the captain turned to the Indians and told them their stolen object had been found. The Indians' smiles were almost as broad as the captain's. In a few moments Marlette saw the talisman brought from below. It was an uncarved gray stone shaped like a fish. An agate, looking very much like a real eye, glimmered from a hole in the fish head.

Gay moaned and struggled to a sitting position as the Indians disappeared over the rail of the ship. No one moved until the torches were plunged into the water and the swish of canoe paddles receded.

Marlette found her voice. "Father," she said vengefully, "I wish to recommend that Mr. Taylor be discharged from this expedition."

Gaylord struggled to his feet, a sheepish smile on his face. "Oh, come on, Marlette. It was all in fun."

The captain answered for her. "All in fun? Ye could've had us all burnt to a crisp."

"I wouldn't let it go that far, Captain. I'd've given it up if I didn't think you could handle it."

Captain McNeal grabbed Gay by the coat front and shook him. "I agree with Miss Brightwood, ye should be sent home. But not on my ship. Ye can damn well walk clear across the damn continent as ye'll never get passage on any ship I can spare from ye."

The captain stalked off, leaving Gay surrounded by a ring of angry eyes. Marlette turned away, leaving him to the men, disgust overwhelming anger.

Marlette stood on deck next morning as the ship got underway, gliding in a southeasterly direction, before the eastern sky had quite turned pink. She watched with growing pleasure as the sun splashed a shifting panorama onto another majestic mountain. The ship began tacking through a series of low gravel islands, changing her view. It occurred to her as she gazed at the overgrown islands, brighter green against the somber stands of timber, that she no longer felt as threatned as she had before by the gloomy stands of trees. With less anxiety than she had felt for days, she went below and began logging the events of the past twenty-four hours.

A subdued-looking Gay joined them for breakfast, his jaw swollen and badly discolored. She soon realized he had not changed, merely that his jaw hurt, hindering the appearance of his cocky smile.

Not too convincingly he said, "Gentlemen, and Miss Brightwood, I forthwith humbly apologize for causing last night's excitement. I promise, wholeheartedly, no more jokes if you will reconsider and not abandon me."

There was a heavy silence around the table. No one met his eyes. After a long while he sat down, his confidence wavering only slightly.

Joshua finally looked up and said, "Marlette, it is up to you whether he stays or goes."

She looked at Gay, remembering everything since he had joined them. Most of the memories were bad, but he had taught them French and kept them entertained with his jokes, stories, and songs gathered in his life of leisure in Paris and London. For herself she knew she would be glad to escape his ploys to seduce her, but for her father and his long friendship with Gay's father, she had to give him another chance.

At last she said, "He can stay, but not because he deserves another chance." She stood up abruptly and left the table.

She didn't see Gay again until supper. He was the same overconfident and clever Gay of yesterday. Already she regretted her leniency.

After supper Marlette returned to her seat on deck, watching the beautiful landscape with anticipation. The range of mountains, aligned from north to south, stood in majestic splendor. As she sat, intent upon the glorious view, Gaylord Taylor came up behind her.

"Good evening, Miss Brightwood."

Marlette looked at him and nodded coldly. "Good evening, Mr. Taylor." Immediately she turned back to the view, but Gaylord was not to be put off so easily.

"Magnificent country, don't you think? Those mountains remind me somewhat of the Alps."

Marlette murmured politely, "Yes, they are beautiful."

"You don't sound convinced. How do you really feel?"

She said icily, "I find it wild and forbidding."

Sarcastically he asked, "How *will* you get along without the good captain to protect you?"

"Well, I am certainly glad the captain was here last night. We need someone to protect us from your idiocy."

With a smile, Gaylord agreed, "You do need protection, but not from me. Which brings me to what I wanted to talk to you about. I'd like to take his place. After all, you and I are the only two on this trip who know we don't belong here. We're going to have to look out for each other."

She realized he meant well and repressed her anger. "Thank you, but you know what the plans are."

"Yes, I know. But do you really think any of them will be concerned about you when their own lives are at stake?"

Her anger returned and she retorted sharply, "My father would not let me be harmed."

He laughed derisively. "He's an old man. Without his glasses he can't see the end sight on the rifle. Be realistic, Marlette."

There was too much truth in what he said. Their eyes locked in silent appraisal; hers, coldly negative; his, confident and hopeful. The momentary silence was suddenly broken by the plaintive bawling of a cow. Marlette turned with surprise in the direction of the sound.

While they had been talking the ship had sailed into a narrowing channel. On the south bank she noticed cattle and horses grazing on lush meadows among groves of trees. It was such a welcome sight that tears sprang uncontrolled to her eyes.

Hopefully she asked, "Have we reached Vancouver?"

"The captain said earlier that the Hudson Bay Company had a farming operation on an island a few miles below the fort. This must be it."

The captain joined them at that moment and confirmed Gaylord's words. "Aye, 'tis Wapato Island. 'Tis always a welcome sight."

Still feeling very homesick, Marlette breathed, "Yes. For a moment it reminded me of the farms around Philadelphia."

Gay winked knowingly and said in a sly voice, "Well, I'll leave you two alone now. Don't forget what we talked about, Miss Brightwood." He bowed with mock gallantry and turned away.

The captain frowned disapprovingly. "Was he vexing ye?"

Relaxing, Marlette answered, "No. Not really."

She stood and stretched her shoulders, breathing deeply of the cooling air. They stood silently for a long while watching the sun set. The anchor rattled noisily and hit the water with a heavy splash. The sound of cattle and horses nearby was comforting and she looked forward to the next day.

The captain cleared his throat. She turned to him and found him gazing at her intently. "This'll be your last night on my ship, lass. Is there any hope ye'll change your mind? 'Twould pleasure me to show ye the world."

She was stunned for a moment, realizing just how much she had hoped for such an invitation, yet knowing she could never accept. She turned away quickly, hoping to hide what she felt. "No," she answered firmly, "I can't turn back now. I could never leave Father here. I think you understand."

She felt his disappointment as he returned, "Aye, lass. I understand." After a period of silence broken only by the puffing of his pipe, he asked, "I feel like a cup o' coffee. Will ye join me?"

She smiled in the darkness and answered, "Yes, thank you." He took her arm in his and kept his hand firmly over hers as they walked to the stairway that led below.

Fort Vancouver

THE SHIP'S CANNON boomed as they approached Fort Vancouver. Marlette, standing at the rail, looked with growing excitement at the imposing log stockade standing in the middle of a small plain. The ship docked and the crew began bringing up their equipment. They planned to buy only horses and fresh food at the fort.

The gates of the fort swung open and a group of men came out and were joined by a larger group of people assembling on the road near a village of cabins clustered a little distance to the west of the fort. As the crowd walked toward them, Marlette easily picked out their leader. He towered above the rest, his hair white and flowing, and he walked regally, seeming not to need the cane he had in his hand. She recognized him immediately as John McLoughlin, the governor of the vast Oregon Country.

The group waiting on the bank was a colorful one. There were dark-haired, swarthy French-Canadians in cotton shirts and leather leggings, wearing beaded moccasins and brilliantly colored sashes at their waists. Their Indian wives were dressed in a mixture of calico and buckskin and their children ran about in various stages of undress. Even more incongruous, but just as colorful, were McLoughlin's Kanaka house servants, from the Pacific islands, in cotton sarongs.

The members of the expedition assembled on deck with their baggage, dressed for the first time in months in their best clothes, and waited to disembark. Captain McNeal descended to the dock first to greet Dr. McLoughlin. There could be no doubt they were friends and countrymen.

McLoughlin's voice boomed, "Welcome, Captain McNeal. What have you brought me?"

"Friends from the States, Doctor." The captain turned to Marlette's father, now standing beside him, and Marlette quickly stepped to her father's side as she was helped from the ship. "Dr. McLoughlin, this is Joshua Brightwood from Philadelphia, and his daughter, Marlette."

McLoughlin extended his hand to her father and said heartily, "Welcome, sir. This is James Douglas, chief clerk for the Hudson Bay Company." Her father exchanged McLoughlin's hand for Douglas's as McLoughlin took hers saying, "It is indeed a pleasure my dear. We do not see many white women here."

Marlette felt the warmth rising to her cheeks and was grateful to curtsy deeply. The introductions went on and Marlette stood aside watching with awe as the chief factor for the Hudson Bay Company greeted each man with genuine warmth.

Finishing the introductions, McLoughlin said, "Come, come. You must be tired. My house is yours for as long as you wish. My men will bring up your luggage." He turned away, precluding all opposition. He was obviously master of all he surveyed and that now included their small company.

Marlette followed immediately behind Dr. McLoughlin, Captain McNeal, and Douglas, clinging tightly to her father's arm. Her eyes missed nothing as the procession walked up the slight hill. She would never have imagined a structure as large and impressive as the fort set in the midst of this wilderness. It was a huge rectangle, nearly twice as long as it was wide, built of sharpened logs near twenty feet high. Two large gates opened on the long south wall facing the river. The village to the west, although crude, was arranged in some semblance of order on narrow roads. The road they were walking on led north past the fort toward a low line of timbered hills, with a cultivated field between the fort and the road separating it from the cabins. In the area surrounding the fort there appeared to be an orchard and more cultivated ground.

Coming down the road some distance from them, Marlette noticed a man and a woman. Unlike the Frenchman she had seen, this man was dressed entirely in buckskin and carried a rifle in one hand and a basket in the other. The woman was wearing a bright calico dress and Marlette supposed she must be one of the few white women McLoughlin had mentioned. The couple separated and the woman took the basket and hurried across the field, disappearing into the orchard. The man stood watching Marlette's group as they proceeded toward the fort gates. She did not see the woman again.

As they passed through the easternmost gate Marlette was again impressed with the number and size of buildings inside the walls, although everything was unpainted and built of sawed lumber in post and sill construction. The only conspicuously different building was the one they were walking toward. It was a two-story structure, painted white, with a wide porch and lush green vines covering the posts. Two stairways curved gracefully upward from the ground toward the center of the porch. On the ground, facing the gate were two, black, ominous looking cannons with neatly piled cannon balls behind them, and even stranger was the profusion of bright marigolds blooming around the cannons.

Doctor McLoughlin stopped and turned toward the crowd following him. In a commanding voice he directed the luggage bearers to take the visitors' trunks to an apartment in one of the buildings and their other equipment to the storehouse they had just passed. Marlette's trunk and her father's were carried ahead to the two-story building by the Kanakas.

As the men dispersed, McLoughlin drew them nearer and quietly advised them, "It would be best not to mention the nature of your visit here, whatever it might be, to any of the men. After dinner, if you are not too tired, I invite you to my office for a talk. Until then, please make yourselves at home. If there is anything you need for your comfort let me know and it will be provided, if possible." Turning to Douglas, solemn at his side, he added, "James, see these men to their quarters and see that they are made comfortable."

With a curt nod, Douglas led the men toward their quarters. Dr. McLoughlin offered Marlette his arm and she and her father walked toward his home. She felt more awed by this man than any she had ever met. Even Jason Lee had not affected her as profoundly as this commanding person did.

Inside the house they entered an ample dining hall, where she was immediately struck by the elegance of the room. Above the polished surface of a banquet-sized dining table was a large, ornate, gold-framed mirror of such depth and clarity that she could see herself without distortion. There were also serving tables, a buffet, and a china cupboard, as well as a handsome black horsehair sofa by the window. It was hard for Marlette to believe that such luxury could exist in this wilderness.

McLoughlin stopped before a door and explained, "This is my apartment and Douglas has the other side of the house. You will stay here."

He opened the door and Marlette stepped into a sitting room. A stout, swarthy woman laid aside her embroidery and rose with an uncertain smile.

McLoughlin took her hand and brought her forward proudly. "This is my wife, Madame Margaret McLoughlin. She does not speak English. Do you, perhaps, speak French?"

Joshua smiled and answered, "A little. One of my men tried to teach us French on the ship."

McLoughlin smiled. "Good, good!" Then in French he said, "My dear, here are Joshua Brightwood and his daughter Marlette all the way from Philadelphia."

Her smile grew more certain. "Welcome to Fort Vancouver, monsieur and mademoiselle. You must be exhausted after your long voyage. May we show you to your rooms so that you may freshen up and rest before dinner?"

Marlette smiled and tried her faltering French. "Yes, madame. We must look travel worn."

Her father followed McLoughlin into another room and Madame McLoughlin led Marlette into a pretty, obviously feminine room. Lace curtains fluttered gently in the window and a dainty ruffled spread covered the double bed. There was even a mirror over the dresser.

For a moment Marlette hesitated. "I'm not taking your room am I, madame?"

"No, no! This is our daughter Eloise's room. She and her husband are in California now. May I have the servants bring up a bath for you?"

"Madame, you must have read my mind."

She nodded understandingly. "Please make yourself comfortable. I will order the bath."

Marlette unpacked her clean clothes the moment the door was closed. Water had been such a luxury on the ship. She had been able to wash clothes or bathe only on the rare occasions when the ship stopped for fresh water or food.

Several moments later two husky, smiling Kanakas carried in a metal tub and buckets of warm water. As soon as they left she lowered herself into the steaming tub and exulted in the sensual pleasure of a hot bath as she never had before.

Later, she stood before the window drying her long hair and looking out toward the buildings in the corner of the stockade. A man came out of one of the buildings and she noticed it was the same buckskin-clad man she had seen with the woman on the road when they had arrived. She knew it was the same man. His particular shade of dark chestnut hair was unmistakable.

She was about to turn away when another figure came through the door behind him and moved ponderously to catch up with him. It was a young Indian woman dressed entirely in buckskin and terribly pregnant. She caught up with the man and they talked. The girl tugged pleadingly at the man's sleeve and he finally allowed her to lead him into an alleyway between the buildings. Once between the buildings the girl turned and threw her arms around the man in what looked, to Marlette, like a passionate embrace. Marlette turned away in embarrassment but curiosity and something else she couldn't name compelled her to look again.

The man was trying to free himself from the girl's embrace and when he finally held the girl away she appeared to be tearfully pleading with him. She broke away from him and stumbled from between the buildings brushing away tears. For a moment Marlette couldn't decide what to think about the scene and then an awful thought struck her. Holliway had told them of the low moral character among the Indians and with rising disgust she wondered what kind of a man this was. She had seen him with another woman and yet here was this woman begging him for—she didn't know what. Was this his wife pleading with him to stop seeing the other woman? Or worse yet, was the other woman his wife and this one carrying his child and asking for help?

The girl disappeared out the back gate and Marlette turned an angry gaze on the man standing by the buildings watching the girl.

To Marlette's further irritation the man now followed in the same direction. Marlette turned away and stood brushing her hair furiously as she wondered if after rejecting the girl the man had now changed his mind and was going to give her some crumb of affection. She flung her hair back contemptuously and noticed her angry reflection in the mirror and after staring at it for a moment, burst out laughing. How silly and ridiculous she was to let something that was none of her business affect her so. She swept the scene from her mind but as she did so she studied her reflection for some hint of beauty in her gaunt face. Finding none she turned away, thinking herself a complete fool. She lay down on the bed and closed her eyes, relaxing.

Some time later she was aroused by a soft rap on the door. She quickly shook herself awake and went to the door.

Madame McLoughlin stood smiling up at her. "Pardon, mademoiselle, but dinner will be ready soon."

"I must have fallen asleep. I'll dress and be out shortly."

In a few minutes she was dressed and her hair combed into the neat bun. Feeling considerably better she went into the sitting room.

Madame smiled and said, "Ah! You looked refreshed. Our dinner will be served in here. It is the custom here for the men to eat alone."

"I will be glad to eat here with you, madame. I'm afraid I have eaten with men for so long, a woman's company will be a pleasure."

There was a knock at the door and madame said, "Entrez."

The door swung open and one of the smiling Kanakas carried in a large tray from which rose a mixture of delightful smells. He set the tray on a round tilt-top table near the window and Marlette's eyes reveled in the steaming plates of baked salmon and roast venison accompanied by—she could hardly believe her eyes—fresh vegetables. It was several minutes before she could stop eating long enough to compliment her hostess on the delicious food.

"Madame you have an excellent cook. And these vegetables! Do you raise them here?"

"Oui, mademoiselle. Burris will appreciate your compliments."

"I hope you'll excuse my rudeness if I don't talk and just enjoy this marvelous dinner. Fresh meat and vegetables were scarce on our voyage."

"Of course. I understand."

When dinner was over, Marlette began to take note of her surroundings. The delicate crystal goblet she drank from was a far cry from the tin cup she had on ship. In fact she could have been having dinner at a friend's home in Philadelphia.

"You have a far more comfortable home than I would've imagined, madame. I find everything lovelier than many I've seen in Philadelphia."

"Thank you. The good Doctor would not have me bear any discomfort."

"But don't you find it lonely living here?"

"Not at all. There is always someone coming."

"Are the only other women here the Frenchmen's wives outside in the village?"

"Oh, no. But I forget. You have not met Madame Douglas or Dr. Barclay's wife."

Marlette thought it strange she hadn't been met by these women. Madame must have seen her puzzlement and said, "Our men are very protective of us. We have learned to withdraw when any strangers arrive. You will meet them later."

Marlette suddenly remembered the captain and asked, "Is Captain McNeal still here?"

Madame McLoughlin's face fell. "Ah, forgive an old woman's memory. The captain came to say adieu, but when I told him you were resting he would not let me awaken you."

There was an increase in the noise outside the sitting room as the men finished their dinner. The door from the dining hall opened and John McLoughlin smiled in at them. "Miss Brightwood, your father tells me you cannot be left out of our meeting. Are you ready to join us?"

"Of course. Will you excuse me, madame?"

Madame nodded and Marlette was escorted into the Doctor's study. It was a good sized room, furnished tastefully and comfortably. As soon as everyone was settled, McLoughlin took the initiative.

"Gentlemen, and Miss Brightwood, we can now discuss your business here and how the Hudson Bay Company and I can be of service. However, I must warn you that I will not approve an endeavor which I feel will not benefit this country or which may be against the policies of the Hudson Bay Company."

They well knew from talking with Jason Lee what McLoughlin meant. While England had agreed to joint occupation of this territory with the United States it was well understood that the Hudson Bay Company considered Oregon its private trapping territory. While McLoughlin was hospitable to all who came to him, he nevertheless ruled his men and the Indians with a strong hand. Those who tried to bribe the Indians with whiskey were dealt with harshly and any other means of competition was soon doomed to failure because the French-Canadians had so well integrated with the Indians that few were willing to trade their furs to outsiders.

Marlette looked at her father and saw a confident smile on his face. The other men remained quiet and expressionless. They had all agreed that Joshua Brightwood would be their spokesman since his honest and sincere manner invariably won confidence in his listeners. Although the doctor's warning meant her father could not reveal the entire truth about their expedition she felt confident he would gain Dr. McLoughlin's approval.

"First of all, Doctor, let me assure you that we are not here to exploit the country or the people for personal gain. We hope that what we are doing will be of some benefit to both our countries. I'm sure you must know of the Oregon fever that has been spreading in our eastern states? Ever since Jason Lee toured our cities in '38 describing the beauties of this territory in his attempt to raise funds, hundreds, probably thousands, of people have formed groups and are considering a move to the Oregon Country.

"Many of these people lost everything during our recent depression and hope to begin a new life in the Oregon Country. Many can ill afford the gamble that they will be taking.

"These gentlemen and myself have formed this expedition in order to determine the feasibility of westward migrations, and to prevent, if possible, an unnecessary, ill-fated move, should we discover unfavorable conditions."

"Ah! I see," McLoughlin nodded gravely. "Yours is purely a philanthropic undertaking. I have heard of growing interest in this territory. Although some of the land is rich, I must, in all honesty, point out that tools are necessary to farm this land, and they would be costly to ship and impossible to bring by wagon across the mountains. Furthermore, the best land has already been claimed by retired employees of the Hudson Bay Company, so you need go no further."

"Yes, Mr. Lee said some of the French-Canadians had settled in the valley, but in such a large territory there must be more good land? And isn't it true, as Dr. Whitman claims, that a wagon can be brought over the mountains?"

McLoughlin laughed heartily and the men around Marlette shifted uneasily in their chairs. "Yes, yes. He has told me that many times. But he left his heavy wagon at Laramie and finally abandoned his two-wheeled cart at Fort Boise. So you see, even he himself has not done it. And as for good land, yes there is probably more. We are now farming some, north of here, but the Indians are stronger to the north, and to the east the country is vastly different and the Indians are even more hostile."

"Doctor, would you grant us permission to explore the country and decide for ourselves whether a wagon road over the mountains is possible or not?"

"Of course," the doctor smiled, "but my permission is unnecessary. Our countries have a joint occupation agreement."

"Thank you, Doctor. There is another matter; even though we have brought most of our own supplies, we still need to buy horses and some of our food from you. We were also hoping to hire a guide, if you can recommend a good man."

The bushy, silver brows knit together in a frown as McLoughlin thought for a moment. "The horses and food I can provide, but there is no French-Canadian here who would guide you. However, there has been a free trapper at the fort recently. If he is still here I can bring him to you."

"What kind of a man is he? We must have someone we can trust."

"I would not recommend anyone I didn't believe would do his best for you."

"We will leave our lives in your hands then, Doctor."

McLoughlin smiled benevolently at them and rose, signaling the end of the discussion. "Very well, gentlemen. Will you join me in the bachelors' quarters, if Miss Brightwood will excuse us?"

Marlette rose and nodded silently. The doctor escorted her back to the sitting room where Madame McLoughlin was again embroidering. Marlette, feeling restless, soon excused herself, and retired to her room to go to bed.

She was roused the next morning by a bell in the yard and opened her eyes to a cool sunlit room. Dreamily she watched the pattern the curtain made as the sun shone through it. A knock at her door brought her out of bed.

"Good morning, mademoiselle. Breakfast will be here soon."

She yawned, "Thank you, madame. I'll get dressed immediately."

She heard madame's soft "Oui" through the door and forced herself to dress. Presently she heard the sound of breakfast arriving and opened her door expectantly, gazing eagerly at fresh milk, eggs, tender wheatcakes, and smoked ham. She felt guilty about taking a second helping but madame urged her on saying, "Please, mademoiselle. You eat now, while you can. Too long, I think, you have not eaten."

Sipping tea after their breakfast, Marlette asked, "Would it be possible to see your gardens and the rest of the fort?"

"Of course. I'm sure our gardener, Bruce, would be glad to show you. He gets so much pleasure in showing off his hard work. I will call him now if you like."

"If it isn't inconvenient."

"No, no. I'm sure not."

Bruce was sent for at once, and madame introduced them explaining that Marlette wished a tour of the fort and gardens. His strong face softening at her delight, he led her westward toward the buildings that divided the yard into two distinct areas. It appeared that the fort area had once been only half as large. "Was one part of the fort built before the other?" Marlette asked.

"Aye. We've more than doubled the size of the fort since we first built it. These two buildings on the north are the pastor's house and the school building. Toward the center is the clerk's office and there, now, ye can see the bell."

They walked between the office and another badly decayed structure that Bruce indicated had been a chapel for a while.

"Used to be a carpenter shop there, too, but 'tis already torn down. That's a granary on the north wall and there are stores along the west wall." He pointed to a brick building tucked into the southwest corner. "That 'tis the powder house and on the south wall we store furs. On this side of the gate is our hospital and a trading area for the Indians."

At her request, Bruce then led her to one of the buildings and they stepped into the dusky light of the store. It was a rough reproduction of a general store in Philadelphia. Plank tables were piled with everything from traps to harness. There were even bolts of calico and fine-steel needles. She discovered a bolt of beautiful silk, undoubtedly from China.

A young clerk with a thick Scottish brogue showed her fur pelts, smoothing them out on a small marble-topped table that could have graced any fashionable home in the States.

An Indian woman entered the store with her young children who were several shades lighter than she. The clerk went to help her and Marlette watched with fascination as they conversed in a mixture of French and Indian. The woman purchased some food and some of the cotton material Marlette had admired earlier. There was no money exchanged, but the clerk wrote everything down in a ledger.

They left the store and walked through the well-tended gardens and orchard beyond the stockade walls. Bruce pointed with pride to the large crop of apples and other fruits ripening in the September sun.

Marlette heard a voice calling and turned to see one of the Kanakas coming toward her.

"Doctor want Miss Brightwood," he said, somewhat out of breath. "Now."

Bruce said, "Tell him we're on our way."

The man's grin grew broader as he nodded and trotted slowly back into the stockade, Bruce and Marlette at his heels. As they all entered the dining hall, the doctor turned and smiled at her.

"Ah, here you are. Did you enjoy your walk?"

"Yes, thank you. Your orchard and garden are without compare."

Bruce beamed proudly and McLoughlin said, "Bruce does a splendid job." He turned to the men of the Brightwood party gathered near the fireplace and said, "Come in to my office, gentlemen." Marlette took his arm and led the others into the office, where McLoughlin waited till they were all seated and then announced, "I have good news. The man I told you about yesterday is still here and I have sent someone to bring him to meet with you."

At that moment there was a knock at the door and McLoughlin called, "Entrez."

The door swung open and a man strode into the room. He was tall and well-built with thick chestnut hair that curled very slightly above his buckskin shirt and Marlette felt a rush of dislike spread in her. This was the man she had seen with the white woman and the Indian girl. Her hand clenched into a fist in her lap as she appraised him with suspicious eyes, taking in every detail from the solid, muscular body to the deeply bronzed face and the hands cradling a rifle.

He stopped just inside the door, his dark eyes sweeping the room boldly, taking in everything and revealing nothing. He looked more like an Indian than a Frenchman although his features were not similar to those of the Indians she had seen. His nose was straight, lacking the width and flare of most Indian noses and his mouth, above a wide, square jaw, was unexpectedly full. Two objects hung around his neck on leather thongs. One, a small, strangely decorated skin bag, dangled against his bare chest. The other, a copper medallion, hung below the laced opening of his shirt.

Doctor McLoughlin rose and said in English, "Chesnut, here are Joshua Brightwood and his daughter." The man did not reach to shake Joshua's hand. Only his eyes moved, flicking over Marlette briefly as he nodded silently to her father, glancing keenly at each man in turn as McLoughlin introduced them.

McLoughlin sat down and Joshua smiled as he prepared to interview Chesnut.

"Mr. Chesnut, Doctor McLoughlin tells me you might be interested in guiding us through the Oregon Country. Can you give us some idea of your knowledge of the area?"

Marlette didn't know what she had expected his voice to sound like, but she was not prepared for the softly husky, unaccented, and perfectly intelligible answer.

"I've been over most of the country on both sides of the mountains."

Joshua smiled, unabashed by the lack of detail. "Under what conditions and at what price would you possibly consider guiding us to the Rocky Mountains and back?"

"Does the woman go?"

"Yes."

"I don't advise it."

Joshua laughed. "I'm afraid none of us has succeeded in convincing her of that."

"Then you'll have to find somebody else." He turned away, his hand reaching for the door.

Joshua strode to the door, anxiety straining his voice. "Sir, I'm sure we can make it worth your while. My daughter, I assure you, will not be a burden. And she is necessary to the expedition."

Chesnut turned and scrutinized Marlette boldly. Anger flared in her and she couldn't restrain it or control the unreasoning dislike she felt for this man. She heard Holliway stir restlessly beside her and glanced at his face. She was not the only one who distrusted Chesnut.

Her father was saying, "Please state your conditions and price and we'll see if we can meet them."

He answered without hesitation, "If I accept I must be in complete command and the woman would have to stay here. My price is five hundred dollars in gold or silver to be left with Doctor McLoughlin before we leave."

Major Holliway jumped to his feet. "What are your reasons for insisting on complete command?"

Chesnut turned calmly toward Holliway, his eyes missing none of the major's contempt. "I can't be responsible for anyone unless I know they'll do as they are told."

"We're not a group of irresponsible greenhorns. We have some idea of what to expect and we will act accordingly."

There was a detectable gleam in his dark eyes as he replied calmly, "Then you don't need me."

Joshua broke in, his voice placating, "You misunderstand, Mr. Chesnut. We *do* need a guide and I'm sure we can come to some agreement."

"I have stated my terms."

Soothingly Joshua asked, "Are they entirely necessary?"

"For your safety and mine, yes."

"What do you consider our greatest hazard?"

"Everything."

Joshua tried not to show impatience, "What about the Indians?" he asked. "Are they friendly?"

"When it benefits them."

The major broke in again. "I see you wear an Indian medicine bag. Where did you get it?"

"It is mine."

Holliway scowled. "What is your relationship with the Indians in the area we want to explore?"

"I walk as a brother in most of the villages."

The major's scowl deepened and his eyes narrowed, "Are you a blood brother?"

With no change of expression Chesnut answered, "I was born in a village of the Sioux."

The major stiffened visibly and his eyes blazed with undisguised hatred. He turned to Joshua and declared, "I can't accept this man."

Gaylord Taylor spoke, frank amusement in his face and voice, "I think, Major, that you have no choice. You heard McLoughlin say there is no other guide."

The major was about to retort when McLoughlin stood up. "Now then, gentlemen," he said firmly, "let us settle this without argument. I'm sure you'll agree, Mr. Brightwood, that the only way is to discuss this among yourselves and do what you Americans do when making decisions—take a vote. If you'll excuse us?"

No one spoke as McLoughlin swept out taking Chesnut with him. Marlette sighed and unclenched her fists.

There was a long silence as the men tried to relax and consider their decisions. Marlette had already made hers, and her thoughts turned to the man. His speech was educated, but he said he had been born in an Indian village. It was entirely possible he was neither white nor Indian but a half-breed.

Joshua interrupted her thoughts, "I think McLoughlin is right. We'll have to take a vote. I have the major's vote. Gaylord, do I assume your vote is yes?"

"Right. We have no other choice if we want to complete this expedition."

"All right. Anyone else ready to vote?"

Smiling gently, von Hout stood up. "I wish to vote. Gaylord is right. If ve vant to go on ve must accept this man. I don't tink the good Doctor vould send us vit a man he didn't trust."

Von Hout sat down and Isaac Thompson rose, stretching himself as tall as his banty rooster body could reach and pacing nervously.

"I don't agree with von Hout or Taylor," he said, waving his arms theatrically. "McLoughlin would have everything to gain if we didn't survive our trip. For years the British have wanted possession of this territory and it wouldn't surprise me if he hired this man to lead us off into the wilderness and kill us."

Evan Long jumped up angrily and forced the smaller man into his seat, shouting, "Well no damn Britisher or his skulking Injun hireling is keepin' me from doin' what I set out to do. There's only one of him and seven of us. One of us can keep an eye on him day and night. He couldn't pull anything with us watchin' him. I vote we go on with what we came to do." He turned to Proctor and bellowed, "Well, Proctor, what do you say?"

Andrew Proctor cleared his throat nervously and with a somewhat quavering voice that grew stronger as he talked, declared, "I'm afraid I don't relish being led into the wilderness by a man we know so little about. I do know more about the major, and I'll have to trust his superior judgment in this matter."

Long gave Proctor a scathing look and turned expectant eyes on Joshua. Joshua turned to Marlette and asked, "And your vote, daughter?"

"I don't wish to vote."

"Why not? This matter may mean life or death for all of us."

"My vote would be prejudiced by events outside of this room."

"But how can that be? None of us has seen this man until today."

"Please, Father, I don't wish to discuss it. I don't want to vote."

Joshua shrugged his shoulders in bewilderment and she noticed Gaylord Taylor watching her with keen interest. The others also looked at her with questioning eyes, but she held herself aloof and turned toward her father.

"Well," he said at last, "that leaves only my vote. I'll have to agree with Long, Taylor, and von Hout. We came this far to do a thing we all felt was important to thousands of people back in the States. McLoughlin has offered us every kindness and I think he is above plotting our deaths. As Chesnut stated there are natural enemies to take care of us. I think we can watch this man closely enough to prevent his abandoning us. The only thing we can't control is any contact with the Indians, but we all knew there would be risks when we formed this company. Any of you who voted against Chesnut can feel free to resign up until the time of departure. After that we will all have to work together regardless of our votes. Agreed?"

Every head nodded agreement. Joshua stepped to the door and called McLoughlin and Chesnut back into the room. McLoughlin immediately took the initiative.

"Well, gentlemen and Miss Brightwood, have you come to an agreement?"

Chesnut stood impassively while Joshua replied, "We have agreed to hire Mr. Chesnut, but we *must* take exception to his terms. My daughter will go with us, and we reserve the right to discuss and approve any commands we do not agree with. Will you agree to that, Mr. Chesnut?"

Chesnut stated coolly, "No."

Beginning to look perplexed, Joshua asked, "Why, sir?"

"This is no trip for a white woman and there won't be time to discuss commands."

Joshua, growing irritated, said loudly, "We need more explanation than that."

Chesnut explained, his eyes narrowing, "There won't be a need for orders unless there is trouble, and when there is trouble there won't be time to discuss orders. You will be going through rough country for a man, let alone a woman, and this late in the season the weather could change overnight. We may have trouble with the Indians, and a white woman would be a prize worth fighting for. None of you would be able to protect her."

McLoughlin commented, "Everything he says is true. It would be against my better judgment to take a woman on such a trip."

Joshua nodded in acknowledgment. "We all know the hazards. My daughter is not afraid, and we are equipped with superior guns capable of withstanding any kind of attack. When you see them I know you will understand my confidence. We have all been trained to use these weapons, even my daughter. Now, sir, is there any possible condition under which you *would* permit my daughter to go? More money perhaps?"

Chesnut turned probing eyes on Marlette and she felt uncomfortable under his penetrating gaze. "Yes," he said at last, "and if I decide she can go she will have to be in my complete charge."

Joshua's face relaxed and a slight smile touched his lips. "That sounds reasonable."

Marlette jumped to her feet, shocked. "Father! I will not be in this man's charge."

Before Joshua could answer, Chesnut said flatly, "You will, or you will stay here."

Heatedly she retorted, "I refuse to stay here."

Chesnut looked at Joshua. "Then you'll have to get another man." He turned toward the door, and Marlette saw two years'-worth of plans fade to nothing with his departure. In a split second her mind registered every look in the room. Her father's face fell in total dismay. Holliway was still angry, but faintly disgusted too. Von Hout shook his head sadly and Andrew Proctor turned his eyes downward in rejection of a temperament so nearly like his wife's; a temperament he had tried to escape. Isaac Thompson glowered while Gaylord Taylor looked slightly amused. Evan Long seemed ready to burst into a profane rage and McLoughlin was frowning.

Marlette swallowed hard and lifting her chin defiantly, said, "Wait!" Chesnut turned an indifferent gaze on her. "Just what do you mean when you say I am to be in your complete charge?" she asked.

"You will take orders from me and obey those orders without question. Can you take orders?" She detected a gleam in his eyes. His insolence was almost more than she could bear but she answered determinedly, "Yes."

"All right, then, your first order is to stay here."

Clenching her fists she stormed at him, "I'll obey any order but that order. I am necessary to this expedition and I intend going. If you don't want our money, I'm sure we can find someone else who does."

Unconcealed amusement flickered in his eyes, and hearing a chuckle from Gaylord she realized she had just agreed to his terms. She sat down, suddenly shaken.

Less arbitrarily he said, "No matter who takes you, your own men won't want to turn back once they've started."

"I realize that," she said, soberly, "I don't intend to turn back. I'm prepared to do my share on this trip."

Joshua Brightwood placed a proud hand on his daughter's shoulder and added, "You can depend on what my daughter says, Mr. Chesnut. She is made of sterner stuff than one would think."

There was the barest suggestion of humor in Chesnut's voice when he said, "She'll need to be," but his eyes were grimly serious.

McLoughlin spoke again. "Your horses will be here in the morning. We can gather your supplies as soon as you wish."

Chesnut asked, "Who's bringing the horses?"

"Tom McKay."

"We'll talk later. Don't pack anything until I return." He turned and left the room.

Holliway sprang to his feet again. "That impudent—!" He checked himself remembering Marlette's presence. "Where is he going?"

"Calm yourself, Major. I imagine he is going to select your horses."

"I wish to be allowed to do that myself."

"Believe me Major, Chesnut is far more capable of choosing what you will need for your journey."

McLoughlin continued, "It is almost dinner time. I suggest we relax, and after dinner we can look at your supply lists. This evening I have arranged a social for you in the bachelors' hall."

Joshua responded, "Thank you, Doctor. I'm sure we could all use a little diversion before our departure."

"Good. Miss Brightwood, I will be honored if you would have the first dance with me."

"Thank you, Doctor, I'd be happy to."

McLoughlin smiled broadly and stood up, ending the meeting. Marlette gratefully retired to her room and lay on the bed trying to forget about Chesnut, and regain her composure. She wondered if she would have judged him so harshly had she not seen him prior to the meeting. Although she knew she would have been fairer, his easy self-possession, and his assumption of control would have infuriated her anyway. She relaxed only after coming to the decision that she would be wary of him, and watch him closely, too.

It was getting dark as she walked with her father and the McLoughlins toward the bachelors' hall, already noisy with sounds of music and laughter. The French-Canadians were singing their rousing voyageur songs accompanied by fiddles and mouth organs.

When the doctor crossed the threshold the music stopped and the men turned expectant eyes toward the door. Marlette's cheeks flushed as she found herself the object of their attention. Two dark-haired women dressed in white women's clothes but obviously of Indian heritage moved toward them. She was sure the younger, slimmer woman was the one she had seen with Chesnut on the road the day they arrived.

"Ah, how lovely you look tonight, Maria." The young woman smiled. McLoughlin continued, "Miss Brightwood, Maria is Doctor Barclay's wife, and this is Madame Douglas."

Both women curtsied slightly and murmured greetings in French. McLoughlin signaled the musicians to play and she was swept onto the floor by the stately doctor.

The next hour seemed a fantasy as she whirled around the floor, dancing with each member of the expedition and some of the braver clerks, amidst the Indian women and their boisterous French husbands.

At last she escaped from the warm, noisy room and stood outside in the cool night air. The stars were bright and close overhead, the moon silvering the buildings in a faint glow. She remembered seeing a well on her walk that morning, and the thought of cool water for her face and hands drew her across the empty, shadowy yard.

She found the well at the west end of the granary and lowered the bucket. She dipped her handkerchief into the cool water and patted her face and arms. The water felt so good that she failed to notice a figure coming toward her from the gate in the south wall.

"What are you doing out here by yourself?"

Marlette whirled around, knocking the bucket into the well in fright. She almost screamed but caught herself in time and turned to face the man who had startled her, recognizing Chesnut's voice and figure. With great effort she brought herself under control and asked, "Why? Isn't it safe here?"

"It might not be."

"You don't waste words do you?" she snapped.

"Usually I don't need to."

"I didn't realize I was in danger, at least not under McLoughlin's command. Would you mind telling me what I'm in danger of?"

She thought she noticed a brief smile on his face before he answered. "Not even McLoughlin can protect you when you're out of
his sight. In this country you must always stay on guard."

"Thank you. I'll try to remember that." Then, trying to be fair
to this man, she asked in a friendlier tone, "Are you coming to the
dance?"

"No." He paused, and matching her attempt to be friendly, added
"I don't dance."

She nodded and turned away, walking back across the yard. She
felt his eyes on her and knew that he followed her until she was safely
back in the hall, yet when she turned in the doorway she could see
nothing.

Late next morning the horses arrived, and everyone gathered to
see them. They were driven to a corral and Chesnut and a tall, dark,
thin-faced man stood near them.

Chesnut walked toward Joshua and introduced the man as Tom
McKay, adding, "You pay him for the horses."

Joshua extended his hand and the big man took it briefly. "They
look like fine stock, Mr. McKay. Do you raise them here?"

"Yes. I have a couple of farms across the river."

"Are they broke to ride."

"Either ride or pack. Ross, here, saw to that."

"Excellent. How much do we owe you?"

"Fifty dollars a head and I'll buy them back when you return for
twenty-five dollars a head."

"That sounds fair enough. Can my people look them over for
approval?"

"Go ahead. I'll be up at McLoughlin's."

The men began saddling and riding each horse in turn and Marlette watched Chesnut carefully. She had to admit that he handled
the horses better than Long. He had a gentle firmness that the horses
responded to with calm respect.

When the horses were all approved, Joshua went to settle with
Tom McKay and turning to Holliway he said, "Major, will you and
Mr. Chesnut go over the supplies and maybe we can get packed and
on our way by morning."

After dinner everyone brought their packs to the dining room. Lists were made of things to be bought from the fort store. Items Chesnut considered unnecessary were taken out of the packs to conserve space since they each had only one extra horse to carry all necessary food, utensils, extra ammunition, and trade goods. When Chesnut got to Marlette's pack he pulled out everything she had painstakingly chosen to take. She was determined to remain calm until she saw him set aside her small tent, spare tarp, and extra clothes.

She protested vigorously, "I need those things. Surely we have enough horses to pack everything?"

"The less weight your horses carry, the longer they'll last. Your life may depend on it."

Joshua spoke up in Marlette's defense, "We can manage the tarp and one change of clothes. We'll leave something else behind if we need to."

Chesnut shrugged his shoulders, stood up and turned away. Marlette, flushed with anger, looked after him.

Her father patted her shoulder. "Don't worry. We'll manage it even if we have to get another horse." He followed Chesnut toward the warehouse where their supplies were stored.

Marlette resentfully stuffed most of the discarded articles into her trunk to be stored at the fort, but left out one bar of soap, a towel, a hairbrush, hairpins, and a comb. She closed the trunk without a second glance, vowing to make the best of things. She asked one of the Kanakas to take the trunk away and retired to her room.

The next morning everyone was awakened before sunrise. The horses were brought into the stockade and Chesnut began assigning them. Holliway, without waiting for Chesnut's approval, took a trim little buckskin from where it was tied. He had started saddling it when Chesnut stopped him.

"Pick another horse."

Holliway reddened immediately. "You're carrying your command too far. I'll choose any horse I want."

Chesnut pulled the saddle from the buckskin's back and dropped it on the ground. "Any horse but this one. This one is for the woman."

He led the horse away from Holliway, handing the reins to Marlette, and chose a small bay for Holliway. Joshua appeared and took the rope from Chesnut, attempting to placate the angry major. Marlette had to marvel at the man's audacity and wondered how long it would take before one of the members of the expedition took a swing at him.

Everyone was saddled but Marlette. Gaylord Taylor, never missing a chance to impress her, came over to help. Chesnut was right on his heels.

"Everyone takes care of his own horse, Taylor."

"But she's a woman."

"Not on this trip she isn't." His eyes flicked quickly to Marlette and studied her disapprovingly from head to toe. She wore the latest in fashionable riding clothes. A grandly veiled, high, silk top hat was perched on her head. Her black, fitted jacket, complete with white cravat, topped a gathered skirt that contained so much yardage it would drag the ground when she was mounted.

"Is that the only outfit you have?"

"Yes," she answered stiffly, squaring a chin that almost matched his in physical dimension.

"Come with me." He turned and strode toward the McLoughlin house. Gay grinned at her slyly, but the grin fled when Chesnut turned to see why she wasn't following him. She reluctantly went toward him, remembering unhappily that she had placed herself in his charge.

He knocked on the McLoughlin door and when a Kanaka answered he asked for Madame McLoughlin. She came from her sitting room in a few moments and Chesnut spoke to her in perfect French.

"Madame, I need your help. Miss Brightwood has no other riding clothes but these. Can you make these more suitable?"

Madame looked at her and smiled. "Oui. Come, mademoiselle, and we shall remodel your costume."

Chesnut said, "Give me the hat."

Marlette removed her hat and handed it to him. She gasped in protest as he tore the veil from the hat and handed the ragged material to her.

His indifferent eyes reminded her of her place, and she stood, furious, as he took the hat and left. Madame McLoughlin touched her arm and she followed her into the sitting room to have her skirt remodeled.

The process of remodeling Marlette's skirts detained them until the next day. She had another good night's sleep and another pleasant breakfast with Madame McLoughlin, although Marlette was beginning to find her appetite faltering. Madame McLoughlin tried to reassure her.

"Do not worry, mademoiselle. The women here make long trips often by horse or boat. To us it is a great occasion. But if you wish to stay, there is time to change your mind."

Marlette shook her head. "No, thank you, madame. I must go. And thank you for your hospitality. I will look forward to coming back here after weeks on the trail."

Madame smiled understandingly and they went to join the men assembling in the yard.

They found Gay saddling the buckskin with a man's saddle. He winked at Marlette grinning, "Orders from headquarters." His eyes, taking in her barely ankle-length divided skirt, brightened with approval.

Chesnut approached and handed her a beige broad-brimmed hat, complete with leather strings to tie under her chin. Without a word he turned to the horse and checked the cinch, looking toward Gaylord. She knew by his look that the next time she had better be prepared to saddle her own horse.

The Trail East

CHESNUT MOUNTED and started off, leading a packhorse. The rest of the party lined up to follow him, Marlette guiding her horse to follow her father's. The McLoughlins and Douglases stood on their porch, the doctor waving his cane in a farewell salute. Outside the gates the French-Canadians and their families were gathered, singing and waving adieu as the expedition trotted eastward across the plain, the sun in their faces, the snow-capped mountain across the river standing guard over them.

A few miles upriver, riding on small, timbered hills, they passed the fort sawmill, and a mile later, the grist mill. Eastward, Marlette could see bluffs rising from the water's edge narrowing the river into a gorge, while just ahead a smaller, timbered river course wandered in from the north to join the Columbia.

Chesnut stopped at the river and rode back toward Marlette. "You'll need help to cross this river," he said dryly, "I'll take the packhorses over first and come back for you. All of you stay here until I get back."

He took her packhorse, tied it to his own, and started across the river. The horses waded easily for several yards, then plunged into a deep channel and had to swim, seemingly losing to the current that swept them downstream. Chesnut kept them going toward the opposite shore and soon the horses had footing again. He left the packhorses and rode upriver before he entered the river once more, letting the current carry him back to them.

He came alongside Marlette and took the lead rope that was already tied to the horse's halter advising, "Whatever happens, don't let go of your saddle horn." He glanced over the rest of the party and added, "Give your horses plenty of room."

Chesnut led her horse into the water and Marlette dutifully held the saddle horn with both hands. Her buckskin plunged into the deep water and went under, carrying Marlette with him. Her hands instinctively clawed for the surface and the current pulled her from the saddle. She was swept away from her horse and found herself desperately struggling to bring her head out of the water. She fought her way to the surface for one brief moment before the current and weight of her clothes pulled her down again. Panic gripped her, and she made one last powerful effort to surface, her lungs aching for air. Her head bobbed briefly above the water and something caught her hair and held her. She coughed and choked, gasping for breath, and realized she was being dragged. Something heavy bumped her and she clutched at it and hung on for dear life. She raised her dripping head and saw the leather-clad leg she was gripping, the wet horse, and Chesnut leaning over her. Her feet scraped across the bottom and she let go of him, losing her footing and stumbling until he caught her arm and steadied her. Jerking her arm away, she waded toward shore, uncomfortably wet and cold and unreasonably angry at Chesnut.

Joshua was in the water and wading to her, relief filling his face. "Thank heaven you're all right! What happened?"

"My horse went under and I was swept out of the saddle."

Chesnut, wading his horse past them, stopped and said, "Next time remember to hold on to the saddle horn."

She snapped, "I did hold on to the saddle horn."

Calmly he pointed out, "If you had, you'd have been on the bank instead of in the water."

She was ready to retort angrily but her father reminded her, "Marlette, he saved your life."

The anger faded and she murmured, "I'm sorry, I'm still a little upset."

Chesnut moved on and Marlette and her father followed him to the bank, where he dismounted and said, "We'll eat something here."

Marlette had been looking forward to getting out of the saddle but now she felt no relief. She was wet and cold, her long unused muscles ached and there were burning sore spots along the inside of her legs. She couldn't blame the horse. He had a very smooth gait and if she hadn't disliked Chesnut so much she might have appreciated the fact that he had chosen this horse for her.

After lunch, Chesnut let them walk for a while. The land rose gently through groves of trees alive with birds and chattering squirrels. They walked until they came to another small river, just as Marlette was beginning to feel dry. This time they made it across without mishap but there was no rest afterward.

Abruptly the hills ended in a high bluff forcing them over the rocky, steep barrier. Chesnut had them dismount and lead the horses up the indistinct trail. It was a long, difficult climb and Marlette had to stop frequently to catch her breath and rest her aching legs, but Chesnut didn't let her rest for long.

Once on top the view of the gorge ahead and behind was spectacular. A waterfall cascaded, frothy and cool, down the black rock cliffs across the river and above it towered the majesty of the snow-capped mountain. Chesnut continued on and they soon descended into the timber and after an arduous downhill hike they were near the river on a brush-and tree-choked level. Chesnut stopped to make camp for the night. Gratefully Marlette slipped from her saddle and found a comfortable place to sit but Chesnut quickly shattered her ideas of immediate rest. He put everyone to work, tending the horses, getting wood, and cooking supper.

While the men drew water and prepared a fireplace under his direction, Marlette found the coffee in the food packs and measured out just enough to make a cup for each one. The wood and water arrived at the same time and Chesnut very carefully built a fire, skillfully nursing a small spark into a large fire without any perceptible smoke.

In an amazingly short time a kettle of beans was set to boil, and even more amazing were the fresh fish Chesnut brought from the river and hung over the fire to roast. As the smell of broiling fish and perking coffee drifted enticingly to Marlette, she forgot how tired and sore she was.

After an eagerly consumed meal, they sat around the fire with their coffee, tired, sore, and ready to relax their aching muscles. Joshua and von Hout lit pipes and savored the luxury. They had been out of tobacco for some time aboard ship.

Finally Joshua spoke. "Chesnut, I think it is time we discussed our plans. McLoughlin didn't want us to talk about it at the fort, but now you must know our purpose. We are looking for mountain passes which will enable wagons to come clear to the Willamette valley. We have heard that Marcus Whitman thinks it possible. Are you familiar enough with the mountains to know if any such passes exist?"

"There are passes, but all of them would be difficult if not impassable for a wagon. The only pass that a wagon might make is around the south side of the mountain you see across the river."

"Good. We'll want to come back over that pass, but first we would like to visit the Whitman mission since he has knowledge of the trail from there on east."

"Are there wagons coming?"

"There may be. We heard rumors of groups wanting to leave last spring."

"Then it wasn't your intention to stop their coming?" Marlette caught a sudden tightness in his tone of voice, although he remained outwardly calm.

Joshua laughed shortly. "I'm afraid no one can stop their attempts. All we can do is advise them against it if we don't find a feasible means of passage."

"There will be trouble if they come."

"What kind of trouble?"

"The Indians and the men of the Hudson Bay Company will not give up this territory easily."

"But McLoughlin welcomes everybody. He has helped everyone who needed help."

"That's McLoughlin. The French-Canadians will not be as friendly if the settlers make it to the valley and take the land they consider theirs."

Joshua sighed deeply, "It becomes obvious why he brought you to us."

Holliway broke in, eager to find out if Chesnut could be trusted, "And where does your loyalty lie, Chesnut?"

Chesnut looked at Holliway without a change of expression or tone of voice, "I give my loyalty to no one."

Hatred was evident in Holliway's voice as he asked, "Then should we expect you to betray us to the highest bidder?"

Marlette rose quietly and moved away from the circle, too exhausted to listen further to this kind of belligerent questioning. She walked toward the river, found a log close to the water's edge, and sank down on it.

Already the deep blue of night was shadowing the river's molten and shimmering flow toward the setting sun. Across the river another waterfall gleamed white, like a ghostly veil against the sheer black cliff. Hardy evergreens clung to narrow ledges. It was a strangely peaceful golden moment. The awesome grandeur of the country somehow made Marlette think of Chesnut. There was no way of knowing what lay hidden beneath the forbidding cloak of forest draped dark over much of the landscape, anymore than she could fathom the mystery of the man. It bothered her that she could not pigeonhole him as she could most people. Except for the brief moments she had glimpsed him with the two women, she knew very little about him.

The river glowed gold, then slowly turned dark blue as her eyes closed and her thoughts drifted with the last light of day. She was suddenly aware of something or someone watching her and her throat tightened with fear. A scream gathered in her throat, but before it burst forth she realized that only Chesnut would frighten her like this.

She pulled herself together and calmly said, "Mr. Chesnut, would you please stop trying to frighten me."

She sat perfectly still trying to hear him, holding her breath and hearing only the wild thumping of her heart. Not until she saw the leather-clad legs and moccasined feet did she know for sure that it was he. The relief she experienced as she looked at his dark expressionless face, and realized that it could have been some savage Indian or wild animal left her weak.

"I thought I made it clear the other night that you were not to be alone."

"But I'm not over a hundred feet from the fire."

"This isn't Philadelphia. You don't know how quiet an Indian can be."

She stood up, looked squarely into his shadowed face and said, "I'm beginning to." She turned and walked quickly back to the fire.

There was some clean, warm water in the bean pot and she carried it to a log, close to where her tarp was draped over a rope, and washed. As she dried she saw Gay coming toward her.

He leaned nonchalantly against a tree and grinned at her. "I see

you and Chesnut are getting pretty friendly. I didn't know you'd go
for his type."

He grinned again and she resisted the urge to hit him. She wished
she were witty enough to say something that would put him in his
place. All she could do was turn his own words to her use and say,
"I know I *don't* go for your type of humor."

He laughed and said, "Well, well! You're finally learning something from me. Maybe there's hope yet." He chuckled again and left
her in a state of defeat. Instead of crushing him she had succeeded
in flattering him.

She sat down with a tired sigh and crawled into her bed. It was
a few moments before she realized she was not lying on the hard
ground. Someone had made a bed of boughs and leaves for her. Her
aching body relaxed gratefully into the softness and she wondered
who had thought of it. On the fuzzy edge of sleep she knew there was
only one person who would know how to make a comfortable bed
out of this wilderness.

She woke with a start sometime in the middle of the night, feeling
chilly and achingly stiff. Peering out into the darkness beyond the
edge of the fire that was just beginning to crackle with renewed vigor,
she saw a shadowy figure move to the fire and carefully placed more
wood on the flames. The light flickered across Chesnut's face and she
thought he looked less formidable, perhaps because of the firelight.
She turned over and went back to sleep.

There were many groans in the pale morning light as the camp
stirred to life. Before Marlette opened her eyes she could smell the
inviting aroma of coffee and bacon but the stiffness and ache in her
muscles made her fight getting up. She moved her legs and found the
sore spots on the inside of each leg extremely tender. She would have
to wrap them with something to be able to ride at all today. With
a groan she forced herself from her bed.

After breakfast they packed and rode off, the silence broken by
the occasional groans of aching, saddle-sore men. The trees thinned
a little on the narrow level they had reached. The horses walked
quietly, the friskiness of yesterday worn out of them. Deer bounded
through the thickets, noiseless shadows whose feet were muted by the

soft resilience of the forest floor. The sun rose over the top of the gorge and warmed the stiffness in Marlette's bones. It felt good and she closed her eyes with relief.

Ahead of them a huge rock pinnacle rose from the river's edge. Marlette looked closely for a way around the rear side of the rock but it was part of a steep ridge. Worry invaded her. She tried not to imagine what could happen in the deeper and stronger Columbia if she were to be swept off her horse again. She looked across the broad, sparkling water. It was beautiful, but not very comforting.

As they reached the base of the rock, Marlette was relieved to find there was footing, although it was narrow and slippery. Chesnut had them dismount and lead their horses around. The walk in itself would have been welcome had the footing been better, but her boots slipped treacherously and she had to step carefully.

Beyond the rock, to the east, a low, timbered plateau rose from the river's edge, with rugged hills rising to the north, confirming Marlette's suspicion that their easy riding was over. Nearer the abruptly rising plateau their going was muffled by the roar of the river. Marlette caught glimpses of the cataract through the trees where it poured over the edge of the plateau constricted by basalt cliffs and a large rock-faced island. Chesnut dismounted at the base of the ridge. They all did as he did and one by one started up the rocky trail toward the top. The climb stole Marlette's breakfast and she was ravenous and eager for lunch by the time she reached the top, but Chesnut mounted without a pause and started off into the forest on a narrow, brushy trail.

They rode for several miles before stopping in a clearing. Gratefully Marlette sat on the ground with her back against a rock, chewing on smoked fish and the bread brought from the fort. Although there were still tall trees standing, the underbrush had been cleared to look like a wide crossroads. Trails ran in each direction away from the broad intersection. Her curiosity was aroused and she wandered down the avenue that led south toward the muffled rush of the river, to the edge of a rocky bluff. Water thundered through the gorge over great slabs of rock that lay like some ancient fallen bridge to the other side. She watched intently, unaware that Chesnut had followed her until he spoke close beside her. She whirled around in surprise, the loose stones under her boots rolled with the sudden movement, and for one split second she felt herself falling over the cliff into the roaring river below.

Before she could cry out, Chesnut had caught her arm and pulled her from the edge. She stood trembling with fear and anger. "Would you please stop sneaking up on me like that."

"If you'd stay where you belonged I wouldn't have to follow you."

"Surely you aren't going to tell me it's dangerous to walk out here in broad daylight within full view of all of you?"

"No place is safe. Especially this place."

She laughed skeptically. "You can't be serious. What's special about this place?"

"It is a sacred place to the Indians."

"What do you mean?" her curiosity was aroused. "How could such a place be sacred to the Indians?"

"The Indians say there was a stone bridge across the river at this place."

"If it was true, why is it so special?"

"Because it was a gift of their Great Spirit."

Marlette was intrigued. Here was a chance to learn something about the Indians and perhaps provide a good tale for her friends in Philadelphia. "Would you mind telling me the story?"

He nodded and continued, "As I said, the Great Spirit built the bridge and gave it to his people. To guard his gift he sent Loo-Wit, a wise old woman, to stand watch over the bridge, and also sent his sons, Wyeast, who stands across the river and—"

Marlette turned to follow his gaze across the river, fully expecting to see an Indian standing there. "Where? I don't see anyone."

"Wyeast is the snow-covered mountain you see to the south."

"A mountain! That's ridiculous! Are you making fun of me?"

"I only tell you the legend of this place."

She saw by the seriousness of his eyes and face that he was not joking. "I'm sorry. Please go on."

Without any change of expression he continued, gesturing northward, "and Klickitat. Everything was peaceful until beautiful Squaw Mountain moved into a small valley between Klickitat and Wyeast, and rivalry for her affections sprang up between them. Although Squaw Mountain grew to love Wyeast, she thought it great fun to flirt with Klickitat. At first they only growled and rumbled, but soon they began to stomp their feet and spit ashes and fire in the air and darkened the sun with great clouds of smoke. They threw white-hot rocks at one another, setting the forests on fire and driving the people into hiding. They threw so many stones on the Great Cross-Over and shook the earth so hard that the bridge broke and fell into the river.

"Klickitat, the bigger of the two male mountains, finally won the fight and Wyeast, admitting defeat, gave over all claim to Squaw Mountain. This was a severe blow to Squaw Mountain and though she dutifully went to Klickitat, her heart was broken and in a short time she fell at Klickitat's feet in a deep sleep and has never awakened.

"This in turn broke Klickitat's heart and he dropped his head, which was once taller than Wyeast, and has never raised it since.

"In the meantime, Loo-Wit, a very old and homely woman, was badly burned and battered by the rocks thrown by the two fighting mountains. She dutifully stayed at her post during the battle trying to save the bridge. The Great Spirit heard of her faithfulness and promised to grant her any wish. She asked to be made young and beautiful once more, but when her wish was granted, her spirit was still old and she did not desire companionship, so she moved away to the west by herself."

Marlette waited for him to go on, but the story was finished and he watched her intently for her reaction. "Why, it's no more than a fairytale," she said wonderingly, "Do you really believe all of it?"

"Stories of the Great Cross-Over are even known among the villages of the Sioux. The rocks in the river below are flat like no others I have seen in this river." He paused and shrugged noncommittally, "But my belief is not important. The Indians here *do* believe and any violation of their sacred place could mean death."

Marlette shivered slightly at the word "death" and turned to look once more at the huge stone slabs that partially obstructed the mighty river's flow. Everything she saw in this vast, rugged country seemed both beautiful and forbidding. She turned away and walked back toward the horses. The men were getting ready to mount, and Gaylord's knowing smile made her blush. Chesnut remained expressionless.

They rode out of the clearing and into the brush. Marlette looked back toward the clearing. Shafts of sunlight coming through the trees gave the place an ethereal appearance, as if some spirit still lingered there. She quickly turned away, but the story would not leave her thoughts.

The trail led ever upward and became rougher, but Marlette's thoughts were so filled with the legend she didn't notice. At first it seemed silly but as she began to probe into the meaning of the tale, it seemed more like a Bible story. She began to realize that the Indian was far from being an unreligious heathen. The story plainly told of a God, and of love and temptation. It was something to ponder.

She began to fit the story into a human context and imagined herself as Squaw Mountain. Gaylord Taylor was Wyeast and Klickitat, the taller and stronger Chesnut. She smiled wryly at the thought of herself as the beautiful Squaw Mountain, with two men vying for her love. More likely she should be Loo-Wit, the guardian of the bridge. It was a frivolous bit of thinking and totally unlike her, but it did help to pass the aching hours.

At last they made camp for the night. After supper she felt rested enough to record the progress of their trip. She got out her journal and began logging every detail of their journey from the fort. She decided to record the Indian legend thinking that it might help someone to understand the Indians of the area. As she finished she noticed Gay watching her intently. He sauntered over to where she was sitting and she shut the journal quickly.

"Well, well! Our little secretary is busy tonight. And what exciting events did you record in your book?" His tone was bantering.

"I try to record everything. Especially things that might help someone else coming here."

"And does that include walks in the woods with the Indian guide?"

"Don't you have something better to do than to make up gossip?" She was unable to keep the irritation out of her voice.

He laughed and squatted down in front of her. "Sure I do. How about reading what you've written?"

"I'm sure it wouldn't interest you."

"Why not? Maybe I can add things you've forgotten."

He snatched the book from her lap and rose before she could stop him. "Gay, please." She pleaded.

"Oh ho! When you ask like that I know you're hiding something." He walked back to the firelight and sat down. Marlette followed somewhat hesitantly, knowing she couldn't stop him.

He read for a while, and began to grin broadly at Marlette.

Evan Long caught the look and became curious. "What you got there, Taylor?"

"You wouldn't believe it, Evan, but our little secretary has been filling the journal with Indian fairytales."

Holliway, curious now, asked, "What are you talking about, Taylor?"

Gay needed no more encouragement. He leaned toward the fire for better light, the eagerness of the entertainer sparkling in his eyes. Marlette stood in dismay. She wanted to stop him, yet she hesitated, unsure if it was only her imagination giving the incident greater importance than it actually had.

Gay began to read aloud and Marlette wondered nervously how Chesnut would react. Gay threw himself into the story with gestures and facial expressions, made even more exaggerated by the flickering firelight. Before Marlette knew it he had cast the characters as she had. At first the insinuation had been subtle as she caught his glance from her to Chesnut. Then he grew more open in his characterization, until she felt everyone must catch his meaning. She was glad no one could see her face. She watched Chesnut, but he sat without expression, apparently oblivious to Gay's portrayal.

The men were enjoying the fun and Marlette walked away, feeling humiliated. A few minutes later Joshua brought the journal back to her.

"I'm sorry, Marlette. I would have stopped him if I'd known."

"Send him back to Vancouver, Father. I can't stand his insinuations any longer."

"I can't do that, but I'll speak to him about it if you like."

Marlette sighed. "It wouldn't do any good. Do you think I should tear the legend out of the journal?"

"No. It's an interesting insight into Indian culture."

"That's what I thought, too, but I didn't want it to humiliate anyone."

"I know, I know. But don't let it keep you from learning everything you can. That is our purpose here."

Marlette nodded. Joshua patted her affectionately on the shoulder. "Better get some rest, now."

She kissed his cheek and watched him walk to his bedroll. The rest of the men started settling down for the night and Marlette gratefully crawled into her makeshift tent.

Next day they left the thick fir forests of the western slope and emerged through open pine forest leading onto the high plateau east of the mountains. The sun was warmer and the trail dustier. It was a hard climb before Chesnut stopped for lunch.

They rode on after lunch and Marlette was soon aware of the heat her black riding costume drew in the midday sun. She removed her jacket and for the first time wore the wide-brimmed hat Chesnut had brought her the morning they left, embarrassed, but grateful.

In contrast to the thick green tangle of the western slope, vast open spaces stretched ahead, silvered by sage. The hilltops flattened into plateaus dotted with the vertical corrugated rock of the narrow gorge.

Late in the afternoon they dropped down into a narrow canyon with a swift, shallow river in the bottom and followed the river until they reached a narrow, rock-strewn valley where the ground showed evidence of a recent campsite.

Holliway rode up to Chesnut and asked, "Is this an Indian camp-site?"

Chesnut, already dismounted and unsaddling his horse, looked up and said, "Yes."

"Friends of yours?"

"Possibly. They're on their way to the rapids up the Columbia for the annual Indian gathering."

"Then there's likely to be more?"

"Yes."

Holliway was getting irritated and his voice sharpened, "Well aren't we taking an unnecessary risk camping here?"

"We run a risk camping anywhere now."

Holliway exploded, "And I say this is a damn poor place. You take us to a safer camp, or we'll leave you here and go on by ourselves."

Joshua interrupted in a soothing voice, "Major, let's not be hasty. Mr. Chesnut knows these people better than we. We'll have to consider his judgment." He turned to Chesnut, "Do you think they will be hostile?"

"It will depend on the Indians."

Holliway said, "If he can't guarantee our safety I don't think we should take the chance."

"I can guarantee nothing from any Indian."

"Then why stay here?"

Chesnut answered patiently, "Because there is water here and if we follow this river it will lead us away from the main gathering on the Columbia."

"I thought our purpose was to contact the Indians?" Taylor asked. "Why don't we ask ourselves what Chesnut will gain by keeping us away from the Indians?"

Chesnut's voice had not risen nor had his expressionless face changed, but his words were ominous. "You might gain a few more miles, alive."

Evan Long roared contentiously, "And what the hell does that mean?"

"My presence doesn't guarantee your safety. My life is in as much danger as yours."

Joshua nodded, accepting what Chesnut said. "Then I think Taylor has a good point. We need to know the temper of the Indians before we can evaluate whether immigrants can safely travel through this country. Why not contact these Indians? If they are on their way to a social gathering they can't be looking for a fight."

"Normally that's true. But they may feel threatened by your presence. All of the tribes in this area know the Cayuse Indians are unhappy with the Whitmans' attempts to civilize them and are suspicious of their presence here. How this will affect you is hard to know until I see their reaction. If they seem friendly, how far do you want to deal with them?"

"Of course we would like to trade with them and gauge their friendliness, but we'll have to trust your judgment as to how far we go with them."

"All right, but you must let me handle things and you must do what I tell you to do. Is that clear to everyone?"

The major was not agreeable. His eyes burned with hate and distrust, his back was ramrod-stiff with resistance. "I think you're making a big mistake. If he handles everything, we'll have no idea what's going on. One of us should do the talking and I have some experience dealing with Indians."

Chesnut turned cold eyes on Holliway and asked quietly, "How would you deal with them, Major? Like you deal with me?"

"You dirty redskin—!"

Joshua broke in. "Gentlemen, gentlemen! This will settle nothing. I think it's time we heard how the rest of you feel about Chesnut's plan. Evan, what do you think?"

"I don't like it neither. He could have his friends kill us and no one would be the wiser."

Isaac Thompson pushed his horse over next to Long, his shrill voice agreeing. "Long is right. I think we should let Major Holliway handle any contact with the Indians."

Gaylord laughed derisively. "Sure he should. Then we can be certain our scalps will be lifted."

Holliway gave Gay a black look and asked, "Are you voting this time, Marlette?"

Marlette knew why he picked on her. His tales of Indian torture of white women captives had frightened her especially and he counted on her agreement. She looked at the two men, Holliway seething with hatred while Chesnut stood calmly, watching her intently. It was a hard decision, but she knew Holliway's hatred was a sure sign of failure. "No. You don't need my vote."

Gay laughed. "I'd say an abstention was the same as a no-confidence vote. What do you say von Hout?"

Von Hout frowned at Gay. "You should be more serious, Herr Taylor. I know how da Fraulein feels. It is hard to choose a man you do not know over one you do know, but it is vat I must do."

The major stiffened and turned toward Andrew. "Well, Proctor?"

Andrew shriveled under Holliway's withering gaze. He swallowed and looked around the ring of faces. He wasn't used to making decisions but he found the courage to speak. "Major, I don't want you to feel I've let you down, but I think Gaylord is right. Your years on the frontier have given you experience, but they've also embittered you against the Indians. I can't say that I trust Mr. Chesnut either, but both ways are a gamble. I'll gamble on Mr. Chesnut."

Marlette smiled her approval at Andrew. Maybe he would regain his self-esteem after all. Joshua was saying, "It looks like we do things Chesnut's way. Will you agree to that, Major?"

Holliway snapped, "No!"

Chesnut said, "You can follow the river back to Vancouver."

"I didn't say I was leaving."

"If you go with me I must have full command. You agreed to that, remember?"

The stiffness went out of Holliway, the rigid lines of his leathery face sagged. Anger and pride still vibrating in his voice, he said, "I remember. I've always kept my word and I'll do so now, but let me warn you, Chesnut, if you make one wrong move I'll shoot you or kill you with my bare hands if I have to. *You* remember *that!*"

Chesnut nodded and went back to his horse as if nothing had happened. The rest of the men dismounted and began unsaddling in quiet watchfulness. Marlette eased her tired body out of the saddle. The sun had almost dropped behind the canyon rim, and already the air was growing chilly.

Von Hout, unsaddling next to her, asked, "You look troubled. Are you frightened? Do you vish to return to Vancouver?"

"No, Papa Hout. I was just wishing I had time to wash and dust my clothes before dark.

He chuckled, "Vat a girl! Being dirty bothers her more than the Indians. I take care of your horse. You go vash. Ja."

She smiled at him. He looked as dirty as she felt. Dust had yellowed his white beard and the ruff of hair around his bald head. "Thank you," she said ruefully, "but I doubt Chesnut would approve."

"Vat can he do to an old man? Kill me? Death makes no vorry in an old man vith nothing to live for. Now you go vash."

"Papa Hout! Don't talk like that. What would your family think if they heard you?"

The smile left his face and a mist blurred his faded blue eyes. "My family? Vy you tink I'm here? Ahh, but you don't know about my family. Vell I vill tell you. I have two sons and two daughters. All they vorry about is who gets Papa's money. Who gets Papa's land. Who gets Papa's house. Who gets Papa's furniture. Who gets Papa's cows. Vell vone day Papa tell them, 'You take the land, the cows, the house, and the furniture, but Papa take the money. You have to earn that like Papa did.' And so I am here, looking for a good place for cows. Now you go to the river."

Marlette put her arms around the stout figure and kissed the dusty cheek. "Papa Hout, you are too good for them."

Softly he agreed. "Ja. You is right. Maybe I vas too goot to them."

The Indian Camp

IN THE MORNING they followed the river through the narrow canyon to a steep trail that led to the top. Once out of the canyon they approached the edge of a vast, golden plain stretching toward pine-forested mountains on the west and north. The snow peak of Klickitat glistened in the morning sun. Several miles to the east two grass buttes dominated the plain and a blue haze wavered in the distance.

The tall grass was alive with small birds whirring up from under their feet and the air was filled with song. Rabbits raced away in sudden bursts making the horses snort. They rode over a gentle undulation and came upon a level area filled with flat-topped Indian lodges. A sudden flurry of activity there brought a party of horsemen thundering toward them. Chesnut sat his horse in cool unconcern as the Indian riders came on at full gallop.

Over his shoulder he advised, "Stay here and don't make any move toward your guns unless I give the signal." He moved his horse ahead several yards and stopped again. The Indians pulled their horses to a halt a hundred feet away, their weapons at the ready.

Chesnut raised his hand and one of the Indians separated from the rest and came slowly forward, stopping a few feet in front of him. From the smile on his face it was evident that he recognized Chesnut. They greeted each other, Chesnut rode forward, and the two shook hands and talked for several minutes.

Chesnut came back to the other members of the expedition and motioned them into a circle. "This is a band of Klickitats," he explained. "They're on their way to the Columbia to trade. They've invited us to spend the night with them, and I've accepted. Don't show off these guns and keep them with you at all times. They will want to trade all they have for guns like these and they're very cunning traders. Also, they're not above stealing. Wear your pistols and keep them covered with your coats so that they can't be pulled from your holsters. Stay together and let me do the talking. Any questions?"

Gay asked with a grin, "Do they provide maidens for visiting dignitaries?"

Chesnut's cold look should have been answer enough, but he replied quietly, "If you want to stay alive, leave the women alone."

Holliway reminded him, "Don't forget what I told you yesterday, Chesnut."

Joshua raised a placating hand. "Please, gentlemen. We came here to make friends. Let's concentrate on doing that and allow Mr. Chesnut to do his job."

Chesnut pulled his horse out of the circle and turned toward the Indians, and they came charging forward, encircling the small group. Marlette's heart pounded as she looked at the intently curious black eyes staring from fierce, bright vermilion faces. It was some comfort that they were not totally naked. They wore leather breechclouts and leggings from moccasin to hip. Their long black hair, slick with grease, was formed into a single braid.

They all rode into a camp noisy with barking dogs and children darting about. New smells assailed Marlette's nose, some of them unpleasant. People came running from everywhere to see the white visitors. Unlike the Indian women of the lower Columbia River, these women were fully dressed in buckskin. Their hair hung in two oily braids and their faces were ludicrously smeared with the same red paint as the men. Jewelry was heavy on arms, necks, and ears. Marlette felt extremely self-conscious as they watched her intently, jabbering and pointing among themselves.

They stopped near the center of the camp and the Indian who had spoken with Chesnut slipped from his horse and went into a lodge nearby. As far as Marlette could tell the lodges were no more than poles covered with woven mats and animal skins. She counted nearly fifty lodges before the Indian emerged and stood aside as another Indian stepped from the dim interior. This man was slightly shorter and heavier than the first, and as he came forward a slow smile touched his thin-lipped mouth. Chesnut dismounted and went to meet the older Indian and Marlette detected a respectful friendliness in their voices, although she could not understand their words.

Chesnut turned around and motioned them to dismount. Hesitantly, Marlette left the security of her saddle for the dust of the ground. Chesnut brought the Indian forward.

In English he said, "Chief Three Bears, these are Joshua Brightwood, his daughter, and his men."

In halting English the chief greeted them. "Chief Three Bears welcomes the friends of his brother to his camp."

Joshua extended his hand with a smile, "It is an honor, Chief."

The Indian took the hand and grunted, showing his teeth in a smile. Then he turned and ordered the onlookers to disperse. Marlette felt the perspiration roll down her back and she sighed as the crowd scattered.

The chief spoke to Chesnut in his native tongue, and Chesnut turned to them.

"Remove your rifles from their scabbards and come into the chief's lodge. Sit on the rifles if you have to."

They loosened their rifles and followed Chesnut into the dim interior of the lodge. Chesnut showed the men to seats around the fire pit. He directed Marlette to a low fur-piled couch behind the circle of men.

"Can you be quiet?" he asked in a low voice.

She nodded, feeling simultaneously frightened and indignant at his question. He returned to the circle and sat down cross-legged next to the Indian chief. More Indians filed in, quietly lowering themselves to the ground around the walls of the lodge. In a few minutes the lodge was full.

The chief raised the pipe he was holding and after a short ceremony, took several long meditative puffs and passed it around the circle until each of the men had taken a puff.

Carefully placing the long-stemmed feathered pipe before him on a flat rock, he looked directly at Joshua and asked in his slow English, "Why you come?"

Marlette heard the surprise in her father's voice as he returned, "Didn't Mr. Chesnut tell you?"

"He tell. Now you tell."

Recovering his composure her father smiled his most charming smile. "You have heard that my people are interested in this country?"

The chief nodded grimly.

"It is true. And though I am not a chief in my country I want to see if this is a good place for the white man to come."

The chief raised a hand for Joshua to stop and turned to speak to Chesnut. Chesnut's answer was slow and studied. There was an ominous murmur in the room as the others listened intently.

The chief raised his hand for silence and the lodge instantly quieted. "You bring people?"

"No, Chief. But they will come unless I tell them they are not wanted here and will be unable to settle."

Again there was a consultation with Chesnut. Then, silencing the crowd once more, the chief said, "We no want white man here. You tell."

Joshua smiled with relief. "Yes, Chief, I will tell them."

The chief smiled in satisfaction. "Good." He rose regally, putting an end to the discussion. "Now we make feast for you." With crisp commands he sent the other Indians in the lodge to various tasks and then spoke again to Chesnut. Chesnut nodded and rose just as effortlessly and regally as the chief.

"The chief says our lodge is ready. We may go to rest, and they will bring some food."

There was a smile and a nod of courtesy from every man around the circle as they rose. Chesnut beckoned to Marlette and she walked toward her father and tucked her arm through his.

They filed out of the stuffy lodge into the warm sunlight and Chesnut led them to another lodge. Their horses were all unsaddled and hobbled nearby. Naked children and a pack of sniffing dogs followed after them, their low growls and bared teeth making Marlette shudder nervously until they were safely inside the lodge.

Holliway immediately questioned Chesnut. "All right, Chesnut, what was all the jabbering about?"

"The chief doesn't like white men or their missionaries. He asked me the same things he asked Mr. Brightwood. Right now he believes us because he trusts me and because Mr. Brightwood's answers agreed with mine. Don't do anything to change that belief. Now it would be wise to check our packs."

He pulled his pack from the pile and started checking it's contents and they all bent to sort through their belongings.

Evan Long finished sorting and said, "Nothin' missing here. How about the rest of you?"

Joshua answered, "Mine seems to be intact. Maybe Mr. Chesnut has misjudged these people. Wouldn't the chief be more suspicious if we carry the guns with us, especially if we take them to dinner?"

"Probably, but it's too great a temptation for them if we leave the guns unguarded. It would be bad for them to discover the value of these weapons."

They all knew this was the truth. The guns they carried were not the single-shot rifles that most of the frontiersmen owned. Joshua had ordered them from a gunsmith in New Jersey by the name of Colt. The guns had been the reason for their late arrival in the territory because they had been delivered several months late. They incorporated a brilliant new invention by Colt and were called repeating rifles and revolvers. They were beautiful and deadly weapons and were prizes worth any man's daring.

Marlette tucked everything back into her pack and ventured to ask Chesnut. "Is there someplace I can wash?"

Without looking at her he answered, "I asked them to bring water for you."

There was a noise outside the entrance and two stocky Indian women entered the lodge carrying a platter of food and a woven basket of water for Marlette. They turned to Chesnut and waited to see if he wanted anything else. He said something to them, and they left.

Marlette dipped water into the bowl and washed. To her surprise the water was quite hot. "Why, they've heated the water. I hope you thanked them for me?"

"There's a hot spring here. That's why they camp here," Chesnut said shortly.

It was well past lunchtime and Evan didn't hesitate to help himself before washing. Chesnut picked up the platter and offered it to Marlette. She found the food similar to what they had eaten at the other Indian village, and she took some smoked fish, camas cake, and some other dried meat.

After lunch, Joshua asked, "What happens next, Chesnut?"

"They will probably have a show of their hunting and riding skills to impress you with their power."

"That sounds interesting. Will my daughter be allowed to watch?"

"Yes. But she will have to stay close to one of you."

Gay spoke up quickly, "I'll volunteer to be Miss Brightwood's escort, since the other women are off limits."

Marlette was about to protest when Chesnut said, "Holliway, you take charge of Miss Brightwood."

Still smiling, Gay asked, "Didn't you hear me, Chesnut? I said I'd take care of her."

Chesnut stood up and looked sharply at Gay. "I heard you. Holliway is going to take care of Miss Brightwood." He turned his back on Gay and left the lodge.

The smile left Gay's face and he sprang after Chesnut but Evan Long grabbed him at the opening of the lodge.

Joshua said, "No need to be upset. I doubt you'll change his mind."

Guy wavered and finally shrugged bitterly. "You're probably right. He's a stubborn bast—." He broke off, remembering Marlette's presence.

Evan laughed. "Don't look like you made any points being on his side."

Gay's arrogance returned and he said, "Chesnut's no fool. He's keeping the opposition happy by giving him an important job."

It was Holliway's turn to be insulted. Angrily he retorted, "He gave me the job because I'm the only one capable of protecting her."

Von Hout nodded soberly, "Ja. Da major has more experience than you, Mr. Taylor. You let him take care of Miss Brightwood."

Andrew Proctor spoke up. "I'll stay here with you, Marlette, if you don't want to go."

Marlette smiled at him. "No. It might be some sort of diplomatic insult if we didn't go. I'll be all right."

Joshua agreed. "You're probably right. I think we all have to go and we have to trust Chesnut."

Evan Long, who had been standing solidly in front of the door, moved back to his bedroll and sat down. "Well at least they fed us before they kill us."

Isaac Thompson, still pale and trembling at the mere presence of

Indians, mopped his balding brow and asked in a strained voice, "You don't think they're going to kill us do you, Major?"

Holliway shrugged. "It doesn't look like it, yet. But then they can shake your hand and scalp you at the same time."

Thompson shuddered. Long grinned at the poor man's discomfort. "Don't worry Isaac, your scalp ain't anything they'd want."

They all settled down in silence for a brief rest. Marlette closed her eyes but she couldn't shut out the noise of the camp or her own fearful thoughts.

In a little while Chesnut came quietly through the doorway and startled them. He stood looking at them and Marlette wondered what he was thinking behind that cool, expressionless exterior.

"They're ready to begin," he said at last.

They rose and followed Chesnut out of the lodge. The entire village was gathered at the edge of the camp on the grassy plain, the chief in their midst, and Chesnut led them to where he stood. The Indians who were to perform came riding around the circle of lodges in full warrior regalia. They were now completely naked except for breechclouts and moccasins. Their bodies were painted and their hair was decorated with feathers. The manes and tails of their horses were decorated in similar fashion.

A target of deer hide mounted on a wooden frame was dragged out onto the plain. The Indians rode a short distance away and turned. With piercing yells they charged across the plain at breakneck speed. As they neared the target, they aimed their bows and pierced it with amazing accuracy as they raced by. It was a thrilling and totally terrifying display.

Again the Indians rode their horses a few hundred yards down the grass arena and rushed back. This time they hurled their hatchets at a slab of log. Chips and splinters flew as the axes sank into the log with sharp whacks that made Marlette flinch.

Next they hurled lances and knives and Marlette watched with growing respect and fear as the sharp weapons whistled through the air to strike the log with unerring accuracy. Then the Indians separated into teams for a brutal form of jousting; trying to unseat one another while charging at full gallop. Their skillful horsemanship awed Marlette and she found herself wondering how Chesnut would perform at these games.

When the display was finished, one of the more daring Indians took a rifle from someone in the crowd and rode toward the chief and Chesnut, stopping in front of them. He smiled coldly and although his face was painted in a grotesque way there was an evil glitter in his eyes that was no illusion.

He held up his rifle and spoke loudly, pointing at Chesnut's rifle. Chesnut apparently declined his offer and the Indian spoke again, the taunt in his voice unmistakable. Again Chesnut calmly declined the challenge.

Gay stepped forward and Marlette gasped. Approving murmurs stirred through the crowd.

In a quiet voice Chesnut ordered, "Back off, Taylor."

Gay's smile was defiant. "If you're not man enough to save our face, I will."

Chesnut stepped toward Gay. Marlette couldn't see his face but she could see the contempt in Gay's eyes.

"Give me the gun, Taylor."

Gay replied in a tense whisper, "You *take* it, Chesnut."

There was hate in his eyes and Marlette realized that Gay wanted to surpass Chesnut, not the Indian. Chesnut reached for the rifle strapped to Gay's back and Gay recoiled and swung with all his strength but Chesnut was even quicker. He ducked the first fist and caught the second one at the wrist, spinning Gay around effortlessly and hurling him to the ground. Evan Long and von Hout leapt on Gay immediately, restraining him while Chesnut removed his revolver and rifle.

Buckling on the extra guns, Chesnut asked, "Are you going to behave or shall I tie you up?"

The anger in Gay's eyes slowly dimmed and he smiled crookedly at the thought of being tied up. "You win, Chesnut, I'll behave, for now."

Chesnut turned away and returned to the chief, who stood with an amused expression, accepting Chesnut's apparent apology.

Turning to Joshua, Chesnut said, "I think this would be a good time to bring out your gifts."

The chief spoke loudly to his people and waved his hand toward camp. The Indians turned toward their lodges with excited voices. The packs were brought out and gifts were given to the chief and to the ranking members of the village. Minor gifts of needles and beads were passed out to the women. The more desirable items such as tobacco, pipes, steel knives, and other tools were to be traded for Indian handicrafts.

Prized articles intended for the trading market on the Columbia were brought out. Marlette watched in fascination as the women ruthlessly shoved each other out of the way in order to get their basketry or beadwork exchanged for a pair of scissors. Joshua was overwhelmed by the variety of goods and asked Chesnut to judge the work. One woman worked her way close to Chesnut and stayed next to him. She appeared to be helping Chesnut, advising him on the workmanship of the articles and enjoying her new status. She grew increasingly bold and it became obvious that Chesnut interested her as much as the trading. It would have been amusing if Marlette hadn't found it so disgusting.

As each lucky woman had her article chosen she was given a pair of scissors. With broad grins they stood showing off their prizes to the less fortunate, but apparently did not know how to cut with them. Joshua was soon giving a demonstration to a group of giggling Indian women.

Marlette smiled and asked Holliway, "Are they like the Indians you knew?"

"They're all the same to me."

Marlette caught the undercurrent of hate in his voice and asked no more questions. The women of the camp were disappearing from the trading area and the men, who had been standing back enjoying the spectacle, were now coming forward to trade for the articles they wanted. It was a quieter and more earnest group. They looked longingly at the rifles but traded for knives and tools instead. Chesnut was having a difficult time bargaining with the men because he wanted to be fair and yet obtain a representative sample of the Indian crafts for Joshua.

At last the men were thinning out and some of them went into a nearby lodge. The Indian who had caused the trouble earlier came up to Gay and motioned him away from the crowd. If Chesnut saw him he said nothing. Gay followed the Indian into the lodge and Marlette could hear the sound of male voices raised in song, then yells of approval and grunts of disappointment.

The trading was finished and the sun began to disappear over the mountains. The chief, who had been observing the trading from a polite distance, came forward and talked to Chesnut. Chesnut told Joshua, "The chief is having a feast for us after dark."

Joshua smiled and nodded to the chief. The chief nodded in return and walked to his lodge. Joshua started picking up his assortment of Indian articles and Chesnut went to retrieve Gay.

Marlette asked Holliway, "What do you suppose they're doing in there?"

"Probably gambling."

Marlette cast a worried eye toward the lodge. She almost wouldn't blame Chesnut if he tied Gay up. With a shrug, she turned and followed the men to their lodge. A fire had been built and the interior was warm and well-lit. They began to sort through the articles they had received, examining the quality of the Indian craftsmanship. Gay and Chesnut came into the lodge and Marlette looked sharply at Gay to see if he was angry, but he appeared quite calm.

Holliway questioned, "Well, Taylor, did you win or lose?"

"I wasn't doing too bad when the constable here broke up the game." He threw an impudent glance at Chesnut.

Evan was immediately interested. "What kinda game you playin'?"

Gay sat down, eager to tell of his experience at Indian gambling. "It's like the old pea and shell game only they use two small bones, one with decoration and one plain, and they pass these back and forth in their hands to confuse you and you try to guess which one is in which hand. If you guess right they give you a stick from their side and if you're wrong they take one away from your side. Whoever ends up with all the sticks wins."

"What'd you win?"

Gay chuckled. "I don't know. I didn't have all the sticks yet."

"I'd like to try that. How about it, Chesnut?"

"You can't beat them at their own game."

"Maybe not, but it'd be fun tryin'."

"No. What if you lost your rifle? Would you fight the winner to get it back? Forget it."

Long's eyes smoldered with resentment but he said nothing more. Gay had resigned himself to the fact that Chesnut was more than his match, but Evan Long was not yet convinced.

They continued to go over the articles and Chesnut explained how some of the things were made and the significance of the designs, as Marlette made notes. As they began packing things away there was a commotion outside and Chesnut rose as the door flap was lifted. Several Indians stood outside with a number of horses tied together. The trouble-maker from earlier incidents spoke to Chesnut. Chesnut's answer was short and apparently disagreeable. The Indian motioned Gay to come outside.

Chesnut stopped him with, "Stay where you are, Taylor. He wants to trade you his horses for your gun."

Gay smiled at the Indian and shook his head negatively. The Indian motioned outside and an Indian woman came forward. She was quite young and still fairly slender. Her face was rather pretty. He pointed to her and then to Gay's rifle. Gay's grin grew broader and his eyes looked appreciatively at the woman. Chesnut gave Gay a warning look and Gay shook his head sadly. The Indian grunted and said something venomous to Chesnut. Chesnut remained completely impassive. The Indian, eyes glittering with hate, spat into the dust and turned angrily away.

They all sat in apprehensive silence until Chesnut said quietly, "We'd better go."

They trooped after him to the chief's lodge and were seated in a semicircle around a huge fire out in front. Other fires were lit in the open area until a large circle of ground was covered with soft, flickering firelight. Rabbits and quail were roasting over the large fire. The chief's wives and daughters came out of the lodge carrying wooden platters laden with food.

Chesnut received the first platter from the oldest of the chief's daughters. He paid little attention to the girl but her eyes remained on him constantly. Marlette was immediately suspicious. A younger girl served her and she didn't hesitate to try the succulent rabbit and fowl as they sizzled on her plate. More cautiously she dipped her horn spoon into the pasty substance and tasted it tentatively. It was barely palatable. The berries and camas cake were far more tasty.

Holliway, sitting next to her, ate stolidly. He looked at her sideways and asked, "How do you like Indian cuisine by now?"

She smiled slightly. "It lacks salt but it's edible. However, this pasty stuff has me wondering. I hope it isn't dog, or something equally distasteful."

He smiled briefly, his well-trimmed mustache turning upward as his teeth flashed briefly. "Don't worry. I don't think we're eating dog."

"Do you know what it is?"

"Some sort of pemmican."

"What on earth is pemmican?"

"It's a mixture of dried berries, dried meat, and marrow mixed with fat."

Marlette grimaced. "Please don't tell me any more. It tasted better when I didn't know what it was."

He smiled again and Marlette felt a little more comfortable in his presence. Perhaps she only imagined that his hatred for Indians was so intense and unpredictable. She wondered what had happened during his years of commanding frontier forts that had made him bitter and desperate for glory. Was it a fault in the man himself or in the system that placed men in impossible situations without reward?

As Marlette finished her plate she noticed the young girl again kneeling before Chesnut, her eyes boldly seeking his as she offered him more food. He let her take the plate and she returned in a few moments with more camas cakes and berries.

Drummers began to play a muted rhythm somewhere outside the circle of fires. A flute was added and the Indians began to chant softly. There was a movement in the shadows near one of the fires and a line of men came into the circle in a bent, slow-stepping dance. The cadence of the drums accelerated and the dancers increased their tempo. Then, at the other end of the circle a lone figure appeared in the skin and head of a large bear. Marlette realized the dancers were simulating a hunt and their studied movements indicated that this was a ritual they had performed before. In due course, the bear had overcome all the hunters but one and a battle ensued between animal and hunter until the hunter was finally forced to use his bare hands. It was a brilliant display of wrestling and agility and Marlette watched in fascination as the hunter overcame the bear. Then the younger maidens of the camp set up a chant of victory and came dancing into the circle singing praises to the hunter and ridiculing the bear. In words and action the bear was skinned and his pelt tossed from girl to girl as they laughed and sang, joined by more members of the camp, until both men and women were performing to the driving rhythm of the drums.

The chief's daughter separated from the rest of the maiden dancers and, swaying in a slow undulating motion, came toward Chesnut in an unmistakable invitation for him to join her. Marlette peered at Chesnut's face in the flickering firelight and saw no sign of interest. Gay immediately rose from his place and started to imitate the girl's steps. She looked pleadingly at Chesnut's impassive face, and then turned to Gay and with him moved to join the rest of the dancers.

Evan Long watched and fidgeted and then jumped to his feet, sweat glistening on his wide face. He shuffled into the ring of dancers and Marlette looked quickly at Chesnut but all she could see was a slight narrowing of his eyes. The rest of the men remained still, and Marlette, her own body feeling sticky, watched in fearful fascination. Chesnut leaned toward the chief and after a short exchange, the chief rose and all motion ceased instantly. The chief spoke and the dancers started to leave the circle. His daughter walked toward them and Gay returned to his place, a detached smile on his face. Evan Long started after one of the women but was blocked by two Indian men. For one long moment Marlette didn't breath as Evan faced the two Indians.

Quickly Chesnut was on his feet and striding to where Long stood. He laid his hand gently on Evan's shoulder and Evan turned slowly toward Chesnut, his face flushed and hungry with desire. The chief moved toward the two men and spoke rapidly to Chesnut. Chesnut kept a restraining hand on Long and answered with controlled calm. The chief, unsatisfied by Chesnut's answer, turned to Long and said, "You want woman? I give for gun."

Long looked confusedly from one to the other of the two men. Slowly the passion died in his eyes. He shrugged Chesnut's hand from his shoulder and lumbered back toward his place, looking pale. Now that the scene was over Marlette felt the blood rushing to her face and was relieved no one could see her discomfort in the firelight.

She leaned toward her father and asked, "Do you think it would be all right if I went to bed?"

Joshua gave her a startled look, distressed that she had witnessed this scene. He regained his composure and replied, "I think it would be a good idea for all of us to go to bed."

He stood up as Chesnut and the chief came back to the fire. "Chesnut, I think it would be wise to end this evening."

Chesnut nodded in agreement and spoke to the chief. The chief agreed with a grunt and the men began to stand, looking awkward and a little embarrassed themselves. Gay rose and turned toward the chief's daughter who stood in the doorway of her lodge. He smiled and said good-night to her, but the girl didn't respond, her eyes on Chesnut. Gay followed her gaze and frowned.

In a few minutes they were all inside the lodge, except Chesnut, who hadn't come with them. Silently they all turned into their beds, but no one slept. Marlette wondered with disgust where Chesnut was spending the night and she knew at least two of the others were probably wondering the same thing. It was beyond her comprehension that women should openly react so strongly to him. Exhaustion finally claimed her and she slept.

The barking of dogs awakened them in the morning. Gay raised his head and surveyed the dim lodge and Marlette followed his gaze to Chesnut's undistrubed bed.

"Well, I see the 'chief' didn't come sleep with us."

Evan Long sat up, saying sarcastically, "I guess you know who *he* slept with last night."

Joshua cleared his throat loudly, reminding them of Marlette's presence.

Andrew Proctor rubbed his eyes and asked, "You don't suppose he could really be a chief?"

Gay answered bitterly, "He sure acts like one."

Evan added, "Yeah. He's too damn high and mighty to my thinkin'. What do you think, Major? You know about Injuns."

Holliway finished rolling a cigarette and took a long drag before he answered. "He could be. Have any of you taken a good look at that medallion he wears? If he got it legally it means he is somebody important among his own people."

Marlette was intrigued and asked, "What do you find significant about it?"

Holliway expelled a curl of smoke and watched it rise to the smoke hole. "It's made of copper and engraved with a chief's headdress. Usually something like that is an object passed down in a chief's family. But he could have gotten it some other way."

A shaft of sunlight penetrated the lodge as the door flap was raised and Chesnut stepped in. Everyone looked at his face wondering how much he had heard of their conversation. His face was impassive, as usual. He stepped to the fire pit and began to rekindle the fire. It was an unspoken signal for all of them to get to their assigned tasks.

After a breakfast of coffee, bacon, and biscuits, and some fresh berries, they were ready to start packing. The Indian camp was already in the process of being dismantled. To Marlette it was a mass of noisy confusion with dogs barking, children dashing about, women yelling, and horses snorting as they were brought in to be loaded. Before their own party was packed the camp around them was ready to move.

The chief and his son came to say their farewells to Chesnut. Joshua stepped forward to shake hands and gave the chief and his son each a special gift of real glass mirrors. Both men smiled with childish delight, but hastened to remind Joshua of his promise. "You no forget. White man not wanted here."

Joshua smiled and nodded, "I'll not forget."

"You tell chief of whites." It was a command, not a question.

"I'll tell my chief."

The Indians grunted with satisfaction. They mounted their horses and galloped after the line of Indians already disappearing over the gentle rise toward the south. The Brightwood party headed eastward toward the twin grass buttes.

The Renegades

THEY STOPPED beside a small stream for their midday rest and lunch. Marlette was covered with fine, white dust that turned to mud where she perspired. It was difficult to think of her horse's comfort before her own but Chesnut's stony glare forbade anything else. At last she found her soap in her saddlebag and went to the stream. She knelt at the water's edge and plunged both hands into the cool water. Suddenly, she heard a sharp whirring rattle and the unknown noise filled her with terror. For a split second she was immobilized until she caught sight of the coiled snake only inches away. Then she screamed, her muscles gathering to spring away.

Chesnut's voice sounded loud as he commanded, "Don't move!"

A shot shattered the hot, motionless air and the hissing head exploded into shreds before her eyes, the lifeless body uncoiling and sliding into the creek. Marlette jumped to her feet and whirled around. Both Chesnut and Gay stood behind her, but Gay held the pistol. She expected to see a smile of self-assured arrogance but saw something entirely different. His hand suddenly went limp and frightened eyes stared out of his normally suave face at the rock where the snake had been.

Marlette ran to him and threw her arms around him, shielding him from the others. His body trembled against hers as she whispered, "Thank you, Gay. You saved my life. If it hadn't been for you—!" He sagged against her as her father rushed up, his face almost as white as Gay's.

"Did it bite you?"

"No, Father. I'm all right. Thanks to Gay."

At the sound of her words, Gaylord straightened, and smiled a thin, weak smile and she knew he would be all right. Chesnut turned away and the rest of the men all started talking at once.

Von Hout called, "Lucky you is such a goot shot, Gaylord."

Marlette, with greater caution, returned to the water and Gay went back to his horse without a word.

They rode on in the hot afternoon sun across the treeless, arid land shimmering a pale, dry gold through the heat waves. Gay was riding ahead of Marlette and she looked at his slumped posture and worried. He hadn't said a word since the rattlesnake incident. She had been relieved to realize that the brashness and self-assurance that so irritated her were all a front, understanding now why he was so obnoxious. But as the day wore on she began to wonder if he would be able to stand another crisis. She had been subconsciously relying on his strength and now that she had reason to doubt it, she found herself deeply disturbed.

Her thoughts were distracted when Chesnut strung the bow he carried and fired at a fleeing cottontail. The rabbit was skewered to the ground with one shot and Marlette now knew the answer to the question she had posed to herself at the Indian camp. By evening camp he had a rabbit for each of them, dressed, wrapped in canvas, and ready for roasting.

After a succulent supper, Marlette looked with longing at the stream near the camp and wondered how she could possibly manage a bath. She turned to her father sitting relaxed next to her, his eyes half-closed in weariness. "Father, do you suppose Chesnut would let me go for a bath away from camp if you came with me?"

Joshua turned thoughtful eyes on her and replied, "I doubt it, but I can ask." Wearily he rose to his feet.

She started to call him back but he had already turned away and was striding toward Chesnut. Chesnut listened to him, looked at the sun, and came toward her. Marlette got up, feeling embarrassed but determined. He stopped before her and eyed her dusty clothes, powdered skin, and hair.

"We'll be crossing the Columbia day after tomorrow. You'll get wet then."

"But that's not a bath! I need to wash my clothes, too."

"You can do that at the mission. They'll never dry in the night."

She had to admit he was right. The night chill had already set in. "How about in the morning?" she asked hopefully.

"No. We need the cool part of the day for travel." He turned on his heel and walked away, her unspoken protest dying on her lips. Every eye was on her and her face flamed with the embarrassment and humiliation that seemed to culminate every encounter with this man. Her eyes blazed after him in hatred.

Joshua put a consoling arm around her and said gently, "I'm afraid he's right, Marlette."

The anger went out of her and she nodded. "Isn't he always?"

She awoke near dawn without knowing why. It was still dark but she sensed someone moving about. She raised her head slightly and peered into the darkness. Something stepped between her and the faint glow of the nearly dead fire. She could just discern the lithe, silent shape of Chesnut, his buckskins a shade lighter than the darkness. The feet disappeared and didn't return. She heard the soft snuffling of the horses a few yards from camp and felt increasingly suspicious. She looked about intently for the other man who was supposed to be on watch, but could see no one else awake. Quietly, her anxiety turning to dread, she crawled from under her tarp.

Cautiously, she picked her way toward the horses, her eyes searching for Chesnut's shadow against the grayness of the landscape. She caught a movement some distance ahead near the stream and went toward it, taking her eyes off the shadow to watch her footing on the rocky ground. She suddenly realized she had no gun and was helpless to bring him back if he was deserting them. Yet she knew she would lose him in the darkness if she turned back. If she yelled to alert the men it would also alert Chesnut and she would never know what he was up to. She decided to follow him and see if he was really leaving, or perhaps meeting someone.

It was becoming lighter now and she could see Chesnut more easily. She dropped back a little and tried to stay hidden behind the rocks along the stream. Chesnut disappeared behind another pile of rocks and Marlette crept from her hiding place and followed him, hurrying across the open space. She reached the rocks and paused again. Carefully she peered around each rock before she proceeded. The jumble of rocks became impenetrable and she had to turn away from the creek to find an easier route. She began to fret that she had lost him when she spotted the faint imprint of his moccasin in the dust. He was headed toward the water and she followed cautiously.

The first golden rays of rising sun were just gilding the distant mountains and Marlette stopped for a moment to watch the yellow light spread over the peaks, setting them on fire. It was a moment to treasure in this strange, barren country. Remembering her mission, she walked on.

She scrambled over more rocks, hearing the muted rush of water. She rounded a huge rock and stopped, her hand flying to her mouth to stifle a startled cry. A few yards away, knee-deep in the water, Chesnut stood, his head bent as he washed his pale, naked body. She tried to step back quickly before he saw her but her foot rolled on the loose rocks creating a small landslide.

She stood paralyzed, clutching the boulder, as Chesnut swiftly grabbed the rifle near him and pointed it directly at her. She shoved herself away from the rock and ran, not stopping until she was out in the open. Breathlessly she stood looking behind her, knowing he would come after her and afraid to let him catch her.

She saw him coming, vaulting through the rocks like a deer, and she started running again. After a few yards she knew it was useless. Her lungs were aching and her feet were leaden. She stumbled and fell. She pulled herself up in a last desperate effort, but he was there and whirled her around with a firm hand on her arm. There was a rage in his eyes that frightened her as he demanded, "What do you think you're doing out here?"

She tried to pull away from his iron grip and gasped, "Take your hands off me!"

"Not until you answer me."

Her fear was replaced with angry indignation and she snapped, "I was following you."

"Why?"

"I thought you were deserting us."

The rage faded from his eyes and his grip loosened on her arm. She jerked herself free and stood glaring at him.

"Then why didn't you call one of your men?"

"Holliway would have killed you."

"And what did you expect to do?"

"I wanted to know where you were going. If you were meeting someone or deserting us."

If she thought he would be grateful for protecting him from Holliway she was mistaken, for he asked, "Do I have to start tying you up at night?"

She clenched her fists and shouted, "You're insufferable!"

"And you're a fool. I almost shot you, back there."

She was too angry to say more. She gave him one last angry look and turned away just as Holliway and Proctor appeared out of the rocks behind her. Holliway stopped a few yards away and leveled his rifle at Chesnut.

"What the hell are you doing with her out here?"

Marlette stepped between them. "He's bringing me back to camp. I went for a walk and Mr. Chesnut came after me." She thrust out her chin, daring them to question her explanation, grateful Chesnut had dressed before coming after her.

Holliway roared, "Miss Brightwood—!" He stopped, his face reddening with rage.

Andrew broke in quickly, "You had us all worried. We didn't know what had happened to you. You'd better come back with us now. Your father is extremely upset."

"I'm sorry I worried you. I couldn't sleep and it was so lovely and peaceful this morning, I just went for a walk." Head held high, she walked briskly between them and followed the trail back to camp.

They ate a cold, hurried breakfast in strained silence. Questions and insinuations had accomplished nothing except to make von Hout miserable because he had fallen asleep on duty. Chesnut said nothing and Marlette would only say that she had gone for a walk. Gaylord said nothing about the incident, much to Marlette's surprise and she worried about his strange behavior. He had been silent since noon yesterday and he averted his eyes when she looked his way.

They rode out and with nothing to occupy her mind, Marlette relived in blushing detail her encounter with Chesnut that morning. She angrily derided herself for such shameful thoughts, but found it impossible to forget him. The other naked Indians she had seen had not affected her like this, indeed she had found their squat, bowlegged bodies repulsive. However, the memory of Chesnut made her heart pound with a strange excitement. She closed her eyes against the picture, but she could still see it clearly—the dark hair, the strong, broad shoulders, and hard, muscled expanse of chest, disfigured with ugly, purplish scars, tapering to a lean, flat belly. She tried desperately to shut it out of her mind, but the image persisted. She could still see the narrow hips, the powerful thighs, the strong legs and all that was between them. Even in her embarrassment she had to admit he was a magnificent animal, not unlike a fine, blooded stallion. Once she had overheard one man call another "stud" and now she knew the aptness of the name.

But there was something else that bothered her about the image of Chesnut in the stream. She consciously tried to recall the picture until the incongruity came to her. It was the whiteness of his body. His face and hands were dark, but his body had been as white as hers. Surely then, he was not Indian as they all believed. At least not a full blood and probably not even a half blood for the French-Indian children at Vancouver were much darker than he. Contrary to her other feelings about him, she found it reassuring that he wasn't totally Indian and continued to speculate on his ancestry. It was one way of diverting her mind from the morning's incident. Whenever their glances crossed she turned away feeling the swift warmth of embarrassment. There was no indication in his face or eyes that anything unusual had happened and she wondered if it was due to Indian indifference or gentlemanly behavior. However, her memory of other encounters with him convinced her that he didn't know what it meant to be a gentleman.

A bloodcurdling yell interrupted her thoughts and she looked about wildly as more yells rent the air. The men bunched up in quick reaction as a small pack of Indians thundered down a steep slope toward them. Chesnut immediately pulled his rifle and cocked it. There was unanimous clicking of cocked rifles behind and ahead of her as the rest of the men laid rifles across their thighs, ready for instant use.

The Indians raced gaunt horses around them, brandishing their own weapons. With slight relief Marlette counted only two antiquated muskets in the bunch. The Indians finished their terrorizing circles and halted in a ragged line a few yards away. Their naked bodies looked thin and dirty, their hair was matted with grease, and caked paint cracked on their hostile faces. The Indian closest to Chesnut held up his hand and spoke in clipped, guttural tones.

Chesnut replied in the same quiet voice he used to everyone, in a language she could not understand. The rest of the Indians were eying everything intently, pointing and remarking to one another. Marlette felt a shiver of apprehension. Chesnut and the Indian leader were still talking. The Indian had an evil look about him and he fastened leering eyes on Marlette. Chesnut's voice snapped like a whip and his rifle muzzle rose slightly. The Indian didn't miss the movement and spat contemptuously into the dust. Marlette heard a chuckle and her eyes darted to the other Indians. They were all looking at her, making gestures she could understand and she looked away, shaken with anger and humiliation.

Chesnut turned to Joshua and said, "They want gifts."

Joshua dismounted, went to one of the packhorses and took out a gift bundle. He unwrapped the package and spread the canvas on the ground between Chesnut and the Indian, setting out the trinkets attractively. The Indian looked disdainful and again spat into the dust. He jerked his horse backward and yelled contemptuously at Chesnut who shrugged. The leader said something to his men and they eagerly slid from their horses and crowded around the canvas, grabbing and pushing for the articles.

After the Indians returned to their horses the leader spoke again. Chesnut nodded to the few scattered trinkets that were left on the ground. The leader yelled angrily at Chesnut and pointed to Marlette. The hair rose on her neck and her palms began to sweat where she gripped the reins. The rest of the Indians moved their horses menacingly closer, their faces threatening masks of evil. Chesnut spoke and they stopped. They waited in tense silence until Chesnut spoke to Joshua.

"He demands something of greater value than what is left."

"What do you suggest?"

"Try a mirror first, but whatever you try don't give him a weapon."

Joshua moved again to the packhorse and rummaged in the sacks of trade goods. He found a mirror and started toward the Indian.

Chesnut cautioned him, "Put it on the canvas and come back."

Joshua, sweating and wary, placed the mirror on the canvas and quickly stepped away. The Indian rode forward and looked down at the offered gift. He sneered and smashed the mirror with his musket butt, shouting unintelligibly to Chesnut.

After another long silence Chesnut asked, "What else do you have?"

Joshua looked bewildered. He pushed his silver-rimmed glasses higher up his nose and said, "I haven't anything else except knives or pipes. How about a pipe and tobacco?"

"Try it."

Again Joshua went to the packs and laid the offering of a beautiful, expensive pipe and a treasured packet of tobacco on the canvas. The Indian turned his head away in scorn and signaled one of his men to accept the gift. One of the Indians leaped to the ground and with a broad grin ran to scoop up the pipe and tobacco, sticking the pipe in his mouth. His commander yelled at him and the Indian, looking resentful, removed the pipe and stalked to his horse. Then he looked at Marlette again and, in a hissing voice, made another demand. Chesnut shook his head. Rapidly the Indian spoke again, and Chesnut again shook his head. Marlette looked back at Holliway. He was ready to explode; his leathery face was purple and his hands nervously raised and lowered the rifle.

Joshua stepped to Chesnut and whispered something to him. Chesnut nodded and Joshua opened his coat and removed his gold pocket watch and chain. He opened the case and the sun flashed on the gold cover as the tinkling strains of a lovely Strauss waltz drifted across the sage to the Indian. The Indian's eyes glittered with interest as Joshua handed the watch to Chesnut. Chesnut held the watch up and said something to the Indian as the watch spun slowly, flashing brilliantly in the sun. The Indian rode closer and Chesnut smoothly tossed the watch to him. He caught it expertly and held it up to his ear, pleasure spreading over his face as the music played again. The Indian looped the chain lovingly around his neck and carressed the smooth metal. Then, with a last lewd glance at Marlette, he yanked his horse away from Chesnut and galloped southward with the others, over the next ridge and out of sight.

Chesnut didn't move or say a word until they had been gone several minutes. When he turned his horse around, the nervous silence instantly filled with the sounds of tense men relaxing.

Holliway kicked his horse violently and rode up to Chesnut.

Harshly he demanded, "What did they say?"

"They're renegades looking for guns, ammunition, horses, and food."

"What did he want Miss Brightwood for?"

"Among other things, a hostage to trade for guns."

Joshua spoke up, wiping the sweat from his thin, white hair, "But couldn't they see we were better armed than they?"

"Yes. But they can sell information, too."

"Does that mean they might come back with more?"

"It's possible. Get what you want to eat now. Miss Brightwood, I want you to ride with me. We'll ride until evening camp."

Holliway stopped their hurried rummaging short by demanding, "Why change Miss Brightwood?"

"I want her where I can protect her."

"What makes you think you can protect her better than the rest of us?"

"Maybe I can't, but if she's at my side, I won't have to look to see what is happening to her."

Joshua agreed, "He's right, Major. Since he is the one taking the responsibility for my daughter, she should be where he can protect her without having his attention diverted."

It was clear Holliway didn't agree, but he yanked his horse around and rode back to the rear. Marlette moved her horse forward and stopped behind Chesnut. He turned and said, "Move your horse so that I can see him out of the corner of my eye."

She moved closer until the buckskin's head was almost against the leather-clad leg. He looked at her again and she could now see that his eyes were dark brown, not black. He said, "Put that gun on and keep it on."

"Am I in danger?" It sounded silly and she stammered, "I mean in that much danger?"

The softness of his voice belied the seriousness of his words, "We're all in danger."

They covered a lot of ground that long, hot afternoon, pushing the horses as fast as they dared and watching for any sign of Indians. Marlette discovered there was one benefit in being up front. She had far less dust in her face.

Late that afternoon they rode over the low treeless ridge that marked the course of the Columbia River. They camped in a narrow canyon formed by a small stream that flowed into the big river. The grass was green and trees crowded along the shallow stream, their roots barely covered and water-soaked in the swampy draw. It was a pleasantly cool haven, sheltered from the sun, and Marlette didn't mind the damp or the voracious mosquitoes, as the party avidly ate their first warm meal of the day and comforted their tired bodies with coffee. As the others talked and slowly relaxed, Marlette noticed that Gay was still withdrawn.

He finally got up and wandered away from the fire, only to find a new place to sit a few yards away. The worry that had been side-tracked by the renegades now returned. Had he really lost his self-confidence? Without it, he was no good to the rest of them because they had to be able to depend on one another. She had to try to help him regain his assurance, even if it meant torment for her again. She rose quietly and followed the direction the men took to relieve themselves.

Evan Long saw her and called, "Don't get lost out there now."

She turned for a moment and saw all their eyes on her, all eyes except Chesnut's. She answered, "Don't worry, I don't intend to."

Long laughed and turned back to the conversation, forgetting about her. She made a side step to get her jacket and when she looked back Chesnut was watching her and she could almost feel the threat in him. With all the defiance she could manage she left the protection of the fire.

On the way back she came by the rock where Gay was sitting. The water rippled softly, drowning out the hushed voices around the campfire. If Gay was aware of her he didn't show it. Darkness was settling over the narrow canyon as she stood beside Gay trying to think of something to say, something that would alter their old, antagonistic relationship.

"Did you ever see so much lonely and desolate land?"

He answered without looking up, "No."

She sat down close to him. "It frightens me," she said, "I don't see why any woman in her right mind would want to come here to live."

He looked at her then, obviously interested in what she was saying. Then he looked away. It was a long moment before he looked back and said, "I didn't think you were frightened of anything."

"There are lots of things that frighten me, Gay. I just have learned not to let them show."

"Well, then, you are to be congratulated. No one would ever know." There was a tinge of bitterness in his voice.

"I know we haven't gotten along very well and I'm sorry." Her voice was gentle, "I'm not very tolerant of people I feel are making fun of me."

He looked at her with surprise. Then he shook his head and laughed softly. "You know, you're right. I guess I *have* been making fun of you. I didn't mean to, but you're about the only woman I haven't been able to charm off her feet. I guess I was just getting even for being the last choice in poor competition with men like the captain —and especially Chesnut."

It was Marlette's turn to laugh. "Do you really think I'm interested in Chesnut?"

He shrugged. "There are women who find men of a different color more exciting."

"I can't believe that! Are you making fun of me again?"

"No. I didn't think you would believe it, but it's true."

"Well not for me. I despise the man."

He laughed again. "You probably won't believe this either, but hate is very close to love."

She thought about his words and said lightly, "I have despised you, too."

"Well, that is encouraging." His teeth flashed white in the darkness.

She stood up quickly, afraid she had gone too far and said, "Well, I'd better get back before they come looking for me."

Gay rose, too. "Yes, I suppose so. It wasn't a very good idea to wander off as you did this morning."

"I know. Will you take me back?"

"Of course. You'd better take my arm so you don't fall."

Marlette awoke with a feeling of well-being. Chesnut already squatted by the fire, nursing it back to life. She looked closely at his bent head, trying to detect if his hair was wet. It occurred to her that he possibly bathed every morning, but that seemed ridiculous because the other men were supposed to be watching him. The men were stirring in their beds, making the first grumpy noises of awakening.

She took down her tarp and rolled up her blankets in it. Gay smiled at her, not in his old arrogant manner, but with a shyness completely foreign to him.

As they ate breakfast, Holliway asked, "Will we still reach the Whitmans', day after tomorrow?"

"We should if we don't run into trouble."

Joshua asked, "Isn't there another Hudson Bay post before we get to the mission?"

"Yes. A good day's ride from here."

Holliway still had Indians on his mind. "Are we likely to run into more Indians?"

"Yes. There are quite a few in this area."

Joshua asked again, "Are we going to stop at the post?"

"We'll have to stop as we come back from the Whitmans' to get supplies for the trip back."

Isaac Thompson's shrill voice cut in, "Why not before we get to Whitmans'? I'd welcome an unworried night's sleep."

"You won't get it at this fort. McKinley doesn't have the control over the Indians that McLoughlin has and the French aren't sympathetic to Americans."

They finished breakfast in silence, afraid to voice their apprehension. They led the horses out of the brush and rode along the steep side hill to the Columbia, where they turned upriver.

A huge island, as high and as barren as the treeless ridge of hills behind them, divided the river. Chesnut checked everything carefully, tightening cinches and placing the ammunition high on the horses. He gave their two packhorses to Long and Holliway and led Marlette into the river.

Marlette held her breath. She was terrified and the river seemed wider with each sucking step her horse took into the seemingly calm water. She knew her horse was far more experienced than she, but that was of little comfort as he left the bottom and struck out after Chesnut's sorrel. She hung on desperately as the great force of the river swept them downstream. She wanted to cry out but she bit her lip to silence herself. They drew closer to the island and as she realized Chesnut's strategy, some of the fear left her.

Their horses regained footing and Chesnut rode a little way through the water and turned to wait for the others. Now that she was safe for the moment, she felt the crossing thus far had been easy enough, but Chesnut looked grimmer than usual. She had time to look at the island as they waded along the shoreline and noticed strange platforms and canoes and other signs of Indian habitation. She asked, "Is this an Indian camp?"

"No. It's a burial ground."

She shivered, looking with fearful curiosity at the silent remains of the dead, and was almost relieved when they were again swimming toward the south shore. The uneasy feeling didn't leave her until they left the water and rode to the top of the south bank, wet but safe.

Two Chiefs

CHESNUT SCANNED the vast, rock-filled wasteland. There were no trees and only a few dry tufts of grass among the restless, naked tumbleweeds. Mountains loomed dark and steep to the southeast. One by one the men gained the top of the bank and formed a ragged, dripping circle.

Holliway spoke first. "Okay, Chesnut, what now?"

Chesnut's dark eyes swept the landscape once more and came to rest on Holliway. "We'll make it to the river near the Whitman mission by night, if we don't have trouble. I think it would be safer for us to camp with Indians if there are any camps between here and the river. If we do, the same orders stand as before. No gunplay, no women, and no talking. These Indians will understand more English than the Klickitats."

Evan Long rubbed the black stubble on his face and asked, "You still worried the renegades will come back?"

"Yes." Chesnut moved his horse, ending the questioning. Marlette touched her heels to the buckskin and fell in immediately behind him.

They followed the curve of the river through the rolling sageland until they came to a stop for a rest and meager lunch within view of a large, flat-topped, rock butte. Chesnut was constantly alert, surveying the land for any unusual signs.

They continued on after their brief, silent rest. As they rode on again, they noticed with pleasure that the sun was not as hot as it had been and Marlette suddenly became aware of the lateness of the season. She had not thought to worry about snow, but now the weather became another threat to their safety.

Late that day they came to the Walla Walla River. After miles of wasteland the pleasant little river valley was a welcome sight. Low rolling plains added to the feeling of tranquillity as they rode down into the shallow valley and followed the meandering river through willow thickets and grassy flats. A dozen Indian lodges stood in a grassy flat at the river's edge. Marlette expected to see another charging welcome, but none came. They were quite close before it was even apparent that they had been seen.

Several men with ghostly white faces came and stood at the edge of the camp, eying them with a watchful apprehension, somehow more discomforting than the hostile curiosity of the Klickitats. Chesnut led his wary group across the shallow stream and rode up to the Indians, greeting them in their language. If they recognized him they didn't show it, but after a few minutes of rapid questioning Chesnut dismounted and the Indians' faces relaxed into smiles as they shook hands with obvious friendship.

They dismounted at Chesnut's signal, still holding their guns, and gathering around him for the introductions.

"Standing Elk, this is Joshua Brightwood, his daughter, and these are his men."

The Indian offered his hand with a smile, "Welcome to my camp and my lodge. We will smoke, eat, and talk."

Joshua smiled warmly, "Thank you, Chief, we will be honored."

Chesnut spoke again, "Standing Elk tells me a party of near a hundred whites are on their way to the valley."

Marlette, momentarily stunned, saw her father stiffen at the news, and slowly, began to sag. She reached out to support him, noticing briefly the grim, dismayed faces of the men. They had come so far and endured so much to discover now that their journey was meaningless. It had to be hideous joke.

Her father regained his composure and asked in a slightly weak, but hopeful voice, "Did they come in wagons?"

The Indian answered, "No wagons, just horses, mules, and some cattle."

The fire returned to Joshua's eyes and his shoulders lifted. The Indian gave orders to his men and their horses were led away. They followed the chief to his lodge; Marlette, at her father's elbow, noticed that their presence caused little stir among these Indians.

The Indian entered his lodge and gave orders to the two women inside. Unlike the Klickitats, he seemed to have only one wife. The second woman was his daughter, a girl of about sixteen. His two younger sons stood nearby. Once again, the guests found themselves placed in a circle around the fire and the chief brought out his pipe, observing the ritual ceremony before passing it around the circle.

In the silence that accompanied this ritual, Marlette noticed the similarity between these Indians and the Klickitats. The women wore the same style of dress, two deerskins sewn together and decorated beautifully. The patterns differed, she saw, and their legs were protected by leggings above their moccasins. Their faces were covered with a thin layer of whitish clay, and earrings of bones, claws, and teeth, hung from pierced ears and matched necklaces that clanked as they worked. A fishy odor came from their thickly oiled hair that hung in two heavy braids.

Their host was naked to the waist; his hair in a single well-oiled braid. He, too, wore earrings and necklaces similar to those the women wore, but his were made from the more valued bits of shell from the coast.

The lodge was low and flat-topped, covered with woven mats and brush cut from the riverbank. The beds looked comfortable, filled with fur blankets and elk robes.

At last the smoking ritual was over, and Standing Elk asked, "You did not know the people of your country were coming?"

Joshua smiled a little sadly. "No. I am totally surprised. When we left to come here we knew of no others planning to come. It was our intention to warn people against coming if we found it was not good them to do so."

Standing Elk smiled in approval. "So my brother, here, has said. It would be wise to prevent more from coming. There will be great trouble if more come. There is much talk of war in the villages of our people. Do you have the power to stop your people from coming?"

"No. I can only tell them what we see and advise them against coming. It would take an order from our great chief in Washington to stop them from coming."

"Then you must speak to this chief and tell him not to let his people come here. This land belongs to the Indian."

With troubled eyes Joshua asked, "Would you make war on the white people even if none stayed in this land but all went on to the valley on the other side of the mountains?"

Solemnly the Indian replied, "I do not know. We have been taught by Dr. Whitman that making war upon the white man is bad and will anger the white man's God, and the white man's chief in Washington will have us all killed. But also, Dr. Whitman tells us it is wrong to steal. Yet is it not stealing for the white man to take the land from the Indian, to take our food, the animals that provide us with meat and clothing, and pay us nothing? If the white God does not want any man to do these things, how can the white man do these things and not be punished?"

"You ask me a question that I have no answer for."

Standing Elk smiled without warmth, "And neither do your white men who say they speak with your God. I have lost my belief in the strength of the white man's God. I do not believe he will punish us for killing the white man any more than he punishes the white man for killing my people or stealing our land."

Marlette felt the creeping discomfort of fear and knew by the slight nervous stirrings of the men that they felt as she did. Her father's face looked pale in the faint light. Only Chesnut sat motionless, unmoved and unimpressed with the portent of the Indian's words.

The women appeared with bowls of water for washing, kneeling before Standing Elk and Chesnut first. Marlette watched as the girl held the bowl for Chesnut, her face hidden, but the very tilt of her head boldly revealing her consciousness of her guest. Marlette thought she detected acknowledgment in the slight movement of Chesnut's head. Next, the girl kneeled before her father, and then before Marlette. Marlette gazed at her with interest and found her somewhat more delicate of feature than the Klickitat girl. She smiled at the girl deliberately and the girl turned her eyes down, a small quirk of her full lips answering Marlette's smile.

Wooden platters of food arrived and Marlette watched as the girl served Chesnut, briefly touching him as she handed him the platter. He watched her openly, but expressionlessly. Marlette looked away, a blush rising to her face as a picture of him standing naked in the stream flitted through her mind. It wasn't difficult to imagine now why women found him attractive. He had probably been with these people before; bathing in this very river. Her embarrassment turned to loathing as she wondered how many women he'd been with. He was like a tongue-dragging dog running from one bitch to the next, and it repelled her.

Her platter was filled with much the same food they had eaten at the Klickitat camp and she ate it without trying to taste it or think about what it might be. Their host finished his platter which was taken away by his wife. The daughter stood ready to answer any request of Chesnut's, her black eyes unable to conceal the expectancy and excitement she felt in his presence.

Standing Elk spoke. "My brother tells me you mean no harm to us but you met some Indians who might do you harm. I have no anger against you and you are welcome to stay here for the night, but know I am not able to protect you against any of my people who might want to harm you."

Joshua nodded, "I understand," he said, and paused. "Tell me, Standing Elk, what good has Dr. Whitman done for you or what do you think needs to be done so that our people and your people can live in peace?"

The Indian frowned and Marlette thought she saw Chesnut look approvingly at her father. Standing Elk answered carefully, "Dr. Whitman has done little good for us. It is true he is more powerful than our medicine men but he tries to make farmers of us and now look at us! Once I had many horses and many wives. This is another thing your white God does not allow. Your Dr. Whitman tried to teach us to grow our own food, but without my wives to do this I have barely enough to feed us. Without my wives to take care of the meat and hides I bring in from hunting I no longer have enough. I am now a poor man, an object of laughter among the other tribes. I think I will no longer do what your Dr. Whitman tells me." He paused and then continued more definitely, "There can never be peace between us unless you stay in your land and let us stay in our land and make all your Dr. Whitmans go home and allow us to live as our God wants us to live."

"Do the rest of the chiefs feel this way?"

"Yes. We have talked with many other tribes. All will fight to keep their land. Would not you fight to keep your home and your land and protect your children?"

All eyes looked away except Holliway's. Joshua nodded gravely,

"Yes. I think we all would fight for that."

"Then you must tell your people that we will fight and many will be killed."

"I will tell my chief in Washington, but you must understand—I am but one man and my chief may not listen to what I say. However, if you and all the other chiefs would come and speak with him, then maybe he would listen."

Standing Elk looked thoughtful. "You speak with wisdom, but such a thing is not easy. To trade and to talk on neutral ground is one thing, but to gather enemy chiefs together for such a thing would be a great and difficult task."

Joshua shrugged with the air of a man who had just unloaded a heavy burden onto another. "The things of greatest value are the hardest to achieve."

Standing Elk smiled broadly, his teeth flashing in the failing light. He dropped a hand on Chesnut's knee and chuckled. "My brother brings to me a man who can speak with the pureness of heart of the Indian."

There was the faintest suggestion of a smile on Chesnut's lips. "What do you think, my brother, is his heart true?"

Chesnut looked intently at Joshua for a moment and Marlette waited breathlessly for Chesnut's answer.

In his quiet, husky voice he answered, "I think Mr. Brightwood speaks true. If all the tribes would agree to send a man to talk to the white chief it would show how strongly you all feel and that you can unite against a common threat if necessary. It would be a sign of greatness to the man who could do such a thing."

Standing Elk smiled with warmth at Chesnut. Clearly he respected and liked the man. "It is a good thing to think of. We must talk of this among our people." He lit his pipe and once again it was passed around the circle.

When the pipe was returned to Standing Elk he laid it carefully in front of him and rose with dignity, his broad face reflective. "It is late," he said. "Your lodge is ready. Sleep well."

Chesnut stood in one lithe movement and the rest followed. The Indian said something to Chesnut in his own language and Chesnut answered. The Indian nodded and Chesnut led them out of the lodge.

A cold wind stirred the willows and Marlette looked up quickly.

Gray clouds sailed across the dark sky blotting out brilliant, twinkling stars. The camp was very quiet in the soft glow of the firelight. A mournful coyote barked in the distance and provoked a medley of plaintive yips from every direction.

They reached their lodge. The fire was crackling and their packs were stacked together. Chesnut ordered, "Check your packs."

Isaac asked fearfully, "Can we trust him not to kill us."

Chesnut answered, "Yes."

Holliway straightened up, his eyes narrowed and his voice was tight. "Why don't you tell him what would happen to us if those renegades track us here?"

Chesnut looked up at Holliway. "I think Standing Elk made that clear."

Holliway leaned forward threateningly. "You're damn right he did. He'd hand us over to those renegades in a wink. And so help me, Chesnut, you better not be close enough for me to get my hands on you if that happens."

Chesnut ignored Holliway's threat and went back to his pack.

Long said caustically, "Save your breath, Major. These Injuns ain't goin' to let you kill their brother."

Joshua broke in, "Gentlemen. Let's not accuse Mr. Chesnut of anything we have no basis for."

Von Hout ran his fingers through his dusty beard. "Ja. Ve all tired. Let's get some sleep instead of all dis argument."

Chesnut closed his pack and left the lodge silently, every eye looking after him distrustfully.

Long chuckled with envy. It was ovbious to everyone where he was going. They spread out their beds and fell in with sighs of exhaustion.

Long chuckled again. "That bastard's got endurance, anyway."

No one said anything and the silence grew uncomfortable. Andrew stirred in embarrassment for Marlette and Long finally mumbled apologetically, "Sorry, Miss Brightwood."

There were more sighs and groans as saddle-weary bodies relaxed and soon they all slept.

They were awakened early to the whining voices of children and barking dogs. The fire was almost out and there was a chill in the lodge. Peeping between the mats, Marlette saw naked children driven by stern mothers toward the river to bathe.

She saw Chesnut duck through the door of Standing Elk's lodge and stride out of sight upriver into the brush. She again remembered how he looked in the water, naked and dripping, as the children were now. She closed her eyes and let the mat fall back into place.

Holliway rose and rekindled the fire, while Marlette prepared coffee. Gay was eager to help her and hurried out of the lodge to fill the pot with water.

Long, who had been looking outside, let his mat drop and said, "I don't see nothin' suspicious out there."

Isaac asked, "Are the horses still there?"

"Yeah."

"Do you see Chesnut?" Holliway asked sourly.

Long grinned. "Naw. You didn't expect me to, did you?"

Holliway didn't answer. He moved to the coffee pot and poured out some of the hot liquid, apparently deep in thought.

At that moment Chesnut stooped into the lodge. He surveyed them and then poured himself a cup of coffee. "Better get something to eat with this. We'll be leaving shortly," he said.

Marlette moved to find them some food and her hand touched Gay's as they reached for the same pack. He held her hand briefly with a reassuring squeeze.

After a brief breakfast of the leathery dried meat they called jerky, they packed and loaded their horses. The whole camp was gathered to watch their departure.

Standing Elk came forward and Joshua smiled. "Thank you for letting us stay with you. I have some gifts for you and your people."

The Indian smiled with pleasure. Joshua opened the pack and the Indians murmured approval as they pushed closer to see the gifts. Joshua was more generous with these few Indians than he had been with the larger camp of Klickitats. Many of the Indians expressed their delight in English as they picked out the things that appealed to them.

Standing Elk nodded with a broad smile. "You have brought good gifts. Standing Elk will not forget."

The expedition mounted while Chesnut returned to the Indians and talked with them briefly. There was a solemn handshake with each before Chesnut returned to his horse and also mounted. A slender figure appeared from Standing Elk's lodge to watch them leave. As they rode past the lodge Chesnut turned his head to the girl and nodded slightly. She watched with sad eyes and then ducked back into the lodge. Marlette felt both anger and pity; pity for the girl and anger at Chesnut.

It was easy riding along the level river valley and Marlette forced herself to stop worrying about the danger and concentrate on the beauty of the pleasant valley. Every thicket was alive with deer or game birds and snow-topped mountains rose in the distance.

Soon they saw the first signs of Indian habitation and attempted agriculture. Across the river, a dugout house stood against a hill. A small patch of tilled ground extended to the river, looking pitifully forlorn. A family of Indians came riding toward them on the other side of the river but they made no effort to cross and passed with only curious looks. They looked lean and poor.

A few miles later a lone rider came slowly toward them on their side of the river. He carried himself with distinction, his black frock coat carefully arranged over his horse's back, a silk hat squarely on his graying head. He could have been a judge, but as he approached they saw he was an Indian. Chesnut stopped and the older Indian watched them intently.

He raised his hand in greeting, bringing his horse to a halt in front of them, and staring at Marlette in a manner that made her uncomfortable.

He smiled at Chesnut in obvious recognition and said in excellent English, "Does my brother from the Dakotas betray his people by bringing white men into the country of the Indian as does the white doctor known as White?"

"No, Five Crows. These people do not stay. They will visit with Dr. Whitman and return to Fort Vancouver and back to their own land."

The Indian smiled again. "That is good. Then I, Five Crows, chief of the Cayuse, welcome you. Perhaps you would like to visit my home? The white woman will find it very comfortable."

"Your offer is generous, but already there is new snow in the mountains and we must return before winter."

The Indian gazed at Marlette with a burning intensity. "I will let the woman decide if she wants to come."

Marlette almost stopped breathing. There was unconcealed invitation in the Indian's eyes. But Chesnut replied quietly and firmly, "She cannot go with you."

The Indian heeled his horse forward trying to get closer to Marlette but Chesnut turned his own horse in front of her. The Indian said indignantly, "I want to speak to this woman."

"No." Chesnut's voice was taut.

"Who are you to speak for this woman?"

"She belongs to me."

Marlette stirred in protest but kept silent. She felt the blood drain from her face. There was a rattle of hooves as Holliway, unable to contain himself, rode up. Chesnut heard him and looked at him threateningly, shaking his head. Holliway stopped, uncertain, but his hand rested ominously on his revolver.

Five Crows demanded, "Let me ask the woman. Maybe she would rather belong to a chief of many than to you who are chief of none. I will give you twenty horses and three of the loveliest virgins for her."

With cold finality Chesnut answered, "No. She is not for sale at any price."

The Indian straightened with determination. "Then you refuse to let her talk with me?"

"She will tell you the same."

They stared at each other for a long moment, measuring each other's strength. Then the Indian turned his eyes back to Marlette. "I am a far richer man than this one. You will have a nice home and anything you desire. You will have many slaves and will never have to work if you come with me."

Chesnut looked at her in wordless warning. She shook her head negatively and looked away trying to appear aloof. Out of the corner of her eye she saw the Indian nod dejectedly and turn his horse away.

When he had gone, Holliway moved his horse closer to Marlette in a protective manner. "All right, Chesnut, what do you intend to do in case he doesn't believe your little story?"

"I'll worry about that when the time comes."

Joshua rode forward. "Major, I'm sure Mr. Chesnut did what he thought was best."

The major lifted his head, anger blazing in his eyes. "Well I think

he could have invented a different story. That Indian might come back
to see if your daughter is sleeping with Chesnut."

"Is that true?"

Matter-of-factly Chesnut answered, "Yes."

Marlette felt the blush that had been rising at the thought of
sleeping with Chesnut, suddenly flee, leaving her pale and apprehensive.

In a harsh voice the major suggested, "You might tell them what
will happen then."

Chesnut replied calmly, "Then Five Crows will challenge me with
the lie." He surveyed all the faces that looked at him angrily. "Unless
one of you wants to take my place?"

He didn't have to say anymore. Even Marlette understood that
it might mean fighting for his life because of her and she shuddered.
Chesnut turned his horse eastward and Marlette followed. The rest
fell in silently.

The Whitman Mission

THE RIVER swung to the south following the low barren ridge. Chesnut led them toward a solitary hill rising steeply from the valley floor, and ahead Marlette saw the gleaming white adobe of the two-story mission building. Past a stream and fields of golden wheat stubble, the sun flashed on glass windows framed in slate and a bright apple green door shouted welcome. Marlette felt weak with relief.

Eagerly her eyes sought every detail of the mission. She noticed a young, yellow-leaved orchard flourishing to the south near the river. They crossed an irrigation ditch and rode around the north end of the mission, following the main irrigation ditch which ran from a large pond east of the mission. Another two-story house stood near the pond. Between this house and a single-story wing extending from the mission stood a barn and corral.

The place was noisy with men working and she was surprised to see that they were white. A tall, husky man in buckskin pants and homespun shirt laid down his hammer and came striding out to meet them. His brown, gray-flecked beard split into a wide smile when he recognized Chesnut. Chesnut dismounted and the two shook hands. "Chesnut!" the man exclaimed, "What a surprise! And these people! Are they the long-prayed-for help for my mission?"

"I'm afraid not, Dr. Whitman."

"Well, no matter," Whitman said as he strode forward, "Welcome to Waiilatpu. Our home is yours."

Joshua was on the ground and moving forward with his hand extended as the rest of the men slowly dismounted. "Dr. Whitman, this is indeed a pleasure. I'm Joshua Brightwood of Philadelphia and this is my daughter, Marlette, and the members of my expedition."

Marlette dismounted as Joshua introduced them. Marcus Whitman took her hand and shook it firmly, his dark blue eyes warm as he smiled at her. "You must be tired," he said briskly. "Let's get your things and find out where Narcissa wants to put you." He turned toward the mission and called, "Narcissa! Narcissa, we have company."

Narcissa Whitman came around the end of the mission wing, her bright, high-necked calico dress swishing against her legs as she strode toward them. Her hair was caught in a neat bun like Marlette's and reflected the sun in its pale copper sheen. She recognized Chesnut and smiled happily, saying, "Ross! How nice! Are these our reinforcements?" In that moment Marlette saw a different man; his face magically transformed by the first smile she had ever seen there. His face softened and his dark brown eyes filled with warmth. He was strikingly handsome in that moment and at least ten years younger than she had imagined. But the smile was only for Narcissa and when he turned with her to meet the others, the smile was gone, and Marlette wondered if she had imagined it.

Mrs. Whitman took Marlette's hand warmly and repeated her husband's welcome. "How tired you must be. Come to the house and make yourself at home. Whatever we have is yours."

Marlette smiled at the sincere blue gray eyes on a level with her own and protested, "But you already have company. Surely we will be imposing."

Narcissa waved away the thought. "Nonsense! You are not imposing. That is what we are here for—a place of rest in the wilderness. Now come and we'll get you comfortable and fix something to eat."

As they walked toward the mission Narcissa asked, "From Philadelphia, your father said. Is that the same Brightwood who builds such fine carriages?"

Marlette replied with a surprised smile, "Yes. But how did you know?"

Narcissa laughed easily, "Surely everyone knows that name."

Marlette said, pleased, "I doubt that, but at times I'm sure Father thought so."

They rounded the end of the building and Marlette saw the remains of a neatly tended vegetable garden spreading toward the river.

Her mouth watered for the golden corn and ripe red tomatoes. Narcissa stuck her head into an open door near the end of the building and said, "All right, children, you can go play now. We'll finish later."

Two young girls and a boy, all obviously part Indian, came shyly down the steps. Narcissa smiled at them affectionately and explained, "These are my special charges, MaryAnn Bridger, Helen Mar Meek, and David Malin." The girls smiled and curtsied, but the boy stared solemnly with round, watchful eyes. "Now run along, but be careful to keep David away from the river." She turned back to the door and locked it.

Marlette followed Mrs. Whitman to another door and entered a large, cool, clean kitchen. Narcissa asked, "Now what would you like first, something to eat, a bath, or just plain rest?"

"I don't think I could do another thing without a bath and clean clothes, if it isn't too much trouble?"

Her companion laughed, "Of course not. It's what every white woman wants the minute she gets here."

She went to a door behind the big table and knocked lightly before she opened it. "Girls, get a wash fire started and heat some water. Our guest would like a bath. Take the large tub upstairs for her."

Two Indian girls of about twelve or thirteen came out of the room and hurried outside.

Marlette asked, "Do you have many Indians living here?"

"Oh, no. Just these two girls. They are here to go to school and I persuaded their father to let them stay to help me. And I've certainly been glad I had them as we've had near a hundred people stop here on their way to the Willamette valley. But you probably passed them on your way here?"

"No. We haven't seen anyone but Indians."

Narcissa's smile faded as she inquired, "No unpleasant experiences I hope?"

"Yes and no. We stayed one night with a band of Klickitats. They were very interested in our guns and I wondered if we would live through the night. After we left them we ran into some renegade Indians. Fortunately they were few and ill-armed but we have been going at a terrific pace to get here before they came back with reinforcements. Chesnut thought it best to stay with Indians for protection, so we spent last night downriver at a camp. I'm *very* glad to be here!"

Narcissa nodded with understanding. "I can imagine. What was the name of the chief at the camp you stayed at last night?"

"Standing Elk. Do you know him?"

She nodded. "Yes. They are part of the Umatilla tribe. If you followed the river in you saw some of their cabins. They are more tractable and easier to work with than the Cayuse."

"We met one of those, too. We ran into him just before we got here. He tried to buy me!"

Narcissa laughed. "That must have been Five Crows. He was just here trying to talk one of the immigrant women into going with him. He thinks he can become civilized if he has a white wife."

"Well, he certainly had me worried. He was so insistent."

"I know what you mean." Narcissa noticed Marlette's strained expression and added cheerfully, "Come, I'll show you to your room."

Marlette followed her upstairs into a small bedroom with a double bed, table, chair, and wash stand.

"It's not very pretentious, but I hope you'll find it comfortable."

Marlette smiled, "It'll be a welcome change from the ground."

The men came up the steps and were led into a large room at the other end of the wing. Gay brought her pack and left her to bathe.

Marlette stripped off her dusty outer clothes and sat brushing the days of trail dust from her hair, recalling Chesnut's face as he greeted Mrs. Whitman. She had caught a look of something close to love, however the thought seemed ridiculous, quite incongruous with everything she had seen of him so far.

After bathing and washing her hair she dressed and turned to the mirror above the wash bowl to pull her fine, shining hair into a smooth bun. She hardly recognized her tanned, hollow-cheeked reflection.

She opened the bedroom door and was enveloped in the delightful aroma of baking bread. A sudden pain growled through her stomach and she felt shaky from hunger. She steadied herself against the door casing, waiting for the feeling to pass. Her breakfast of jerky had been many hours ago.

Down the hall the men's door opened and Chesnut came out,

freshly groomed. His alert eyes caught the anguish in her face and he asked, "Is something wrong?"

Marlette straightened, blushing under his observant gaze. "No, no. I'm all right."

He came to her and, as if perceiving her trouble, said, "Dinner will be ready soon. I'll take you to the table."

He took her arm and she hesitantly let him, feeling terribly self-conscious as they walked down the steep steps. The men were already seated around the table, discussing their trip and their future plans. Gay threw Marlette and Chesnut a curious look as she entered on Chesnut's arm. She smiled reassuringly at him but he still seemed a little hurt. Marlette took an empty chair and Chesnut seated himself quietly, listening intently. It was remarkable how he could appear completely aloof and seemingly unobtrusive when he was anything but that.

Narcissa dished out the array of vegetables and meat onto platters and they filled their plates eagerly, enjoying their first complete meal since Fort Vancouver. They ate their fill in relative silence and leaned back to enjoy pipes and coffee.

The dishes were removed and the children ushered out of the room before Whitman broke the silence. "As I was saying, it is still vital to find a pass through the mountains. Even if we can get the wagons to the Columbia it is a risky job to raft them downriver, and the portages around some of the rapids would be impossible for a wagon. I've always maintained that there has to be a pass somewhere in those mountains, but so far, I have been unsuccessful in discovering it." He looked hopefully at Chesnut and continued, "If any man can find a pass for you, it's Chesnut."

Chesnut said nothing, but Joshua nodded and said, "Yes. He has assured us there are passes. I'm hoping to take the most likely one on the way back and chart it for future use. If we can at least do that, I will consider it worth the journey."

"You are quite right, Mr. Brightwood, and I wish I could go with you, but I have more urgent business." He sat in frowning silence for a long moment, his face a study in determination and endurance. It was little wonder that he had been able to do so much in the six years since he had come to the Oregon country.

"I haven't mentioned this because I dislike speaking of personal difficulties, but Dr. White brought us orders from the Mission Board to close down Waiilatpu and Lapwai. I have already decided to ride east within the week to try to rectify the matter. It would be disastrous to close down this station, especially now." He paused again, running a hand through his dark brown, unruly hair that was beginning to gray at the temples. "If I finish my business in time I will accompany next spring's immigration."

Joshua asked, "Is there anything we could do to help?"

"Not with the Mission Board, I'm afraid, but I am worried about the protection of future settlers. I have not been very successful in winning Indian acceptance of the white man. Dr. Spalding is doing a better job at Lapwai. The Nez Perce are not as warlike as the Cayuse. I can boast some success in getting them to farm the ground but I have had a great deal of difficulty with them. And now that the fur traders have disbanded east of the mountains, the Sioux will undoubtedly be a menace to anyone not traveling in enough strength to protect themselves.

"I do know that Senators Linn and Benton of Missouri have a bill in Congress concerning establishment of law in the Oregon Country. I think we need forts all along the route to help protect these people and to serve as posts for mail riders. Do you realize it takes a year or more for a letter to reach us here? It is this very lack of communication that forces me to take the trip east at this time of year."

Joshua smiled and nodded his understanding. "I'm sure we can all sympathize with your position, Doctor. We, too, feel the need to protect these people. Now that the first group has come, many more will come. Our hope is in Mr. Thompson, here. His partners have influence in Washington and we hope that after we return with a full report we can get these men to back a presidential candidate sympathetic to the Oregon question."

Whitman leaned forward enthusiastically. "I had been half-thinking of going to Washington myself and now I know that I must. If I can talk to President Tyler, present the facts to him as we know them, perhaps we can delay the ceding of this territory to Britain until there are enough of us here to form a majority in favor of the United States."

Joshua, his eyes moist with emotion, stood up and raised his cup in salute to Marcus Whitman, saying, "Godspeed for Oregon!"

Marlette rose with the rest of them and repeated the invocation. Only Chesnut remained silent and seated. It was a moment of renewed dedication and intense emotion. Finally Whitman spoke, "Then there is no time to delay. I will leave Monday for the States. Now if you will excuse me, I'd better make some preparations."

Marlette suddenly felt very tired and went to kiss her father good-night, feeling at home in the secure surroundings.

Gay caught up with her and said, "Let me see you to your room."

She took his arm and they went upstairs. He opened her door, lit a candle in the darkened room, and turned to her, a soft smile on his lips. "Well, you should sleep well tonight."

"I've been looking forward to it."

He chuckled. "I must admit, I never thought you could take it."

"Neither did I think you'd make it," she retorted.

He laughed and this time Marlette laughed with him. Their laughter relaxed them and she leaned against the doorway, strangely at ease.

He looked at her for a long moment, his blue eyes soft and serious. "You make me almost want to return home and make something of myself."

"You flatter me, but I hope you are not just flattering me."

He moved closer to her and stood with one hand braced against the wall behind her. "And what does that mean?"

She ducked under his arm and stood holding the door. "It means I hope you will still feel like making something of yourself when you get home."

He smiled thinly. "I was afraid that was what you meant."

She saw the hurt in his eyes again and said, "Nothing has changed since the other night."

He smiled warmly at her. "Good night. Sleep tight." He reached for the door, his fingers closing over hers and left, pulling the door closed behind him.

Marlette awoke the next morning from the first sound sleep she had had in days. She opened the window and a cool autumn briskness swept into the room. She heard chickens clucking in the yard and somewhere a cow bellowed insistently. She got dressed and went down to breakfast.

Narcissa greeted her pleasantly. "Good morning. Did you sleep well?"

"Too well. I may want to stay."

She laughed merrily, "Then you would be welcome. Come. Breakfast is almost ready and then it will be time for church."

"Church? Is it Sunday?"

Again Narcissa laughed. "Yes. I hope you and the men will come."

"I'd almost forgotten about church. It seems so far removed from what we've been through."

"Oh, but I'm sure that isn't so. You have come so far with so little difficulty, I'm sure God has been with you."

Marlette smiled faintly, remembering a time when they had gone to church every Sunday. But that was before her mother died. "Where do you hold your services?"

Narcissa stepped to the door at the bottom of the steps and unbolted it. It opened onto a large room with a fireplace in the north wall and a few benches filling the empty space. "This is the Indian room."

"Do you have many Indians attending services?"

"The number varies with the time of year. There won't be many today since they have not all returned from the fall hunt. We never have many because the Cayuse are difficult people to persuade in the ways of the Lord. We can't even get them to work for us. They find it beneath their dignity."

"Then you have built all this by yourselves?"

Narcissa laughed at Marlette's astonishment. "Hardly! Dr. McLoughlin loaned us some of his Kanakas and we've hired Americans at times and the Walla Walla Indians will work for us. The two girls you saw are from the Walla Walla tribe."

"Surely, if nothing else, you've been able to communicate with them, teach them our language?"

"Unfortunately, no. That is another of our great difficulties. They are reluctant to learn English. We've learned the Nez Perce dialect which most of the Indians in the region can speak." She smiled ruefully. "It does sound as if we've done all the learning and they've done all the teaching." She waved a hand. "Well, let's have our breakfast."

After breakfast the Whitmans excused themselves to hold Sunday school and services for the Indians. The rest of them sat around the table talking and drinking coffee. Presently Marlette heard Narcissa's voice rising in song. All talking stopped as they listened to the lovely, clear voice.

The Whitmans reappeared sometime later and began to prepare for the service for the white people at the mission. Everyone went into the Indian room. The benches were filled with the immigrants staying at the mission. Narcissa glowed with happiness as she spoke to the gathering people. Joshua sat down on the last bench and Marlette followed, Holliway behind her. She was surprised to see Chesnut standing behind them near the outside door.

Dr. Whitman opened the service with the Lord's Prayer, and then Narcissa led them in hymn singing. As Marlette clasped her hands and closed her eyes to give her own special thanks for their safe journey, she heard Narcissa's soprano voice soar over the room again with angelic sweetness. She turned her head toward Chesnut who stood behind them. His head was not bent in prayer and he watched Narcissa with an admiring smile.

The service ended after a stirring sermon by Dr. Whitman and regretfully they stood. The men filed out the door with the rest of the congregation, but Marlette waited uncertainly. Narcissa started to gather up the hymnbooks and Marlette moved to help her.

They carried the books through the sitting room and into the Whitman bedroom. As they turned to leave the room, she saw the feather comforter on the bed and exclaimed, "A featherbed! How on earth did you manage to get it here in one piece?"

Narcissa smiled and touched it lovingly. "I didn't. Mrs. McLoughlin helped me make it when I stayed there while Marcus started our first house."

Marlette shook her head in wonder. "You both make this wilderness seem almost civilized."

They returned to the sitting room and Narcissa motioned Marlette to sit with her on a settee. The older girls were entertaining the younger children with stories and quiet games on the other settee.

Narcissa continued, "We have been fortunate in some things, but not without great cost to both of us." She looked away, a little sad and withdrawn. When she looked back the sadness was gone and she said thoughtfully, "You know, it's like bearing a child. The pain of the moment dims in time and memory, and you remember only the joy of having done something special."

Marlette concurred, "And you are doing something special. I've never heard anything more inspiring than Dr. Whitman's sermon this morning."

Narcissa smiled warmly, "Then we have helped each other. It was your father's hope that helped renew my dear husband's spirits. He works so hard and by this time of the year he is near collapse. After all the guests we have had and the letter Dr. White brought, well, I'm afraid he was as depressed as he has ever been."

Marlette nodded. "Father, too. This has been such a hard trip for him especially after learning that people were already on their way to the valley. He really needed what Dr. Whitman gave us this morning. We all did."

Laughingly Narcissa said, "If only our Indians could be so easily inspired. If they were all as willing, intelligent, and as civilized as Ross, our work would be so much easier."

Marlette's eyes widened with surprise. She would hardly have considered Chesnut willing or civilized. Narcissa noticed her expression and laughed. "I see you don't agree with me, but if you dealt with as many uncivilized people as we have, he would seem quite the opposite in comparison."

"Tell me," Marlette asked, "what do you know about him?"

"Not very much. He says little about himself."

"Oh? I thought he had talked to you. He seems to become a different man in your presence."

Narcissa shook her head and smiled. "You are observant. He told me once that I reminded him of someone he knew. He has never said anymore than that."

"Well he certainly is hard to understand. I'm not sure I trust him and he exasperates me so. I'm afraid I dislike him."

"I can see where you would. But I think he's trustworthy. He has helped us at times and we've always found him honest."

"I'm relieved to hear that, but could it be because of his liking for you?"

Narcissa laughed again. "Goodness, no! Honesty and friendship are not necessarily one and the same with the Indian. In my short

experience I would have to conclude that honesty is a rare quality
in these people. Ross is a man with unusually high principles. When
we first came here we didn't know the language and even after we
learned it we didn't understand the Indian way of thinking. Ross spent
quite a bit of time here and through him we gained some insight into
Indian culture. But he never went so far as to bring the Indians to
our point of view. He would explain our point of view but he refused
to convince them, because he doesn't believe we should change the
Indians."

Marlette shook her head. "He's too complex for me. Why would
he help you at all if he doesn't believe in what you do?"

"He realizes, with the increase in settlers, that the Indians will
eventually have to share this country with the white man. He knows
what is coming, but doesn't want it to come."

Marlette nodded. "Yes, I can see that. But I do wish he was easier
to talk with."

"You would get used to that if you lived among the Indians. It
all has to do with dignity, honor, respect, and whatever else they feel
at the moment."

"Do you really think he is an Indian?"

Narcissa looked thoughtful. "I'm not sure. Whenever he is with
me, I know in my heart that he is white—that he is some poor white
child captured in infancy by the Indians and raised as their own. But
when he is with the Indians he is one of them. I've never presumed
to ask him. I always hoped he would tell us on his own if he wanted
us to know, although I suppose it's quite possible he doesn't know
himself."

Marlette stood up, suddenly restless and needing the release of
movement. "I've sat too long. Would it be all right if I went for a
walk?"

Narcissa rose and smiled. "Of course. I'll come with you and we'll
make the grand tour."

They strolled around the mission grounds, then leisurely walked
toward the hill and started up the trail, passing through a thin scatter-
ing of trees that circled the lower slope. Marlette noticed a grave
mound with a marker, beside the trail. She stopped to look at the
marker and read the name ALICE CLARISSA WHITMAN. She looked
from the marker to Mrs. Whitman with unspoken curiosity.

Narcissa tenderly touched the marker and her eyes held the same sad, far-off look Marlette had seen earlier. "This is our daughter's grave. She drowned in the river three years ago."

Marlette reached out and touched the hand that still rested on the marker. "I'm so sorry."

"It was God's will." Narcissa turned away, with a visible straightening of her shoulders, and started once more up the trail.

They reached the top a few minutes later and stood viewing a vast panorama of hills, pine-clad mountains, and river valley. The river sparkled as it curved in serpentine loops westward.

Narcissa beckoned Marlette to sit on the weathered bench on the highest point of the hill. "My husband made this bench for me and I often sit here when he is gone and watch for him."

Marlette felt the loneliness implicit in Narcissa's words and she nodded with understanding. "It must be very difficult for you at times."

Narcissa sighed and said candidly, "Yes. I do so miss my family and friends and the happy society of civilized people." She quickly threw off her mood and became animated again. They chatted of things in general discussing the latest fashions and other trivia of civilization that Narcissa missed.

Wandering down the west slope of the hill, they stopped in a small, grassy clearing in the middle of the trees. It was another burial place and Narcissa was telling Marlette about the people buried there when Chesnut came through the trees toward them. Marlette could guess why he was there.

Narcissa smiled and greeted him. "Ross! Were you looking for us?"

"Yes. It's time Miss Brightwood came back to the mission."

The smile faded from Narcissa's face, and she looked concerned. "Is there something wrong?"

"No. But she is a stranger here. For her there might be danger."

"I'm sorry, I didn't realize. You're right, of course."

Marlette felt humiliated and angered. He treated her like a child. He even talked around her as people do with a child. She turned on her heel and started down the trail without waiting for Chesnut or Narcissa.

The men were seated at the big kitchen table when she entered.

Papa Hout bounced a chuckling David on his knee while the girls giggled with delight, waiting for their turn.

Joshua asked, "Did Chesnut come back with you?"

Trying to keep the anger out of her voice she answered, "He's coming with Mrs. Whitman."

As she spoke the door opened behind her and Narcissa and Chesnut came into the kitchen.

"Ah, Chesnut, there you are. Dr. Whitman has suggested we accompany him as far as Fort Boise to map the trail through the Blue Mountains if you think there's time?"

"It's too great a chance to take. We should leave tomorrow for the fort at Wallula if we want to make it to the valley before snow falls in the mountains."

Whitman agreed. "If Chesnut thinks it's too risky, I'll have to go along with his judgment." To Narcissa he said, "Narcissa, I'm sure our guests must be hungry. Is there something we can prepare for them?"

"Of course. I'll get something right away." She crossed the room to the pantry and Marlette followed.

"May I help?"

"Yes, if you like." Slicing the meat and bustling about the kitchen she added, "I'm sorry, I didn't realize you weren't suppose to leave the mission. I hope you're not angry with me."

Marlette smiled. "It wasn't your fault. I should have known better than to wander off. Heaven knows Chesnut has warned me often enough."

"Well," Narcissa said, relieved, "I'm glad you're not angry with me."

They finished preparing the simple dinner and set it on the table. The men helped themselves to the bread and meat and continued talking. Marlette helped Narcissa clear away the dishes and when they were finished Narcissa asked, "Do you mind if I tend to some letter writing now? If Marcus insists on leaving in the morning I shall be up all night getting things together."

Marlette smiled, "Of course not. I have some writing of my own to do."

With a lovely smile Narcissa bade the men good-night and left the room. Marlette was not surprised that she could bring out whatever love lay hidden in Chesnut's heart. Anyone who entered Narcissa Whitman's presence would find her endearing.

Marlette had been writing for a long time when someone knocked at her door.

"Who is it?"

"Gay. May I come in?"

She put down her pencil and closed the book turning in her chair, her arm aching. "It's not bolted," she called.

"Am I interrupting something?"

"I'm just catching up on my journal."

He sat down on the bed, their knees almost touching, and with a hint of former mischievousness he asked, "Heard any more Indian legends lately?"

Marlette smiled at the memory. "No."

"You were really angry with me that night, weren't you?"

"I thought it was terrible of you to humiliate us that way."

"Would you believe me if I said I'm sorry it happened?"

"Yes. I think you've changed a lot since that night."

There was a strange, wistful smile on his face as he said, "Yes, I think I have. I never thought at the start of this trip I would end up wanting to dedicate my life to making you smile."

The serious look in his eyes belied the lightness in his tone. She felt a flush warm her face. "Gay, are you teasing me?"

"No, Marlette. For the first time in my life I'm serious."

She stood up in embarrassment, but he rose with her, taking her in his arms. She stood stiffly as he kissed her. His lips left hers and moved over her face and neck, stopping only to whisper words of endearment in her ear. When his lips returned to hers she was no longer unyielding. Her heart skipped erratically and she felt strangely giddy. She pulled away and looked into the blue eyes so close to her own, not really believing what was happening.

"Gay, is this a proposal?"

He looked at her in amazement. Then he laughed. She watched him laugh, feeling confused and embarrassed that he should laugh at her. "Always the proper Miss Brightwood. Well, then," he made a sweeping bow and kneeling gallantly before her, said, "Miss Brightwood, will you accept my hand in marriage?"

His eyes were dancing and she couldn't tell if he was serious or not. She pulled away from him, dismayed.

He rose and took her into his arms again, the merriment gone. "Marlette, I do mean it. We could be married tonight if Whitman would do it or as soon as you like. But I'm serious, I love you." He kissed her and she responded warmly.

She couldn't believe it was really happening to her. This charming and handsome man had just asked her to marry him. How long ago she had abandoned all idea of marriage! She wanted to say yes, wanted to shout it, but practicality ruled and she pulled away from Gay's embrace. She didn't want to lose this chance, yet she wasn't sure enough of her own feelings. Things had happened too quickly.

Turning back to Gay, she said, "Gay, will you forgive me if I'm not sure? I need more time. I feel this is the wrong place and the wrong time."

He came to her with a smile and swept her hands up, pressing them to his lips. "Of course, my darling. Maybe by the time we reach Fort Vancouver you will know and we can honeymoon all the way back to New York."

She smiled at the thought and nodded. He embraced her again and kissed her forehead. "Now I think I'd better let you finish your writing."

He left her standing by the window and she gazed after him a long while, all thoughts of writing gone. Another knock on her door brought her back to reality.

"Who is it?"

"Chesnut. Are you all right?"

With a frown she crossed to the door and opened it wide so her room was in full view. He came past her and crossed to the table to light the candle. She crossed her arms indignantly at his intrusion. He turned from the table and looked at her. The color rose in her cheeks and she wondered if she was disheveled from Gay's embraces. Angrily she asked, "Is there anything else?"

"We'll be leaving first thing in the morning. Be ready."

With a slight nod, he left the room. Marlette stood for a moment seething with anger. She gave the door a hard shove and with little satisfaction heard it bang. He was so infuriating!

She awoke before dawn to dress and pack. Quietly, she opened her door and tiptoed down the stairs to the kitchen. There, she found

Chesnut laying the fire in the stove. She got the coffee pot, filled it from the water bucket in the pantry, and measured in the coffee.

Chesnut stood up and they eyed each other coldly. "Are your things ready?"

"Yes."

Before any more was said Narcissa Whitman came in. She looked tired but said brightly, "Good morning."

The coldness went out of Chesnut's eyes and he smiled. The two Indian girls opened their bedroom door and came in. Their eyes immediately fastened on Chesnut. He said something to them in their own language and their dark eyes sparkled with pleasure as shy smiles curved their lips. With a nod to Narcissa he left the house.

Narcissa told the girls, "Go get the children up and dressed for breakfast."

They obediently went to do her bidding, smiles still on their faces.

As soon as they were gone, Marlette asked with barely controlled curiosity, "What did he say to the girls?"

"He told them they were an honor to their father."

Marlette could only utter a soft, uncertain, "Oh."

"I see you two are speaking this morning."

"Just barely. He manages to infuriate me every time we meet."

Narcissa looked at Marlette seriously for a moment. "Maybe there's a reason why you react to him that way. Maybe you're in love with him."

Marlette laughed. "Hardly! I find him rude and aggravating. Tell me, why did he spend so much time here, of all places?"

"He wanted to learn to read and write."

Marlette looked astonished. "You mean he has only learned our language since you've been here?"

"Oh, no. He spoke it just as well then. He was at Vancouver when I stayed there. Dr. McLoughlin encouraged me to teach the children there and I did. Ross learned I was teaching them and asked me to help him, too. He actually accomplished the basics before I left Vancouver, but he came to help us here in the summers as repayment."

"Didn't you find that odd?"

"Yes, but everything out here is not what it seems to be. I did wonder that he learned to read and write so quickly. It was as if he had been to school before, but for some reason had never finished."

The door opened and the two Indian girls came in with the smaller children. They were whispering and giggling but when they saw Marlette's disapproving frown their faces returned to masklike impassiveness. She couldn't help but think that Chesnut was the reason for their giggles. She found it disturbing that these two young girls could be attracted to Chesnut, too.

Marlette heard voices as the rest of the men came downstairs. She gathered up the cups and carried them to the table. Thompson, who had been relatively uncomplaining since they'd come to the mission, was again grumbling at the prospect of long days in the saddle. Evan was chiding him. Gay's face was glowing. She returned his smile and poured him a cup of coffee. Eggs and bacon were sizzling and the tantalizing aroma drew everyone into the kitchen.

They ate without much conversation, sad to leave this tranquil place and reluctant to express their fears.

Warning at Fort Walla Walla

THEIR GOOD-BYES were short. They shook hands with the Whitmans, spoke hopefully about future meetings and rode away from the security of the mission toward Fort Walla Walla some twenty-five miles away.

Later that afternoon they reached the fort which stood on the banks of the Columbia, looking small and overwhelmed by the high, barren bluffs lining the river. A few small cabins stood near the fort and a handful of Indian lodges were clustered near the river.

Their arrival inside the fort brought only watchful, curious looks from the French-Canadians; but the tall, redheaded Scotsman, Chief Trader McKinley, greeted them warmly, "Aye, 'tis a pleasure to meet you, Mr. Brightwood, Miss Brightwood, gentlemen. Will ye nae stay the night and dine with me? Sarah has gone down to Vancouver to visit, but I think we can manage."

Joshua, warned by Chesnut not to stay, replied, "Thank you for your hospitality, but we can't delay. Chesnut is worried about the possibility of snow. We can stop only long enough for supplies."

McKinley turned to Chesnut, "Surely, mon, they can stay for dinner? It'll take a wee bit to get the supplies ye need."

"If one of your men can help me, they can have an hour to eat."

McKinley smiled broadly. "Good. Get Stuart to help ye." He turned to Joshua. "Come in. I'll get the cook to start dinner."

McKinley led them into a small, comfortable house.

"Now tell me about your trip Mr. Brightwood. I've heard ye were at the mission."

"Yes. We were much impressed with all Dr. Whitman has accomplished there."

"Aye. But he has had his troubles. There are many who do nae accept the Christian teaching. I fear some day they will turn on him. It is nae safe anywhere for missionaries or strangers." A solemn tone in his voice sent a shiver of fear through Marlette. "I have heard ye are seeking the Indians' friendship so American settlers can come here. I must advise ye that while they will take your gifts, they will be little bound by them."

Joshua smiled and nodded. "You advice is well taken, but our primary purpose is to learn about the country and the people so that we can warn potential settlers of any dangers if they are foolish enough to believe their fortunes lie here."

McKinley smiled, "Aye, mon, that relieves me. I'm assured ye will tell them this is a hard and dangerous country, nae suitable for families?"

"I'm afraid we would all have to agree with you there, sir."

The door to the kitchen opened and an Indian woman spoke to McKinley. He rose and said, "Dinner is almost ready. They've brought water for ye to wash."

Dinner did not compare to the meals at Vancouver or the Whitman's, but after a long morning of riding, Marlette was too hungry to care. While they ate, McKinley continued to question them, particularly about the guns they diligently carried in with them. Although he seemed friendly and genuinely interested in their safety, his insistence gave Marlette an uneasy feeling. Finally she excused herself from the table and wandered through an open door into McKinley's office.

The room was dim and stale with smoke. She went to the window and pulled back the heavy curtain. Idly watching the few people that moved about the buildings of the fort, she saw an Indian woman come through the gate and stand waiting near one of the buildings.

Chesnut and another man came out of the provision store across the yard carrying packs which they loaded onto their waiting horses.

The Indian woman stepped away from the wall and came toward Chesnut. She looked vaguely familiar. They talked for a few moments and the woman seductively ran her hand down Chesnut's sleeve and took his hand in both of hers, stepping away from him. Marlette watched in dismay as he followed her outside the gate.

She was instantly angry. He barely allowed them time to eat, yet he found time to run after any Indian woman who chased him. She suddenly realized the woman was Standing Elk's daughter. Turning away from the window, she sat in McKinley's chair, trembling with anger and disgust.

She returned to the window and was surprised to see Chesnut striding through the gate. She went back into the dining room and announced, "Chesnut is coming."

The men rose noisily, and thanked McKinley for their meal. Marlette turned to the door as Chesnut came in and caught the grim set of his face. He looked more like a man who had received bad news than one who had enjoyed a lover's embrace. He came across the room and gave the clerk's bill to McKinley. Joshua went over it with them and paid for the supplies.

They walked across the dusty yard toward their horses. McKinley came with them and Marlette stepped forward, mustering a smile of thanks as the tall Scotsman took her hand in a farewell handshake.

They mounted and rode out of the fort. Marlette felt more relaxed once they were away from the unfriendly faces of the Frenchmen and the decidedly hostile stares of the Indians who had gathered to watch them leave. They rode south toward the Walla Walla River, and forded it, leaving the pleasant little river valley behind as they started across the rolling wasteland.

It was almost dark before they came to a small stream where Chesnut decided to camp. They ate a cold supper of jerky and biscuits, aware it wasn't wise to make a fire.

Marlette crawled into cold blankets and lay awake listening to the chilling bark of coyotes. The stars were so big and brilliant in the cold, crisp air that they seemed unreal. At last she fell into a sound sleep.

In the morning Gay helped her to load her horse, as he had helped her unload the night before. She thought she saw Chesnut give them a disapproving look, but he said nothing. Before noon they left the rolling plain and rode into a rough, rocky terrain. Mountains loomed rugged and majestic to the east, their jagged peaks glistening with snow that never melted.

They stopped in an open area for lunch. Chesnut built a small fire and they had a hot meal and coffee. As they were finishing their coffee a single rider appeared in the distance. Chesnut was standing, rifle at the ready, before the rest of the men could put down their cups.

When the rider was close enough to be recognized, Chesnut warned them, "Don't tell this man anything. He's your enemy."

The rider stopped a few yards from their camp. He was a tall, dignified Indian, and he walked toward them with deliberately measured strides. There was an aloof half-smile on his unpainted face. He stopped a few feet from Chesnut and his smile broadened. "Ho, my brother. May I sit with you awhile?"

Chesnut, standing in relaxed readiness with his rifle held waist-high in front of him, answered with unusual crispness, "We have enough time to hear why you are here, but no more."

The other man laughed, "What is this? My brother rejects me?" He turned in mock dismay to gaze at the other men around the small fire. His eyes came to rest on Marlette and he smiled. Marlette looked at Chesnut's grim face and felt uneasy as the Indian asked, "I hope my brother does not speak for the white men here? I come in friendship, to offer you advice for your safe journey."

Joshua stood up. "Forgive Mr. Chesnut. He is only concerned for us. I'm Joshua Brightwood and these are the members of my party and my daughter. We welcome any advice you may have to offer."

The Indian, still smiling, stepped forward with his hand extended and returned, "I am Tom Hill."

Chesnut moved behind Marlette and for once she welcomed his presence. She felt something sinister in this Indian's appearance and Chesnut's attitude only heightened her fears.

Joshua replied, "The pleasure is mine, sir. Sit if you will and have a cup of coffee."

The Indian lowered himself majestically to the ground and sat cross-legged. He accepted the coffee Joshua offered and sipped it. A smile of pleasure sprang to his lips. "Ah, Mr. Brightwood, this is good coffee. You must have been to Fort Walla Walla?"

"Yes. We've just come from there."

Chesnut broke in, his voice noticeably sharp but still controlled, "State your business, Hill."

"Ah, my brother is impatient. Mr. Brightwood, I must warn you that there is great danger for you in this country. I do not want to see any harm come to your people or to my people, but since I cannot control the Indian radicals, I wish to offer my help to you."

Holliway asked impatiently, "What is your proposition?"

"Simply this, to see you safely downriver to Fort Vancouver." He smiled benignly.

"How much will it cost us?"

"You misunderstand. I offer this only to prevent a tragedy. Of course you will understand that we have no way of transporting your horses and other unnecessary equipment downstream. But you will not need horses or guns once you are at Vancouver."

Holliway's face was red with anger.

Joshua broke in quickly, "Mr. Hill, your offer is appreciated, but we can hardly accept such terms. Our horses and equipment cost us a good deal of money."

"Consider, sir, what a small price a few horses and guns are in exchange for the lives of your people, or mine," said the Indian, still smiling pleasantly as he deliberately rose to his full powerful height. "This is a matter not to be decided by one man. I will leave you to discuss this thing in privacy. I will be with my horse when you have reached a decision."

He turned away, walked with apparent casualness toward his horse, and led the animal even farther away. They all watched him in silence until he was well out of earshot.

Holliway turned to Chesnut, angrily, "Who the hell does he think he is? Is this some kind of a trick, Chesnut? Are you in cahoots with him?"

Joshua laid a restraining hand on Holliway, "Major, let's be reasonable. I don't think Chesnut is responsible for this." He turned to Chesnut, "Who is this man, Tom Hill? What reason could he have for stopping us?"

"This man needs no other reason than his hatred for the white man."

Holliway snapped, "That's no answer. Now you tell us what you know about this man and you'd better explain how he knew we were out here."

Chesnut replied without anger, "Those renegades we ran into were on their way to Tom Hill's camp. Hill is a Delaware Indian, educated in a white man's school. He has become, more or less, an advisor for all the renegades who break away from their tribes. He keeps them stirred up for his own personal gain."

Holliway exploded, "Then you knew he would be out here! And you let us come! You dirty son of a Sioux bitch!"

Holliway grabbed his gun and pulled the hammer back. Marlette, not stopping to think, jumped up to protect Chesnut behind her and cried, "Don't!"

Chesnut's hand pushed her down and she saw his rifle pointed at Holliway. His voice was a deadly whisper as he said, "If you kill me, you kill yourselves. Take his gun, Taylor."

Gay rose with surprising calm and placed a hand on Holliway's arm, slowly forcing the gun down until he removed it from Holliway's grip.

Facing Chesnut, he asked quietly, "If you knew what was going to happen, why didn't you tell us at the fort? We could've gotten a boat there and gone downriver."

"Don't you think Hill would know that? Our only chance is to stay in the open."

Joshua asked, "What would he gain by killing us? Surely, he doesn't want trouble with our government?"

"He wants the guns and horses. If he can't get them by bargaining with us he'll anger the Indians into killing us by telling them you will bring more whites into the country. He's too smart to kill us himself."

Thompson's voice shook with fear as he urged, "Let's give him the guns and horses for safe passage downriver."

Gay glanced worriedly at Marlette and asked Chesnut, "Would we have a chance if we made a deal with him?"

"I doubt it. He wouldn't want McLoughlin to know he had even talked to you."

"Then it doesn't look like we have much choice."

Holliway suggested coldly, "I say we kill them both and go back to the mission."

"You'd never make it, Holliway," Chesnut snapped. "Without me, your lives aren't worth the guns you carry."

Joshua interrupted. "That's enough!" he said firmly. "We have a decision to make. Now, what do we want to do?"

Evan Long snorted. "What decision? You mean we have to decide between one damned Injun or another? I'll take my chances with this gun." He rested a hand on the rifle beside him.

"All right, Gaylord," Joshua continued, "what's your opinion?"

Gay looked hesitantly at Marlette as if she held the answer. Then he looked at the unsmiling Chesnut and grinned with a return to his old arrogant manner. "I'm a gambler, Mr. Brightwood," he said, "I'll stick with Chesnut."

Joshua nodded. "Isaac?" he said, turning to Thompson.

Isaac cleared his throat, glancing nervously around the circle, "I'll have to go along with the Major and Long. Our only hope is to make it back to the mission."

"Andy?"

Andrew Proctor turned pale and glanced first at Chesnut, then at Holliway. He asked Chesnut, "Are you sure we couldn't make it back to the mission?"

"Hill didn't come out here by himself. His renegades will find you no matter which way you go. If you made it to the mission you would put them in the same danger that you're in. The Cayuse wouldn't need much urging by Hill to burn the mission and kill everyone there."

"Then I'll go along with the majority," stammered Andrew.

Von Hout spoke up angrily, "Vell, I tink you damn fools if you don't stick with Chesnut. He is goot man."

Joshua looked at Marlette and asked gently, "Marlette, how do you vote?"

Marlette looked up at Chesnut's impassive face. She suddenly realized why he had returned so quickly after seeing Standing Elk's daughter. He hadn't been sure Tom Hill would be after them until he had seen the girl. He could have abandoned them at the fort, but he hadn't. Now his life was in danger too, unless—? She rejected the thought. Narcissa Whitman had trusted him and his concern for the mission vindicated that trust. She took a deep breath and said, "I think we should stay with Mr. Chesnut."

Joshua smiled. "And I believe we stand a better chance with Chesnut than with Hill. Gentlemen, do you concur?"

They nodded their agreement and Chesnut called out to Hill. They watched him silently as he approached, the tension almost palpable.

Tom Hill stopped a few feet from them and dismounted, a smile

of confidence on his arrogant face. "You have reached a decision?"
Joshua smiled slightly. "Yes. We thank you for your offer, but we
have decided to stay with Mr. Chesnut."
The smile left Hill's face. "You are making a serious mistake, Mr.
Brightwood. I think you should reconsider, for the sake of your
daughter. Maybe my Sioux brother should tell you what happens to
women who are captured—."

He didn't get the chance to finish. Chesnut stepped forward, the
cords in his neck pulsing under the dark skin. His eyes were filled
with intense hatred, but his voice was still in control as he said,
"They've given you their decision."

His rifle was aimed squarely at Hill and the Indian stared back
at Chesnut malevolently. He vaulted onto his horse and yanked it
away.

Joshua pulled a rumpled hankerchief from his pocket and mopped
his sweating face. "What happens now?"

"I'll tell you what happens!" Holliway snapped, "We get attacked!"

Joshua mopped his face again. "Well, what do we do?"

There was complete silence while Chesnut watched Tom Hill
disappear. At last his arms relaxed and his rifle barrel fell to his side.
He turned toward them, and they saw that all trace of tension had
left his face. "It'll take Hill a little while to get to the rest of them.
Let's get moving."

They broke camp in a flurry of feverish haste and galloped away.
Finally Chesnut found a rocky upthrust with a small spring that was
big enough to protect the horses and small enough to give them a
defensible position.

It was still early and there was no sign of Indians. They chewed
on some jerky and planned their method of defense. Marlette forced
herself to describe the events of the last two days in her journal as
the men talked, and picked their positions.

After dark Gay came to sit with her and quietly took her hand.

"When does Chesnut think they'll attack us," Marlette asked.

"Most likely, first thing in the morning."

"What are our chances?"

"He thinks they're pretty good. We've got water and can defend
this place pretty well. They can't sneak up on us, so we've a good

chance of keeping them from getting close enough to use anything less than guns. Are you frightened?"

"Would it disappoint you if I said yes?"

Gay laughed softly and put his arm around her. "No. I'm more than a little scared myself."

They sat quietly for a while and Marlette leaned her head on his shoulder. The desperation of their situation drew her to him for comfort. In that moment she was sure that she had found love, and was content.

Finally Gay broke the silence. "You know, Marlette, I'll have to admit I'm getting to trust Chesnut. He's a strange one, but I think he knows what he's doing."

Marlette glanced up, surprised. She had wondered if Gay's past support of Chesnut had been intended merely to aggravate the rest of them. A week ago she would have been sure of it but now she felt he believed in Chesnut. She kissed his cheek lightly.

"Say! What was that for?"

"A token of my appreciation."

"For what?"

"Let's just say for being you, now."

He smiled at her and pulled her closer for a real kiss. She didn't resist. He held her for a little while, then sighed, "Well, I'd better get some sleep before my watch. Need anything before I turn in?"

"No, thank you. I think I'd better get some sleep, too."

He kissed her again lightly and then walked to his bed. Marlette got up and crawled into her shelter. Everyone was in bed except for the two men on first watch. The sounds of the night soon took over. Near their small spring a frog croaked softly and the crickets' sounded loud in the darkness. Somewhere a bird whistled a mournful song and Marlette turned restlessly in her bed.

The Attack

LONG BEFORE DAWN Marlette awoke with a start. She peered out into the darkness but could see nothing. There was no campfire, and she was stiff and cold. A bird called out of the darkness with startling clarity and a shiver of dread ran up her spine. The major had told them that Indians frequently used bird calls as signals.

Something big moved in front of her tent and she held her breath in panic. Then she reasoned that it wasn't an Indian since there was no smell of grease. She reached out and touched soft leather. A hand closed over hers and Chesnut leaned over until his lips brushed her ear.

"Get ready. I'll come for you in a few minutes."

Quietly, she pulled on her boots and bound up her hair. She searched for her gun and strapped it on. She waited silently for his return and jumped when his hand touched her shoulder. He pulled her up beside him and holding her tightly, guided her to a safe spot in their rock fortress.

Gay was already there and they sat huddled together waiting for the first pale light of dawn to creep over the mountains. They listened to the bird calls that seemed to come from every bush around them and Marlette shivered as the tension built inside her.

Chesnut returned just as it was beginning to get light. Gay squeezed her hand and crept away to a large boulder a few yards away. Chesnut kneeled down close to her.

"Let me see see your gun."

She handed it to him and heard him check it. He handed it back and said, "Keep it out and don't be afraid to use it."

She nodded and rose to her knees, cautiously peeking over the top of the boulder. Chesnut pushed her down and whispered, "Keep down."

Suddenly, a bloodcurdling yell pierced the silence. Chesnut's hand dropped to her shoulder and held her down. Silently they waited. Minutes passed before Marlette heard the ominous thunder of hooves and the howling of what seemed like hundreds of Indians. She wanted to look but Chesnut's hand remained heavily on her shoulder. A shot rang out somewhere around the circle and Chesnut removed his hand. His rifle exploded and deafened her.

She rolled over on her side and looked out of a narrow crack between two rocks terrified by what she saw. Indians were riding at breakneck speed around the rocks, their faces painted and their voices lifted in frightening whoops. Arrows and bullets whistled around them and clattered harmlessly against the rocks. Chesnut and Gay were firing repeatedly and two Indians fell from their horses.

The mad circling continued for several minutes but the Indians were unable to get close enough to the rock fortress to be effective. Despite their courage and their superb horsemanship, they were unable to withstand the Brightwoods' superior rifles, and soon there were only a dozen left. The remaining Indians bunched together, and in one desperate attack, rode at breakneck speed toward the spot where Chesnut, Gay, and Marlette crouched. The horses looked almost riderless as they came thundering in, their riders clinging to their sides for protection. Unable to get a clear shot, Chesnut yelled at Gay to shoot the horses.

Marlette wanted to close her eyes as the horses crashed to the ground squealing in pain, but it was impossible to do more than blink in horrified fascination.

Five horses made it to the rocks. Two Indians leaped on to the boulders close to Gay and he fired rapidly as a third Indian jumped to the rock where Marlette cowered. She looked up as he let out a maniacal yell. Chesnut fired point-blank at the Indian's chest and he fell backward off the rock. At that moment another Indian leaped over the rock and grabbed Chesnut's rifle, his upraised tomahawk flashing in the sun.

The fifth Indian vaulted over the rocks beyond Chesnut, holding a deadly hatchet aimed at Chesnut's skull. Marlette raised the pistol she held, aimed and fired with an expertise born of desperation. The Indian staggered and fell against the Indian struggling with Chesnut, knocking him off-balance. Chesnut wrenched the tomahawk from the Indian and sank the weapon deep into the Indian's neck.

He slipped from Chesnut's grasp and fell across Marlette, his blood spraying her face and soaking her skirt. She cried out in horror. Chesnut quickly pulled the body from her as she sank back against the rock, her eyes closed and her stomach convulsing. She felt a gentle hand lift her face and opened her eyes to find Chesnut wiping away the blood.

Gay dropped to her side and took her in his arms.

She buried her head against his chest, clinging to him fiercely. Her father's voice called her and she realized that the noise she still heard was the pounding of her own heart. She hadn't had time to think of anyone else. She rose and went into her father's arms.

"Marlette! Thank God you're all right." Then turning to Chesnut he asked, "Will there be any more?"

"Yes. But they'll go for reinforcements. We'd better clear out and make as many miles as we can."

The rest of the men left their stations and came scrambling through the rocks. Evan Long had a nasty flesh wound in his side. He'd gotten so angry that he had stood up during the battle and a bullet had creased his side. It was oozing a little blood and burning painfully. Andrew Proctor had small bleeding cuts all over his face where rock chips had showered him. He tried to stop the bleeding but there were too many cuts and his shirt was wet with blood.

Chesnut surveyed them quickly and gave his orders. "Miss Brightwood, take Long and Proctor to the spring and take care of their wounds. The rest of us will get packed."

Marlette got her only towel and wash cloth and soaked them in the cold spring water. Evan Long lay on his side softly swearing as she placed the cold towel across his wound. Andrew splashed cold water on his face and leaned back against the rocks, his face ashen as Marlette pressed his cuts with the cold wash cloth.

The cold water soon numbed Evan's side and he got up.

Marlette asked him anxiously, "Are you sure it'll be all right?"

"Yeah. Only thing more we could do for it would be a shot of whiskey."

"For you, or the wound?"

He started to laugh, but found it too painful and walked off clutching his side.

Marlette wrung out Andrew's cloth and pressed it firmly against the only cut that was still bleeding. He smiled weakly at her and said, "You're a brave girl, Marlette. Your father should be proud of you."

"I don't think it was bravery," she said ruefully, "more like self-preservation. I was terrified out there."

"Yes, I'm afraid I'm not cut out for this kind of thing," Andrew agreed.

"I don't think many of us are."

He sighed. "If only I'd realized that a year ago. I was a fool to think I could become something I'm not."

Gently she asked, "Could you go back and be happy with the way things were?"

"No. No, I don't think so."

"Then you've changed more than you think."

The realization brought a smile to his face and he said more confidently, "You may be right."

Before she could say more, Chesnut approached them. "We're ready."

Andrew got up and went for the horses. Marlette bent to rinse out her cloths and stood up to find Chesnut standing there. She looked squarely into his eyes and wondered what he wanted.

He held a black bundle out to her. "I brought your skirt, if you'd like to change."

She took it gratefully, remembering the bloodstains on the one she wore. "Thank you."

Stepping behind another boulder, she quickly changed her skirt. When she straightened up, he was still standing there. She blushed and bent over quickly to roll up the soiled skirt, hiding her face. She wondered if she would ever stop feeling insecure and embarrassed in his presence.

He stepped aside as she came out from her rock and followed her toward the waiting men. Gay raised his eyebrows at her and she looked away, still feeling the warmth on her cheeks.

As they mounted, Long asked, "Hey, Chesnut, ain't you goin' to scalp them dead Injuns?"

Chesnut looked at Long contemptuously. "No. They died with honor." He turned his horse away and started off at a gallop.

They rode for several hours before they got off their horses and walked them, eating stale bread and jerky as they walked. When Chesnut felt the horses were rested enough they rode again.

At the end of the long day they camped in the open near a small creek. There were a few scattered junipers among the tall pungent sage, dry weeds, and grass. They didn't build a fire and fell exhausted into their bedrolls after a cold supper.

Marlette woke, coughing, in the middle of the night. Smoke filled her lungs and she heard the ominous crackle of fire in the distance. She opened her eyes in panic but the smoke was so thick her eyes instantly filled with blinding tears. She started to crawl from her bed only to be stopped by something in front of her. She struck out in unreasoning terror, choking and blinded by smoke. Strong arms encircled her and held her still. She felt the smoothness of leather against her cheek and realized it was Chesnut, and she quieted.

"Get your bed rolled up and your gun on. I'll be back for you in a little while. Hurry."

He released her and she tried once more to open her eyes. A wind stirred the air and the smoke was briefly blown away. She could see the men around her silhouetted against a fierce, leaping fire that was rushing in a huge half-circle toward them. The wind changed again and the smoke blocked off all vision. With a pounding heart she began rolling up her bed. Someone came to her side.

"Marlette, are you all right?" It was Gay.

"Yes," she choked.

He bent to help her with her things but Chesnut returned. "Taylor, I told you to stay with the horses." His voice was muffled and harsh.

"Miss Brightwood needs help."

"Get back to the horses. I'll help her."

Gay gripped her arm and left. Chesnut held out a cool, damp cloth. "Put this over your nose and mouth."

She held the cloth in place and felt some relief from the suffocating smoke as he tied it around her head. He picked up her bedroll and guided her toward the horses who were restlessly stamping and whinnying with fear in the creek. The men tried to keep them from bolting by covering their tossing heads with wet cloths.

The heat was intense and the crackling fire roared as it swept around them. Just when Marlette was sure they would all be burned to a crisp the fickle wind changed and blew the smoke and heat away. A juniper nearby exploded in flames sending a shower of sparks within yards of them. Her horse shuddered but stood his ground. He was as stoical as Chesnut, and in that moment, priceless.

Chesnut shouted instructions and while the rest of them held the frightened horses, Holliway, Taylor, and Chesnut ran into the darkness and disappeared into the smoke.

Long fearful moments passed and Marlette prayed for the rain she hoped would put out the fire. As wind blew the smoke away, she looked heavenward for the clouds she felt sure would be there. Only then did she realize that she had heard no thunder; seen no lightning. With horror she realized the Indians must have set this fire. No wonder Chesnut had not led them away immediately. He knew the Indians were ahead, waiting for them. Several yards further on, faggots of sage blazed into life and the three figures carrying them separated and lighted a wide path. The fire spread quickly, fanned by the same wind that fanned the fire so terrifyingly close behind them.

The men returned and Marlette gratefully felt Chesnut's strong hand take the reins of her nervous horse. Slowly they urged the horses forward, almost completely encircled now by fire. She heard the nearby horses snort and plunge and the men curse as they tried to hold them. Choking and blinded with smoke they walked ahead on foot leading the horses until they reached the newly burned ground. Cautiously Chesnut stepped onto the smoking earth, stopping when the heat burned through his moccasins.

Behind them the fire reached the creek where they had been only minutes ago and another juniper exploded, sending hot sparks across the creek to ignite the unburnt sage.

Slowly they moved forward until they were away from the intense heat and flames. Marlette saw the fire smolder and die as it reached the burned ground behind them and understood Chesnut's strategy. A cool breeze fanned their scorched faces. Chesnut mounted and led them south instead of following the fire that was far ahead of them moving across the rolling sageland.

They kept riding long after dawn, tired and blackened. When it grew light, Marlette saw what they had used to cover their faces and the horse's heads during the fire. The extra shirts of the men and even some of her things hung around them in nearly unrecognizable condition. Her bloodstained skirt had been thrown over the ammunition pack and was torn and singed.

In the afternoon they came to a good-sized river and Chesnut let them stop to wash, rest, and eat. Unhappily, Marlette surveyed the ruin of her extra clothing and towel. Since she had no clothes to change into she bathed in the river in her clothes with the rest of the men, except for Chesnut. He stood watch on top of the ridge and appeared to be rubbing his buckskins with handfuls of alkali dust.

They sat around chewing the leathery jerky, washing it down with river water. Before they had finished Chesnut came down the hill and said, "It's time to go."

Holliway immediately protested. "Look, Chesnut, the horses are about done in and we need some rest and a decent meal. I haven't seen an Indian since yesterday morning, so why not camp here?"

Chesnut looked coldly at Holliway. "No. You know as well as I do who set that fire last night."

No one argued with him. They had known it but hadn't wanted to admit the truth. Slowly Holliway got up and went to his horses, the rest of the men following.

Chesnut went to the river and plunged his head into the water rubbing his face briskly. Marlette watched him, wondering how long he could keep going at this pace. She knew he rested less than any of them. He rose from the water and came to his horse. If Marlette had been less tired she would have readily grasped the fact that Chesnut had not been able to wash all the dark smudges off his face. She had accepted the fact his smooth face was due to his Indian blood, but now he looked like the rest of the men with a two-day growth of stubble.

They continued in a southwesterly direction toward a range of pine-timbered mountains. By sundown they were in the timbered foothills. Chesnut unerringly led them to water and they made camp in a small cluster of pines near a clear, cold creek. The small meadow had enough grass for the horses and the little hill they camped on was easy to guard.

Chesnut made a small fire and they had their first hot meal in two days. Even Isaac Thompson was quiet for the moment, grateful for a hot cup of coffee. Exhaustion soon overtook them and everyone except those on first watch turned in. Marlette was asleep almost instantly.

In the morning they took a more westerly direction, heading across sagebrush-covered hills. To the west across a vast plain Marlette saw the immense mountain range they would have to cross. The view of the black peaks still frosted with a thin layer of snow was breathtaking. To the north she recognized the mountains that overlooked Fort Vancouver and had been familiar landmarks on their way east.

Marlette hadn't realized they were riding toward a gorge until they reached the rim, overlooking spectacular, black basalt cliffs. Hundreds of feet below the almost perpendicular cliffs, she could see a thin ribbon of water. Faint columns of smoke rose from somewhere in the depths of the canyon and Chesnut motioned them away from whatever lay below.

He turned south and when his direction was apparent, Holliway rode forward and intercepted him.

"What are you doing, Chesnut? We need to go north to make that pass."

"We have to find a place to ford this river. There are few places north of here to get down to the water and those few are Indian camps. There's another canyon almost like this one coming in from the east. We have to get across that one and two more before we can head north."

Holliway stared at Chesnut, trying to decide if he was lying. Threateningly he said, "You'd better be telling it straight, Chesnut."

Chesnut rode on and Holliway sat watching until the last man passed. They rode toward a rock formation that marked the western reach of the mountains they had skirted. As they neared the towering rocks they encountered the smaller gorge. Chesnut followed it until he found a place where they could get down to the river that ran through the bottom of the gorge.

He dismounted and walked along the edge of the steep canyon looking for the best way to descend, purposely rolling rocks with his feet.

He returned to Marlette and said, "Get on your horse. I'll lead you down."

She mounted and he reached to take her packhorse's lead rope, his arm brushing her thigh. She jerked her leg away feeling the warmth rise in her cheeks. If he noticed her flinch he ignored it. He tied her packhorse with his and told the rest of the men, "We'll go down one at a time. Leave your saddle horse on top and take your packhorse down first. Don't start down until the man in front is almost at the bottom."

They started down the steep bank, the horse's hooves sending a small landslide of rocks around Chesnut's feet. Rattlesnakes crawled away from the shower of stones and recoiled on sun-warmed rocks rattling ominously. Marlette hung tightly to her saddle horn as her horse slipped and plunged in the loose shale. Chesnut held him steady and they made it to the river in a cascade of rocks. She looked back to see her father already started down the trail. She held her breath until he was safely at the bottom.

The men made another hard trip up and down the steep slope before all the animals were down. They rode easily along the wide bank lined with sage and juniper trees. A few hundred yards up the curving river a low bank marked an easy exit from the canyon.

They made camp on the bank, and facing the rosy glow of late afternoon reflecting off the buff-colored canyon walls, they built a fire and had a hot meal. Marlette felt some of her anxiety drain away as she watched the tranquil beauty of the canyon. The men relaxed also and the grim silence of the past days ended as they once more took time to discuss and map their journey. Marlette took out her journal and moved away from the men so that their low conversation wouldn't interrupt the flow of her thoughts as she wrote.

She had to write swiftly because the sun was dipping slowly behind the jagged upthrust of rocks. Out of the corner of her eye she saw Gay coming toward her. He sat down beside her, his face freshly shaved but his eyes tired.

"Mind if I interrupt?"

She smiled at him, glad of this moment with him. "Not if you can be quiet while I finish this."

He leaned back against a rock, seemingly content to wait. She resumed her furious writing until it was too dark to see the words on the page. She closed the book and Gay encircled her with an arm. Leaning against him, she watched the shadows envelop the canyon walls.

Gay broke the silence. "You know, I could like this country under different circumstances."

Before she could agree a silent shadow loomed over them and Marlette started up. She sank back down as the shape took on familiar lines.

Gay protested mildly, "Damn it, Chesnut, will you quit sneaking up on people."

Unperturbed, Chesnut advised, "You'd better turn in."

Marlette stood up as Chesnut walked down the slope toward the river. Gay stood beside her, his arm around her.

"I wonder where he's going?"

"Probably to take a bath."

Gay's voice took on a note of strained surprise. "And how do you know that?"

She blushed as she remembered the source of her knowledge. She couldn't tell Gay about that. Hastily she answered, "Just a wild guess."

But he perceived the embarrassment in her voice and insisted, "Marlette, you're not being honest with me. I've asked you to marry me and I have every right to know how far this has gone."

Angrily she retorted, "It's gone nowhere. You debase me to even think that it has." She turned on her heel and walked away.

Gay leaped after her and held her arm. "I'm sorry, Marlette. I keep forgetting you're not like the other women I've known. It makes me jealous that he's always so close to you and I'm not."

Quietly she said, "Forget it Gay. It's not important." She tried to walk on but he held her firmly. Slowly, she turned back to him and raised her head, knowing he would kiss her. His lips took hers roughly, his body bruising her in his passion. She was frightened by his desire and pushed away from him. "Please, Gay. This isn't the time or the place."

He released her, realizing that she was right. "I'm sorry, but now you know how much I care for you. Now, please, let me walk you back to the fire."

Without a word she took his arm and walked the few yards to the fire. The men were going to bed and her father stood by the fire waiting for her. He smiled wearily at her. "Are you all right, my dear?"

She kissed him on the cheek, slipping a tender arm around him. "I'm fine, Father. And you?"

He patted her shoulder. "Tired, but I've been more tired. Chesnut says we'll cross the river the Frenchmen call Deschutes tomorrow and we'll be on our way north. We should be back at the fort in three or four days."

"I can't say I won't be glad."

"I know. I'm sorry I let you talk me into letting you come. I never imagined trouble like this."

"Don't worry about me, Father. I'll make it, just as we all will." She tried to inject a note of hope in her voice.

He hugged her and smiled warmly, his eyes openly filled with love and pride for her. "We'd better get to bed now, eh?"

"Good night, Father." She watched him crawl into his bed, her heart filled with the warmth of his love. She went to her own bed and crawled under the cool blankets, looking toward her father once more, savoring the long-awaited unleashing of his love for her. Tears stung her eyes as she wondered why the moment she had striven for so fiercely had come in this place of desolation.

Chesnut moved across her line of vision, surveying the camp in silence. She watched him kneel to pull the fire apart and bury the burning limbs with dust. The night of a million stars took over and she fell asleep without counting any of them.

She awoke early, feeling more rested than any time since their departure from Waiilatpu. Chesnut was cooking breakfast over a new fire. He'd even filled a pan with water for her and it waited on a rock close by. Surely, she thought, taking time to make breakfast and to bring her water meant they were out of danger. The very thought of it flooded her with relief. But she tried to keep the relief in control, wise enough to know that nothing could be certain.

Massacre on the Deschutes

THEY HEADED southwest that morning toward a distant line of low hills. The going was easy and Ross Chesnut let the horses pick their own pace.

Before noon they reached the rimrock ridges that marked the breaks along the Deschutes River. Instead of going toward the river he turned south, skirting the rough river canyon, looking for the east-west trail used by the Indians.

A mile or so later, he saw the wide, plainly marked trail. He leaned over his horse to scrutinize the tracks and could see no fresh Indian sign. Turning to the men behind him, he said curtly, "Stay here."

He scanned the ground on either side of the trail for several hundred yards in all directions riding at a trot, and found nothing. Yet he couldn't rid himself of a persistent feeling of danger. He looked toward the mountains west of them and saw the unmistakable signs of a brewing storm, roiling white thunderheads over the darkened peaks. He felt instinctively that it would be safest to go farther south and cross the river in the open, although if the storm dumped rain in this area it could delay their crossing and mean snow in the mountains. Any further delay would severely deplete their food supply and there was an unmistakable chill in the air. Their time was running out.

He rode back to the waiting group of men, weary and haggard from their long hours in the saddle. In the last three days they had lost some of their contempt for him and when he spoke, they listened with clear respect.

"This trail will take us to a crossing. I don't see any fresh Indian signs, but this is good ambush country. It would be safer to ride south and cross where it's flatter tomorrow, but there's a storm building in the mountains and any rain could raise this river so fast it might delay us an extra day or more."

He saw Holliway take in the cloud formation and nod in agreement.

Taylor broke the silence. "Well, then, what's the problem, Chesnut? You said you didn't see any sign and with these guns—."

Holliway interrupted, "The problem is a potential Indian ambush which would give them the advantage of surprise."

Joshua asked, "Do we have a choice, Chesnut?"

"The only choice is being able to pick the spot where we fight."

Joshua nodded, "True, but we can't fight the weather. I see no reason why we should delay any longer."

In a quiet voice Ross said, "There is one reason, Mr. Brightwood, your lives."

They stared silently at his expressionless face and at one another.

After a few moments Joshua asked, "Is there anyone who would rather ride south?"

Ross could see uncertainty in two pairs of eyes as they waited for someone else to answer. Thompson glanced at Holliway and Proctor looked unhappy, but no one spoke out.

Ross broke the silence. "Everyone keep a sharp lookout. Holliway, I want you to keep watch behind us when we're down in the draws."

He turned his horse and started along the trail leading up a gentle slope. He saw the woman fall in at her accustomed place and looked briefly at her gaunt face, admiring her determination. She had been less trouble than he had expected, except for her stubborn and total disregard for orders earlier on the journey. He felt she deserved a quick end to this trip. It would be especially hard on her if they were caught in cold weather.

As they neared the top of the rise, he motioned her to stay back. He dismounted and stealthily made his way to the top of the hill, but saw nothing on its downward curve. He felt a nagging sense of danger again, but there was nothing visible to indicate that things were not right.

Returning to his horse, he led them across the hill and down the slope toward the steep draw, watching intently for any overt movement. He turned and saw Holliway watching from the top of the hill.

He waved him forward as they rounded a rock wall and made their way cautiously up another steep ridge.

Once on top, he could see the trail descend into another deeper canyon. The canyon was almost hidden from view by junipers that grew thickly on both sides of the trail. He didn't like the look of it. His eyes caught a movement below and he waited, tense. A doe and fawn crossed the trail unconcernedly and stopped to nibble along the edge of the trees. He felt slightly relieved by their presence.

He motioned the other riders forward and sent his horse down the trail. The deer bounded down the trail away from them and he watched them closely. The canyon widened presently, its sides rounding gradually as they opened toward the river and the junipers thinned out. The deer easily ran up the slope and Ross felt some relief now that the uneasy group of riders wasn't entirely boxed in. The thirsty horses eagerly headed for the river. The crossing would be difficult in the swift boulder-strewn water and he stopped at the water's edge, signaling a brief rest.

The men were dismounting to get drinks themselves when Holliway, still behind them up the canyon, fired his gun. Ross turned around quickly. Holliway was riding at breakneck speed toward them shouting, "Indians!" More shots rang out and Holliway reeled. At that moment Indians began pouring over the top of the canyon from both sides. Ross grabbed the halter rope of the woman's horse and wheeled his horse along the bank, yelling for the startled and momentarily stunned men to mount up.

The woman cried out as another volley of shots struck the frantic men trying desperately to mount. Thompson and Long were hit and their horses struggled to get away. Ross couldn't worry about them now. The level bank ended in a tumble of rocks a few yards ahead and he had to turn up the slope pulling the woman's horse after him.

They were partway up the slope when a group of Indians came thundering over the crest of the hill above them in a wild, yelling charge. Ross fired, aiming at the horses and bringing two down. It slowed the other Indians, but only for a few moments. Kicking his horse he turned across the slope and down into another shallow draw.

When they reached some open ground, Ross fired again, picking off two more Indians before racing on. Another line of rimrock rose in the distance and he headed toward it. He needed the protection of canyons for a defensible position. Their already tired horses could never outrun the Indians' fresher mounts.

They weaved in and out of rocks, the woman's face white with fear. They ducked into a smaller intersecting canyon with high steep walls. Ross was afraid to think that the canyon might be a trap for them as well as for their pursuers, but his luck held. The canyon ended in a steep, crumbled rock slope. It was too steep to ride up, but they could lead the horses up.

There was no time to lose and he dismounted and motioned the woman to dismount. She sat frozen in her saddle and he pulled her down, speaking harshly, "Take your horse and get up that bank as fast as you can."

She blinked and scrambled up the slope. He followed, hearing the shouts of the Indians as they found their tracks at the mouth of the canyon.

They reached the protective rocks at the top of the slope just in time. He pulled the rifles from their scabbards before he ran the horses out of sight and pushed Marlette down behind a large rock. The Indians came into view. There was no time to replace the nearly empty cylinder in his rifle. He leaned over a rock, waiting until the Indians reached the slope they had just climbed. Taking careful aim, he fired, knocking down the last two horses with two shots. The horses fell, screaming, their riders yelling as they scrambled away from their thrashing mounts. The middle Indian wheeled around but found his retreat blocked by the fallen horses. The other two Indians fired at Ross, emptying their single-shot rifles. As the balls slammed harmlessly into the rock, Ross picked up Marlette's rifle. He fired at them with deadly accuracy, picking them off one at a time in rapid succession. Silence settled over the small, narrow canyon and Ross stood up, his face dark with distaste.

Marlette raised her head. "Are they gone?" she asked in a shaking voice.

"Yes."

She slowly rose and glanced toward the canyon floor with wide, fearful eyes. She jerked her head away, shuddering at the carnage she saw.

He took her arm and said quietly, "Let's go."

She looked at him with horror, pulling away from his touch. "You killed them all!"

His mouth tightened and he said firmly, "We have to go. There'll be others looking for us."

"What about Father, and the rest? We can't leave without them. We've got to go back and help them."

"We can't help them, now."

"But we've got to!" Her voice rose in desperation.

More gently he said, "Miss Brightwood, understand, it's too late to help them."

Her face crumpled momentarily with disbelief and he thought she was going to cry. She turned away and covered her face with shaking hands. He left her there and went after the horses. He replaced the empty cylinders and returned the rifles to their scabbards. Without the packhorses there would be no more ammunition for the guns.

He led the horses back to where the woman sat hunched on a boulder. She had regained control and mounted her horse without protest. He headed once more toward the river. The storm clouds were beginning to drift over the mountains and looked threateningly close. The sky was darkening ominously.

Finally he found a place to ford the river. For the woman's sake he would have waited until morning to cross as it was getting cold and she would have no dry clothes to change into for the night. But there was no doubt in his mind that the Indians would be on their trail. Rain also threatened and looked more likely every minute. If they didn't cross now and it rained all night the river might be too high by morning to cross. Without a second thought he urged his horse into the river.

As they rode onward brilliant flashes of lightning and thunder preceded the inevitable storm, followed by a steady gray veil of rain. Soon the black-timbered butte he was using to guide him was all but lost in the onrushing downpour.

Ross looked for a place to camp where they would be sheltered from the storm. They had moved into a fringe of pine that spread out from the mountains and he looked for a downed tree or a thicket of young pines over which he could spread Marlette's small tarp to keep them dry.

He finally found a spot and quickly made a shelter as the first heavy drops of rain penetrated the tall pines. He got Marlette under cover and gathered wood for a fire, aware that they hadn't eaten since breakfast.

Unfortunately, most of their food had been on the packhorses. All they had with them was some dried meat. He got the fire going and mentally calculated how long he could make the food last. He handed her her ration, but she took only one small piece and put the rest back into the saddlebag.

The rain pelted down and the thunder and lightning crashed violently around them. Wind whipped through the trees and limbs creaked and brittle branches broke and plummeted to the ground. The Indians wouldn't be able to trail them after their tracks had been washed away by driving rain and Ross felt a little easier about their situation.

Darkness came swiftly and he had to put out the fire. The chill air soon drove Marlette, wet and exhausted, under her blankets, but she did not sleep, and Ross could feel her watching him fearfully in the darkness. He crawled into his own blanket and let himself sleep in the security of the rain and darkness.

He awoke long before morning and sat listening to the heavy stillness of the sodden forest. He started the fire again and put his blanket over the sleeping woman.

She awoke, stifling a sneeze, looking uncertainly at Ross huddled close to the fire. He offered her some more of the jerky and she took more this time, chewing it silently.

He rose to saddle the horses and she mounted without a word. As they rode through the pines, Ross unslung his bow and strung it. The first rabbit he saw became lunch. He stopped on the shore of a good-sized lake and built a fire. The woman stood close to it, warming her damp skirt and staring with unseeing eyes toward the beautiful blue green water.

After lunch they rode on. The trail grew steeper and there were traces of snow as they climbed toward the top. They reached the summit of the pass, where fresh snow frosted the firs, and a chill wind whipped across the snowy flanks of the jagged pinnacle they had passed, warning Ross of things to come. He guided his horse onto the narrower trail around the sheer face of a cliff which overlooked a deep canyon. From here, Ross could see the bleak gray cloud mass in the west. It didn't look good. They entered another forest of firs and hemlock, denser than the one they had left. Underbrush crowded the trail and the vine maple was turning into brilliant shades of yellow and red. Winter was imminent.

Late in the afternoon they came to another lake. Ross led the way through the marshy, shallow edges of the lake to the opposite shore and made camp in the shelter of the thick underbrush. It was early yet and Ross took time to put together a makeshift fishing line and within minutes had two nice trout for their supper. While the trout were cooking he caught two more for their breakfast.

Marlette ate but still made no effort to talk or even cry. Ross was concerned for her but didn't know how to help her. Any move he made toward her brought stark fear into her eyes and he realized that only time would heal her wounds.

He slept badly that night, knowing the Indians might well have picked up their trail, but heard only the sounds of the forest. A mountain lion screamed once from some distant place and the wind sighed through the trees, the sound punctuated by the mournful hoot of a lonesome owl.

At dawn he built up the fire and roasted the fish. The air was chilly and he kept his blanket around him until the fire warmed him. He went to cover Marlette with it and she sat up with a start as he dropped the blanket around her, but she remained silent. A ghostly fog was rising from the lake and although Ross knew they should be moving on, he let Marlette stay by the fire, even after they had finished eating the fish.

At last, when he knew that the sun would be high enough to warm them, he moved to saddle the horses as Marlette, moving automatically, rolled up her blankets and wrapped them in her tarp. He was about to put out the fire when the mist lifted from the lake revealing a small band of Indians grouped near the far shore.

There was no time to run and no place to fight. He heard Marlette gasp behind him as she saw the Indians moving through the shallow lake toward them.

He went to her. "Can you act like you're out of your mind?"

For the first time in almost two days, she spoke. "Why?"

"If they think you're crazy they may not kill you. They believe that killing a crazy person releases the evil spirit in that body to enter the body of the one who killed it."

She nodded her head and he turned away to watch the Indians come ashore. They split into two lines and formed a semicircle around them. Ross recognized the leader and some of the others. He was surprised that these Indians were part of the war party. They had little to do with the eastern Indians under Hill's influence. He had been welcome in their camps along the lower Deschutes many times. Hill's influence must be greater than he had imagined, to turn these usually friendly Indians into manhunters. Since they didn't immediately slaughter him, he believed they had a chance.

He held up his hand in greeting and spoke in their dialect. "Welcome to my camp, Antelope Runner. My brother is far from his lodge. I have not much but you are welcome to share it."

The muscular Indian stared at him silently with dark, uncertain eyes. Ross knew the man had strength and courage, but saw that he now appeared to find his job distasteful.

Ross was aware of a murmur among the Indians and heard a soft unintelligible sing-song noise behind him but he didn't dare turn his gaze from the Indian in front of him.

Antelope Runner spoke, "My brother, too, is far from the great White Eagle's nest. I wish my brother had not strayed from his nest."

"Antelope Runner speaks sadly. Have I caused you sadness?"

"My people have looked upon you as their friend and brother. You have been welcome in our lodges. It pains us that you have brought these people to steal our land."

Ross smiled slightly. "The one who told you these people came to steal your land lies. They have taken nothing. Now their great chief in the east will be angry because they have been killed."

At that moment the woman let out a cry and Ross turned quickly. She stood on her feet and stared, glassy-eyed, toward the water, crying, "Father, Father! I'm coming, Father."

She walked, as though in a trance, toward the water. Again he had to admire her courage. The Indians were visibly shaken by her apparent lunacy. They murmured worriedly among themselves. She kept walking and Ross wondered what she would do. She didn't stop at the water's edge but kept right on wading into the lake. He felt apprehensive as she continued deeper into the lake.

Suddenly she dropped out of sight into a hole. He ran and plunged into the lake before he had time to consider the consequences. She bobbed to the surface just in front of him and he made a grab for her. She slipped beneath the water again just out of reach and he dove after her hauling her up by the collar of her coat. She gasped, and he whispered angrily into her wet ear, "That was a stupid thing to do."

He carried her ashore and placed her by the fire and she rocked back and forth humming the same senseless tune as if nothing had happened. He turned back to Antelope Runner. The Indian spoke first, his polite diplomatic speech replaced by necessary shrewdness.

"What is wrong with the woman?"

"You saw for yourself, my brother. The sight of her father and the others being killed has affected her mind."

"What you do with her now?"

"I will take her back to the Eagle's nest where she can take one of the white man's ocean canoes back to her home in the east."

The Indian's eyes clouded. "This is what must not happen."

"Do not fear. She cannot tell what has happened. She will bring no harm to you." He could see that the Indian was considering the situation. Bluntly he asked, "Would you kill her?"

A startled expression appeared on the Indian's face at the thought of releasing the evil spirit. Careful not to allow his fear to show, he said shrewdly, "If it is as you say, there is no need. Antelope Runner does not kill unnecessarily. You must be a witness to this, that I, Antelope Runner, spared her life. Because you are held as chief among your people and respected in my village and I know you to be a man who speaks true, I will trust you to make sure this woman brings no harm to my people." He paused, but Ross knew he was not finished and waited for what he knew would follow. The Indian continued, "However, I must also protect my warriors from the anger of our chief. I must take your horses and guns to prove we have not failed to find you and kill you as was ordered."

Ross nodded. "I understand." He unbuckled his gun belt and handed it to Antelope Runner. The Indian motioned to his men and they immediately took the horses. The rest of the guns and his bedroll were already on the horses. Silently, the Indian wheeled his horse around and trotted back to the water, his warriors following.

Jacques

Ross WATCHED as the Indians plunged their horses through the marshy edge of the lake and disappeared through the trees. He looked up at the cloudy sky. It had been quite cold last night and the cloud formation indicated snow before nightfall. If they had only been able to keep the horses, they might have made it to Jacques's cabin before the day was out.

Impatiently, he turned from thought to action. He went to the log where Marlette's bedroll had been bundled and pushed out of sight. At least they would still have her blankets for warmth. He unrolled the pack and took one of the blankets to her. She stood up, wrapping it around her wet, shivering body, looking at him with unconcealed hopelessness. He made a roll from the remaining blanket and tarp and tied it across his own shoulders. He hated to take her away from the fire, but they had to get started before it snowed.

Turning back to the fire he started kicking dirt over it. She didn't say anything, but her look was enough to let him know her thoughts. Gently he reminded her, "We have to go."

Obediently she turned and followed him through the trees. He found it difficult to walk slowly enough for her to keep up. By himself he would have set off at a dogtrot and he felt increasingly anxious as they trudged slowly under the graying sky. At least there was a faint trail which made it easier for them to get through the thick underbrush.

In a couple of miles they reached another stunted growth of pines. He left the trail and turned in a northwesterly direction. Marlette was keeping up with him and he didn't stop for rest. They approached an ancient lava flow and he let her rest because he knew it would be difficult walking through the lava.

After a short rest, he took her arm to help her through the jumble of rough, black, porous rocks. Halfway through Marlette removed her blanket and he noticed that her face was damp with the effort of scrambling through the rocks. He found a tree that afforded some shade and let her rest while he rolled her blanket and folded it over his pack. His eyes restlessly searched the sky as his mind ticked off the seconds of delay.

He didn't let her stop again until they reached the cushioned floor of the forest. Here, the waning warmth of the sun was cut off in the dense shelter of the trees and he gave the blanket back to her and went on.

They stopped for water at a tiny stream, resting a few minutes from the struggle with the underbrush. She was taking a beating and he knew it but he couldn't let her rest too long. She said nothing, and when he rose, she rose doggedly and followed him.

He came across a game trail which made the going somewhat easier, but the air was growing colder and Ross could feel the signs of impending snow. He wanted to move ahead more rapidly but he knew she couldn't keep up with him. The wind died suddenly and an ominous quiet fell over the forest with the first small intermittent snowflakes. Looking back at Marlette, he saw the worry in her eyes.

Within an hour flakes were falling, huge, fluffy, and thick. The wind picked up again and Ross found it difficult to see in the driving, swirling snow that quickly obliterated the trail.

He took Marlette's arm and led her off the trail in search of a shelter. It was difficult in the blinding storm but he finally found a huge tree that lay on its side, with a depression large enough for them under it's sheltering trunk. With his hatchet he stripped the surrounding smaller trees of branches and made a thick layer in the depression. Spreading the canvas tarp over it, he placed the blankets on top. He motioned Marlette into the bed and cut bigger boughs to prop along both sides of the log enclosing the depression.

He crawled into the snug shelter and placed the last branches over them, brushing the snow off his buckskins and starting to get under the blankets, thoroughly chilled.

Marlette gasped, "What are you doing?"

"What did you expect me to do?"

She remained silent, but she turned and moved away from him. A cold draft filled the space between them. Patiently he said, "Miss Brightwood, if we want to live through the night we must keep warm. Don't worry about what I'm not going to do and come here."

There was no response, not even the sound of her breathing. There was nothing to do but force the issue. He reached out and put his arm around her waist to draw her near.

She twisted out of his grasp and hissed at him in fury, "Don't touch me! You tell me not to worry about what you're going to do. Two people who meant very much to me are dead along with five others and you tell me not to worry!" Her voice rose with emotion. She was close to hysteria and he was helpless to reason with her. She went on in another anguished burst. "I've done nothing but worry for a long time. I've worried about the deaths that left my father without a wife or a son to carry on his business. I've worried about filling that void. I've worried about getting older and plainer as the years passed. Now the only man who ever wanted to marry me is dead. Do you find it surprising that someone wanted to marry me? Gaylord did and now I'll never know what it means to be loved and fulfilled because I'm going to die in this Godforsaken wilderness!"

She started to cry and he hoped it would relieve some of the unbearable tension locked inside her. He reached out to hold her and his touch broke down her last vestige of control. She turned on him, beating her fists against his arms, face, and chest while she sobbed hysterically. There was surprising strength left in her and he felt sure she would make it if they lived through the night. He let her pound on him, covering his head against her blows, until she had exhausted herself and cried softly against him.

He straightened the covers over them and held her while she cried. Gently he stroked her hair, hoping to quiet her. At last she raised her head and he felt her body grow taut again.

Gently he whispered, "I'm not going to hurt you. Relax and trust me."

Her voice was controlled as she answered, "I find that hard to believe."

He had never understood why she disliked and distrusted him. Although he found it irritating, he knew that hate would give her strength for what still lay ahead. However, he was curious about the reason for her animosity and he asked simply, "Why?"

Coldly, she said, "From the first time I saw you there have been women after you. I could hardly come to any other conclusion."

He smiled in the darkness. "Why should that bother you?"

"Because I find it disgusting that you use women, even married women. I don't trust any man who does that."

He sighed. In one sense, she was right, but how could he tell her it only appeared to be true. She wasn't ready to believe the truth yet. He pulled out the knife he carried and placed it in her hand.

She jerked back from the cold steel. "What are you doing?"

"It's my knife. You can have it if you'll feel better about sleeping with me."

She laughed harshly. "Would it make any difference?"

He answered honestly, "No."

"Then what are you waiting for?"

She was trying his patience but he kept himself under control. "Miss Brightwood, regardless of what you think of me, I don't intend to hurt you. Now be reasonable and go to sleep."

He felt her stiffen with anger. "Why not? Is it because I'm so, so—plain? What if I said I wanted you to. Yes! Why not? I'm going to die anyway. Why not know what it's like to be made love to?"

She turned to him stiffly, placing her arms around him, her lips cold against his cheek. He remembered another time and place with another woman and gently removed her arms.

"You only want to hurt yourself. The act of love should be a beautiful thing between two people. You must want to give of yourself freely. I can't do what you ask because you want to punish yourself."

She lay there for a long time silently. At last she turned away from him. Firmly he pulled her toward him and her head rested on his arm. She didn't fight him this time and he felt her muscles slowly relax, as she finally fell asleep. He closed his eyes and forcibly pushed away the memory of another woman who had lain at his side and given him her love.

He awoke in the gray gloom of morning in their shelter. Listening intently, he heard nothing. Even the animals had fled the snow and the forest was absolutely still. He heard the faint swish and soft plop of snow sliding from the trees to the ground. He realized it had stopped snowing and that it wasn't freezing. It was time to go.

Marlette was still cradled in his arms, her pale hair flowing out over his arm, shoulder, and chest, so close he could smell the dust and sweat of it. He put his hand on her shoulder and shook her very gently. She stirred and murmured but didn't wake. He shook her again and she rolled away from him and lay on her back. Her eyes sleepily surveyed her surroundings and then rested on his face. She was far from plain in that unguarded moment with the dimness of the shelter disguising the gauntness of her face. He brushed away a tendril of hair that clung to the corner of her mouth. A soft, tentative smile curved her full lips and softened her prominent jaw.

He knew they should be going but he hated to break the spell of the moment—the only moment they might ever have without her suspicion dividing them. Only half-realizing what was happening, he felt himself drawn to her soft, slightly parted lips. They touched and clung, gently tasting the sweetness of the moment. Her eyes closed and his hand caressed her hair.

Whether it was a movement he made or something she heard, her eyes suddenly flew open and the magic moment was gone. She moved away from him and he, somewhat regretfully, rose to push through the boughs lining the shelter. Flakes of ice fell on his face and the cold shocked him into full alertness. Their shelter had been warmer than he had realized. He remembered his knife and retrieved it among the blankets.

Quickly he cleared the boughs away and helped Marlette through. She shivered as the cold hit her and he draped one of the blankets over her head and shoulders. She clutched it around her, her face grim; all previous softness gone. He rolled up the tarp and remaining blanket and slung them across his shoulders.

He looked around until his unfailing sense of direction showed him the way. Bending over quickly, he took a small ball of snow, putting it in his mouth to quench his thirst. She immediately did the same and he cautioned her, "Not too much, just enough to wet your mouth and throat."

He started off and she followed. The snow was only a few inches deep and walking was not too difficult, but their feet were soon wet and cold. He had suffered cold before and could steel his mind and body against it.

Just a few hundred feet from their shelter there was a fairly wide stream. This had to be the main stream that ran by Jacques's cabin. It was still a long walk and he doubted they would reach the cabin before it snowed again.

They followed the stream for some distance until they were confronted by a steep ridge. The other side was still level and he decided it would be wiser to cross the stream than to attempt the steep hill. However the rocks he could use for stepping stones to the other side were too small and slippery for her hard-soled boots.

He turned to her. "Do you know how to ride piggyback?"

She nodded and he squatted down so she could climb on his back. She was surprisingly light even with the heavy clothes and blanket. And it was no wonder, he thought, as he felt a sharp pang of hunger. He would have to get them some food.

He carried her precariously across the stream and they walked on through the snow, following the stream. Nothing moved in the silent forest and they forged on, hunger increasing their weakness.

They hadn't gone nearly as far as he had hoped before it started snowing again. The snow gradually increased and there was a sharp wind that seemed to push them backward. He heard Marlette fall and turned to see her sitting in the snow. He let her rest for a few minutes and then helped her to her feet. They went another mile before she stopped again.

"I can't go any farther."

"You can and you will." The severity of his voice brought a spark into her weary eyes.

Bitterly she said, "Why don't you leave me?"

"We can both make it, but you've got to keep going."

"Make it to where? To my death?"

"Just a few miles down this stream is a cabin. If we can make it that far, we'll be safe."

She repeated, "A cabin?" Hope tinged her voice.

He nodded and saw her body steady with determination as they continued. The snow was getting deeper and they began to flounder in and out of unseen hollows and trip over downed limbs hidden under the snow. They couldn't see more than a few feet in front of them and Ross had trouble hearing the rush of the stream through the howling wind.

Marlette stumbled and pulled them both down. He held her close in the chill snow and felt the shaking weariness of her body. He tried to lift her but she looked up tearfully.

"I'm so tired. Can't we rest?"

He knew it was a mistake, but his own body was growing weary. He sat holding her as they rested. When he felt too comfortable and sleepy he urged her to go on.

The snow whipped about them and it soon became impossible to see anything. He realized that the only sure path was the stream. He headed for it and slid down the bank into the chill water. She followed, crying out as the water filled her boots. The footing was just as bad on the slippery stream bottom, but at least it was a trail he could follow in the howling blizzard that isolated them in a cocoon of blinding whiteness.

It soon became obvious that Marlette was completely exhausted. Resting didn't help and she began to stop more frequently. Ross knew every delay only lessened their chances of reaching safety. He had no choice but to carry her.

He lifted her onto his back and, for a while, made better time. However, his own strength began to decline under the double load. In the tradition of his Indian upbringing, he forced everything from his mind except his goal. Time and again he stumbled and fell with weariness but he continued on.

It was growing perceptibly darker and colder and he began to wonder if he had passed the cabin in the blinding snow. He struggled on, arms and legs numb with cold, and his apprehension turning into near panic. He stopped to rest, letting Marlette down by the edge of the stream. She didn't move and he bent to peer into her snow-encrusted face. She was either asleep or unconscious. It made little difference—either was a deadly sign. He wrapped her up and lifted her over his shoulder. It was harder to carry her this way but he would never get her onto his back again without her help.

Tenaciously he went on down the stream. Reason told him they had not gone far enough. He could only guess at how many miles they had covered.

His weary mind dwelled on the cabin and its warm fire in the rough stone fireplace. He staggered on, falling to his knees and dimly aware he wasn't feeling the water anymore. The water had been getting deeper as smaller streams flowed into it and he realized he wouldn't be able to stay in it much longer.

Half-wading, half-swimming, clutching at rocks and roots along the bank, he went on. The cold was beginning to tear at his lungs and he had difficulty breathing deeply. Stopping long enough to find a dry piece of blanket to cover his face he struggled on, desperation driving him.

All strength was gone. The deeper water dragged him down and he realized he would have to leave the stream and leave Marlette if he was to make it to the cabin. He would have to go on alone and send Jacques back for her. He dragged himself and Marlette's lifeless body out of the water and fell exhausted on the bank. It was imperative to move on but his body failed to respond to his command. Anger at his weakness feebly stirred his muscles and he raised himself to his hands and knees. Suddenly, he caught a faint, illusive whiff of smoke in the biting wind and relief flooded his mind. He must be near the cabin. Jacques kept the canoe pulled out of the water and hopefully he would fall over it if he walked next to the stream. He struggled to pick up Marlette, but fell again after only a few steps. Crawling then, he dragged her in the deepening snow until he hit something and reached out with numb fingers to test its outline. He felt the whole length before he was satisfied that it was the canoe.

Wrapping a shaking arm around Marlette, he crawled on his hands and knees, inch by inch, toward the cabin, mentally calculating the distance. A shiver of panic shot through him before he saw the faint glow of light from a shuttered window. He stood then and lifted Marlette. He took one step forward, stumbled over the steps, and crashed into the door. Inside he heard a rumbling growl.

He called out desperately, but no sound came from his frozen throat. There was a thud of feet and the sound of a bar being raised. The door swung open and Ross felt his iced face crack in a grateful grin as he saw the big Frenchman standing before him, his black beard fast gathering snow.

After an astonished oath the Frenchman lifted the lifeless woman from Ross's arms and turned to the fire. Ross followed, feeling suddenly stronger now that he was safe. They kneeled over Marlette and Jacques bent to listen for her heartbeat. His black, hairy face split into a grin as he listened.

"Ah! There is still life."

"We'd better get her out of these wet clothes. Get some blankets."

Ross started undressing Marlette while Jacques climbed the ladder to the loft above to get blankets. Jacques's pet, a full-grown black bear, watched curiously as Ross's frozen fingers fumbled to remove the woman's clothing.

Jacques came down the ladder and took over the undressing since Ross's hands were too numb.

As they removed the last piece of frozen clothing, Jacques exclaimed, "Mon Dieu, Chesnut! Why you pick such a skinny woman? She no keep you warm on cold nights!"

Ross grinned, feeling his chapped lips crack. He was relaxed in Jacques's presence and could do and say things he seldom did anywhere else. "Jacques, it's not the flesh that keeps you warm, it's what's in the heart. Hand me that blanket."

He wrapped her thin body in the blanket and bathed her frostbitten feet and hands until some of the blueness left her skin. There was nothing more they could do except keep her warm. Jacques carried her to the fur-piled bunk at the end of the fireplace.

Ross stood weakly and began stripping off his wet clothes. Jacques brought him some dry clothes from the loft and he dressed with shaky slowness.

Jacques asked, "How long since you eat?"

"Yesterday morning."

He muttered an oath. "Why you not say so?"

"I was getting around to it."

Jacques went to the small cupboard and pulled a pot from the outdoor pantry. He hung it over the fire. "You know, mon ami, I never understand you. Are you white man or red man?"

Ross smiled and shrugged, "A little of both, I guess."

Jacques sat down in his comfortable fur-lined chair and said, "Now you tell me what happened."

Ross moved from the fire to sit in his own familiar chair and told briefly of the persistent Indian attacks, the massacre, and their escape. The pot of stew was bubbling when he finished and Jacques dished up a healthy portion for Ross. He sat down and mused on the story while Ross ate.

Finally he said, "You know, I think that damn Delaware Tom

needs killing. He crazy, power mad."

Ross nodded in agreement and sipped the hot coffee that always stood ready over the fire. He got up and checked on Marlette. He thought he saw a little color creeping back into her skin.

Turning back to Jacques, he said, "I'm going to bed. If she wakes up, her name is Miss Brightwood, and she may be difficult."

Jacques chuckled. "I take care of her. You go sleep."

Ross climbed the ladder to the loft and gratefully crawled under the warmth of the blankets and furs that covered the beds he and Jacques had built. He fell asleep instantly, for the first time at peace since he had left Vancouver.

Hours later he was disturbed by a shattering scream and instinctively scrambled from his bed. As he started down the ladder, he heard Jacques yell at the bear. Jacques was standing by the bed as Ross reached the floor. He glared at Ross. "I fall asleep and that damn bear he get up on the bed with the woman."

Marlette looked fearfully at Ross and burst into tears. He went to her and she let him take her in his arms while she cried.

When the sobbing quieted he asked, "How do you feel?"

In a weak, trembling voice she answered, "I'm not sure."

He took the hand that still clutched the blanket around her body. It felt warm. "Do you have feeling in your hands and feet?"

He found her foot and squeezed it through the blanket. "Yes, I can feel," she said. She realized then that she had no clothes on and she drew away from him. "Where are my clothes?" she gasped.

"We hung them by the fire to dry. Are you hungry?"

She answered, "Yes," her tone betraying dismay and resignation.

Jacques, who had been watching intently, suddenly came to life and hung the stewpot over the fire. Ross suddenly remembered that Jacques was still a stranger to her.

"Miss Brightwood, this is Jacques Broulette. The bear is his pet, Ivan. He won't hurt you."

Her eyes lost their apprehensive look and she lay back weakly. He stood up. "Jacques will take care of you." He climbed the ladder back to his bed.

It was dark when Ross finally awoke. His stomach rumbled with hunger and he rose, feeling weak, but rested. The lamp was set on the small table in the middle of the room below and Jacques and Marlette were eating.

Jacques grinned broadly. "Ah, my friend, you at last wake up. You are hungry, no?"

"Yes."

Ross was aware of Marlette watching him with uncertain eyes. She was dressed and her hair was combed into the familiar unbecoming bun. "How do you feel now, Miss Brightwood?"

"Much better, thank you."

Ross washed and joined them at the table. Jacques had outdone himself in preparing a nourishing meal for his half-starved friend. Roasted venison, potatoes, carrots—even biscuits.

Never one to worry about a mess, Jacques let Ross clean up while he and Marlette sipped their hot coffee by the fireplace. Ross didn't mind. It was an arrangement that worked, but he wondered how Marlette felt about the rank, animal smell of the place. He asked, "Is there enough food for the three of us all winter?"

"Oui, there is enough."

Marlette straightened in her chair, instantly protesting, "I can't stay here the whole winter. I must get back east at the earliest possible moment."

"But, Mademoiselle, it is not wise to travel now. The water is too low for the canoe and the snow too deep for walking. A storm come and—" Jacques threw up his hands in despair, "you freeze to death."

She leaned back, her eyes flashing with protest, but she remained silent.

Ross continued, "How's the fresh meat?"

"Not much left. We ate the last roast."

"Are the deer moving yet?"

"Oui. Everything tell Jacques she going to be a bad winter."

Ross nodded his agreement. "I'd better go hunting early in the morning. Did you bring me a bow?"

"Oui. I brought everything you wanted."

Marlette sprang from her chair, her body rigid and her eyes blazing in rage. "You planned on staying here this winter! You knew what was going to happen to us! You knew from the beginning!" She fought back a sob, "And I was beginning to trust you. Why am I still alive? Or did you have something special planned for me? Am I to be sold to the highest bidder? Tell me! I have a right to know!" She glared at him in fury, her hands clenched into fists.

Ross sighed deeply. It was no use trying to talk to her; she hated him so intensely, she wouldn't believe anything he said. He rose slowly feeling that it was going to be a long winter. Looking her in the eye he said wearily, "Miss Brightwood, my only plan is to see you safely on the first ship out of the Oregon country." He turned away from her tense challenge and walked to the ladder. He lay down on his bed and closed his eyes but couldn't sleep. In a few minutes his sharp ears caught Jacques's voice from below.

"Mademoiselle, you judge my friend too harshly. He had me bring extra supplies for you and your people. He knew the great danger you faced. He knew you might need supplies to finish the journey to Fort Vancouver. He did all these things for you."

"But why did he have his things brought here?"

Jacques chuckled softly, "But why not? He spends *every* winter here."

No more was said and in a few moments Ross fell asleep.

Winter in the Mountains

ROSS AWOKE HOURS LATER, feeling refreshed. He listened with keen ears and heard nothing but Jacques's snores. All was very still, and he wondered if the snow had stopped. The loft was cool and still dark, telling him clearly as a clock that it was close to dawn. He rose quietly and went below. The bear raised his head as Ross reached over him for wood to feed the waning fire. He sliced a few hunks of the roast and took the leftover biscuits to eat. He put on his heavy, fur-lined clothes and slung the bow and arrows over his shoulder. Sensing that Marlette had awakened, he turned toward her bed, but she remained still. He left the cabin and followed the path toward the game trail. Every year they brought salt to attract the deer and usually it worked.

He reached the stand and sat down in the darkness to wait, chewing on the cold venison and scraping his face clean of stubble with the small, straightedge razor he carried. The darkness slowly and imperceptibly turned to gray gloom as the sun rose. It began to snow very lightly and the sudden chill helped to sharpen his senses as he waited.

A dark shape suddenly emerged at the edge of the clearing. He waited patiently as a doe, followed by her fawn, cautiously moved into the opening, pawed away the snow, and bent to nibble at the grass beneath. In a short while, another larger shape moved into the clearing. It was growing much lighter now and Ross could clearly see horns. The cautious buck sniffed the air and swiveled his sharp ears in every direction before moving to join the doe. Ross slowly raised his bow and arrow. He aimed carefully and the arrow pierced the buck behind the shoulder and through the lungs. The buck cried out and the three deer leaped into the brush. Ross jumped up and followed in swift pursuit. The buck was bleeding and left a vivid trail in the snow. Luckily the deer was well hit and unable to escape. Ross found him a few hundred feet from the clearing. With speed born of experience he bled and gutted the animal. He made carrying straps by inserting the front legs through slits in the back legs and shouldered the heavy animal for the return trip.

He was weaker than he realized and he had to rest several times before reaching the cabin. He dragged the deer into the shed and lit the lantern. Only a few furs were stretched on the frames stored in the shed. Some haunches of meat and several slabs of bacon hung from the rafters.

Jacques appeared in the doorway with a happy exclamation. "Say, that one nice buck!"

Ross smiled as Jacques helped him hang the deer up. The effort brought more sweat to his forehead and Jacques was quick to notice. "You go in and eat. I take care of this one."

Ross nodded. The understanding between them needed no words. He entered the cabin and Marlette glanced at him thoughtfully from her seat by the fire. He wanted to say something to her, but didn't know the right words. He dished up what was left of breakfast and ate silently.

When Jacques came in, Ross was doing the dishes. The sensitive Frenchman looked at them both thoughtfully. Ross knew he was aware of the quiet hostility that hung unspoken between the woman and himself.

"Ready for me to help cut him up?"

"Oui. He is skinned out."

Ross put on his heavy coat and boots and followed Jacques out the door. It was starting to snow in earnest as they went into the attached shed. They worked silently for a few minutes, until Jacques asked, "What you plan to do about the way she feels about you?"

"Nothing."

"Nothing!" he snorted. "Jacques never think he see the day you could not have a woman without half-trying."

Ross grinned, unable to deny his obvious physical charm. He was not always the stoic Indian he had been the past couple of weeks. In the company of friends, his dark eyes emanated warmth and humor.

But his attraction went beyond the physical. He was endowed with a deep compassion for women and they instinctively felt it and were drawn to him. Those who knew him lamented over his good fortune and Jacques, who knew him best, cajoled him for not taking advantage of it. He let Jacques think he was being virtuous but he knew that wasn't the case. "This woman is different. She doesn't like Indians."

"You haven't told her?"

"No. I don't think she would believe me."

"Well, then, I will tell her."

"No, Jacques. She must want to know before she will believe anything we tell her."

Jacques laughed wisely. "Oh, Jacques think she want to know. I see now why the battle she wages inside herself is greater than the one she wages against you."

Ross laughed. "Jacques, my friend, I think you could imagine amour in that door." He pointed with his knife to the open shed door.

Jacques laughed heartily and then sobered. "You laugh but I tell you, I see it in her eyes."

"She's nothing more than a job to me, and not an easy one at that. But if you want her, you try charming her."

Jacques laughed happily, "Oh, ho, mon cher! What a glorious winter Jacques would have, no?" He mused joyfully at the thought of sharing his bed with a woman for the long winter. Then his face lost its smile and he sighed deeply. "But no. This one is too much a lady. She not want a bear like Jacques. She belong to you. You need the woman more than I."

Ross shook his head. "You have chosen the wrong woman for me. This one will leave on the first ship in the spring and that is not what I want."

Jacques laid an understanding hand on his shoulder. "Jacques know what you want. But it is a long winter. Maybe one of you will change your mind, eh?" And he grinned hopefully.

Ross knew that the incorrigibly optimistic Jacques would do everything in his power to bring that about now that he had decided that the woman was to be Ross's. However, Jacques didn't know how stubborn and independent Marlette was. It might be interesting for a change to let someone else try handling her.

They finished cutting the meat and carried the scraps outside for the bear. They went into the cabin and found Marlette sitting rigidly in the chair. The bear got up and came eagerly to smell Jacques's hands for a tidbit.

"Ho! You will not find food here. Outside my friend."

The bear went to the door and rose on his hind legs, lifting the bar as a man would. This sparked some interest in Marlette and she asked, "Did you teach him to do that?"

"Oui, mademoiselle."

"Was he hard to train?"

"No. I have him since he very young. It is easy to teach them when they are young. And then, there is nothing better to do here in the winter. Some six, seven springs ago, maybe, this she-bear was raiding my traps. Jacques have to kill her but she have this small cub. It was lonely before Ross come to keep me company, so I take this small cub and raise him. He come now every winter to hibernate with me."

"It must be comforting to have such an animal to protect you."

"Oui." Jacques laughed. "The Indians never bother here."

"Why did you name him Ivan?"

Jacques smiled. "That is simple. When I was a small boy in France my grand-père would take me to see a troupe of traveling Russian bears perform. The trainer's name was Ivan. He looked so much like the bears, big and black. In fact he look like Jacques look now." Jacques slapped his knee and laughed heartily.

He made their supper and they sat down to eat. The men talked about the trap line and their work while Marlette sat listening in withdrawn silence. The evening passed in this subdued manner and they settled in for a few days to wait out the snowstorm raging outside.

When the storm finally passed, Jacques decided it was time to check the trap line. "If the weather hold I will check the whole line. If not, Jacques be back tonight." He shouldered his pack and picked up his rifle and snowshoes. "Come, Ivan. It not time for sleep yet."

The bear lazily got to his feet and ambled after the bundled Frenchman. Jacques paused outside to fasten the snowshoes, then with a grin he said, "You take care of things." Slushing off through the snow, his devilish laugh carried back to them on the wind.

Ross turned back into the room and looked at the clutter and dinginess in the bright, cold sunshine. His nose rebelled at the rank smell of the bear and of their own stale bodies. It was time to dig out, as he had often done before in the untidy Frenchman's wake. He left the front door wide open and strode to open the back door, saying, "You'd better put on a blanket for awhile. It's time to air this place out."

He took up a ragged, makeshift broom and began sweeping the littered floor. Marlette watched for awhile and then, with the contagion of cleaning stirring her, she took a rope from a peg near the door and tramped into the snow to tie it between two trees. She carried out all the blankets and whacked them thoroughly with a snowshoe. Ross found himself grinning as he watched her. Perhaps it wouldn't be such a long winter after all.

Together they cleaned every inch of the small cabin and Ross shredded a chunk of cedar; its fragrance filling the room. He made some lunch and Marlette sat down at the table looking a little flushed from her work. A stray strand of hair hung limply and she tried to tuck it back into the bun at her neck. Remembering her dislike for being dirty and his own desire for a bath he offered, "Would you like to wash your clothes and bathe?"

She brightened considerably at the thought, but suspicion quickly clouded her face. "Thank you, but I have no other clothes now."

"I can fix that if you want."

"How?"

"I have some nice deerskins and I can make a dress for you."

She looked thoughtful for a moment, then murmured, "No. Thank you, but I couldn't—." She stopped, her face coloring as she cast her eyes down in embarrassment.

Then he remembered the night he and Jacques had undressed her. It was the first time he had been exposed to the intricacies of a white woman's undergarments. "I think I can fix that, too."

He swung up the ladder and found the bundle he was looking for. He brought it down and laid it on the table, unwrapping the cover. It was a bolt of fine white cotton printed with dainty red rosebuds. She touched the soft cloth and looked at him strangely.

"You bought this for someone else."

He remained silent and she perceived who it was for.

"You bought it for Mrs. Whitman, didn't you?"

"Yes. But that doesn't matter. I can get more. I want you to have it."

She ran her fingers over the material again and then withdrew her hand. Her jaw squared stubbornly. "No. I couldn't accept it."

Exasperation filled him, but he was determined to make her agree in spite of herself. He smiled and said, "If you don't take it, I will make it for you and I'm sure that you're more skillful at making your clothes than I am."

She smiled then and he knew she had wanted it all along. She nodded and touched the material again. Shaking his head at her perversity, he went to get some water to heat.

While the water was heating over the fire, he fashioned a dress out of buckskin and she watched with interest. She had apparently accepted the fact that she would have to be without underclothes for a while and she had not, to his surprise, questioned his motives.

He wasn't quite through with the dress when he decided it was time he took his bath. He went to the loft to strip and with a blanket wrapped around him, he ran outside toward the cold river. It wasn't as pleasant as the tub near the fire, but he got the job done and raced back to the cabin.

She stood up in shocked silence as he entered and strode to the fire. She quickly averted her eyes although he was completely covered in the blanket. He grinned at her stiff back and the redness that colored her neck. If she had been another woman he might have teased her, but he understood that what he found natural, she did not. He rubbed himself briskly and climbed the ladder to dress.

He returned in a few minutes and emptied the hot kettles into the partially filled tub. Gathering up the dress and the lamp he headed again for the loft as she stood in watchful silence. He called down behind him, "Let me know when you're ready for this."

He lit the lamp and sat down to finish sewing the dress, hearing no movement below. After ten minutes or more he heard the sound of splashing water as she bathed. He smiled a pleased little smile.

It took her a long time and he was able to finish the last stitches on the dress before she called. He rolled up the garment and tossed it over the edge of the loft.

In a few minutes she called, "I'm dressed."

He descended the ladder and stood motionless, admiring the transformation. She had washed her hair and it shimmered more silver than gold in the firelight, hanging long and damp, once again seeming to flesh out her thin face. But his gaze bothered her and she wrapped a blanket around herself and turned away.

He was fixing supper when he heard Jacques return. Jacques unslung his pack and revealed half a dozen prime mink and ermine furs inside. Marlette rose to look and Jacques noticed her Indian dress.

"Oh, ho! My good friend, what you do? Already you have turned the mademoiselle into one charming Indian maid," he winked gleefully at the two of them. "Jacques hope to see some camaraderie between you two, but how far you go, eh?"

Marlette blushed and Ross quickly cautioned Jacques, "She may look like one of the Indians you have known, but she is not."

The sternness of Ross's voice was not lost on Jacques and he quickly became apologetic. "Mademoiselle, forgive me? I only make the joke."

She smiled briefly to indicate forgiveness and went back to her chair by the fire. Jacques winked and shrugged his shoulders at Ross.

While they ate, Jacques regaled them with fluent details of his day on the trap line. Later, nodding to sleep in his chair, he decided it was time to go to bed. He rose and stretched noisily. "Well, my friends, it is time for Jacques to turn in. Good night." He left them alone and was soon sleeping soundly.

Ross asked, "Are you tired?"

Absently she answered, "No."

He sat silently watching her troubled and distant gaze fixed on the crackling flames. After a long while, he asked gently, "Do you want to talk about it?"

Slowly she shifted her gaze to him. "Talk about what?"

"Whatever's troubling you."

"Why are you concerning yourself?"

She always put him on the defensive and it irritated him. He answered defensively on purpose. "I was paid to take care of you. I'm just doing my job."

"I hardly think my father meant for you to take your job so

literally." Her laugh did not ring true.

"Maybe not then, but what about now?"

She rose a little stiffly and he felt her hostility as she stared into the fire. "If you are worried about your money, I will see that you get it, provided I reach Vancouver alive."

He stretched his legs. "I'm not worried about the money."

"Do you expect me to believe that?"

He half-smiled and shook his head in wonder. "Miss Brightwood, if you will for one moment be honest with yourself, you know you can believe me."

She turned toward him suddenly with accusing eyes. "How can I believe you? I can only believe what I know. I saw my father and the others killed by Indians and you are an Indian. Somehow I escaped and I still don't know why. I was beginning to trust you until they trapped us at the lake and you spoke with them as if you knew them, and they let us go when they should have killed us. You knew them all and you talked to them all, all along the way. How do I know what was said? And then to have your things here waiting for you. I can hardly believe a man like you could have foreseen what was to happen unless it was planned from the beginning."

Ross rose, his patience wearing thin. Controlling his anger with difficulty, he replied evenly, "It all comes down to a man like me. That's the only basis for your suspicion, isn't it? In the first place, I didn't have to tell you it was dangerous to come here. You knew that. It was the chance you all took. And if we are to talk about the truth, let us add that you hired me without telling me the whole truth. Three days later I learned the real reason for your expedition. I should have quit then." He stopped, a feeling of frustration flooding him as he admitted, "I made an enemy of every Hudson Bay man by guiding you. And you can say that a man *like me* couldn't forsee the dangers and plan for them? I was under the impression that was part of my job!"

He could see that he had outflanked her and she retreated with, "I don't see any point to this conversation."

"The point is, Miss Brightwood, that you don't trust me because of what you think you know about me, not what you really know about me."

He turned away abruptly and climbed the ladder to his bed feeling more frustrated than victorious. She was the most difficult person he'd ever dealt with.

The next couple of days, Ross kept busy with the furs Jacques brought in. He was skillful at cleaning and stretching the hides on frames for maximum size. It was an art few men had mastered as thoroughly as he. Marlette watched with interest but the tension between them remained. Jacques, however, talked enough for both of them.

The weather changed suddenly one morning. The snow stopped and patches of blue showed through the clouds. Ross knew it might be his last chance to hunt so he dressed quickly and went out to scout for game. He took Jacques's muzzle-load rifle, a lunch of jerky, and a sled on which to bring back his kill. He wanted an elk and the gun was the best way to insure a quick kill.

He followed the trail to the salt lick and made a silent circle around the clearing, looking for signs. He found nothing in the fresh snow and decided to go farther north toward the other game trails. He didn't relish the thought of hauling a five- or six-hundred-pound elk very far but they needed the meat for the winter months ahead.

As he neared the next known game trail, he again abandoned the sled and snowshoes for greater stealth and scouted the trail. Fresh tracks indicated the elk were moving through. If he was lucky there were still more coming. He found a small opening along the trail where he would have a good view of the animals passing and settled down to wait. He double-checked the temperamental old gun and lay down in the snow for maximum accuracy.

He heard the elk long before he saw them and was ready to fire when the first elk stepped into the small opening. It was a yearling cow followed by an older cow. Momentarily two more cows and a yearling spike.ambled by while Ross waited for the bull he was sure would be with them. The cows were gone for several long minutes and Ross was damning himself for waiting when he heard a snort in the brush up the trail.

Finally a young bull elk appeared in the opening and stood suspiciously sniffing the air. A sudden bound carried him halfway across the little opening and Ross fired as the animal's forelegs touched the ground. The force of his bound and the impact of the ball sent him crashing to the ground. Ross discarded the gun and ran toward the stunned elk who was struggling to his feet, blood streaming from his wound. He swung his head toward Ross and bellowed, glaring with enraged eyes. Ross threw the hatchet with all his strength, splitting the animal's skull between the eyes. Slowly the elk sank into the blood-tinged snow and heaved a last, gasping sigh. Ross lost no time. He moved in to slit the animal's throat and prepare him for the sled.

It was dark and snowing by the time Ross returned to the cabin, tired, cold, and very hungry.

Several nights later, when the storm had passed, the two men went outside to relieve themselves before going to bed. The sky was clear again and stars twinkled brilliantly in the crisp cold air.

"Look like Jacques can check the trap line again. You go with Jacques this time?"

"No. I can't leave Miss Brightwood alone."

"Maybe you should go and I should stay this time, eh?"

Ross laughed. "Changed your mind about charming her?"

The Frenchman chuckled wickedly. "Jacques think one of us should take advantage of this wonderful opportunity, no?"

Ross shook his head. "No."

Jacques placed his hand on Ross's shoulder. "You know, my friend, Jacques think you blame yourself for what has happened. You should not. Nothing you could have done would have prevented it."

"Maybe not. But I can't escape the fact that I knew I shouldn't lead them in there. I could feel that things weren't right."

"Oui. But the fact is that everything was against you. If not the Indians, it would have been the weather. Jacques think either way they had to die. It was their fate."

Ross shivered, not from cold alone. "You may be right. Let's go to bed."

Jacques left in the morning and again Ross spent part of the day doing household chores. Marlette sat watching and it bothered Ross to see her so inactive. It wasn't good for her to sit and dwell on the tragedy. He had to get her interested in something. He remembered the material and retrieved it from the loft along with a small package of sewing equipment that Jacques had brought with his things. As soon as she saw the scissors, needles, and thread she came to the table.

Picking up the scissors she asked suspiciously, "Where did you get these?"

"I got them from your father before we left Vancouver. I thought you'd want to start on your sewing."

She ran a slender finger along the shiny scissors, then placed them carefully on the table as if setting aside a delicate memory. When she looked up, her eyes were filled with desperate futility. "Is there any point to doing this?"

"That's up to you."

Her expression changed immediately and she glanced at him distrustfully, misinterpreting his words as usual. "What do you mean by that?"

"Only that you are safe here. Do what you would do in your own home, among your own people."

"If I do, then what happens when we leave here? Will I be turned over to the Indians?"

"If I had wanted to turn you over to the Indians I would have done so back at the lake."

She smiled knowingly. "Not if someone else had offered you more money for me."

Ross smiled too, in admiration of her shrewdness, although he was saddened by her mistaken logic. "I have no use for money. The most important thing to me is my freedom, and I have that. I don't need money for food, clothing, or shelter. When I want something, I make it or trade for it."

Her hands must have ached from the ferocity of her grip on the back of the chair, for she slowly uncurled them and rubbed the stiff fingers.

"How I wish I could believe you. It would be such a relief," she said quietly. "But I know so little about you—who you are—what you are, and who you really work for. Someone wanted to make sure we were all killed. Who was it? Was it the Hudson Bay Company or British concerns outside of the Hudson Bay Company?"

Ross pulled out a chair and settled across from her. "I don't know of any British interests other than the Hudson Bay Company. But I do know that the Hudson Bay Company is here only to make money. They aren't worried about keeping any of the land south of the Columbia since it is no longer profitable for the fur trade. If Doctor

McLoughlin had wanted to stop you he simply wouldn't have helped you. He would have sent you back on the first ship. He would hardly risk a war with the United States by allowing you to be killed. The French-Canadians, however, feel differently because this land has become their home. Most of the retired employees have settled in the valley with their families and they would feel threatened by any attempt of the United States to claim their land."

"And what about you? Wouldn't you do anything to help your Indian brothers?"

"Yes. You can't deny that this land rightfully belongs to the Indian. If I believed that your deaths would stop further American migrations I would've killed you myself. But you and I both know the Americans will come in spite of what may happen to a few of them."

"Then you still say it is Tom Hill, alone, who wanted us dead?"

"Yes. He hates the white men and he needs the power of your guns. The Indians will listen to the man with the most power and Tom Hill wants to be that man."

Marlette was interested. "There is one thing I still don't understand. Why did you agree to guide us when your sympathy is with the Indians?"

"I wanted to know what you were really doing here."

"And now that you know, what do you plan to do about it?"

"Nothing."

"Nothing! I can hardly believe that."

"What have you really learned by coming here? Have you found the Indians friendly and the mountains low and smooth? Will you tell your people that money hangs on every tree and everyone should come?"

She looked at him for a long moment and shook her head. "No." Her face crumpled and her eyes filled with tears. "The whole thing was for nothing. My father's death—." Her voice broke and she couldn't finish.

He waited until she had regained control before he said, "Not for nothing. You can save many of your people from making a fatal mistake by telling them the truth."

She raised her head and looked at him, her face tearstreaked. "But I have already failed at that, too. One immigration has already reached the valley and another will probably start west in the spring."

"All you can do is tell the truth. Maybe some will listen and those who don't will be better prepared for what they will find here."

"But that is exactly what you don't want, isn't it?"

"You're right. I don't want them to come. It will ruin the land, but I'm afraid nothing will stop them."

"What will you do if the country becomes settled?" she asked tentatively.

"I haven't really thought about it. Maybe I would leave; follow the Hudson Bay Company north."

He stood up, suddenly feeling restless. "I'm going outside for a little while if you want to get started on your sewing."

She nodded absently and he left the cabin.

When he finally returned he felt somewhat better. Physical exertion always helped to relieve his tension. He opened the door and meeting Marlette's silent glance he realized that something more than her hostility divided them. She was frightened again and it was because Jacques was not there.

He quietly went about cooking their supper. When it was ready she came to the table and took a very small helping. She avoided his eyes and ate quietly.

He took a deep breath and said gently, "Miss Brightwood, it's going to be a long winter and your fear will only make it tougher for you."

She dropped her eyes and stared at her plate, attempting to conceal her anxiety.

"You're mistaken if you think Jacques will protect you from me."

She pushed her chair away from the table and walked to the fireplace, her hands clasped fearfully in front of her.

He finished his supper and cleaned up their dishes, then filled his cup with coffee and sat down comfortably in Jacques's chair, studying her rigid back. In a soft, strangely husky voice he asked, "Would you like my knife?"

She stiffened at the memory. In a more normal voice he said, "You can't stand up all winter so you'd better sit down and try to relax."

Her shoulders drooped suddenly as she acknowledged the truth of his words.

"Tell me, what is it like where you come from?"

She relaxed even more and turned toward him, gazing at him intently. "How do you mean?" Her voice was still defensive.

"Is it as big as Fort Vancouver?"

She smiled involuntarily at his question. "There is no comparison. Philadelphia is much larger."

"I have never seen a white man's town, except for Vancouver," he said simply.

Her eyes widened a little and her haughty attitude melted away. She sank slowly into her chair and Ross handed her a cup of coffee.

"Imagine a town the size of Vancouver and all its area including the cabins outside, the fort, the orchards, the fields, nearly the whole plain in fact, covered with buildings and houses. There are streets in all directions linking each building. The larger buildings are several stories tall and many are made of brick. Most of the homes are built of smooth boards or brick much finer than Doctor McLoughlin's. There is no stockade around the town and some of the streets are laid with stones so that they are never muddy or dusty. The people with money live in beautiful homes and some people still live in cabins."

"What is your home like?"

Her lips trembled at the memory but she fought off the tears and answered softly, "It is not as elegant as the best, but it is very nice. My father built it himself from brick and wood. There are five large rooms downstairs and the bedrooms upstairs and—." She stopped abruptly, memories overcoming her.

Ross went on. "Do you have any family at home waiting for you?"

"No. My mother died some time ago. I have close relatives, but none of them live in Philadelphia."

"What do you plan to do when you get back?"

Her chin rose with determination. "Carry on Father's business."

"Is there someone taking care of it now?"

"Yes."

"Who is he? Is he someone you can trust?"

"Of course. He's been with us a long time. When my mother got sick after my brother died, Father hired a woman to take care of us. She was a widow and had a son about my age. Father liked Tom immediately and started him working at the shop after school. Tom was hardworking and he learned quickly and seemed to have the talent to create what people wanted from my father's designs. Father made him foreman over the shop when he was twenty."

"How do you feel about him?"

She thought a moment before answering, as if she had never thought about him seriously before. "I think he's capable and hardworking and even talented."

Ross uncrossed his legs and leaned forward, resting his elbows on his knees as he cradled the coffee cup in his strong, lean hands. "I mean is he a man you could marry?"

She looked momentarily startled at his question. "Why, I'd never thought about it. But—no—I wouldn't even consider it."

"Maybe you should."

"Why?"

"You say you can run the business and I have no doubt that you can, but this Tom and the men working for him now may not like you coming back and taking over."

It was clearly something that she had not thought about and she looked troubled for a moment. Then her jaw squared in an expression he recognized. "I will just have to take that chance, now."

"Why? If not Tom, there must be someone else you can marry who can take over for you?"

She stood up facing the fire and said slowly, "Yes. I suppose I could. But I don't want a man that way. I want to be married for love, for *myself,* not for my business." She looked at him bitterly. "It could have been possible with Gay. His family has money and he didn't need mine. However, I'm not naive enough to think that Gay would have married me, merely because he asked me, or that any other man would."

Gently he asked, "Don't you think it's possible for more than one man to love you?"

"Yes, it's possible. But I'm not growing any more beautiful and each year the chance lessens."

"There are more important things in a woman than beauty."

"That may be, but you must admit that the first thing a man sees is beauty."

He nodded in agreement and leaned back once more. "That's true. So why do you hide the beauty you have?"

She straightened suddenly, shocked into confusion, and stammered, "I don't know what you mean."

Her reaction convinced him that she knew very well what he meant, and he felt that something more was involved than merely her looks. However he didn't press her, knowing he had already inadvertently put her on the defensive. As tactfully as possible he said, "I don't know what you looked like before you came here, so I can only tell you what I have seen. With your hair down and your mouth full and soft I saw a woman who was pleasing to the eye."

She turned away from him abruptly, but he caught the fear in her eyes. He remained silent, feeling he had already said too much. She stood, her fear evident in her sudden rigidity, and he shook his head mournfully. No matter what he tried to do it only made things worse.

He said good-night and swung up the ladder to his bed.

When he awoke in the morning, he dressed and started down the ladder quietly. He paused midway on the ladder and looked down, stopping suddenly in surprise. Marlette was standing before the small mirror that hung next to the back door of the cabin. She was combing her hair around her face and it flowed softly over her shoulders and down her back. It looked darker than it really was in the dim light of the room.

She moved slightly and caught his reflection in the mirror. Quickly she pulled her hair back to the base of her neck and with deft fingers formed the usual bun and pinned it into place. He swung lightly to the floor, wishing she had lost those pins in the lake. She watched him warily while he restored the fire.

Swinging the buckets, he left the cabin to fetch water. It looked as if the weather would hold until Jacques could make it back. The sky was already a clear pale blue and no wind stirred the snow-laden trees. The only sound in the vast quiet forest was the pleasant chatter of the stream. He breathed deeply, smiling with contentment.

After breakfast Marlette sat down with her sewing and Ross brought out some skins and began cutting moccasins. By the time he was ready to sew them together, Marlette's attention was riveted to his work.

He looked up and smiled at her. "Would you like a pair? They'd be more comfortable than your boots in the cabin."

Her cheeks colored slightly and she stammered self-consciously, "I didn't mean to—. It would be too much trouble. Thank you, anyway."

"It's no trouble. Slip off your boot and I'll measure your foot."

Her color deepened. "No. Please don't. Really."

He pulled a chair out and held it for her. She sat down reluctantly and he bent to help her remove her boot. She sat in flustered silence as he placed her stockinged foot on a piece of leather and traced an outline there. He set to work fashioning the smaller moccasins for her slender feet.

At last she asked, "I remember seeing some with decorations on them. Is that difficult to do?"

He smiled easily, "No, but it takes a long time."

"I thought it was the women who made most of the clothes. Or do they just do the decorating?"

He smiled again. "No. All of it is woman's work, but they don't feel it is work. They take pride in the making and decorating of their things. Each woman tries to outdo the others in making her clothes, utensils, and especially her husband's things the handsomest in the village."

Something was obviously on her mind, and he worked quietly waiting for her next question. "Why do you do all this yourself when you could undoubtedly have a woman to do it for you?"

He grinned ruefully, and couldn't resist the temptation to tease her a little. "The women in this country aren't of my tribe."

She didn't smile or give any sign that she knew he wasn't serious. He continued his work and she returned to her own.

After lunch she seemed restless and looked longingly out the window. Ross worked more quickly on the moccasins hoping to take her outside if he finished early enough. Until he finished them she would have nothing dry to put on her feet. So far her trips outside had been limited to necessity.

He finished the moccasins and stood up, stretching his tired muscles. "I'm going for a walk. Do you want to come?"

She turned away from the window, her eyes lighting with anticipation. "Yes. Will you mind?"

She had answered without a trace of fear and he smiled, feeling a small sense of accomplishment. "No. You need to get out."

Quickly she wrapped herself in a heavy blanket as Ross pulled on his boots and coat, and they stepped out into the brisk afternoon air.

He took the trail that led to the salt lick and they proceeded slowly, finding it difficult to walk without snowshoes. When they reached the clearing where he had shot the deer, she swept off a log and sat down, breathing heavily. He let her rest as he skirted the clearing for any deer signs. He found nothing and returned to her. She watched him without fear, her cheeks pink from exertion and cold, and he again felt that they could work out the differences between them.

He said, "This is where I shot the deer."

She said nothing and looked away from him. Too late he realized it was wrong to speak of killing. He sighed inwardly at his stupidity and said, "We'd better start back."

The return walk was somewhat easier and they reached the cabin just as the sun dropped behind the ridge. Ross helped her off with her wet boots and she pulled the moccasins on her feet and padded to the fire. He went to work on supper knowing that Jacques would be in shortly and ravenously hungry after two days on jerky. From the cellar under the floor of the cabin he brought up carrots and potatoes to boil from their precious store of vegetables and had venison steaks ready to put over the fire when Jacques came.

They soon heard the Frenchman's boisterous voice outside. Ross put the meat on the fire and went to help his friend. Jacques burst into the cabin like a frozen hurricane, noisily dumping his skins and pack on the floor. The bear snuffled happily and shuffled to the fire.

"Ah, my friend, Jacques is glad to be back. You got something good to eat, no?"

Ross grinned at him as he discarded his clothing and gear indiscriminately. "How'd you do?"

"Ah," he sighed, "a little better than last trip, but not much. It is as you have said, we soon will have to relocate."

Jacques ate heartily and described his trip along the trap line in detail. It was not an unusual trip in any respect, but Jacques had a flair for storytelling and could make the dullest events sound interesting. Ross noticed that Marlette seemed to find his recital entertaining, and every now and then a slight smile curved her lips. But Jacques soon felt the effects of the warm cabin and the big meal and left them to go the bed.

The fire crackled cheerfully, punctuated by infrequent rumbling snores from the bear. Ross sat back contentedly and decided he could use a good smoke. When he lived with the Indians, smoking had been a normal part of his existence. Since he had left, he had given up the Indian ritual of smoking, but every now and then he longed for a good pipe. He found the pipe and tobacco that he had traded some prime furs for some years before and began the pleasurable ritual involved in packing and lighting it.

As the fragrant smoke filled the room Marlette looked up thoughtfully and asked, "I've smelled that before. Where did you get it?"

"I traded a sea captain out of it a few years ago. Why?"

"No reason, really." She got up and moved away in a restless, constrained manner.

"I'll put it out if you don't like it."

"No. It's one of the few I like. Did you get it from a Captain McNeal? He smoked the same kind."

"No." He watched her closely, she seemed eager to talk about it.

Again she asked, "Do you know Captain McNeal?"

Honestly he answered, "No. I don't think so."

She sank back in the chair, clearly disappointed, and gazed wistfully at the fire, flooded with sudden memories. Her face softened and at that moment she was lovely. Whoever Captain McNeal was, she obviously enjoyed the memory of him. A sudden noise distracted her and all traces of the softness disappeared. She stared thoughtfully into the fire and Ross doubted that she would speak again.

He was mildly surprised when she asked, "What will the Hudson Bay Company do if the fur business runs out?"

"They'll probably close this fort down and move their operation farther north."

"How much longer do you think it will be profitable enough to stay?"

"From what I understand they are barely breaking even now, but McLoughlin feels his farming can bring in as much profit as the furs. But from what McKay has told me, he is having trouble getting company approval."

"I can't imagine him leaving Vancouver."

"I don't think he will when the order is given. He's claimed land at the falls in the valley. He wants to retire there and build a sawmill and a grist mill."

"Would they let him do that?"

"I don't know. But I don't think he'll do anything he doesn't want to do."

"And if the United States is successful in claiming this territory, I wonder what will happen to him then?"

"If that happens they'd be wise to make him governor. He's the only one who can control the Indians."

She leaned forward, gazing at him intently. "After what happened to us, you can still say that?"

"Yes. This is a big territory. He can hardly stop what he doesn't know about. But when he learns what happened, you can be sure he will do something about it. He has to, otherwise his own men wouldn't be safe."

She sat back looking doubtful. "I hope Dr. Whitman succeeds in getting some sort of military protection for this country, if for no other reason than to clean out out those responsible for my father's murder."

He stood up, the feeling of contentment gone. He knocked the ashes from his pipe and returned it to the mantle. "That would only make matters worse. The Indians already feel threatened, and there would be war if soldiers move in. I can understand your desire for justice, but you must understand the Indian point of view. To him, *you* are the one in the wrong. Probably if Tom Hill had not stirred them up this would not have happened, but open war is not the answer."

"Then what is the answer?" she asked quietly.

He shrugged his shoulders and bent to throw more logs on the fire. "The only one I know is to let McLoughlin handle it."

"Doesn't Dr. Whitman realize what might happen if he should succeed in bringing soldiers here?"

"He should, but he unfortunately believes that the Indians are accepting his teaching."

"And you don't think they are?"

"No. The Whitmans are in more danger than they realize."

She looked troubled. "That's what McKinley said, too." She paused, looking at him questioningly. "Then why don't you do something to help them? Mrs. Whitman told me that you would only act as an interpreter for them. Couldn't you have done more?"

His face clouded at the thought of the tenuous situation at Waii-

latpu. "Yes, I could have done more, but it would be against everything I believe in. Dr. Whitman wants to change the Indians, but a
man won't change unless he wants to. The Cayuse don't. Of all the
Indians in the territory he picked the ones least likely to accept him.
The Cayuse didn't ask for missionaries as the Nez Perce did. Most
people don't understand that the Indians who want the white missionaries aren't interested in spiritual gifts, but rather in material gifts and
the means of obtaining them."

"But he's been so good to them, would they really harm the
mission?"

"That's just the point. The Cayuse don't feel he's been good to
them. If you want to gain an Indian's respect you must first learn what
he respects. Dr. Whitman doesn't have their respect because he can't
or won't learn their ways. They feel it beneath their dignity to work
as he does. He refuses to bargain with them and in their eyes he lacks
dignity."

"It sounds like a hopeless situation."

"It is. The Whitmans would be better off if they followed the
orders Dr. White brought them from Boston."

She sighed and sank deeper in her chair. "Well, there's still a
possibility that he'll change his mind after seeing the Mission Board."

"There's little chance of that. Part of their problem is that they've
had trouble getting along with each other, Spalding in particular.
That's why the Board wants to remove Spalding from his mission.
But if Whitman can convince the Mission Board that they've worked
out their difficulties, things will probably remain as they are."

Her magnificent chin rose stubbornly. "Well, maybe I can do
something when I get back east."

He had to smile at her determination. "For the Whitmans' sake,
I hope you can, but be sure to consider the consequences. Good
night."

The next few days were busy ones for Ross as he cleaned and
stretched the furs Jacques had brought in. Jacques took over the
cooking duties gladly and his voluble delight in his culinary skill more
than made up for their limited menu. The atmosphere in the cabin
had become one of ease and acceptance, and Jacques was quick to
take advantage of it. He found a well-used pack of playing cards and

they began a nightly game to fill the long, wintry evenings.

When Ross finished working with the furs, their card games started earlier in the day and they soon grew bored with them. Jacques however, with his usual ingenuity, came up with a new diversion. Like a great many Frenchmen, he delighted in music and always carried a mouth organ. He brought it out one night and, with much ceremony, he began to play. Marlette immediately brightened and Jacques played every gay tune he knew. When his repertoire of lighthearted music was exhausted he looked at Ross with twinkling eyes. "Now, my friend, it is your turn to entertain the lady."

Ross looked up and shook his head negatively, feeling vaguely embarrassed. Marlette's eyes were bright with interest.

Jacques laughed. "Ah, ha! My friend is strangely shy. Maybe if the mademoiselle asked him, he would favor us with a song, eh?"

Marlette smiled at him. "Please, Mr. Chesnut, I'd like to hear you sing."

Ross didn't understand why he felt suddenly foolish. He had a good voice and he and Jacques had spent many long evenings singing and playing. He sighed silently and said, "All right, Jacques, play something."

Jacques grinned and began with a few bars from one of the voyageur songs. Ross sang in French, his voice clear and strong with little trace of the huskiness that veiled his speaking voice. Then the crafty Jacques played the old English ballad "Greensleeves." Ross sang it in French, hoping Marlette wouldn't know it, but she recognized it. It was one of the few songs his mother had taught him as a child.

When he finished she asked, "Can you sing it in English?"

He hesitated a moment, then nodded. Jacques eagerly lifted the harmonica to his lips and played. Ross sang to Marlette, watching her eyes grow dreamy and her lips curve in a soft smile.

When the song ended she smiled with pleasure. "That was lovely. Thank you."

He nodded, still feeling strangely uncomfortable, and retreated to the frozen world outside. Snow was still falling, but the flakes were drifting softly down now as the wind had all but blown itself out. The door of the cabin opened behind him and Jacques stepped out into the snow.

"Mon ami, you flee like the rejected suitor."

Ross smiled crookedly. "It's been a long time since I've had an audience."

Jacques laughed knowingly. "Maybe it is time you had another woman to sing to."

"I can't deny that, but this is not the woman."

"Who are you trying to convince, my friend, me or you?"

Ross chuckled softly. "The one who thinks amour grows on every tree."

Jacques laughed and disappeared into the shadows. Ross shivered and quickly returned to the cabin. Marlette turned as he came in and smiled slightly. He went to the fire and added more logs for the night from the stack along the wall. When he finished, he found her still watching him curiously. He smiled down at her and said, "Good night."

With another slight smile she answered, "Good night."

They spent the next few evenings in the same manner and Ross encouraged Marlette to sing with him. It was enjoyable, as they learned songs from each other and laughed when they forgot the words or sang off-key.

One day the weather cleared and Jacques got his things ready to check the trap line if it held over night. By evening it was extremely cold and even the roaring fire could not keep out the chill. Jacques sat down with his harmonica and started playing lively round dances. Marlette's foot began tapping time to the music and Jacques stopped playing momentarily to ask, "Maybe the mademoiselle would like to dance? Ross, ask her to dance."

Ross shook his head, smiling. "You dance with her and I'll play the mouth organ."

"But, mon ami, you do not know how to play the music."

"No. And I don't know how to dance either."

Feigning surprise, Jacques gestured, "Ah, but it is easy to dance, is it not mademoiselle?"

Smilingly she answered, "Fairly easy."

Jacques grinned broadly and winked. "Ah ha! Then you can teach my friend to dance, no?"

She dropped her eyes quickly and blushed. "Well, I'm afraid I'm not very good."

Jacques pressed on. "But, mademoiselle, you don't have to be good, just patient."

Ross interrupted, "Jacques, you haven't asked me if I even want to learn."

"But of course you want to learn. Do you forget the times you stood around watching the others steal the women away because you could not dance? Remember how you say, 'Ah, if only I—!' "

Ross waved him off in the middle of his dramatization. He looked at Marlette who was watching Jacques's performance with delight. "You can see he doesn't tell the truth, can't you?"

She turned to him with amusement dancing in her eyes. "I do remember you wandering around outside a dance one night looking rather forlorn."

Jacques chuckled. "There! I speak the truth, no? Come, now, what else is there to do, eh?"

Ross studied Marlette. Her eyes were bright but shy. "Only if Miss Brightwood doesn't mind."

She sat looking from one to the other, still a little flushed. For a moment her eyes clouded and Ross felt sure she would refuse, then to his surprise she said, "All right."

Jacques pushed the table against the wall to give them more room and the instruction began. Ross felt awkward as he tried to follow her steps and Jacques roared with laughter when he got mixed up. But the laughter didn't last long. He was quick to catch on and once he learned the steps, his rhythm was good and they danced quite well.

Marlette had to remove her jacket as the exercise warmed them. As she twirled under his arm, her hair was brushed awry and tumbled down around her shoulders. She let it go, obviously enjoying herself too much to interrupt their dance.

Ross was enjoying himself too and he felt long repressed desires stirring in him. As he held her waist he felt the supple softness of flesh where he had once felt bone. He deliberately looked at her face and noticed that it had filled out nicely. She looked lovely as she smiled at him.

Jacques ended the dance and stood up. Ross was strangely aware of her as they stood together, their hands still clasped. The smile on her face dimmed as she became self-conscious under his penetrating gaze.

Jacques spoke, breaking the spell. "Well, my friends, it is getting late and Jacques must go early."

Their hands separated but Ross could still feel the warmth.

Huskily he said, "Thank you. I'll be looking forward to the next lesson."

She smiled slightly, her face still flushed from their dancing. He turned away from her, slipped on his heavy coat, and followed Jacques into the cold, clear night.

"Well, what you say, my friend? Is she not a woman you could desire? Was she not like a feather in your arms?"

Ross smiled in the darkness. "Yes."

"Ah ha! You notice then she is filling out a little, becoming soft to the touch, eh?"

"I noticed."

"And she forget you are Indian tonight. You could have her, my friend, before Jacques get back if you try a little."

Ross grinned ruefully. "You don't know her, Jacques. By tomorrow she'll remember what she thinks I am and she'll be just as she always is."

"You have no faith, cher ami. She want you."

He had to laugh at Jacques's seemingly wild statement. He walked down the path shaking his head and chuckling.

The Wolverine

JACQUES WAS UP and gone before Ross awoke. He'd had trouble falling asleep with the memory of Marlette stirring his blood. He knew it was foolish to even consider her. She would leave in the spring and he would have nothing. But it was hard to forget how she had felt under his hand, or the soft brush of her loosened hair. She had been light on her feet and she had seemed to enjoy herself. Her laughter and her smile still lingered in his mind. He shaved a little faster than usual, eager to see if anything had changed.

Smiling hopefully, he swung down the ladder, but she was not smiling and quickly turned away from his gaze. He stood a moment, wondering if he should tell her and decided against it. He went about his daily chores quietly. She ate breakfast with downcast eyes and he had an almost irresistible urge to grab her and force her to look at him, but he controlled himself.

He was cleaning up their plates when he heard Jacques bellowing somewhere near the cabin. He ran to the back door as Jacques came dashing out of the timber yelling, "Mon Dieu, loup garou!"

Marlette ran out. "What is it? What's he saying?"

"Wolverine. How many traps did you check?"

"Six. Furs torn all to hell. He look like he go onto next trap. Maybe make the whole damn line. Jacques come back quick."

"I'll get my things." Ross turned back into the cabin, quickly stuffed some jerky into a bag, and crammed it into his coat pocket. He slung on his powder horn and shot pouch and picked up his rifle.

Marlette lingered by the door, her eyes wide with uncertainty. Ross stopped in front of her. "I want you to bar this door after me and I don't want you to go outside for any reason. Do you understand?"

She nodded.

"I'll be back tonight if possible. If not, I want you to stay in until I get back. You've got everything you need for a couple of days."

His parting look stirred her and he heard the bar drop into place as she swung the door shut.

He took off after Jacques and they headed for the midpoint in the trap line, near their overnight shelter. It meant going over the hill behind the cabin instead of around it and they lost time struggling through the deep snowdrifts. They were further delayed because Jacques was already tired.

Finally Ross suggested, "I'll go on ahead. You rest."

Jacques nodded and Ross started off alone, shuffling slowly as he neared the closest trap, hungrily chewing on a mouthful of jerky.

Before he reached the trap he could smell the foul animal stench. He picked up the trap, released the mangled fur and stuffed the trap into his pack. The stink followed him relentlessly.

He followed the trail the wolverine made to the next trap. The tracks were only a few hours old. He felt a growing uneasiness when he thought of where the wolverine would end up if he worked through every one of their traps and followed their scent to the cabin. He increased his pace until his lungs ached from the deep, frosty breaths of chilling air.

Each trap was the same. As luck would have it each trap had held an animal before the wolverine got to it. His anxiety increased and he labored on, his load getting heavier as he took up the traps.

Finally he reached the last trap on the bottom slope of the hill, northwest of the cabin. The wolverine's fresh tracks followed the trail on to the cabin and Ross uttered a barely audible threat through clenched teeth. He unloaded the traps and plunged down the slope in fierce desperation. As he neared the cabin he heard a savage growling. Jacques's bear was holding the small wolverine in the corner near the shed. The wolverine was snarling and lunging at the larger bear and it was hard to tell who had who at bay.

Ross checked the rifle and dropped to one knee in the snow. He yelled at Ivan and the bear backed off as the undaunted wolverine charged him. It was the exact moment for his shot and Ross squeezed the trigger.

The ball smacked the wolverine dead center and he dropped into a convulsing heap. Ivan came roaring in and grabbed the lifeless form, shaking it savagely.

Ross rose slowly, feeling weak. He noticed the door of the cabin was open and his anxiety returned. "Miss Brightwood?" he yelled.

Slowly the shed door opened and Marlette stood, pale, a double-bitted axe clenched tightly in her hand. He ran toward her, relief flooding through him. The axe slipped from her hand and her terrified face crumpled. Without thinking, his arms went around her.

His voice trembled when he asked, "Are you all right?"

She nodded and his relief turned to anger. He released her and stepped back.

"I told you to stay in the cabin." The harshness grated in his voice.

She wiped away her tears and said defensively, "I know you did, but I thought I heard something in the shed. I didn't know what it was and I was worried about the meat and the furs being ruined. I had to do something."

"Nothing in here was worth risking your life for."

"I didn't feel I was risking my life. I should have realized that you wouldn't appreciate anything I did."

Less sharply he said, "But you didn't know what was out here. You can't last long in this country if you don't learn its dangers. You should never risk your life unless you know you can win. The odds weren't in your favor with the wolverine."

The spark in her eyes faded as she realized her danger. She shivered and dropped her eyes, abandoning her defense.

"You'd better get into the cabin."

He stepped aside and she hurried past him. He heard Jacques coming down the hill, the traps banging as he ran. Ross waited for him.

Jacques saw what was left of the wolverine and exclaimed, "By damn! He come clear to the cabin! What a devil, no?" He saw the strained look on Ross's face and asked, "What wrong, my friend, you do not look well?"

"Nothing, Jacques. Let's get started on those traps."

They used what was left of the day to clean the traps of the strong wolverine stench. Darkness set in before they were finished and they retreated to the cabin, cold, tired, and hungry. Ross was surprised as he opened the door and smelled the tantalizing odor of cooking meat and vegetables.

Jacques approved heartily. "Ah, a mademoiselle who can make meat and potatoes smell so good is a woman worthy of praise."

She gave Jacques a pleased little smile, but avoided meeting Ross's searching gaze. He wanted to believe it was a peace offering but it was hard to tell with her.

Jacques praised her lavishly as they ate. She had indeed livened the stew up somehow and her biscuits were considerably lighter than either of theirs. Her coffee was more like coffee and less like the solution they used to clean the traps. Ross would have told her so, but she kept her eyes down, forbidding him to speak. Jacques was quick to realize something was not right between them and he grew silent, the smile fading from his face.

The evening was not as companionable as previous evenings had been. Jacques finished his coffee and pipe and went to bed. Ross sat quietly, waiting for Jacques to fall asleep. As soon as he heard Jacques's snores, he turned to face her. She kept her eyes down, still refusing to give him any opening.

In a low voice he asked, "Do you understand what I told you today?"

She nodded curtly.

He continued, refusing to be put off. "I hope you will give Jacques some instructions on cooking. Your supper was better than either one of us can make. What did you do to the coffee?"

She answered finally, "I scoured out the pot."

He smiled. "I'll have to remember that." She looked away, clearly unforgiving. With a sigh he said, "Miss Brightwood, I'm not going to tell you I'm sorry for being rough on you. You know you were wrong."

She stood up, her eyes flashing with anger. "And you won't let me forget that will you?"

He smiled unabashedly, "I hope you don't forget it. It may save your life another time."

She stamped her foot. "You're—, you're—, an uncivilized boor."

She turned away from him and stalked to her bed.

He followed her, strangely enjoying her anger. "If I were any less civilized I'd take you over my knee and spank you."

She turned around quickly, a look of surprise on her angry face. "You wouldn't dare!" she gasped.

He smiled mischievously, watching her anxious face. Finally he said, "No, but where I come from if you belonged to me and you disobeyed, I'd have every right to beat you."

Her anger cooled, and she appraised him in a calmer manner. "I'll try not to forget my place again."

He caught the contempt in her voice and warned her seriously, "Don't think I wouldn't because you're a white woman. If I have to be rough with you I will be, but only if that's the way you want it."

She searched his face. Completely subdued she shook her head slowly. "No, that is not the way I want it."

"Then we understand each other?"

She dropped her eyes and nodded. He breathed easier. "Good night."

Jacques left after breakfast to retrieve the other traps, and they spent the next several days working on the traps while another storm dumped more snow on the cabin, drifting it up over the windows. The atmosphere became easier in a couple of days and it almost seemed as if their harsh words had been forgotten. Although she appeared to have forgotten the incident, Ross knew she hadn't. He felt an aloofness in her that hadn't been there the night they had danced.

The weather cleared again in several days and Jacques set off with the trap-laden sled. As soon as he was gone Marlette became withdrawn. She had been meeting his gaze with lofty appraisal, and now she avoided looking at him. He had hoped her frank appraisal of him since the wolverine incident meant she had forgiven him, but now he knew it was an act.

He was restless with frustration and eagerly undertook the task of shoveling snow away from the doors and windows and clearing the paths. When that was finished he carried in more wood. Marlette got out the material and began measuring and cutting on the table. When he was through he noticed she was working on a new blouse, using her old one for a pattern.

He sat down and rested while he watched her work. When she was finished he offered, "I'll go outside for a couple of minutes if you want to put your blouse on."

She looked up, her expression unreadable. "Thank you."

He went out and heard the bar drop behind him and shook his head. In a couple of minutes she came to let him in. He went to stand by the fire and she sat down with her needle to sew.

"Now I'm sorry I didn't get more material."

She glanced up at him. "Why?"

"You could have made yourself more clothes."

She stopped sewing and met his eyes. "I have a whole trunkful of clothes at Vancouver, if I ever get there."

"You still aren't sure of me, are you?"

Quite simply she answered, "No."

"I think you know I don't want it to be that way, but you seem to misinterpret anything I say. I haven't had much chance to talk to white women, but I never had this much trouble being understood before."

She smiled slightly and said with a trace of contempt, "I'm sure you haven't."

He spread his hands in a gesture of futility. "There! That's what I mean."

She looked surprised and colored slightly. She murmured, "I'm sorry."

"It isn't necessary to apologize. Although I speak your language, in your eyes I still think like an Indian and probably act like an Indian and that is your defense against me. But I don't think you really know what you're defending yourself against."

She looked up at him curiously. He gave her an unexpectedly warm smile, and left her sitting there while he went to take a bath in the river.

He ran back to the cabin, shivering under the blanket he wrapped around himself. Quickly closing the door, he hurried over to the fireplace to warm himself. Marlette stared steadfastly at her sewing as if he didn't exist, but her cheeks were flaming. He smiled at her bent head.

Every time he came in from bathing it was the same way. At first he hadn't realized why she blushed. He was as fully covered as if he had on his buckskins. Then he remembered the morning she had followed him to the river and came upon him bathing. He found it amusing that this memory troubled her so and wondered how she would survive in an Indian camp where the body was not an object of shame. He liked to think she was stubborn and determined enough to adapt. She had come through a lot with only one good case of hysterics, but it would be interesting to know how she would react on a more personal level.

An empty rumble in his stomach cut short his contemplation. It was past lunchtime. He climbed the ladder and dressed in clean buckskins.

Lunch was warmed-over beans and pork. Marlette toyed with her food, taking a disinterested bite now and then.

"Anything wrong?" he queried.

She looked up and sighed. "Nothing that a change of diet wouldn't cure. Right now I'm so hungry for some fresh fruit, an egg, or a cool fresh glass of milk." She shook her head sadly.

He studied her, wondering whether to pique her curiosity again. It was a good opportunity and one he honestly wanted to take. She was becoming more than just a job to him and although he knew it wasn't wise to want her, he would never find out unless they started on equal ground. Deliberately he said, "You sound like my mother."

Immediately her eyes brightened with interest. "Where is your mother now?"

"She's dead."

"Oh. I'm sorry."

"Don't be."

She stiffened in shocked disapproval. "That's a terrible thing to say. Didn't you love your mother?"

"Yes," he said softly.

She pushed away from the table in disgust and glared at him. "Then I don't understand you at all."

Already the memory was painful but he didn't want to stop now. "Let me put it to you this way. If your mother had been captured, raped, and enslaved by Indians, and you grew up watching her die a little each year from hard work, blazingly hot summers and bitterly cold winters, would you be sorry she was released from that kind of life?"

Marlette shuddered and turned away from him, but he caught the sparkle of tears in her eyes. After a long moment she turned back and sat down again, her anger gone.

"I'm sorry. I have been unfair to you. I remember what you said about not knowing you. I'd like to know about you. Would you tell me?"

His face relaxed a little in a faint smile. Here was the opportunity he had been waiting for. He would now either gain her trust or lose it completely, but it was a chance he was willing to take. "Are you sure? It isn't a very pretty story."

"Yes, I'm sure."

He leaned forward, pushing his plate out of the way so he could rest his forearms on the table, his strong hands clasped. He started at the beginning.

"My mother and father came down the Ohio River in 1811. They went north on the Mississippi and settled on land near a new settlement on the Missouri River. They were on the edge of the plains and the Indians raided the area frequently. They were there only a few months when a lone Indian came to their place. My father was working outside and the Indian killed him and came to the cabin to kill my mother. She didn't know her husband was dead and wasn't frightened by the Indian. My mother had very fair skin and hair and she was undoubtedly more beautiful than I remember her to be, because the Indian took her captive instead of killing her.

"My mother had just begun to suspect that she was pregnant and their treatment of her must have seemed all the more cruel, since as your Major Holliway probably told you, it is the Indian custom to rape and enslave female captives. However, once she got over the shock of my father's death and the repeated abuses at the hands of her captor, she decided she wanted to live to bear the child of her murdered husband."

He stopped as Marlette rose suddenly, her face stark and pale. She turned away from him and walked to the window to lean her forehead against the cool glass. Ross got up and cleared the table, feeling his story was ended.

She came back in a few minutes and stood close to him. "I'm sorry. It brings back too many things." She looked away and he knew what she meant.

"I told you it wasn't a pretty story."

She nodded. "Then you don't have any Indian blood in you?"

"No."

He looked directly at her for a long time as she got used to this truth. Finally she whispered, "Please go on. I want to hear it all."

He smiled faintly. "All right."

She turned toward the fireplace and he followed her. He settled into Jacques's chair and continued. "The Indian was the son of a chief. He and his father had been fighting in the war against the United States and his father was killed. He was on his way back to his village when he killed my father as an act of revenge.

"Later he made my mother his wife but at first she was a slave, being used by his wife, Slow Water, and their three daughters by day and by her captor, Snow Cloud, at night.

"Within a few months it became obvious that she was carrying a child and Snow Cloud began treating her a little better. When she gave birth to a son, Snow Cloud naturally thought it was his and my mother became his favorite because she had given him a successor. My mother's life became somewhat easier then because Snow Cloud made sure she was not treated unfairly by Slow Water or any one else in the village.

"For five years I was her only child. She lost several during that time. She spent a lot of time with me and when we were alone she would speak to me in a language that was not used when the Indians were around.

"Then she bore another son for Snow Cloud and two years later a daughter. When I was close to ten summers I began to notice that she did things for me that she didn't do for my brother and sister. She spent time alone with me, teaching me how to read, write, and speak her language and she made me lie in the sun so that I would stay tanned. When there was no sun, she would dye my skin.

"I began to ask her questions and finally she told me about my real father. She had always called me Ross when we were alone and I learned it was my father's name and that I resembled him. I wanted to know more but she wouldn't tell me. She said I could never go back home because my Indian upbringing made me different, and I would only find unhappiness if I tried to fit into a family that couldn't understand me.

"When I was about twelve my real manhood training began and I spent most of my time with other boys my age learning to hunt and raid other tribes. From then on my mother begin to fail and I realized I had to take her back to her own people or she would die. I worked harder than any of the other boys to become a warrior, because only then could I take her away.

"Two summers passed before I was ready to seek my vision."

He stopped and got up, feeling strangely self-conscious. Jacques was the only one who knew even a small part of his story. He had kept it inside for so long that it seemed like a dream now. He poured her a cup of coffee and handed it to her. Her clear, blue eyes were wide with interest. He poured his own coffee and set it on the mantle, dropping his head between his upraised arms. The memory of that trip into the hills to seek his vision and protector was the beginning of the bitterest memory for him. It wasn't going to be easy to talk about it. He heard her voice and was aware she had spoken his name more than once.

He dropped his arms and turned to face her. "I'm not used to being called mister. I'd like it if you'd call me Ross."

She smiled in agreement. "I will, if you will stop calling me Miss Brightwood. Do you know my name?"

He nodded, "Yes. Marlette." He felt a strange sensation as he said it out loud. She smiled at him again, pleased that he knew. He took his coffee and sat down, taking a long sip.

"Would you rather not tell me any more?"

"It isn't that. I'm just not used to talking about these things. I don't know if you really want to hear it all. It will seem too uncivilized and brutal to you."

"I have only heard Major Holliway's version of Indian customs and I must admit it did sound almost too savage to be true. But it can't be as cruel as he said, at least not to the Indians. I'd like to know how you felt living it."

"I didn't feel it was cruel at the time. It was something we all had to do. But now I know a boy can become a man without going through what I did."

"Please tell me about it. No matter what it is, I want to hear it."

He took another sip of coffee and continued. "It was the custom of my village to receive your vision and thereby get your adult name before you could become a warrior. Snow Cloud felt I was too young to seek my vision, but I had successfully completed my other tasks and when I begged him to let me go he agreed. It was decided that his best friend, the head of the warrior society, Buffalo Horn, should go with me.

"We rode north for several days to reach the sacred hill. We arrived there early in the afternoon and I completed all the necessary rituals of purification and prayer to prepare my body to walk upon the sacred hill. By nightfall I had done everything and climbed the hill alone. I took no food, water, weapons, or clothes. I wasn't to eat or drink until I had received my vision and I was at the mercy of the weather and the animals."

He paused momentarily as he remembered the suffering of those three days spent on the hill. He took a deep breath and went on. "By the third day I was weak from hunger and my tongue was so swollen that it entirely filled my mouth. There had been no wind or clouds and my body burned from the sun and my lips cracked and bled. My eyes were almost blind from staring sleeplessly as I waited for my vision.

"I'm not sure just what happened to me on the afternoon of that third day. I may have lost consciousness or been delirious, but suddenly there was such a dazzling white light, so brilliant and intense, that I covered my head in fear that it would burn the skin from my skull. Then a voice that sounded like the howling of a wind and the rumble of thunder—like nothing I'd ever heard before or since—spoke to me. My body cooled and my suffering lessened as the voice told me to open my eyes and see the things that would happen in my life.

"I opened my eyes to the blinding light and saw a figure galloping toward me from the very center of the light. It was a beautiful snow white mare and her mane and tail were pale gold. As the mare galloped closer I saw the smooth skull of a death's-head instead of a horse's head. I was frightened but I couldn't move as it passed over my body and out of sight.

"Next I heard singing and beating drums and as I watched the light shimmered and lifted like fog vapors. I could see the people of my village dancing victory and scalp dances, and dances honoring a mighty hunter. Soon these died away and all that remained was the steady, mind-capturing throb of the sun-dance drum. I saw myself dancing, blood-streaked and triumphant, and then this too faded away.

"I saw a deer coming out of the light, walking toward me on dainty feet. It was a doe and although she was full grown, she still had the faint spots of a fawn. She looked at me adoringly and lay down on my chest. I could feel her soft, warm body and was filled with such a sense of love and happiness that I never wanted her to leave.

"But all too soon I heard the distant thud of hooves again, and the doe disappeared, and another horse came out of the brilliant light. This horse was a small blood bay with slender bones and a black mane and tail. She ran slowly and ponderously because she was heavy with foal. She too had the death's skull as she ran over me.

"I closed my eyes when the light became blinding again and the voice spoke to me, telling me to watch because my vision was not yet complete.

"I opened my eyes slowly and saw a fine stallion standing near me. His front half was white and his hindquarters were reddish brown. His tail was decorated with many eagle feathers. The horse turned and walked away from me and as he walked his brown hindquarters faded into white. A great white eagle rose up from the distance and the now pure white horse lay down in the eagle's nest.

"A haze clouded the vision for a few moments and when the vision cleared again the eagle's nest was empty and two brown spotted horses were galloping away. The light flared again and I closed my seared eyes while the voice spoke to me. It said that my vision was now complete, and it warned me that the wise men might doubt the truth of my vision, since it differed from those of the other warriors. The voice told me to ride north for two days and take Buffalo Horn as my witness. There I would find a cliff where a white eagle nested. I was to climb the cliff and wait for the eagle to return to its nest and pull three white feathers from its tail to bring to my village as a sign of my vision's truth. When my vision had been interpreted, I was to take my eagle feathers and burn them to make my medicine bag. Nothing else was to go into this bag until a certain time came when I would exchange the ashes for another object. I asked when this time would be and what was the object I should look for and was told that when the time came I would know. Then the voice told me that the wise men would be unable to fully understand the last part of my vision, but when it was fulfilled, I would understand it. I was not to attempt to change my destiny by interfering with my vision. All these things had to happen before the last part of my vision could be fulfilled.

"Then the voice said, 'There will be many false interpretations of your vision. Do not heed them. Follow your heart and it will lead you true. Now arise my son and be not afraid.' I closed my eyes as the light grew intense again and my agony returned. I think I must have slept then or blacked out and when I opened my eyes again I found I was staring at the last rays of the setting sun. I tried to stand but could not. I crawled down the hill and reached Buffalo Horn before dark.

"He took care of me for two days before I was able to ride north as the voice had instructed. We found the cliff and I got the white eagle feathers.

"We returned to our village and after we had rested and feasted, I was taken to the medicine men to have my vision interpreted. As prophesied, they felt it was a strange and false vision, except for the white eagle feathers.

"My vision had been so simple that I understood all but the last part before their explanation.

"The first part of my vision came true that winter. My mother died while Snow Cloud, my brother, and I were off hunting buffalo with the men of the village.

"I felt a deep sense of guilt because I had not become a warrior in time to save my mother. I was not able to leave the camp either, although for a while I thought of little else. I received little sympathy from Slow Water or her daughters, but there was one in our lodge who did try to comfort me. She was the daughter of Slow Water's sister. Her parents had died shortly after I was born and she came to live in our lodge because Slow Water was her only living relative. She was about four years older than I was and a spindly, shy, little girl. Snow Cloud's daughters were all older and treated her badly. My mother felt sorry for her and took the girl under her wing. When my mother died she took over the care of my brother and sister.

"I resolved my guilt and accepted my fate as Snow Cloud's heir. He was very good to me and I couldn't have asked for a better father.

I respected him and I suppose I even loved him, although I felt my life would have been entirely different if it hadn't been for him.

"I became the man he wanted in the next few years. In my seventeenth summer I performed the final ritual for manhood. It wasn't necessarily required, but few men had not performed the sun dance.

"It is a sacred ritual in which the dancer is secured to a pole by thongs. These thongs are pinned to the chest by skewers which are thrust through the skin. The warrior then dances the entire day, exerting pressure on these skewers, until at sundown they are torn out of the flesh."

He stopped when Marlette shuddered and turned her face away. He felt dry and strangely wrung out. He went to the water bucket and took a cup of water. He drank his and gave her one. She looked up at him, her eyes filled with anguish. She drank the water and in a barely audible whisper, asked, "Please, go on."

He stood apprehensively by the fireplace, afraid to relive the ensuing memories. He had forced this part of his life out of his mind and the memory always brought great pain. He gazed unseeingly at the fire and continued. "The moment I was free of the thongs I was taken to Snow Cloud's lodge. The girl I told you about, Spotted Fawn, was waiting there to take care of me. She was so gentle and her eyes were the same eyes as the adoring doe in my vision. I hadn't wanted to believe that she was the one in my vision, but I no longer could deny the truth.

"She was well past the age to marry and many wondered why she hadn't chosen a man. There were plenty that courted her as she was very lovely."

He choked on the memory of Spotted Fawn. His heart filled at the thought of her, and he couldn't speak for several moments as he remembered her body, as small and supple as a willow sapling, and the small face with the large, sparkling eyes.

"She laughed when anyone asked her hand in marriage. She told each suitor that when he could sing as sweetly as I, she would marry him. All the time she was waiting for me to come of age. She had loved me for years. She knew what my vision meant and refused to believe we would not have a long and happy life together. I resisted her for a long time, but she said she wanted to live with me as my wife for as many years as she could. I remembered that I had been warned, by my vision, not to attempt to alter the course of my life.

"In my eighteenth summer I took her as my wife and I was filled with the same sense of happiness and contentment that I had known in my vision. I no longer cared about hunting, I wanted only to spend every waking moment with her."

Ross stopped suddenly and strode to the window, standing in agonized silence. How could anyone ever know what Spotted Fawn had meant to him. Tears filled his eyes at the memory of her. Her laugh had been like the cheerful rippling of water. Her eager, uninhibited body had become a drug to his own body. He had lived for her alone. He hadn't cared when he became an object of laughter in the village. Their love had meant more than war parties, hunting, or horses.

He stood at the window for a long time until he was able to control the grief that engulfed him. He heard Marlette stir behind him and turned to see her lifting a log onto the fire. Quickly he shut out the memories and went to help her.

"Here, let me do that." He added more wood to the fire and the distraction helped to ease his tension.

Gently she said, "You don't have to tell me anymore if you don't wish to."

"It's all right. There's not much left to tell now. I might as well finish. In a few months Spotted Fawn was with child. Everything changed then. I was tormented by my vision. Spotted Fawn laughed away my worry and sent me out to hunt, reminding me that we would need food, especially after the baby came. In the fall her time came. For days she suffered unbearably. She was too small to bear my child and they both died."

Ross stopped again and swallowed hard. Marlette uttered a small sob of dismay. "That winter was worse for me than any torture devised by man. At times I thought of promoting my own death. By spring I knew what I must do. There was nothing to hold me any longer, I could leave."

As he spoke he remembered vividly that winter of grief. His depression had been deep and many were sure he had lost his mind. For days he would not eat and at night he could not sleep. Whenever his grief became unbearable he heard the voice from his vision reminding him that these things had to pass or his life would remain unful-

filled. It was during one of these reminders that he suddenly realized
what he had to do.

The men of the village prepared for the first buffalo hunt of the
spring and he went with them. He waited for an opportunity to speak
to Snow Cloud alone. During the hunt they were separated from the
others and they gave up the chase. As they rode slowly back, Ross
approached Snow Cloud.

"Your son would like to speak to his chief."

Snow Cloud reined in his horse and eyed him gravely. "For many
moons I have known the darkness in your heart and have been helpless, waiting to listen if you should speak. You have fought the evil
spirits like a true and mighty warrior. Your father listens now."

"My father remembers the strange vision his son received on the
sacred mountain?"

Snow Cloud nodded.

"I now know what the last part means. I must go away."

Snow Cloud's eyes widened in surprise. "But my son, you are to
be chief."

"There is another who has more right to be chief than I."

"I know."

It was Ross's turn to look surprised. "You know?"

"Yes. For many winters I have known you were not flesh of my
flesh."

"Then why—?" But he couldn't finish and he looked away from
Snow Cloud in confusion. The older Indian's hand closed on his
shoulder.

"Why did I not kill you and your mother? How could I kill what
I loved? You were all the son a man could ask for. Truly you are
capable to be chief as no other. And your mother? Did she not become
a worthy wife of a chief? If you must go, I cannot stop you. It is
written in your life."

A few days later they returned to the village and Ross prepared
to leave. As he gathered his things together in his lodge, his younger
brother stepped into the dim interior.

His brother would soon be fifteen. He was a slender, serious boy,
always in awe of his older brother. His skin was much darker than
Ross's and his eyes black, but his hair was a deep brown. He was
called Brown Hair, but in the intimate circle of his family he was

called Brownie. He stood stiffly, waiting for Ross to acknowledge him.

"Speak, my brother."

"Our father, the chief, tells us you are leaving."

"It is so."

The boy's stiffness crumpled and he threw his arms around his brother. "Ross, you can't go. You are to be chief. How can I take your place?"

Ross placed his hands on the shoulders of his brother. "The gods have decreed that my life is not to be here. Their will has to be done."

"Then if you go, I will go."

Ross shook his head and smiled. "No, Brownie. These people need you. You will be their chief."

He cried out in anguish, "How can I? I am not as great as you. I never can be."

Ross shook him gently. "You can and you will. You never thought about it before because it was taken for granted I would be chief. Now that you know it is not so, you will find the ability."

There was another sound outside his lodge. Ross stepped away from his brother as their sister came in.

She was two years younger than Brown Hair. Her skin was golden and her hair was light brown.

"Father says you are to come, Brownie."

Brown Hair relaxed and turned to Ross. "Good-bye, my brother. I will not let the people forget you, for I will try to become like you."

Ross smiled at him again. "You must be yourself, my brother." He held out his hand and they shook hands warmly. With a sorrowful look Brown Hair strode quickly from the lodge.

The girl stood silently, looking sadly at him. Ross dropped to his knees and held his arms out to her. She came flying into them, her tears spilling over.

Through her sobs she asked, "Is it true? Are you leaving?"

"Yes, little sister."

"Please, don't go. With you and Spotted Fawn gone who will take care of us?" she cried.

"Slow Water will take care of you. She has been good to you, has she not?"

"I guess so, but only because she has to be. She doesn't love me. Take me with you."

"I do not know what lies ahead for me. There may be great danger or even death. But I will promise you one thing, little sister, if I live, I will come back some day to see you."

She thrust herself against him and he held her tightly. In the distance he heard the voice of the village crier calling the people for an assembly. In a few moments Buffalo Horn entered his lodge and Ross stood up, releasing his sister. "Welcome, Buffalo Horn."

"The chief calls you to the council circle."

Ross looked puzzled, but he nodded his assent. Buffalo Horn stepped aside, and Ross took his sister's hand and left the lodge.

The people lined the open space between the circle of lodges and they looked solemnly at him as he passed.

They reached the center of the village where all ceremonies of importance took place. Snow Cloud emerged from his lodge with Brown Hair. As they walked toward Ross the people closed in to form a solid circle around them. As Snow Cloud came to a halt before Ross, he smiled slightly. The copper medallion, a sacred ornament of the chieftainship, flashed in the sun. Snow Cloud turned to address the people.

"I have called you together, my people, because something of great importance must be told you. Many seasons ago the man who was to be your chief had a vision so strange that not even our wise men could interpret all of it.

"Four sleeps ago, my son, White Eagle, came to me and told me the gods have permitted him to know now what our wise men did not know. It brings me great sorrow to tell you that it has been decreed White Eagle must leave us."

A great wailing murmur rose in response to Snow Cloud's words. He raised his hands to quiet them.

"White Eagle would leave quietly, as a truly great warrior would go, without exalting himself. But I know you, my people, would be grieved if you were not allowed to bestow upon him the honor he deserves. What will you do to honor this man who is worthy of being a chief?"

The people scattered to their lodges. In a few minutes they returned and laid their gifts before him, and he stood passively, hiding the deep emotion he felt. They gave him their finest robes, their most beautiful shirts and moccasins, and weapons that had been sharpened and decorated painstakingly. He was overwhelmed, and as the people returned to their places and watched him in open sorrow, he cleared his throat of the lump that swelled there.

"You fill my heart to bursting with your honor. Wherever I go I will not forget this people or the generosity of their hearts. All will know of the greatness of this people from my lips and whatever I do, I will try to deserve this great honor you have given me."

The people smiled and nodded their heads, murmuring approval of his words. Snow Cloud turned to face him and the crowd grew silent again. He smiled with pride at Ross. "I have yet to honor you, my son, and I can think of no honor more suitable for a man who will always be a chief among men, than to give you a symbol of chiefs." He paused and with a slow, deliberate, ceremonious gesture, lifted the medallion from his own neck and placed it over Ross's head. There was a gasp of shock from the onlookers. Snow Cloud silenced them with a curt motion of his arm. "All who see this will know you are worthy to be chief and from this day forward I charge this people to remember you by this sign. I command there be a song in your remembrance, so that if you return you will be honored as a chief and your words will be spoken in council. May the Maker of Visions continue to lead you true."

Ross bowed his head. "Thank you, my chief, my father."

Snow Cloud's strong hands gripped his arms briefly. There was a movement in the crowd and the snort of horses. "They bring your horses."

The crowd parted and some younger boys led his ten horses into the circle. He would need only two horses. He took five of the lead ropes and turned to his brother. A look of joyful surprise swept across the boy's face.

"Here, little brother, these are for you, but I would make a stipulation for earning them. The first mare will be yours when you ride to the sacred hill and the second mare yours when you return with a true vision. You will give their foals away to the people you feel will benefit most from your gift. It will not be easy but you must make the decision and you must decide wisely. When you strike your first coup you may have another, and when you successfully dance to the sun the stallion will be yours. The gelding will be yours when you have given away all the rest for the woman you want, so you will not be a poor man."

Laughter welled around them and Brown Hair's color deepened perceptibly, but he stood tall and proud. "My brother honors me. My victories will be all the sweeter because of your gifts." He took the horses and pulled them after him in a trot for fear the tears in his eyes would be seen.

There were still three horses left to give. Ross took them from the hands of their holders and turned to his sister. She sucked in her breath, her eyes growing wide. He looked at her for a long time, seeing in her the resemblance to their mother. She would be a beauty in a few short years. Already the signs were unmistakable.

"Soon these three will be five, little sister. Learn to manage them wisely and you will have much to bring to your wedding. As you watch and learn from these horses you will be able to tell the good from the bad. Use that knowledge when the young men come singing around your lodge and choose with your head as well as your heart."

Solemnly she nodded her head. "I will do as you say, my brother. If I do not, when you return and are not pleased, you may take them back."

He smiled at her with pride and bent to take her in his arms as murmurs of approval buzzed through the crowd. He lifted her in his arms and kissed her smooth young cheek. "Well said, little sister."

He set her down and turned to pack the remaining horses, expressing his pleasure with each gift as he put it in place. When he was through, he mounted his horse.

He looked for Slow Water but couldn't find her. It was not unusual. She had always been jealous of his mother and him for usurping her place in Snow Cloud's affections. He turned his horse toward Snow Cloud's lodge, and the people parted with surprised whispers. He rode up to the lodge and called out, "The son of the chief has a gift for the wife of the chief if she will accept it?"

After a few long moments the round, stolid face of Slow Water poked out of the lodge. She did not speak.

"The people have been so generous with me that I need nothing in my lodge. It is yours to do with as you choose."

Her only acknowledgment was a look of surprise that he should have considered her at all. He trotted back to Snow Cloud, saluted, and rode out of the camp.

Ross looked up from his locked fingers and slowly relaxed his aching hands. Quietly he finished, "I joined the fur traders on their way to the rendezvous in the shining mountains. There I met Jacques and Tom McKay. We became friends and when Tom asked me to come west to Fort Vancouver, I did."

It was over and he felt emotionally exhausted. Marlette sat silently, looking into the fire. He had to get outside and walk until things were back in perspective again. He put on the warm coat and opened the door. However he found little relief in exercise; his memories now brought to the surface, continued to haunt him.

He finally gave in to his ghosts and allowed his mind to dwell on Spotted Fawn. He knew why her memory was so bitter and why he had been unable to recover from her death. He had taken the guilt upon himself. He had known that the woman he took would die carrying a child. He had let Spotted Fawn talk him into marrying her against his better judgment. He had even allowed himself to believe her when she said his vision might be false.

He had forced himself to forget about her in order to pull himself together. He had been successful but now he remembered her as if it had happened yesterday. She had been so slender and small, with striking large eyes, indeed aptly named Spotted Fawn. And like a fawn, she had been quiet and shy. Yet when they were alone together there was nothing shy about her. At times he had been amazed by her boldness, seeking him as often as he sought her.

He heaved a great tearing sigh, his lungs aching with the sharp intake of cold air. Charging on through the timber, he drove himself until he had to stop, exhausted.

He gradually became aware it was getting dark and he had not been paying attention to where he was going. Looking around to get his bearings, he realized he wasn't too far from the cabin. He started back, feeling tired but strangely calm. He knew his ghosts weren't gone, but maybe he could live with them now.

He entered the cabin a little after dark. Marlette was cooking their supper at the fireplace and straightened up to look at him. She gave him a tenuous smile and said, "Supper's ready."

They ate silently but her eyes never left him. At last she laid down her fork. "Ross, I'm sorry. I have misjudged you and for all the wrong reasons. I'd ask you for forgiveness but I don't think you will forgive me, will you?"

"No."

"Then why did you tell me? I know you don't care what people think of you—they must accept you at face value or not at all."

"That's true. Any other time or place it wouldn't have mattered, but I'm responsible for you now. Your feelings about me aren't important to me but they are to you. I would rather get along with you than fight you. But don't think I've changed just because you know I don't have Indian blood. I'm still just as much an Indian as you thought me before."

"What if I didn't believe you?"

"Then nothing is changed."

She laughed shortly. "I can't believe how narrow-minded I've become. I listened to Major Holliway's Indian stories for so long that I couldn't trust my own judgment about you."

"What was your judgment of me?"

The color heightened in her cheeks. "I'm afraid I had you condemned before McLoughlin ever brought you to us. I saw you the day we arrived. You were walking down the road beside the fort with a woman. When she saw us she hurried off as if there was something to hide. And later that day, from my bedroom window, I saw you come out of one of the buildings with a young Indian woman following you. She embraced you, and I was disgusted when I thought you followed her. I'm afraid I let that and Holliway's stories influence my opinion of you."

Ross smiled. "And now?"

"Now I don't know. I have seen so many sides to you that contradicted everything I believed. I'm still uncertain about the truth, but at least now I can approach you positively rather than negatively."

He smiled and shook his head. No wonder she had never married; what man could stand up before logic like that. He pushed his chair away from the table and started to clear their dishes. She rose to help him. They worked together for a few minutes and her nearness was strangely disturbing, yet comforting.

"Ross, do you mind if I ask questions about you?"

He looked at her for a moment, knowing she would ask about

Spotted Fawn and his mother, and afraid those memories were still too painful. "It depends on what."

"Would you rather I didn't?"

He sighed inwardly. Perhaps airing the memories would rid him of the pain. Very quietly he said, "Ask anything you want."

It was her turn to search his eyes. She was close enough to touch and for a moment he wanted to. He remembered the time he had kissed her in the blizzard and it stirred him. She must have sensed what he was feeling because she quickly turned away. The moment was gone and he regretted it. His feelings toward her were changing and he wasn't sure he wanted them to.

The last dish was put away and he asked, "Do you want a bath before Jacques gets back?"

"Yes, if there's time."

"I can bring in the water tonight and it would be ready by morning."

Her eyes lighted. "Why didn't we think of it sooner. Do you mind?"

He smiled. "No."

Later as they sat before the fire, Marlette broke the silence. "How long have you been gone from the Indians?"

"It will be ten years this spring."

"Have you ever been back to see them?"

"No."

She looked thoughtfully at him. "If they were my brother and sister I would have taken them with me."

"If they had been white, yes, but they are Indian and they wouldn't have been able to adjust."

"Will you ever go back?"

"Yes. I must go and do what I can to help them."

"You mean help them fight the white man?"

"No, not in the way you mean. They can't fight the white man and live. They must learn to survive in the white man's world. The missionaries' solution is no good either. I'm not yet sure what I can do, but I will find the way."

She smiled at him warmly. "If anyone can, I think you can. Would you stay and live with them and marry a woman of their tribe?"

Ross frowned. He had thought about this a lot. "I don't think so.

I couldn't become one of them again if I were to help them."

She was silent for a long time, then in a strange tone of voice she asked, "Do you want to marry again?"

He stood up, uncomfortably, his back to her as he stared restlessly into the fire. "It isn't something I've thought about."

With tenacity she struck to the heart of the matter. "Are you afraid?"

He turned to face her slowly, his eyes clouded. "Yes."

"Ross, don't be afraid," she reassured him gently. "It wasn't your fault. It probably would have happened no matter who had been her husband."

"You wouldn't be afraid?"

Her eyes were wide and her lips trembled as she whispered huskily, "No." Their eyes clung together for a breathless moment, then she dropped her eyes and continued in a surer voice, "I wouldn't be afraid that I couldn't have a child. My only fear would come from my lack of experience."

His face relaxed into a crooked little smile. He had never been able to admit why he had avoided learning to dance, or why he had chosen to spend his winters away from the fort. But now that it had been said he knew it was true. Very softly he said, "Now you know all my secrets."

Her eyes widened as she grasped the meaning of his words and bent her head in confusion, her cheeks growing rosy in the firelight.

Ross suddenly felt tired. It had been an exhausting day for him. He said good-night and went to bed.

When he awoke in the morning he felt light-hearted. It was a relief to have it all out in the open. He shaved and swung down the ladder with boyish eagerness. Marlette was sitting before the fire brushing out her hair. He went to the woodpile but stopped as she lifted her hands to pull her hair into its uncomely bun. He caught her hands and held them as her hair fell about her face. It was thick, but so fine it fell as smooth and shiny as a satin ribbon. It curved upward near the ends. He pleaded, "Leave it down."

"I don't like it that way."

"Why? Are you afraid a man might find you beautiful? No one will see you but Jacques and me." Then he added with twinkling eyes, "And we have already seen you."

She pulled her hands from his and bent her head, her cheeks blazing with embarrassment.

Gently he said, "Last night you made me face my fear. Now it is time you faced yours."

He turned away from her and went on with his chores. He took the water bucket and went out to the river. When he returned she was making breakfast and her hair was still down. She didn't look at him but her cheeks were still flushed. He didn't break the silence and neither did she.

After breakfast he poured her bath water and put on his coat. "I'll be in the shed if you need anything."

Time passed quickly as Ross worked among the pelts. He was mildly surprised that his memories didn't haunt him. It was easy to keep his mind on his work and if it strayed at all he thought only of Marlette. He frowned as he realized how frequently he thought about her.

He finished tying the last bundle of hides and closed up the shed. He rapped on the cabin door and her voice called, "Ross?"

"Yes. Are you finished?"

She was standing in front of the fire in the buckskin dress, her hair hanging straight and damp over her shoulders. The sight of her made his heart lurch.

He heard Jacques shout as he neared the cabin and the spell was broken. Ross opened the door and Jacques stormed in, soon filling the quiet room with his hearty laughter and exclamations. He noticed Marlette by the fire and stopped abruptly, his face breaking into an approving smile.

"Mademoiselle! How glad you make Jacques's eyes." He turned to Ross. "Is she not lovely, mon ami?"

Ross's voice was husky as he replied, "Yes."

Marlette smiled self-consciously and turned away from them. Jacques slapped Ross heartily on the shoulder, his look implying that they shared a secret. Ross shook his head soberly, and leaving Jacques with a quizzical look, he went to find them some lunch.

Spring

THE DAYS AND WEEKS flowed together in a comfortable routine of companionship. They played cards, sang, and danced.
Often, they spent evenings just sitting around the fire, talking.
The weather remained cold and it snowed relentlessly. It was
the worst winter the men had witnessed in the mountains. Snow was
piled so deep around the cabin that there was no window left to give
light. They had to dig steps upward from the cabin door to get outside.

Ross felt increasingly aware of Marlette. He looked forward to
the times they danced to Jacques's happy music. She had left her hair
down since the day he had asked her to and was apparently over her
fear of him. He grew impatient with the continual snowfall and looked
forward to the day when Jacques would be able to check the trap line.
He wondered with eager anticipation if she would be as companionable after Jacques left.

Every day Ross awoke early to check on the weather. Finally, on
a night in February, the weather took a sudden and drastic change.
A warm Chinook wind brought rain and above-freezing temperatures
to the mountains. In a matter of hours snow was melting and sliding
from the roof and trees, waking them before dawn.

Jacques scowled with worry when they went outside in the weak
morning light. "We wash into the river if this keep up. Maybe I better
go check the line before the pelt spoil, eh?"

Noncommittally Ross commented, "Looks like solid rain from
here west."

They slushed back into the cabin and Jacques began packing his
gear. Ross helped him eagerly and Jacques knew why he was being
helped so cheerfully. He winked broadly at Ross as he went out the

door and Ross had to grin. But when he closed the door and barred it, he was once again thoroughly in control of himself. He would have to let her make the first move, otherwise all her fear and doubt would return. He took great care in fixing breakfast, waiting patiently for her to speak.

During breakfast, she finally broke her frowning silence. "Was it wise to let Jacques go?"

"He'll be all right."

"But what if he isn't all right? You should have gone with him."

"I can't take the chance of something happening to both of us and leaving you without anyone."

Persistently she went on, "But he's your friend. Would you let him die out there?"

He began to feel irritated. "We both know the risks. He knows I can't leave you. If he were here and I had gone, he wouldn't come after me and leave you alone."

She shook her head in dismay. "I guess I just don't understand you. I wouldn't have let him go in the first place."

Ross stood up uncomfortably. "If Jacques didn't think he could make it he wouldn't have gone." She looked away from him but he felt a little guilty now, knowing she was right. The anticipation he had harbored faded to nothing. He was angry with himself for letting Marlette become so important that his own good judgment had been impaired. His appetite was gone and he strode to the fireplace in aggravated silence.

Marlette finished her breakfast and came to sit by the fire. He felt her anxious eyes on his back and knew he wouldn't feel better until he acknowledged that she was right. He turned to face her, but she spoke first.

"Ross, I'm sorry. I shouldn't try to tell you what to do."

He waved her apology aside. "Don't be sorry. Your judgment is better than mine. I shouldn't have let him go." Abruptly he strode back to the table hoping she wouldn't ask him why. He cleared away the breakfast dishes and she helped him silently. He avoided her eyes, not wanting to be questioned.

He began to clean the food out of the pantry box because it wouldn't keep there in the warmer weather. Pulling open the trapdoor that led to the pit under the cabin floor, he climbed down into the cool cellar to store the food. If it didn't freeze during the night he'd have to move it again because there would soon be water under the cabin. Marlette stood by the door and held the lamp for him as he rearranged their provisions.

"Are we in much danger here?"

He climbed out of the cellar and closed the trapdoor. "We could be, if it keeps up."

"Do you think the river will flood?"

"I don't really know. I've never seen the snow so deep. If it all melts at once, these streams could go on quite a rampage. I'd be more worried about flooding if I lived in the valley, though. Here, we're more likely to be washed to the river."

She returned to her chair and sat down. "You've never told me much about the valley. Is it as beautiful as Jason Lee described it?"

"Yes. But it rains too much there for me. Somehow I find mud and rain more miserable than the cold and snow."

"I'm looking forward to seeing it. I'm just sorry the rest aren't here to see it too. It was their main goal and they never reached it." She looked away with a sad sigh.

Ross looked up as he heard the slow, shifting grind of the snow on the roof. The additional weight of the rain on the deep snow might cause leaks, or something worse. Needing an excuse for action, he left the cabin and removed the snow off the roofs of the cabin, shed and lean-to. He tried to dig a ditch around the cabin to channel the water away but it was already too late for the shed. Water was seeping in and running across the floor and he had to move everything off the floor. He dug some more in back of the cabin until he had stopped most of the water.

He was getting soaked and began to ache from hours of shoveling, but he didn't want to leave the canoe by the river overnight and went to bring it closer to the cabin.

Thoroughly wet and cold, it was dark by the time he returned. Marlette had supper ready. He changed into dry clothes and ate before the fire.

After dinner, he poured them some coffee and settled down in his chair, wondering how Jacques was. By the lines of worry on Marlette's face as she absently stared into her cup, he knew she was wondering the same thing.

She looked up and asked, "If all the snow melts will we be able to leave earlier than you planned?"

He smiled at her hopefulness. "Don't plan on it. It could start snowing again."

She sighed, "I thought you'd be glad to get rid of me sooner."

He smiled again, showing off his dimples. "I should be, but—." He let the sentence trail off.

She looked at him curiously but changed the subject completely. "What did the Indians call you?"

"I took the name White Eagle after my vision."

"And before that?"

He smiled at her. "You'll laugh, but translated it meant holes in face."

A look of disbelief crossed her face. "You can't be serious!"

He grinned and stuck both index fingers into his dimples. "It's true. I became so self-conscious I wouldn't even smile when I got older, but the name stuck."

She began to laugh and he laughed with her, forgetting for the moment about Jacques.

At last she choked, "I don't know if I should believe you. I think you're teasing me."

He shook his head. "There were some who had stranger names. There was one old man who had been rolled on by a buffalo when he was young. His name was Buffalo Rolls Over. Another man had teeth so large they stuck out even when his mouth was closed. They called him Beaver Teeth."

Soberly she said, "How terribly cruel."

"Not to the Indian way of thinking. These things were marks of distinction, a matter of pride. That is what is so wrong with the way many white men think. The Indian can find beauty and pride in what is natural. It is often considered a special sign from the Great Spirit. You blush any time you think of your body and its functions but if you stopped to think—to really understand—you would see that what is natural is beautiful and man's mind alone has made it ugly."

She dropped her eyes. He finished his coffee and decided to go to bed. He smiled softly down at her. "Good night."

In the morning the weather had cleared somewhat, and by noon the clouds had blown away and the sun came out. It didn't take long for it to warm the already tepid air. The sound of running water filled the air and the cabin smelled damp.

They were putting away the lunch dishes when Ross asked, "Would you like to go for a walk?"

"Do you think it would be safe?"

"What can happen?"

"That's what I'm asking you. Could we fall through the snow or something?"

He smiled. "It's possible, but not too dangerous."

She smiled back. "All right. I've been cooped up too long to refuse."

He got an extra pair of snowshoes for her from the shed. It would be impossible to stay on top of the melting snow without them. The art of walking with snowshoes was not entirely beyond her, but she found it difficult, and they laughed at her attempts as they progressed slowly. After a while she was able to slog along fairly well and they got out of sight of the cabin. They stopped often, as it was strenuous exercise for Marlette.

Near the river, they slowed to watch the muddy stream as it charged past with an almost perceptible rise in water, carrying brush and debris along in its torrent.

Marlette saw a bare log nearby and started toward it. Ross opened his mouth to caution her just as the snow collapsed under her, and she sank up to her armpits in the hole. The snow began to break away all around her and she cried out in panic as she sank deeper.

Quickly Ross pulled his hatchet out of his belt and chopped down the nearest young tree. Carrying it as close as he dared, he pushed it out to her. She caught it and hung on until Ross pulled her onto solid snow. He pulled her to her feet but the snowshoes were twisted and would need repair before she could walk in them. Lifting her in his arms he carried her away from the snow tunnel. She clung to him, her eyes still wide with fright and her lips trembling. He was acutely aware of her and now that he had her in his arms, he didn't want to let her go. He stopped, and just held her close, eyes beseeching hers as he bent his head toward her lips.

She stiffened and turned her head away, murmuring, "Please don't."

Gently, he said, "I ask nothing of you, only to give to you."

She turned and looked at him for a long moment. "Why?"

He moved to a tree a few steps away and carefully seated her on a stout limb. He held her upper arms with his hands, looking at her deeply. "Because you need someone."

"Don't you need someone?"

"Yes."

"But why me, when you have your choice of so many?"

"You have qualities the others don't."

She looked searchingly at him for a long moment. "Because I'm white?"

"Yes."

She shook her head wonderingly. "That still doesn't explain it to me."

"This will be a white man's country. They will drive the Indians away as they did where you come from. I am a white man. I want my children to be white."

"Then you are asking me to stay with you—to live with you?"

"Yes."

A frown furrowed her forehead. "But you don't speak of love."

"Giving is more than loving."

She sighed, "Will I never understand you?"

"You will. When you want to."

She shivered slightly. "You frighten me."

He smiled, softening the seriousness of his face. "I don't mean to."

"I know, but I've never known anyone who can put so few words together so well. Is that the Indian in you?"

"Yes."

"How can you ask nothing of me?"

"I only want to see you happy. If you don't want to stay, I will accept that."

She turned her head away, but he caught the distress in her eyes. Offhandedly she said, "Gay once said he wanted to dedicate his life to making me happy."

"Could he have?"

"I don't know."

"Then you didn't love him?"

She thought about it for a long moment and turned back to him. "No. I guess not."

She shivered with cold and he knelt to straighten her snowshoes. He had said enough for now. She would have to think about it; to grow used to the idea of staying with him. He tied the snowshoes to her feet and stood up. She slid off the limb and they shuffled back to the trail that led to the cabin.

Jacques was there when they returned and Ross was relieved to see his friend, regretting only that he would have no more time alone with Marlette. Having admitted out loud that he wanted her, it would be hard to have her near and not be alone with her, but since she had not declared any feeling for him, it was probably just as well.

The evening passed swiftly as they listened to Jacques tell about the trouble he had had bringing in the furs. The state of his gear was mute, wet testimony to the truth of his words. Everything, including his clothes, was wet and it took most of the evening just to get the mess cleaned up.

The next few days Ross was kept busy working on the furs and helping Jacques fight the deluge of water brought on by the warm temperature. He had little time to wonder what Marlette might be thinking and by nightfall he was too tired to care.

Then the weather changed. The river, which had come close to the cabin on its furious rampage, slowly began to recede as snow returned to the mountains. They welcomed the cold and snow with relief, but the snow meant long hours of togetherness again. Ross felt the tension building in him. He tried to sing and dance with her, but her every touch and look filled him with desire. The only way to fight it was to withdraw.

He worked long hours in the shed and when that work was exhausted, he wandered in the silent forest. He spoke little and Jacques carried the conversation for both of them. Marlette cast worried glances at him and he tried to smile as if nothing was wrong, but he knew they both felt his strain.

Jacques, unable to tolerate his mood, cornered him away from the cabin. "What wrong with you? You like the she-bear with cubs."

Ross smiled crookedly. "Why do you need to ask? You know

what's wrong with me."

Jacques's face lit up. "Ah! Mon ami, you are in love?"

"Yes."

"Well, why you so depressed? Love should make you happy."

"Not when the love isn't returned."

Jacques laughed. "You blind fool. She loves you."

Ross shook his head. "If she does, she keeps it to herself. Maybe it's just as well. In another two months she'll be gone." He snapped a tree branch fiercely.

"Maybe tomorrow you want to check the trap line, eh?"

Ross looked up at his friend. "Yes. I've got to get away. Maybe I can get her out of my system."

Jacques shrugged. "You missing a good chance, but I be glad to stay with her." He grinned wickedly.

The weather held during the night and in the morning, Ross packed his gear. Marlette watched anxiously as he loaded up, but she said nothing. With a feeling of relief, Ross set off for the trap line. He drove himself as hard as he could, working off the built-up tension. He reached the shelter early and found that the melting snow had damaged it. He set about repairing it, finding release in the hard labor.

At dark he built his fire and ate in the snug warmth of the little hut. He rolled into his warm robes and blankets but could not sleep. Thoughts flooded his mind, and he tried to sort everything out. He thought of Spotted Fawn and found the memory more bittersweet than painful now, although her face kept merging with Marlette's. This disturbed him. He didn't want to get the two of them mixed in his thoughts. He knew his life with Marlette, if she'd have him, would be very different from the life he had led with Spotted Fawn. That difference would be just as great for Marlette as for him. Could he live as a white man lived? How far across the line could he go for Marlette? He knew he had to decide that, even if it took the whole night. If she would stay and be his wife, what could he offer her? Vague plans had already formed in his mind during the past few weeks. Although he was not a farmer, he had worked with Tom McKay at his horse ranch down the Columbia. He was good with horses and he knew the valley well enough to be able to haul freight, or log. He felt he could do any of these things, but would they be acceptable to her? What would she have to have? She was strong, but

was she strong enough to endure the discomforts of wilderness living
on a permanent basis? Would his love be strong enough to keep him
tied down to a cabin? He had been contented with her in Jacques's
cabin for a few months but could he do it for the rest of his life?

His mental and physical exhaustion caught up with him in the
early morning hours. He slept until afternoon. He cut more wood and
prepared to stay another night and many more nights if he had to.
The traps in the basin below the shelter checked out, he returned
before dark to eat his dinner. One of the traps had held a freshly
caught rabbit and it made an excellent meal roasted over his fire.

During the night the wind rose, and toward morning a fierce
snowstorm blotted out everything but the nearest trees. He wasn't
worried. He had brought plenty of jerky and he had shelter.

Three days passed before the storm finally spent itself. The time
had sufficed for everything to settle into place. He knew she would
have to return east no matter what he might propose, but he too had
a mission. When he finally left the shelter, he felt calm and untrou-
bled. He knew he loved her and wanted her regardless of the consequences. Now it would be up to her.

He reached the cabin just before dark and couldn't deny his joy
at the thought of seeing her. He unstrapped his snowshoes and
pounded on the door. Jacques's exclamation was followed by the
clump of heavy feet thudding across the floor.

"Ross, mon ami! Is it you?"

Feeling happy beyond reason, Ross replied, "Who'd you expect?"

Again an exclamation of relief as the bar hit the floor and the door
swung open. The first thing he saw was Marlette standing by the table,
her hand close to her mouth as if she expected to see a ghost. He
unslung his pack and set his rifle down without taking his eyes off
her, his smile growing broader each moment.

At last, realizing he was all right and really there, she let out a
choking cry and ran toward him, tears of relief rolling down her
cheeks. She ran into his waiting arms and he held her tightly as she
cried against the cool fur of his coat. He kissed the warm pulse of
her temple, his hand smoothing the softness of her hair. She lifted
her head, her lips temptingly close, and at that moment nothing in
the world mattered. Jacques closed the door and the bang of the bar
dropping into place was like an explosion splitting the intimate silence

between them. Her arms slid away and he let her go.

"Oh, Ross! We were so worried about you. Are you all right? What happened? Why didn't you come back before the storm?"

He grinned with pleasure. She had been concerned about him. "One thing at a time. First, how about some supper?"

They both hurried to take care of him. While he ate, Jacques unpacked for him. Later they sat around the fire and he told them about his trip, making it sound as though he had too much to do to return before the storm. He knew Jacques saw through him, but at least Marlette didn't need to know.

"What you think, mon ami, will we be smart not to come back?"

"I think the area needs a rest."

Jacques puffed his pipe thoughtfully. "Ah, Jacques hate not to come back here." His eyes roamed the small cabin lovingly. He shrugged off the nostalgia. "But, we must eat, eh?"

Ross smiled slightly. Eating wasn't a problem for him. It wasn't for Jacques either, but he had to say something to make the leaving easier.

River Interlude

IN MARCH the weather began to change; it snowed less frequently and the days were sunnier. Ross and Jacques began building another canoe since they needed two to get them downriver. As they worked they made plans for the trip. Ross wanted to be alone with Marlette on the trip and Jacques heartily agreed. However, they had to start out together to help each other through the shallower upper stretches of the river. Once they reached deeper water, Jacques would go on ahead.

Ross watched the weather and the river constantly, with a restlessness that would be eased only when they were on their way. He went through the same anxious watch every spring, but this year he could hardly contain his anticipation.

One day the river finally began to recede. They decided to start immediately so as not to lose the advantage of what little high water they had, and they took off early next morning. Jacques with a happy, "Bon voyage!" shoved off first. Ross and Marlette followed. Jacques soon broke into a gay voyageur song and Ross joined in as he felt his spirits soar.

He breathed deeply of the damp, sweet air. Along the river the brush was beginning to come alive with the first feathery, almost illusionary, greenery. He felt renewed as he always did when spring reached his mountain retreat and released him from the prison of snow.

But this spring the beauty was marred by the ravages of the flood. Huge uprooted trees and barriers of drift clogged the river. Tons of rock had been dredged into new bars and channels. It had always been difficult to maneuver the canoe through the upper part of the river even when the water was high, but now it was worse. In addition to the usual treacherous boulders and shallows they had to move brush and chop through fallen logs and at times unload and carry their canoes around jams too big to clear away. Even when they could rope their canoes through shallows or under logs it meant delay and long hours in icy water.

When they were able to stay in the canoe, Marlette knelt in front of Ross with a grim face, her white-knuckled hands clutching the sides of the canoe. But Jacques and Ross met the challenge with high spirits. It became a race for them to reach the deeper water as quickly as possible and save themselves the hardship of wading. It was a welcome change for both of them from a winter of inactivity and for Ross, especially, it was a release from emotions too long controlled.

Late in the day they sailed into deeper water. Jacques waved good-bye to them and disappeared around a bend. Ross, tired from the unaccustomed work and eager to be alone with Marlette, looked for a place to camp and landed the canoe in a suitable spot.

The air was beginning to chill and he quickly built a fire for Marlette. He rigged a fishing line and caught two large trout which were soon roasting over the fire. There had been little time to talk during the harrowing day and now he found himself at a loss for words. A mild wind swept through the tall lush firs that stretched across the length of the mountains rising steeply on both sides of the river. He felt the chill of his damp buckskins and rose to put more wood on the fire. He returned to Marlette and sat cross-legged beside her. She pulled her blankets around her, shivering slightly.

Ross asked, "Are you going to be warm enough?"

"Since these are all the blankets we brought, I guess they'll have to do."

Without looking at her he said, "No, they don't have to do. We could put them together." He turned quickly to see her reaction.

Her eyes were large and sparkling as they met his and a coy little smile curved her lips. "Are you suggesting I sleep with you?"

He smiled hopefully and said, "Yes."

She looked uncertain. "Do I have to be frightened of you again?"

"No." He paused, attempting to find the right words to express his emotions and feeling suddenly inadequate in English. "Marlette, I'm not sure how to say this correctly, as a white man would say it, but I love you. If there was anything I could say or do to make you stay, I would."

Her eyes softened and she reached out to him in a gesture of dismay. He caught her hand in his and pressed it to his lips. She withdrew her hand and whispered, "You know I can't stay."

"We can work it out if you want to."

"Would you come east with me?"

"No. I don't belong there."

"No," she agreed. "Neither could I live the life you live."

"I don't expect you to live as I have lived. I want to build you a home—."

She didn't let him finish. Shaking her head sadly she broke in, saying, "Please don't. You know I have this duty to do."

"I know. But when you're finished, is there anything to keep you there?"

"I haven't thought about it."

"Well, I want you to think about it. I want you to decide now what you want. After you're back there it'll be too late. I want you here, with me. Think of yourself and think of this, too."

He bent over her and lifted her face to his between his hands until their lips touched. She didn't respond, but her eyes were wide and depthless. He turned away to crawl into his own blankets, feeling depressed and frustrated. For a long time her restless stirrings kept them both awake. The fire died down and he got up to throw more wood on it. Marlette rose on an elbow to watch him.

"Are you cold?" he asked.

"Yes."

He shook his blankets out, laying them on top of hers, and sat down by the fire.

"Ross, I want you to come to bed with me."

The way her voice vibrated made his heart skip but he was careful to control his excitement as he asked, "Are you sure?"

He looked at her intently and saw that she was both desperate and uncertain, but she answered with only the slightest hesitation, "Yes."

He stood up to undress, feeling a long forgotten warmth spring from his groin and flow upward. He raised the edge of the blankets and saw the whiteness of her shoulder and arm revealed against the dark bedding, and realized why she had been stirring. He slipped in beside her and reached to take her in his arms, but she turned her head away quickly and her body cringed at his touch. He withdrew his hand and tucked the aroused member of his body under his bent leg. Fighting down his desire he asked gently, "You're afraid. Why?"

She looked at him then, her anguish apparent in her voice and her face. "Oh Ross, forgive me. I thought I could do it, but I find it's just not that easy to discard a lifetime of impressions and inhibitions."

"Do you want me to go back to my own bed?"

"Oh, no. Please don't go. Try to understand and be patient. I do want you. As the devil is my witness, I do want you! From the time I saw you bathing in the creek, maybe even from the first moment I saw you, that excitement has been there and I can't leave without having you, but I don't know what to do. You said it was something beautiful, but all I've ever heard about was the pain, the shame and degradation. Is that all there is to it for a woman? Is it strictly a man's pleasure? Oh, Ross, please help me!"

Her eyes searched his in desperation. He understood so much more than he had before. Now he knew why many white men who left their families to come west preferred to stay with their Indian wives. And he understood the humiliation his mother must have suffered at having to submit no matter what the hour or audience. He realized now why she had found so many chores away from the lodge during the day. He was suddenly glad he had been raised an Indian.

He reached for Marlette's hand and held it. "I want you to forget what you have heard. It is only important how you feel. If you have already made up your mind that it will be shameful and degrading, it will be. But if you are willing to try to make it something beautiful, it can be. Just remember that you have to want me as much as I want you or it will have little meaning for either of us. There should be no pain after the first time and I will let you control that. I don't think you will find it unbearable. If your desire is strong enough, you will not mind the pain. It is even possible you will have none."

Her hand was limp in his as she thought over his words. He drew her hand to his lips and kissed it. There had been so little opportunity to show her his feelings or to prepare her for this moment, and now because of ideas and fears formed from men who had nothing to do with him, he might lose her.

He was almost ready to consider going east with her when he felt her fingers tighten around his and he knew her answer even before she turned to him, a smile barely touching her lips. She came into his arms and he kissed her, intensely aware of the soft warmth of her body. Her admission reminded him of Jacques's words. All the time she had fought him she had really been fighting herself. He pulled away from her clinging lips. She had reminded him of what he had said months ago in the snow and he knew how hard it would be for him to live up to that statement. He had to prepare her.

"Marlette, I want more than anything to make you happy but I have to tell you honestly that it may not be possible this time. I'm not forgetting what I told you. All of it is true, but not under these conditions. It's been so long for me that I may be unable to wait for you, or your fear may make you unresponsive, but that doesn't mean you can't enjoy it the next time. I don't want you to think I'm using you. This is like anything else. It isn't always perfect and it takes practice to make it perfect. Do you understand?"

She nodded, her face sober and tantalizingly close. He took a deep breath, forestalling his desire as he remembered something else. "I want you to do something for me. Everything I do will be new for you and you may not like it at first, but wait for that reaction to pass and if you still don't like it then I want you to tell me."

Her eyes were wide as she nodded her head again, asking, "But why?"

He smiled at her innocence and her ever questioning mind. "If I do something you don't like it will lessen your response to me and if that happens, you will be less likely to feel what you should feel." She trembled against him and he asked wonderingly, "Are you cold?"

She laughed softly. "No. I just want you."

He laughed in return. "Then I think we have talked enough." He covered her face with kisses, releasing his pent-up desire with each touch of his lips. He bent his head and kissed the soft firmness of her breasts and felt her stiffen at the new sensation. He caressed her with his lips, smoothing her body gently with his hand. He felt a responding warmth flow over her skin as she relaxed and pressed his lips to her breasts.

All sense of time was lost in the sweet, precious interval that followed. When it was over, he was filled with indescribable joy and contentment. He stroked her hair and kissed her, feeling a sudden wetness on his shoulder where her head lay. Remorse gripped him.

"Oh, Marlette," he whispered, his voice husky with concern, "I'm sorry. I thought you were with me."

Her fingers rushed to his lips. "I was. Oh, I was! Have you never seen a woman cry from joy?"

Relief flowed through him. "Yes. For the first time, just now with you." He pulled her head up and kissed her long and tenderly.

She breathed against his cheek, "Now I know why all those other women are so unhappy."

He smiled. "Why?"

"Because they didn't have you as a lover."

He chuckled. ."Do you want to share me with them?"

"Never!" She raised her head to look into his face and asked, "Was I all right? Did I please you as much as—?"

She couldn't say it and he knew then what had driven her. "As Spotted Fawn? I didn't think about her and you shouldn't either. It can only make you unhappy."

"I know. But I can't forget the look on your face when you talked about her. Any woman who tries to take her place has a lot to live up to, and I'm not sure I can."

He pulled her close to shut out the cold air she was letting in. "No woman can take her place. I don't expect or even want you to. She is dead. You are the important one to me now. From this time on I want to remember you, not her. I want to remember how nice you are, how good you feel. For the rest of my life I want to spend every night with you in my arms, trying to give you back the joy and exquisite pleasure I have found in you."

She snuggled close to him, sighing contentedly. "Will I ever stop underestimating you?"

"It is yourself you underestimate."

She was silent for a long while and he was filled with unbounded happiness. Then she whispered in a voice filled with awe, "I could never have imagined how it could be. I'm so glad I didn't let my fear stop me."

He kissed the top of her head, running his hand through her silky hair.

"Mmmm," she purred.

"I think we'd better go to sleep now."

"I don't want to. I feel too good."

He smiled. "Try, anyway. There's always tomorrow."

Her lips caressed his neck and she curled herself against him. He kissed her gently, but she was already asleep, her hand covering his lightly.

He awoke before dawn. The fire was practically out and the air was dripping with the heavy dew of morning. He looked at Marlette curled beside him and smiled happily. Carefully he crawled from the bed to rekindle the fire. The damp air chilled his naked body but he didn't dress. He returned to the bed and crawled in, careful not to touch her with his cold body. He lay on his side, watching her sleep as the ghostly light of morning brightened the forest.

The crackling of the fire roused her and she opened her eyes slowly. When she focused on his face a smile curved her lips. "Ross," she whispered huskily.

His heart filled with joy. She didn't regret last night, at least not yet. Softly he said, "Your smile fills me with the warmth of the sun."

She reached out to touch him, happiness reflected in her face, and he bent to kiss her. Her arms closed tightly around him as their lips touched and his body responded instantly to hers. The shyness for the unknown was gone and in its place was an eagerness to match his own.

Later they lay in each other's arms for a long time, not wanting to break the spell created by their contentment.

When he realized how late it was, he broke away from her embrace and ran to the river, yelling at the shock as the icy water swept over him. Marlette followed him to the river, a blanket clutched around her, laughing at his idiocy. She gritted her teeth as she washed herself in the cold water and quickly retreated to the fire to dress. He came after her and scrubbed himself dry before the fire with the rough blanket.

They started downriver in high spirits. Ross considered the water they would travel today the most exciting and beautiful. The river had a depth and turbulence unknown in the shallower upper portion. There were dangerous falls and fierce chutes that challenged the heartiest of men, and Ross loved every foot of it.

By mid-morning they neared one of the more treacherous

stretches of water. There was a frightened look on Marlette's face as the roar of whitewater reached them. Ahead, he saw the black rock wall at the end of the chute and he repressed his excitement at the challenge echoing thunderously around him.

Ross landed the canoe on the south bank of the river just above the churning water. There was a smile of relief on Marlette's white face when he helped her out of the canoe.

"I thought you were going to run that water."

He grinned back at her. "Not today."

With an incredulous look she exclaimed, "You mean you have!"

"I've tried it but never with anything I'd care about losing."

"Have you ever made it through?"

He looked out over the frothing whitewater with its boulders scattered in such a way that a straight shot was impossible. The water boiled so swiftly that there was little time to maneuver the zigzag course. The stretch ended in a wide deep pool at the base of a solid rock wall which almost blocked the river entirely except for a narrow crevice on the south side. The water ran swiftly through this funnel, at times only three feet wide, depending on the river height.

"I've only made it through this part twice, in higher water. The narrows below are easy compared to this."

He tied a rope to the canoe and eased the craft back into the water taking one last respectful look at the wildly plunging river. It wasn't the most difficult of places to rope through since the shoreline was fairly easy to follow until they came to the base of the rock wall. By then they were at the bottom of the most turbulent water and he could straighten the canoe out before they were swept through the funnel.

In a matter of seconds they were through the crevice and into the wider river below it. Marlette looked back toward the narrow chute to make sure it was behind her and smiled with relief at Ross.

A short way downstream they neared a small falls and Marlette pointed to a black bear standing on some rocks on the north side of the river.

Ross nodded and said, "There must be salmon running in the river." He paddled the canoe to the south shore just upstream from a huge basalt cliff that bordered the falls and watched the bear expertly grab a salmon in one paw. He ignored them until Ross, taking an arrow from his quiver, got out of the canoe, eased himself into the water, and waded toward the falls. The bear growled menacingly, but was reluctant to leave his fishing to plunge into the swift river after Ross.

The current was strong and the rocks slippery but Ross, holding the arrow in his teeth and finding handholds in the rough cliff face, inched his way past the falls to where he could see the salmon milling in the water below the falls. Using the arrow as a spear he lunged at one of the silver bodies plunging headlong into the water. The arrow pierced the salmon and he brought it to the surface. He heard Marlette yelling his name as he kicked for the rocks at the base of the cliff trying to hang onto the thrashing fish. As soon as he got footing among the rocks he dashed the fish against the cliff to still its struggle and laboriously made his way back to where Marlette stood anxiously waiting for him.

"Our lunch."

"Ross, you're out of your mind! What if that bear had come after you?"

Ross grinned. "He's too busy to come after me."

She got into the canoe, not quite reassured. He pulled off his wet shirt, laying it over the fish, and pushed the canoe back into the stream. They bounced over the falls, the bear swiping futilely at them as they plunged on just out of his reach.

Ross paddled quickly, fearing he was getting behind in the schedule he wanted to keep. There was still a bad section of water ahead and another falls. He wanted to be past the falls before he stopped for lunch and his stomach and the sun told him it was nearing noon.

In another few miles Ross heard the roar of the next falls around the bend. Marlette turned questioning eyes on him as she recognized the louder thunder.

"It's another falls. Not much worse than the last."

She looked ahead and saw the falls on a slight curve in the river. Ross lined the canoe up in the center of the river and headed straight toward the falls. Marlette turned a white face toward him just before they plunged breakneck over the edge. She screamed as a wave of water rose and soaked them, but they stayed upright and Ross paddled with all his strength to flee the torrent of water crashing close behind them.

When they passed the falls, Ross looked for a sunny bank where they could dry themselves and eat their lunch. He beached the canoe and helped Marlette out. She looked pale and shaken.

"Are you all right?"

"Now that I'm on dry land I am."

He smiled. "The worst is over. Better check the blankets in case they got wet. I'll get a fire going."

They worked quietly for a while and Ross delighted in their silent companionship. A look or touch was all they needed to convey their thoughts. The warm spring sun soon began to dry their wet clothes and they lay on the grass while the salmon roasted over the fire.

Suddenly Marlette sat up and turned worried eyes on Ross. "We haven't seen any Indians. Why?"

"There aren't many left in the valley. The white man's sicknesses have killed most of them. The few that are left are in the lower parts of the valley where they can dig camas. They won't bother us."

Her face relaxed and she lay down again. The smell of the cooking salmon drifted toward them and she remarked dreamily, "Ummm. I'm getting hungry."

"Only for food I hope?"

She looked at him curiously for a moment, then her cheeks reddened and she threw a handfull of grass at him. He rose with a grin, knowing they didn't have time for anything other than lunch. He took his knife and tested the pink sizzling meat. It flaked cleanly from the bone. He carried Marlette a piece on a tin plate along with a biscuit they had brought from the cabin. They washed down their meal with the icy cold water of the river.

After lunch, they continued down the river. There was less turbulence and Marlette was able to relax and enjoy the beauty of her surroundings. By dusk they had passed the mouth of the south fork of the river. Ross soon found a place to camp and beached the canoe for the night.

While Marlette laid out their blankets, Ross gathered wood for the fire. Then they finished the rest of the fish and biscuits. Gratefully Ross crawled into bed. It had been a long day and his arms ached with weariness. Marlette curled against him and he permitted himself the luxury of kissing and caressing her for the first time since early morning. The tiredness soon left his arms as he lost himself in the warmth of her body.

Marlette broke the silence as they lay basking in the contented afterglow of their love.

"Can it always be this way between us?"

He stroked her hair tenderly. "If you want it to be."

She was silent for a long time and he felt a wetness on his shoulder where the tears slid off her cheek. Aware that she was thinking of leaving, he touched her cheek gently.

"Promise me one thing?" She nodded tearfully. "As long as we can be together, don't think of anything that will make you unhappy." She nodded again, a small smile barely curving her lips. "Now you'd better go to sleep." She kissed him and obediently turned over, snuggling close to him. He ran his hand lovingly down the full soft length of her body and she held it tightly just beneath the fullness of her breasts. He kissed her shoulder and neck and heard her sigh of contentment. He felt extremely happy.

When the early morning chorus of awakening birds roused him, he forced himself to get out of bed and dress. The temptation to hold Marlette would delay the day he had planned and he resisted his desire. Noisily stirring the fire, he tried to wake her up. She stirred and glanced up to see what he was doing. Smiling at her, he continued fixing their breakfast of salt pork and potatoes. She didn't question him but got dressed and started folding the blankets while breakfast cooked. It was this understanding that made his heart swell with love for her. It was hard not to compare her with Spotted Fawn. Spotted Fawn had never questioned or nagged. She had never failed him when he had needed her. He had seen Marlette in conditions that would have tried most men and she had the same strength. Every sense told him he had chosen wisely.

The sun was barely lighting the rippling water when Ross pushed the canoe into the river. Ducks and deer departed noisily as they drifted quietly down the river. Ross had to paddle continuously to keep his schedule since the current was weak and gave them little help. They stopped for lunch and Ross caught fat, frisky trout and soon had them roasting over a fire. While they cooked he lay in the sun with Marlette close to him and rested, recovering his strength for the long hours of paddling ahead.

Shortly after lunch Ross saw his first great blue heron on the river.

The huge bird flapped away from them, uttering a raucous squawk. It meant they were nearing the main river and in less than an hour he saw the high bank that marked the confluence of the two rivers.

When Marlette realized they were entering another river she turned to him eagerly. "Is this the river where Jason Lee has his mission?"

"Yes."

They sailed into the larger, calmer river and a group of startled ducks rose in a quacking cloud ahead of them. Ross reached belatedly for his bow but they were too far away. There were more sloughs downriver and next time he would be prepared.

As he paddled steadily downriver in the slower current, he saw a brushy inlet extending into the river, forming a slough. He touched Marlette and held his finger to his lips. Quietly guiding the canoe closer to the bank he readied his bow as a small bunch of green-headed mallards jumped into the air. Ross took careful aim and shot the arrow, hearing the singing twang as it flew. A fat, gray-feathered drake crumpled and fell. Ross paddled after it as it hit the water near the upper end of the slough.

Marlette picked the floating bird out of the water and turned it over in her hands. "He's so pretty. It's a shame to kill him."

"Just think of how good he'll taste for supper."

"I'll try to."

She laid the bird in front of her and they paddled out of the slough and back into the river. At the next slough he managed to bag another duck and took time to clean them both on the gravel bar. It provided him with a much-needed rest and he was able to paddle on in steady, strong strokes. The sun was beginning to set as they approached a large westerly curve in the river, and Ross breathed a sigh of relief. They were near his goal.

They approached a large island shortly thereafter and Ross was amazed at the change the flood had wrought in the area. The high water had washed away a great portion of the upper end of the island widening a once narrow channel and creating gravel bars in the previously tranquil slough. The island itself was cluttered with piles of driftwood in the tangled brush and fallen trees lay in the water. Ross wondered if there would be a suitable place left to camp.

He landed the canoe on the lower end of the island in a shallow, mudbanked little bay. Leaving Marlette in the canoe, he pushed his way through the fringe of unkempt willows toward the secluded center of the island. He found a small grassy area beneath some huge cottonwoods and returned for Marlette.

They carried their things to the campsite and Marlette kneeled to spread their blankets, breathing, "Mmmm. It smells so good here. What is it?"

Ross inhaled deeply of the sweet fragrance of the place and bent to pick up a small golden hull from the many that littered the ground. He held it near her nose. "It's from these trees."

She took the small, sticky, tear-shaped hull and remarked wonderingly, "How sweet they smell."

In a short time the ducks were sizzling over a driftwood fire and they ate watching the setting sun cover the island and the river around them in a soft cerise glow. It was dark when they crawled into their bed, tired but eager to enjoy their newfound intimacy, falling asleep in each other's arms, breathing the sweet fragrance of the cottonwood buds.

Ross was the first to awake next morning. He rekindled the fire and crept back between the blankets to wait for Marlette to waken. A raucous squawk shattered the early morning air and Marlette jumped up, startled. "What was that?"

He chuckled softly and pulled her down to him. "Only one of those big blue birds."

She relaxed in his arms and asked, "Aren't we in a hurry today?"

"No. I want to show you the valley from heré."

"But how, from here?"

"The hill across from us overlooks the whole valley."

"Are you sure we can take the time?"

"I'm not worried about the time. I'd like to keep you here forever if I could. Besides, I thought you might like to wash your clothes and bathe before we reached Champoeg."

She hugged him, delighted. "You always know just what I need."

He pulled her closer and kissed her. "And you are what I need." Then, as he felt her body flush warm in response, he pushed her away and grinned devilishly. "But not now. We have a hill to climb."

With reluctant determination he pushed himself out of bed and dressed before the fire.

Marlette murmured petulantly, "You're a big tease."

He turned to face her, pulling his shirt over his head. "And you are far too pleasing for any man to deny himself for long, so get up before I change my mind." With quick strides he left her and went to the river.

When he returned she was dressed. They ate breakfast, then paddled to the north bank of the river. The bank was still soft from the recent flooding and Ross knocked down the sharp thigh-high grass to make dry footing for Marlette. He forced his way through the lush growth of the riverbank, making a trail toward the base of the hill. Carpets of snowy white flowers bloomed everywhere, brilliant in the shaded canopy of trees. He pointed out the taller spikes of the blue violet camas flower just beginning to bloom. Part way up the hill, they found a small clearing where several deer, grazing in the abundant green grass, watched the intruders for a long moment before leaping away in gliding bounds.

They continued through the tangled brush and trees until they reached another clearing. Ross stopped, knowing Marlette would be tired. She caught up with him and sighed deeply, brushing away her tangled hair, decorated with bits of twig and leaf.

"How much farther?"

"Not too far now. Sit down and rest for awhile."

Gratefully she sank down into the luxuriant grass. He dropped down beside her and picked the woodland ornaments from her hair as she leaned comfortably against him.

"I feel as if we are the only two people left in the world."

He smiled and nodded. "It's a good feeling."

She was silent for a moment, then said, "I don't think it would bother you to go on living like this forever."

He chuckled softly, "Well, maybe not forever."

She said no more but he knew her thoughts. He brushed her hair back from her neck and kissed her damp, pale skin. She turned toward him and smiled. He kissed her and said reluctantly, "We'd better be going."

It was an easier climb through the grass and he took her hand to help her up the steep slope of the meadow. He stopped and made her turn to see the valley spreading out below them in a multi-colored carpet of green trees and natural clearings. They continued up the hill, finally reaching the highest crest, and they stood looking northeastward toward the Columbia. The southern view had been beautiful, but this view was magnificent. Snow-capped peaks rose east of them, glistening brilliantly against the royal blue sky.

In an awed voice Marlette whispered, "Jason Lee wasn't exaggerating when he said this was the most beautiful place on earth."

Ross laughed, "Nearly, anyway. If you can get used to the rain."

"Where is the Lee mission from here?"

"To the northwest, just over the hills."

She searched for some sign of the mission but nothing was visible behind the barrier of ragged tree-covered hills.

"We'd better start back," Ross said, and Marlette reluctantly followed him down the hill.

When they reached the riverbank, Marlette was disheveled and her clothes were stained and sweaty from the long hike. Ross lifted her into the canoe and pushed off.

"Just look at me! I really need that bath now and I'm starved."

He grinned at her. "We'll have to catch some lunch first."

He paddled the canoe toward the bay and tested the water with his hand on the way. The water was perceptibly warmer in the protected, shallow little inlet. He beached the canoe and gathered drift on the way through the brush to their camp. Soon he had a roaring fire going and went off to the river to fish for their lunch, while Marlette sat in the sun by the fire.

He kept only the smaller fish which would cook quickly and they ate hungrily.

Ross finished the last morsel and asked, "Are you ready for that bath?"

She grimaced. "As ready as I'll ever be."

He started pulling off his clothes and left her to undress by herself. He padded barefoot through the trees and plunged into the cool water. When he turned toward the shore she was standing there in her chemise and pantalets, holding her clothes and the soap she had made before they left the cabin. She waded in gingerly and withdrew her foot quickly from the chilly water. He laughed and showered her with a wave of water.

"Ross!" she shrieked, shivering as the cold water hit her.

He started to splash her again but she stepped forward and kicked a spray of drops over him with her foot. Laughing and playful he lunged out of the water toward her. She turned to run but was soon forced onto the gravel bank to elude him and it slowed her down considerably. He could have caught her easily but he enjoyed her teasing flight and didn't stop her as she limped along on tender feet.

Finally, her feet too sore to run farther, she turned to face him, mock dismay on her face. He picked her up and she screamed in protest, struggling as he carried her into the water. He dropped her into the water and she came up choking and thrashing. He helped her stand and felt the gooseflesh that roughened her chilled arms. "Now off with the clothes."

He reached to help her but she backed away, covering her breasts protectively. Her eyes, however, sparkled teasingly as she gasped, "Sir! I am a lady. And ladies do not undress before men who aren't their husbands."

He stepped toward her, his smile fading as his eyes grew serious. He placed his hands gently on her arms and she shivered. "Maybe by your customs we are not married, but when you gave yourself to me you became my wife for as long as I live and nothing can change that."

She looked at him lovingly and went into his arms. He felt the chill firmness of her breasts against his body as he kissed her wet, yielding lips. His heart almost suffocated with emotion. He picked her up and carried her dripping through the brush to their bed.

He could have stayed there with her until dark, but he knew it would take time for her clothes to dry and it was getting cooler by the minute. Reluctantly he pulled her to her feet. "Come on. The water won't get much warmer."

Then she remembered she had dropped her soap and gasped, "Oh, my soap!"

He laughed as she ran naked to the bank looking for her precious soap. She found the soap where she had dropped it and knelt at the edge of the water, scrubbing her clothes. He brought her underclothes and kneeled down to help her.

She worked earnestly for a few minutes, then looked at him with a self-conscious half-smile. "Look at me! I think you've made a wanton woman out of me."

He did not laugh but looked at her seriously instead. "You were already a woman, I just helped set you free."

She laughed shortly, "Free to do what? Run around naked?"

"No. I want you to be free from shame."

She looked at him for a long moment, the embarrassment leaving her face. She said no more and went back to her scrubbing. He rinsed the clothes and hung them over the willow brush that grew weed-like around the bay.

She gritted her teeth and stepped into the water to bathe herself. When she was through, he picked up her shivering body and carried her to the fire, wrapping her in a warm blanket.

After a dinner of freshwater clams they went for a walk along the broad gravel shore of the island.

When they returned, they went to bed and lay quietly in the flickering firelight, listening to the music of the night. Marlette's eyes were closed and her even, quiet breathing told him she had drifted off to sleep. He closed his own eyes, but they wouldn't stay closed. He wanted to watch her for as long as possible, trying to fill his mind with an indelible picture of her. The voice of a heron shattered the night and startled Marlette from sleep.

He smiled reassuringly at her and whispered, "Go back to sleep," letting her sleep on even though he wanted her again. He knew it might well be their last night alone. Tomorrow they would be camping among the settlers, and in order to remain completely alert he would have to refrain from anything that could catch him off guard.

Ross woke before dawn the next morning and got up to rekindle the fire. When he returned to bed he found Marlette awake and smiling at him. She moved against him and shivered at the coolness of his body.

"Is it time to get up?"

"Do you want to?"

The velvet huskiness of his voice sobered her and she whispered, "No."

His arms went around her and pulled her close.

The sun was slanting through the tall cottonwoods before they finally dressed. They ate a meager breakfast, loaded the canoe silently, and glided away from their secluded island. He paddled slowly, letting the river carry them at its own speed.

Near noon they passed out of the low hills and Ross saw a curl of smoke rising in the distance.

Marlette saw it too and asked, "Is that smoke from the Lee mission?"

"Yes."

"Will we have time to stop?"

He had been reluctant to worry her before, but now he knew he had to tell her about the possible dangers. "I don't think it's wise to stop here. The fewer people who know you are here, the better."

Her face clouded. "Am I still in danger?"

"Possibly. I don't want to take any chances."

She was obviously disappointed. He didn't like to hurt her but she would have to understand. He touched her arm with a gesture of regret and she nodded in understanding.

Several hundred yards downriver they paddled by the mouth of the stream where the mission was located. A half-dozen Indians stood with fishing spears watching for salmon heading upstream to spawn. They were dressed in a combination of white and Indian clothing and they stopped their fishing to stare at the passing canoe. One of the Indians called out over the water and Ross raised his hand in salute. He said nothing, however, and a concerned frown settled over his face as his body assumed an attitude of wariness. Their carefree days were over and he knew he would have to remain on his guard for the remainder of the trip.

Mid-afternoon they passed the abandoned cabin of the first Lee mission. Grave markers barely visible through the tangle of vines were a grim reminder of the heartbreak that went into conquering the wilderness. Marlette stared at the site until it was hidden by trees.

Several miles later they rounded a bend and met an oncoming canoe. Two young French-Indian boys paddled toward them. Ross hoped they wouldn't know him, but as they neared he was sure he recognized a resemblance in one of the boys to a Frenchman he knew well. The boys called out a greeting and Ross answered. They let their canoe drift backward with Ross as they eagerly asked where he had come from and where he was going. He forced a friendly smile but didn't encourage too much conversation, and they soon said goodbye and paddled upriver.

Every now and then they saw the unfamiliar sight of cows, horses, or goats grazing along the river's banks, an additional reminder that they were nearing civilization.

Ross stopped early at a fairly secluded spot on the river. Had he been by himself he would have spent the night at one of the Frenchmen's cabins, but he didn't know how much or how little they might know about Marlette.

He pulled the canoe into the brush to hide it from the river and he didn't build a fire. They ate a supper of cold jerky and hard biscuits. Marlette was silent but he knew she was dismayed at his complete change of attitude. She sat staring unhappily into the darkening thicket around them. He came and sat down in front of her, taking her folded hands in his. She met his eyes and he told her earnestly, "Marlette, I'm sorry things have to be this way. From now on I want you to remember one thing—I love you. Everything I do is for your safety, no matter what happens."

She gave him an uncertain smile and nodded her head. He stood up and she followed him to their bed. He crawled in fully clothed and she followed suit, turning away from him under the blankets. He knew she was still feeling rejected and put his hand on her shoulder. She turned to him and he held her close.

After a while she whispered in his ear, "Ross, I'm sorry for acting so childishly. It's just that what we've had has been so beautiful, I don't want it to end."

"It doesn't have to. We can be married in Champoeg by your custom."

"You know I have to leave."

"Yes. But it may be a week, or more, before a ship comes in. We could be together until then."

"Oh, Ross, I do want you for whatever time there is left, but after I leave, what then?"

"You're my wife. I'll wait for you."

"But what if I don't or can't come back?"

"Then I'll come after you."

Her arms tightened about him. "Yes, I believe you would."

She was silent for a long time, then raised her face to his whispering huskily, "Until we wed." Her lips melted warmly under his in a long kiss.

She broke the embrace and quickly turned away from him, moving to her edge of the blankets. He smiled at her in the darkness and closed his eyes.

Champoeg—2 May 1843

THEY REACHED Champoeg by mid-morning. The riverbank of the settlement was not as Ross remembered it. The flood had devastated the old landing and the large Hudson Bay warehouse was gone completely. Some of the landing had been replaced and Ross turned the canoe in among several boats already lining the muddy bank next to it.

As they landed, Ross heard a group of loud voices raised in argument. He helped Marlette from the canoe and picked up his rifle. They crossed the muddy lower bank on a plank walk, climbing the newly built steps that rose to the top bank.

In a grassy clearing in front of a small new building, a group of more than a hundred men stood. Ross recognized at least half of the men as Frenchmen who had settled in the valley, former employees of the Hudson Bay Company. The rest of the men were American trappers and settlers who had come to the valley with the White immigration.

Ross also recognized Dr. Ira Babcock from Lee's mission, standing on the porch in front of the assembled group. Three men sat in chairs next to Babcock, appearing to take notes. One of the men was William Gray, formerly with the Whitmans and now with Lee's mission. The second man, who also worked with Lee, was George LeBreton.

Babcock was shouting over the murmuring crowd. "Gentlemen, I'm unable to decide. Those favoring the motion will please say aye, those opposed, no."

A chorus of ayes and noes rang out. Ross thought it sounded like a draw and Babcock apparently felt the same way because he shook his head indecisively. LeBreton pushed his glasses up on his nose and stood up. Babcock recognized him and the diminutive LeBreton suggested, "I move we have the men divide. Those in favor of forming a local government to the right. Those opposed to the left."

Gray seconded the motion quickly and the crowd shouted its approval.

A tall man with unruly black hair whom Ross recognized as Joe Meek, pushed his way to the front of the crowd and shouted, "Who's for a divide? All for the report of the committee follow me!"

A near riot followed as men struggled and cursed to divide to the right or left. After almost a half-hour of wrangling the lines were finally formed, except for two men who stood between the jeering, threatening lines. The look on their faces fully conveyed their dismay. It was like being condemned to death and having to choose between the rope or the firing squad.

At last both men stepped to the right and Babcock quickly appointed counters. At the final tally there were fifty-two for the government and fifty against.

Joe Meek shouted, "Three cheers for our side!"

A thunderous yell arose and the losing faction, predominantly French, withdrew a little way down the hill and hung together in murmuring groups. Before the cheering was over, Joe Meek noticed Ross on the bank and came striding toward him.

"Chesnut!" He hugged Ross happily. "Where've you been? We thought you were dead!" Without waiting for an answer he turned to Marlette. "Are you Miss Brightwood?"

Marlette nodded, a little overwhelmed by the giant, black-bearded man. By this time the crowd had encircled them and Babcock came to the front.

"I don't believe it!" He shook Ross's hand. "We were told you were all dead. Are the rest coming?"

"No. The rest of them are dead."

Babcock took Marlette's hand, "For a moment I had hoped—. Thank God at least *you* are safe. But forgive me, I'm Ira Babcock and this is Joe Meek. Are you going to stay, or are you on your way to Vancouver?"

Ross answered, "We thought we might spend the night here."

"Good! Good!" he beamed. "We've just held a meeting and voted to form a governing body. Tell me Miss Brightwood, are you planning on staying in this country or are you going back east?"

"I'm hoping to sail on the first available ship."

Babcock's smile broadened. "Splendid! May we ask a favor of you? Would you deliver our petition to the Congress of the United States informing them that we have voted to form a government in expectation of gaining United States territorial status and protection?"

Ross noticed Marlette's back straighten rigidly as determination filled her. Duty called her again. In a strong voice she answered, "I'd be honored to help you in any way I can."

Babcock turned to the crowd behind them. "You hear that, men? Miss Brightwood will carry our petition to Washington."

A cheer rose from the men on the winning side, while the disgruntled French-Canadians edged closer to hear what was going on.

"But come. You must be tired. Let's get inside and sit down. We want to hear what happened to you."

Babcock took Marlette's arm and led her toward the building. A large group of men crowded in behind them to hear the firsthand report of the massacre.

"Can you tell us, Chesnut, who was behind this attack on you?"

"Tom Hill. He contacted us after we left Whitman's. He offered us safe passage down the Columbia in trade for our horses and guns."

Babcock's face clouded and there were angry murmurs from the men listening. "That scoundrel! I would make it the Army's first duty to hang that troublemaker. You refused his offer of course?"

"Yes. The next morning we were attacked. There were between forty and fifty of them. If it hadn't been for Brightwood's repeating rifles we all would have been dead, but the Indians didn't stand a chance. We kept ahead of them the rest of the day but they caught up with us during the night and set fire to the plain. Two days later near the Deschutes canyon we ran into a large Indian camp and headed south. They ambushed us in a draw leading to the Deschutes the next day. Some of the others had dismounted to get water and check packs. Miss Brightwood and I were nearest the river and hadn't dismounted when Holliway rode over the ridge behind us with the warning. They must have been waiting for us—hidden in the canyons. Whether it was luck or Hill's good guess that put them there, I don't know. Miss Brightwood and I were able to make it up the hill before

they had time to encircle us. We escaped and crossed the river later
that day. It rained that evening and I felt we were safe, but I was
wrong. They found us the morning after we crossed the summit. I
knew the leader and because of our past friendship he gave us our
lives, but he took our horses and guns. The next day we made it to
Broulette's cabin."

There was a long, grim silence as Ross finished the story of their
tragic experience.

Babcock spoke first in a quiet, almost stunned voice. "What a
terrifying experience for you, Miss Brightwood. I can hardly believe
you could survive such an ordeal."

"Believe me, every word is true and perhaps understated. If I
survived it was only because of Mr. Chesnut."

Babcock slammed his fist against the desk. "Every man here
should know now that he has done the right thing in voting to organ-
ize a government to protect ourselves from such attacks. Hill must
be mad to risk such a senseless killing for guns and horses."

Ross spoke up, "I think there is more to it than just the guns. The
Indians are upset about the immigration, and the French-Canadians
don't want to see this territory in the hands of the United States. A
clever man like Tom Hill could use these things to stir up a full-scale
war, especially if it was to his advantage."

There was a murmur of assent from the standing men.

"Miss Brightwood, we understand your mission was to determine
whether mass immigration to the west was advisable. Had your father
drawn any conclusions?"

"On the basis of our knowledge at that point, I feel he would have
advised against it. However, after seeing this valley, I don't know if
he would've changed his mind."

"What is your opinion, Miss Brightwood?"

"Please understand, I am speaking strictly from a woman's view-
point. The valley is as beautiful as Jason Lee described it, but I will
discourage anyone, especially families, from making the trip. However, I will contact Mr. Thompson's associates who have a great deal
of influence in Washington, and I will do all I can to help you."

The men smiled approvingly as Babcock said, "Good! Now you
must be hungry. I suggest we adjourn for lunch and meet back here
in one hour to draft the petition to Washington." He turned to one

of the men in the room. "Ezra Tucker, can you take these people to your place for lunch?"

A slender, bearded man stepped forward, dressed in the homespun attire of a farmer. "Certainly, Judge. I'd be happy to."

Ross took Marlette's arm and they walked through the crowd. There were murmurs of admiration and sincere handshakes as they passed. Ross felt Marlette's grip tighten on his arm and she smiled proudly at him. They were trying to make him a hero but there were seven men who would violently disagree, if they could.

They walked down the road toward Ezra's cabin.

Halfway up the slope Ezra stopped, a worried look on his face. "Could I ask a favor of you folks?"

Marlette quickly answered, "Of course."

"I'd appreciate it if you'd say nothing about your trouble with the Indians. We lost our oldest boy on the way out in an Indian raid and my wife hasn't got over it yet."

Marlette nodded. "I well know how she feels."

Ezra smiled more broadly. "Thank you, ma'am."

They continued up the hill toward the cabin. Ezra opened the door to the one-room home. A thin woman with stringy, gray hair was bent over a very small iron cookstove. Its very presence was a monument to the Tuckers' hardiness and determination.

"Emma, I brought some folks for dinner. This is Miss Brightwood and Mr. Chesnut. Can you throw another potato in the pot?"

The woman turned, self-consciously pushing her wayward hair back into place. She frowned as she faced them. "Ezra Tucker, how many times have I asked you to let me know before you bring company?"

"I'm sorry, Emma, but I didn't know until just a few minutes ago myself."

This seemed to rectify the issue and she smiled a little. "Well, never mind. We got plenty. You folks make yourselves at home. Ezra, call Bessie in to set the table. This stew'll be ready in a few minutes." Ezra went out the back door of the cabin while his wife appraised them carefully. "You folks from around here?"

Ross answered, "No. We just came downriver this morning."

"Well, you don't look like them missionary folks from Jason Lee's."

Marlette smiled and answered, "We're not. We spent the winter in the mountains."

The woman looked thoughtful. "Brightwood you say?" She repeated the name to herself several times, then a strange look appeared on her tired, lined face. "I recollect a stir this winter about some folks named Brightwood. Said they'd been killed east of the mountains."

Marlette glanced at Ross, a pained expression in her eyes, but she answered quietly, "Yes. That was my father."

Without another word the woman turned back to her stove. The back door opened and a teen-aged girl entered. Her dress was patched and her feet were bare.

Ezra followed the girl in and introduced them. "Bessie this is Miss Brightwood and Mr. Chesnut." The girl curtsied politely. "You get the table set for your maw."

Ezra glanced at his wife and sized up the situation instantly. "You folks can wash out back, if you like."

Marlette smiled and she and Ross walked toward the door. Outside, two younger children were stacking wood under a wide roof that extended from the cabin. They paused to stare at the strangers curiously. Marlette stepped off the porch and motioned Ross out of the children's earshot.

"Do you think we ought to stay? That poor woman is so distraught."

"It's too late to leave now, but maybe your strength will help her."

Marlette looked away and nodded her head slowly, then asked, "Is there someone here who can marry us?"

"I'll have Tucker ask Babcock, that is if you're still sure you want to?"

She smiled and there was a seductive huskiness in her voice as she said, "Yes." She looked longingly at him and he would have taken her in his arms right there but she turned abruptly and walked back to the porch.

They washed and Ross knocked lightly on the door before he opened it. Ezra had his arm around Emma. She dabbed at her tearing eyes and turned away to stir the pot of stew.

Apologetically Ezra said, "You folks sit down. I think everything's ready. Bessie you call in Nathaniel and Clara."

As the younger children entered Ezra introduced them, "Clara and Nathaniel, this is Miss Brightwood and Mr. Chesnut."

The children bowed respectfully and took chairs as far away from them as possible. Emma lifted the steaming pot from the stove and carried it to the table. She sat down and bowed her head, the children following suit. Ezra Tucker stood at the head of the table, clasped his hands, and gave thanks quietly. He filled the plates—one ladle for each child, three ladles for his guests, and two for his wife and himself.

It was a meager stew of potatoes, barley, beans, and salted venison in a thin gravy; silent declaration of the hardships faced by settlers who arrived with no food and no means to grow any during the long winter. But the mere fact that they had the ingredients for a stew was an indication that they were better off than most. It took money to buy potatoes, barley, and beans. McLoughlin didn't give credit, at least not easily.

After lunch, Ezra declared, "Well, I got to get back to the meetin'."

Ross and Marlette rose with him and Emma, who had remained silent, suddenly pleaded, "Please, don't go, Miss Brightwood. I'd like so much for you to stay and visit, if you can?"

Marlette looked questioningly at Ross and he nodded his consent. They had nothing else to do.

Marlette smiled, "I'd be glad to stay, if you really want us to."

The smile that brightened Emma's weary face was answer enough. Ezra smiled gratefully. "I'll be back at dark for supper."

Ross followed him to the door and asked, "Would you tell Dr. Babcock I'd like to talk to him when he has time?"

Ezra nodded. "Sure."

The children's eyes all turned to Ross after their father left. With a smile he asked, "Nathaniel, how about me helping you with that woodpile?"

The boy looked uncertainly at his mother. Emma said, "Mr. Chesnut, you don't have to do that. You're our guest."

Ross smiled at her. "But I want to. I need something to do while you visit."

"All right. Nathaniel, you help Mr. Chesnut good. Bessie and Clara, you get at the dishes while Miss Brightwood and I get acquainted."

Ross set to work and the boy watched, gazing with unconcealed

admiration at Ross's muscular body and apparent strength. They
worked in silence for quite some time until the boy lost some of his
shyness and began questioning Ross.

"Is that a real Indian hatchet, Mr. Chesnut?"

"Yes."

"I'd sure like to learn how to throw one." He looked at Ross
hopefully. "Do you think you could teach me?"

"Yes. But I think you'd better ask your mother first."

"She wouldn't let me. But she wouldn't have to know. We could
go into the woods."

"I'd like to teach you but I can't leave Miss Brightwood alone."

"Why not? She's safe here, ain't she?"

Ross placed an understanding hand on the boy's shoulder. "I'm
going to tell you something, Nathaniel, but this has got to be a secret
just between you and me. Understand?"

The boy nodded his head and crossed his heart solemnly.

"Do you know what your father and the rest of the men were
doing here today?"

"I think so. They want to have a sheriff and judge so they can
take care of legal things like when Mr. Young died without anyone
to leave his farm to, and protect us from the wolves and the Indians."

Ross smiled. "That's pretty close. They are organizing a govern-
ment for just that purpose, but it would be a United States govern-
ment. The Frenchmen living here are loyal to the Hudson Bay
Company and England and they are afraid the United States will take
their land away so they don't want the United States to take over.
Miss Brightwood knows people in the East who could possibly get
United States soldiers to protect this new government and fight the
Indians or anyone else opposing them. Someone might want to stop
Miss Brightwood from getting that help."

The boy's eyes grew round at the idea of danger and intrigue.
"Golly!" he said.

"But I'll tell you what I'll do. When I get Miss Brightwood safely
on a boat back to the United States, I plan to come back here and
take up some land. I'll need help to build a cabin and if your father
would agree, I'd like you to come work for me."

The boy's face shone with enthusiasm. "Would you really?"

Ross repeated the sign the boy had made earlier. "Cross my heart."

"That'd be swell, Mr. Chesnut." The boy stuck out his hand to seal the agreement and Ross felt a strange twinge in his heart as he looked into the earnest blue eyes. His own son would've been about this age.

They went back to the cabin and found the two women chatting contentedly. Mrs. Tucker stood up, realizing for the first time that it was getting dark.

"My goodness!" she exclaimed, "How time has flown. I'd better get some supper. Will you stay?"

Marlette glanced at Ross, "We don't want to impose on you."

Emma waved away Marlette's answer. "Ezra brung home a nice venison the other day. And I got plenty of potatoes. I'd be much pleased if you'd let me fix supper for you."

Ross answered, "All right."

Emma smiled happily and asked, "Do you have a place to spend the night?"

Ross answered quickly, "Yes."

She didn't insist and turned to her supper preparations. Marlette went to help and Ross leaned back contentedly, happy for the excuse to watch Marlette.

Ezra came in when supper was ready. They sat down and Nathaniel dashed to the chair next to Ross.

Ezra commented, "Looks like the boy has taken a shine to you."

Nathaniel spoke up with boyish enthusiasm, "Paw, Mr. Chesnut says he's going to come back as soon as Miss Brightwood leaves and he says he'd like me to work for him building a cabin. Can I, Paw?"

Ezra laughed. "Hold it now, Nathaniel. Are you sure you're not jumping to conclusions?"

"No, he isn't. I did ask him, with your permission."

"Well, we'll have to see about that. We've got a lot of clearing and planting to do. It depends on how fast we can get things done." The boy's face fell and Ezra added, "But we could use the money if Mr. Chesnut can pay you and maybe your maw and the girls can help with the planting."

Nathaniel straightened in his chair and gazed adoringly at Ross.

Ross asked, "Did you get to tell Babcock I wanted to see him?"

"I told him, but they're still figurin' out things. It'll be awhile 'fore they're done."

As soon as the meal was over Ross and Marlette thanked the Tuckers and prepared to leave. The Tuckers followed them out onto the dark porch, where Emma Tucker gave Marlette a quick hug.

"Thank you for visitin' with me. You'll never know how much it brightened my day."

"I enjoyed it, too."

"God bless and keep you."

Marlette patted Emma's hand and murmured, "You, too."

She took Ross's arm and they started down the dark road toward a light that shone dimly through the trees a few hundred yards away.

When they were out of earshot Marlette said, "That poor woman. She is so homesick. How terrible it must be for her here."

"Do you expect him to take her home?"

"No. I realize he can't do that. But if they'd only stayed where they were I'm sure they couldn't have been worse off."

"Is that how you'll feel when you get home?"

"I don't know. I only know that right now you're everything."

He took her in his arms and kissed her. There was a movement behind him and instinctively he tried to push Marlette out of the way, but before he could turn around he saw a figure grab her and close a hand over her mouth, and almost instantaneously something hard crashed against his skull. He reeled sideways, caught his balance and came lunging back, his head bursting with pain. Dimly he saw a figure ahead of him and felt someone else grab him from the side. He twisted and dropped to the ground, dragging his assailant with him. Blows were rained viciously on his sides and back as he struggled.

Something flashed above him and he rolled away instinctively, feeling a strange warmth engulf his left shoulder. He heaved with all his strength to the side and broke free, only to feel another jarring explosion shatter his brain. He felt himself slipping into unconsciousness and he fought desperately to keep his senses alert, but darkness engulfed him and he slumped to the ground.

It seemed like hours before he drifted back to consciousness, and he lay very still, trying to ease the unbearable pain in his head. He tried to remember where he was, and in a flash of lucidity he thought of Marlette. He had to find her. As he struggled to get up, a searing jolt of pain shot through his left shoulder. Carefully he touched the area with his right fingers and felt the warm stickiness of blood.

He took a deep breath and discovered a whole series of aches along his ribs. His stomach suddenly churned and he groaned at each painful convulsion as it emptied violently. At last the retching stopped and he lay still, waiting for the waves of pain to subside.

He listened intently through the dull hammering of his head and thought he heard the rush of water nearby. He knew he had to get to that water. The coldness would ease the pain and stop the bleeding from his shoulder.

He carefully gathered his legs and arms under him and crawled slowly and painfully toward the water. He was closer than he had realized and he soon slid down the bank of mud to the river. He lay in the water, letting the chill numb his pain. His knife was still strapped to his leg and tortuously he began to hack off a shirt sleeve for a bandage. A cold sweat mingled with the cold water and ran down his face as he worked. He pulled the sleeve free and draped it over his shoulder, then fumbled for his belt managing to cinch it tightly around the sleeve. He lay back in the water exhausted by his efforts, and tried to decide what to do next.

Steeling himself against the pain by self-hypnosis, he got to his feet and staggered from tree to tree toward the landing. Reaching the landing, he stared intently at the moonlit water. He saw nothing and he slowly realized what that meant. His attackers had shoved all the boats into the current.

He leaned against a tree, trying to sort out his confused thoughts. There had been another canoe, but where? He tried to focus on the events of the day and it suddenly came to him. The canoe had been upriver just above this landing. He pushed away from the tree, and half-running and half-crawling, he stumbled along the riverbank.

He fell over the canoe and collapsed, his head pounding from the effort. He rolled into the water, feeling the merciful relief of the numbing cold. His fumbling fingers felt for and found the paddle and he slid the canoe into the water. He fell in, whispering Marlette's name over and over to blot out the pain. As he paddled by the well-lit Hudson Bay building he wished he had a gun to fire to summon help. He could only hope they would be able to figure out what had happened when they discovered the boats and two people missing.

Every stroke of the paddle was agonizingly painful. Long years of discipline over mind and body was all that kept him going. Mile after mile he paddled, the sweat from his pain-wracked body bathing him in clammy wetness. He rounded a bend and saw a darker shape ahead moving over the black water. Then the shape disappeared around a bend and he forced himself to paddle faster.

He became aware of a disturbing noise and realized it was his own labored breathing. He knew they would also hear it when he got close enough to them. He couldn't take the chance of alerting them to his presence until he was close enough to save Marlette. She would undoubtedly be bound and gagged and if the canoe overturned she would drown immediately. He pulled out the only weapon he had left, his knife, and placed it in his mouth. He would have to keep his mouth closed to hold it.

He drove himself on, the pounding of his labored heart exceeded only by the pounding of his head. Dizziness swept over him in waves and he continued to splash water over his face.

He was gaining on them rapidly. He held the knife a moment and breathed deeply to ease his tortured lungs. He replaced the knife and paddled on. The prow of his canoe was overtaking theirs when the back man turned and saw him. He reached for his knife and threw it with all his strength into the man's back. The man let out a startled cry as he pitched forward. Ross grabbed the canoe as the other man whirled around and reached for his hatchet. Ross had only the paddle left and he hurled it like a spear at the Frenchman. His own canoe rocked crazily and he caught a glimpse of a dark bundle with silver hair in the other canoe. The man reeled backward, letting the hatchet fly toward Ross. Ross ducked and fell across the other canoe as the Frenchman pitched into the water. He grabbed at the only part of Marlette he could see as they both plunged into the water with the overturned canoe.

Her bound body was like a rock pulling him down, but the cold water revived his reeling senses and he stroked frantically for the surface. He broke water gasping painfully. Shifting Marlette so he could hold her under the chin with his left arm he swam toward the canoe drifting a few yards away.

He reached the canoe and grabbed onto the cross-brace for support, but was blacking out again and had to duck his head under the water, realizing with horror that he could have drowned Marlette. Terror-stricken that he had held her under too long already, he let go of the canoe for a brief moment and hoisted her higher in his arms, grabbing the canoe before it floated out of reach. He locked his legs around her and pulled the gag from her mouth. She coughed and gasped. Blackness was closing over him again and he gasped, "Marlette!" His voice sounded harsh from pain. "Try to hook your arms over my shoulder as I go under."

He sank gratefully into coldness again, his brain clearing momentarily. He helped her work her tied hands over his shoulder and rose for air, bringing her high out of the water.

"Oh, Ross!" she cried. "Are you all right?"

He didn't answer and sank under the water again as he felt consciousness slipping away. He ran his hands down her legs and felt the rawhide that bound them. He fumbled at the knot knowing she had to be free to kick against the current if they were going to make it to shore. He finally worked the knot free and eased Marlette back into the water, pulling the rawhide from her wrists.

"Grab the canoe and kick for shore," he ordered.

Together they kicked and Ross felt the current resisting them as they made painfully slow headway. He swam with his head underwater now except when he needed to breathe. Each time he raised his head from the water he groaned uncontrollably from the pain.

When he felt his knees banging the bottom, relief surged through him. With one final effort he shoved the canoe out of the water and collapsed beside it, no longer able to fight off the enveloping blackness. The last thing he heard was Marlette calling to him, but he couldn't answer.

Willamette Falls

IT WAS DAYS later before he began drifting in and out of consciousness. Whenever he became aware of light, it was a whirling, illusive sensation that he couldn't sustain. The black shroud of unconsciousness terrified him, but the more he fought against it, the faster it returned.

Finally, after what seemed like weeks of struggling to remain conscious to his confused mind, but was actually only a day, the whirling kaleidoscope of light stopped and he opened his eyes to see the beams and boards of a ceiling above him. His first thought was of Marlette, and he wondered hazily where she was. He tried to get up and groaned as pain shot through every inch of his body, and left him bathed in a cold sweat.

A door opened and he tried to look in the direction of the sound only to find that too brought pain. He strained to see the upper half of the door as it swung open and Marlette came into his range of vision. Joy burst in his heart at the sight of her. He tried to call to her and found he could only utter a hoarse, unintelligible whisper. She heard it however, and hurried to him, tears of relief rolling down her cheeks as she knelt beside the bed and gripped his right hand.

He became acutely aware of a gnawing void in his midsection. He was starving and had to tell her so. He moved his hand and she looked up, wiping the tears of happiness from her face. It took all his strength just to utter the words, "I'm hungry."

She stood up. "I've got some broth made, it'll only take a little while to warm."

She hurried away and he heard lids banging on the stove as she started a fire. She went to the door and called, "Jacques! Jacques! He's awake."

Jacques burst into the room and strode eagerly to the bed, gazing down at Ross with a wide smile.

"Mon Dieu! It good to see you, my friend."

"Jacques, prop him up. I'm going to feed him."

The big Frenchman gently burrowed his arms under Ross, cradling him as he would a delicate baby. Even then it was painful and Ross grimaced. Jacques shook his head in dismay, "Still the pain, cher ami?"

Marlette stuffed pillows behind his back, and as soon as the broth was warmed held a spoon to his lips. Ross opened his mouth to find that the simple act of swallowing caused pain. He closed his eyes against the twinges and just opened his mouth for each spoonful. He wanted to watch Marlette, but he found it too painful to keep his eyes and mouth open simultaneously. He took one last look at her before he felt himself going under again.

In the middle of the night he awoke with hunger gnawing at him. Listening intently, he heard Jacques's heavy breathing punctuated by an occasional snort. He wondered if Marlette was there too. He wanted her. He tried to look around for her, but the effort brought a sharp pain to his head and he could only whisper her name. There was a rustle of covers and the soft pad of feet on the floor as Marlette rushed to him.

Jacques heard the noise and was at Marlette's side immediately, whispering, "What is wrong?"

"Ross is awake."

Jacques lit the lamp and the room was filled with a soft light. Ross was able to whisper, "I'm hungry."

Jacques laughed. "So! Like a baby he wakes up at night to be fed."

He felt a little stronger this time and could keep his eyes open as she fed him. She sat only an inch or two from his right hand and he wanted to hold her. He moved his hand slowly until he could feel the warmth of her leg through the gown she wore.

When he had all he could hold of the broth, he closed his eyes and mouth. He felt the muscles in her leg tighten as she prepared to stand and he clutched at her gown. She smiled knowingly and sat down again, setting the bowl on the floor. She took his hand and he smiled weakly. He longed to hold her in his arms, but he knew that was impossible. His lips formed the words, "Hold me."

Her face glowed in the lamplight as she carefully leaned over him until he could feel her against him. He slept peacefully.

He was awakened the next morning as Marlette and Jacques moved about the cabin. Turning his head a little, expecting pain, he was relieved to feel only a sharp twinge. He felt he had gained a victory. He was hungry again and the smell of their breakfast delighted him. Marlette noticed that he was awake and came immediately to his side, bending to kiss his forehead. He smiled and tried to raise his good arm to encircle her but the effort was still beyond him.

Jacques grinned knowingly behind her. "See. Only half-alive and still he thinks only of love."

Marlette smiled, her face flushing a little. Ross thought she looked beautiful. She quipped, "It isn't me, Jacques, it's my soup."

Weakly Ross asked, "How about some bacon and eggs?"

The two looked at each other and Jacques asked, "What you think?"

"I don't think it's a good idea just yet. I'll ask the doctor when he comes and maybe tonight he can eat something solid."

Ross frowned, but knew she was probably right. He was beginning to realize what Marlette and Jacques must have had to do for him while he was unconscious. He felt even more depressed when he realized what they would still have to do for him if he couldn't get on his feet soon.

He ate all the broth and felt better. "Next batch put a little barley in it."

"Oui, and you want a half a chicken in it, too, perhaps?"

Ross smiled.

There was a knock at the door and Jacques let in a stocky, bearded man, carrying a black bag. He marched confidently to the bedside and peered at Ross intently, his alert grey eyes missing nothing of his patient's condition.

"I'm Doctor Riley. Glad to see you're better. Now let's take a look at that shoulder."

With great curiosity, Ross watched him remove the bandages. He had not been able to remember much about that night, except the excruciating pain. The doctor rinsed his fingers in alcohol and very gently felt along the wound for signs of infection.

"I'd like to see it."

Marlette brought a small mirror and the doctor held it at the proper angle. What Ross saw made his stomach turn. The wound was ugly and must have been a lot uglier. It was still swollen and angry. It had been so bad they'd had to sew the wound closed, the white knots showing up like seeds in the strawberry flesh.

The doctor pulled the covers away to examine his ribs and he realized he was naked, although no one else seemed to be aware of it. The doctor gently prodded his ribs and Ross flinched.

"Sore, eh?" He held up the mirror and Ross saw massive areas of discolored skin along both sides of his rib cage just beginning to turn a stagnant yellow green.

"How many broken?" he asked hoarsely.

"My guess is that at least half of them are cracked, anyway."

Ross's face, already pale from weakness, paled even more. But the worst part was yet to come as the doctor covered him up and moved closer to his head.

"Does your head ache?"

"Ache isn't the word."

The doctor smiled grimly. "Can you turn it?"

"A little."

"Well, let's see how far."

Ross tried to move his head but the pain was intense. He kept trying until a sweat broke out on his face.

The doctor laid a hand on him. "Don't force it. Jacques, Miss Brightwood, come lift him up."

They raised him to a sitting position and although they did all the work, Ross was wet with sweat. The doctor held his head until they got him steadied, then Marlette took his head in a routine which was apparently familiar to them. Marlette kneeled on the bed beside him and leaned his forehead against her. He would have enjoyed the feel of her if he hadn't been almost blacking out. The doctor's exploring fingers brought waves of pain through his head, but the pain was endurable. He took it as a sign of healing.

Before they laid him down, Marlette brought a towel and dried him. The doctor took a small vial out of his bag and handed it to her. "This is for pain. A drop or two in some water will ease him." She nodded. "How is his head?"

"Better I think." Then he turned to Ross. "You are one lucky man. I've buried people in better shape. Besides cracked ribs, you've got a dented skull. I want you to be as careful as you can be about moving. Absolutely no getting up until I say you're ready. If it hurts, don't do it." He turned back to Marlette. "Is he eating?"

"Yes, and he said he wanted bacon and eggs this morning."

The doctor chuckled. "Did you give it to him?"

"No. I thought it might be a little too soon."

The doctor nodded. "Yes, but if he wants solids, start with mashed potatoes, gravy, and the like. Until he's able to be on his feet, it'll be easier on both of you if you keep his food soft."

Marlette nodded.

"Well then, 'til next time, good day."

Ross closed his eyes. Escape into sleep was a welcome relief from the ordeal he had just endured.

He awoke again at suppertime. Marlette was busy at the stove and whatever she was preparing smelled delicious. Jacques was sitting at the table and holding a pot, mashing its contents. He saw Ross was awake and said, "Ross, you crazy not to keep this woman. She cook," he kissed the tips of his fingers in an eloquent gesture, "magnifique!"

"I was working on it."

Jacques grinned from ear to ear. "I know. She tell me." From the look on his face, Ross knew he understood more than he had been told. Jacques got up and carried the pot to Marlette and she poured spoonfuls of thick gravy over the mashed potatoes. Jacques propped him up and began the slow procedure of feeding him. He hated to be so helpless. He tried lifting his arm to see if he might be able to help himself but he was still too weak. He must have lost a lot of blood to be so weak.

The potatoes were a flavorful panacea to his starving body. He smiled his approval and Marlette asked, "Would you like some pudding?"

"Yes."

She returned with the pudding and it was so good he ate it all. He felt comfortably full at last and contentedly watched Marlette and

Jacques, falling asleep before they had finished their dinner.

He awoke in the morning feeling stronger. He tried raising his hand to his face and found the pain diminished, although he was still very weak. He was finally able to feel the growth of hair on his face and guessed he'd probably had it no less than a week.

Jacques obligingly shaved him several times in the next few days until Ross was strong enough to do it himself. As he grew stronger he grew increasingly restless, impatient for the day when he would no longer be so helpless.

The doctor visited and listened to his plea for meat. He was finally able to raise himself on his elbows without pain and feed himself. But each accomplishment only made him more stoical. He could tolerate almost anything outside of himself, but he found he could not tolerate his own human frailty. He hated to put Marlette and Jacques through the ordeal of caring for him, even though they willingly would have done more.

He was afraid his angry impatience would turn on them, so he became increasingly silent. Although at first he had longed for Marlette, he now kept her away. The sickly sweat of his body was distasteful to him and he didn't want her, above all, to have to be close to him. Those first conscious days she had lovingly washed him daily. Now he wouldn't let her.

One evening Jacques announced he was going hunting the next day since their meat supply was almost gone. Ross didn't object although the thought of being alone with Marlette disturbed him.

Jacques, sensing his distress, placed an understanding hand on Ross's shoulder. "I will be back as soon as I can. You be a good patient and do not suffer for your pride's sake, mon ami."

He awoke when Jacques did and watched him leave. He lay in bed quietly, listening to Marlette's soft steady breathing as she slept. For the first time he found himself wondering if he would ever regain all he had lost. Would he always have headaches whenever he exerted himself? Questions and doubts obsessed him until he swore softly, angry with himself at his indulgence in self-pity. He was unable, however, to completely erase the doubts.

Marlette awoke, and seeing his eyes open, she came over to his bed. He let her come, unable to resist his need for her, made more tantalizing by the soft, clinging gown she wore.

"Good morning. How do you feel?"

"Marlette, you know how I feel."

The smile left her face. "Yes. At least I can imagine how you must feel." Her hand tenderly caressed his face. "Don't you know it makes no difference to me. I can never do enough to repay you for my life, even if I didn't care for you."

He eased himself back on his pillow, only half-concealing his frustration. "I feel so helpless."

She picked up his hand and stroked the long, strong fingers. "You're not helpless. The doctor says any other man would have died. You've improved more than he thought possible."

"How long was I unconscious?"

"Eight days."

"What I must have put you through."

She smiled sadly, "Your ordeal was worse than ours. Our suffering was to watch you suffer."

"Did you learn where those men were taking you?"

"No. They didn't say much." She shuddered at the memory. "I never expected to see you again." She raised his hand to her face and pressed her lips against his fingers.

He pulled her to him and kissed her passionately. She cried then, her tears relieving the untold anxiety and terror she had felt.

At last she whispered against his neck, "For me, having you this way is better than not having you at all."

"Foolish woman. I could never let you marry half a man."

She raised her head to look at him, her face calm with inner determination. "But we are married. You promised yourself to me for life. Are you going to break that promise?"

"No. But it was my promise. I will not hold you to it. I will not become another of your duties."

A slow, wise smile spread over her face. "Do you know the only thing that is really wrong with you?"

How well she understood him and how he loved her. He smiled a little shamefacedly, conceding to her.

"Then this whole argument is ridiculous. You don't intend on being anything less than a whole man, do you?"

"No," he answered, still smiling.

She stood up, her gown draping softly over the fullness of her breasts and thighs. "What do you want for breakfast?"

"You." The husky timbre of his voice made it apparent that he was serious.

She blushed beautifully and her own voice softened with delight at the thought. "And you would try it too, wouldn't you?"

"Yes."

She laughed huskily. "Then I will make sure to stay out of your reach."

"What if I come after you?"

"Then we will have to be married."

He grinned happily; it was the first time in days he felt really sure of things.

"I'd better get dressed before I lose my good sense, too." She took a few quick steps to her bed and pulled the curtain between them.

He lay back with a greater determination to be on his feet as soon as possible. If a boat came and she left before they were married he was afraid she would never come back to him. It was a risk either way but if they were bound in a respectable manner, one that was honorable among her people, it would at least serve to remind her of him.

After breakfast she washed the dishes on the makeshift kitchen counter. The cabin was really primitive. Had it not been for the warm spring weather, they would have been less comfortable than in Jacques's mountain cabin.

Ross asked, "How many boats have come to the fort since we've been here?"

"None."

He looked at her seriously and said, "I want you to be on the first one that comes in."

She turned away from her work. "I won't leave until I know you're able to take care of yourself."

"I don't intend for that to be much longer."

"The doctor and I will be the judges of that."

"Marlette, there is no reason for you to stay. It'll only delay your return. I can mend without you but I don't know how long I can be content as a white man without you."

She wiped her hands on a towel and sat in the chair near him. Her face was troubled. "I wanted to talk to you about that. I was going to ask you when we left the Tuckers what you meant by promising the boy a job?"

"I meant to tell you my plans but I had to see how things were in the valley first. If more people come and we both know they will, I think we could build our home here. I could haul freight and raise some horses and cattle to sell to the settlers. Or I could start a sawmill. It all depends on whether you think you could be happy living here with me. Whatever I do, it will be something that will keep me close to you and our children."

She stared down at her clasped hands. It was hard to tell what she was thinking. Finally she said quietly, "You know I can't promise that I can come back."

"Do you want to come back?"

She raised her eyes and they were wet with tears. "Yes," she whispered.

"That's all I need to know."

She came to the bed and kneeled on the floor, taking his hand. "I love you so much."

It was the first time she had said it. He had felt that she loved him but hearing it made his heart overflow with warmth. He squeezed her hand and wanted to do more but he knew it was unwise.

"Do you have a pencil and paper?"

"Yes."

She started to hand it to him but he said, "You hold it. If I'm going to build you a home, I want to build it to please you."

A smile of pleasure lit her face as she said, "But where shall I begin? I've never thought about building a house."

"Why not the kitchen?"

She looked thoughtfully at the blank sheet of paper and nodded her head. After a few moments she said, "My father was very talented at designing things. He drew the plans for our home in Philadelphia. Except for a few minor changes, I think I'd like to have my kitchen exactly like that."

"All right, draw it."

She set to work and Ross immediately saw that she had her father's talent. He watched her work, interrupting her only to make a suggestion or correction. They were delighted to discover that their ideas were similar, and they worked together in perfect harmony.

Ross felt a sense of peace and contentment as never before.

The time flew and they were surprised when they heard the sound of Jacques's feet thumping across the porch. Marlette rose to let him in but Ross caught her hand.

"He can wait a minute."

He encircled her with his arms and hungrily sought her lips as he pulled her tighter to him. Despite the twinges of pain the embrace felt good.

Jacques pounded at the door again and Ross reluctantly let her go. She unbolted the door and Jacques stepped in, his eyes quickly catching the pretty flush of Marlette's face and the change in Ross's attitude.

"So! I cannot trust you to behave for even a little while?" His black-bearded face split in a broad grin.

Ross grinned back. "What would you do if you had a woman locked up with you for nearly a day?"

Jacques laughed. "Why I make love to her. But you, my friend!" He looked from one to the other increduously and chuckled knowingly. "But you would try, no?"

Marlette blushed and Jacques grinned approvingly. "Whatever you do, it was good for the cross bear."

Ross changed the subject. "Did you bring us anything to eat?"

"Oui. Jacques bring you nice buck."

While Marlette and Jacques worked together to get their supper, Jacques told them of his hunt. After supper Ross relaxed and fell asleep quickly with a newfound peace of mind.

He slept later than usual in the morning. Marlette and Jacques were dressed before he heard them. He was uncomfortably aware of the growing staleness of his body and the bed he lay in. After breakfast he decided that he must have a bath.

Marlette, as if reading his mind, asked, "Won't you let Jacques wash you today?"

"I won't settle for anything less than a bath. Out of this bed, in a tub."

Jacques threw up his hands. "Why not?"

Marlette frowned thoughtfully for a moment. "Well, I do think the bed needs to be changed. Are you sure you can do it, Ross?"

"I won't know until I try."

Jacques went out and soon returned with a borrowed wash tub. They filled the tub with warmed water and Marlette went outside while Jacques helped Ross get out of bed.

Ross would never have believed he could be so weak. The simple task of getting his legs over the edge of the bed and standing on the floor made his heart pound and his head throb. He rested for a minute and then Jacques gently eased him into the tub. The water felt wonderful and more than made up for his earlier pain.

Marlette came in and changed the bed while he soaked. She looked worriedly at him and shook her head before she left the room.

He was trembling with weakness by the time he finished bathing and he gratefully let Jacques carry him back to bed. He lay quietly, trying to fight off the throbbing pain in his head and the shaking of his body.

Marlette came in and rushed to his side. "Do you want some of the drug the doctor left?"

"No" he whispered, not even opening his eyes. She didn't say anything but he could feel her disapproval. He forced a weak smile. "It's weakness more than pain."

She laid her hand on his briefly and then he heard her walk away. He finally dozed, blocking out everything but the throb in his head.

The doctor came the next day and examined him. "Have you tried getting up?"

"Yesterday," Ross answered.

"How'd you make out?"

"I'm a lot weaker than I thought."

The doctor's round face broke into a knowing smile. "But there was no pain in the ribs or at the point of fracture in your skull?"

"No pain to speak of in the ribs. My head throbbed, but it was a different pain from the one I've had."

The doctor nodded. "Well, I think it is safe for you to sit with your feet on the floor for a little while each day, if you don't overdo it or have pain. I'll be back in a few days to see how you're doing." He closed his bag with a snap and walked quickly from the cabin.

Jacques closed the door and turned to grin broadly at Ross. "I feel like one released from the jail."

Ross smiled with relief. "Me too, my friend. Where are my clothes? I want to eat at the table with you tonight."

Marlette brought his buckskin pants but the shirt she handed him was not his.

"What is this?" he asked, holding the gray green cotton shirt.

"I couldn't mend your other shirt, so I bought some material and made you one."

He smiled at her, running his hand over the smooth, lightweight material. "I've never had anything but buckskin." He held it up and slipped his arm into the sleeve and Marlette helped pull the other sleeve on, smoothing her handiwork across his shoulders.

"Does it feel all right?"

He stretched his arms and hunched his shoulders. It felt different but it didn't bind. "It's fine. What happened to my medicine bag?"

Marlette handed him the medallion and medicine bag and he tucked them under his shirt out of sight. "Now you'd better let Jacques help me."

Jacques laughed. "You were not so modest when you were unconscious."

"It's not modesty. It's necessity. You're stronger than she is."

Chuckling, Jacques bent to slip the leather pants over Ross's legs and helped him stand. The same dull throb hammered around his brain and sweat broke out on his temples. He gripped Jacques's shoulder and walked unsteadily the few feet to the table. It was a relief to sit down and he grinned weakly, wiping the perspiration from his face with the hankerchief Marlette handed him.

The throbbing eased a little as his heart slowed to a more normal beat. He looked at his two companions, their faces sober with concern.

"I'm all right. Get on with supper. I don't know how long I can sit here."

They both smiled but Marlette cautioned, "Remember, the doctor said not to overdo."

During the next few days he had to remind himself of that continuously. He was battling time and the insufferable weakness of his body. His contempt for his frail body only made him the more determined to conquer the throbbing, shaking, and sweating that overwhelmed him.

More than once in the days that followed he cursed himself in silent frustration. Then one day he walked across the room and noticed that he wasn't sweating and that even the throbbing in his head was barely noticeable. Jacques and Marlette, who stood by ready to pick up the pieces if he should fall, looked at his happy grin with wonder.

"Is something wrong?" Marlette asked anxiously as she moved hesitantly toward him.

"No," he breathed happily. She was very close to him and he took her in his arms and kissed her joyfully.

She blushed, exclaiming, "Ross! What is it?"

He held her and looked into her puzzled face while Jacques smiled in understanding. "I think I'm going to make it now. You'd better get the minister."

Her arms tightened around him and the happiness in her face was all the encouragement he needed to kiss her again. He heard Jacques clear his throat noisily and he let Marlette go. The strength he had felt was already beginning to fade.

"You want Jacques to go fishing?"

Marlette blushed again and Ross laughed, but not so exuberantly now. "No, Jacques. I'll have to rest before I can even kiss her again."

Jacques slapped his knee and laughed until the tears came. "Ah, mon ami! Maybe on your wedding night Jacques better stay close so he can help, oui?"

Marlette whirled around, her face reddening as she exclaimed, "Jacques!" He had gone beyond her sense of what was proper.

Jacques immediately sobered. "Pardon, mademoiselle. Jacques did not mean to offend you," he stammered helplessly while Marlette glared at him. He turned pleading eyes on Ross.

Ross chuckled and she turned a withering gaze on him. He sat down and rested for a moment before he spoke in Jacques's defense, "Marlette, you know we are uncivilized backwoodsmen. We're not used to having a lady in our company. Will you forgive us?" He couldn't help the twinkle in his dark eyes and she was well aware of it.

She gazed reproachfully at them. "You two are uncouth." She paused, the anger melting into mirth, "And I shouldn't allow myself to laugh at your crude, embarrassing humor, but I can't help but forgive you."

Jacques sighed with relief. "Jacques try not to forget you are a lady again."

Marlette smiled at him and walked toward Ross. "And you!" she reprimanded, "If you wouldn't take such liberties with me in his presence he wouldn't think so bad of me."

Jacques came around the table and stood behind Ross. "Mademoiselle, I do not think bad of you. This thing between us is no more than a jest. I have all winter told him if he did not claim you, I would, but I always know you belong to him, first in your heart and now your—."

Ross threw up his hand to stop Jacques but it was too late. Marlette's face turned white and her eyes turned from Jacques to Ross accusingly.

"You told him?"

Before Ross could answer, Jacques came to his defense. "He would not tell such a thing. But you, mademoiselle, have told me."

"But how?"

"In your eyes, in your voice, the way you touch him, care for him. Only a woman who has found something beautiful with the man she loves speaks of it without words."

Marlette turned away and went to stand near the stove. Ross wanted to go to her, but Jacques went instead.

"Mademoiselle, if I have brought you shame for knowing this, I am truly sorry. I would not want to destroy the love you have. If you say the word, I will go and you never see Jacques's ugly face again."

There was a long silence while Marlette kept her back to them. Jacques stood quietly like a man waiting to be sentenced.

When she finally turned to face Jacques she was calm. "Jacques, I can't blame you for my indiscretion. I don't want you to go. Ross will need someone to look after him when I leave." She paused and a slight smile touched her lips. "Only please don't see so much."

Jacques gave a wicked grin. "But, mademoiselle," he protested, "what a Frenchman does not see he feels, and whenever I stand between you two, it is like standing in the path of lightning."

Marlette laughed in surrender. "You two! Can I have no respect from either of you?" She turned to Ross, "Don't you have anything to say?"

"What can I say? He speaks the truth."

She threw up her hands, shaking her head as her cheeks reddened. "You're both incorrigible." She turned away and made a great clatter of getting their supper.

After they ate, Ross went to bed. It felt good to lie down and he closed his eyes. Jacques sat for a few minutes and seeing that neither of his companions was in the mood for conversation, he rose and stretched noisily.

"Well, I think it is a good evening to catch some fish. I'll be back by dark."

After Jacques left, Marlette remained silent and busied herself with dishes. Ross knew she was still thinking about what had been said earlier.

"Marlette," he opened his eyes and smiled tiredly at her, "come here."

She came reluctantly, her face troubled.

"Sit down." She settled herself beside him and he took her hand. "Does it bother you that Jacques knows?"

"Yes. I felt no guilt, no shame in loving you. In fact I would do it again. And I guess this is what really bothers me. All my life I have been led to believe what I've done was wrong. But I don't see how anything so wonderful could be wrong."

He smiled in understanding. "What we have is good. But it is not always so. That is especially true with your people. For some reason, white men desire to destroy what is good, often not even realizing what they do."

She lay down beside him and placed her head on his shoulder. "If it is wrong to want you, then I hope I never know what is right."

He kissed her forehead, desire filling him. "I think you'd better arrange for our marriage soon."

"How soon?"

He grinned, "Do you think you can wait until the day after tomorrow?"

"Are you sure you'll be strong enough by then?"

"How much strength will it take to stand here for a few minutes?"

She sat up, looking troubled again. "Ross, I know this is asking a lot, but I would like to be married in the church."

"All right."

A hopeful smile brightened her face. "You wouldn't mind?"

He smiled back and ran his fingers along the soft smoothness of her arm. "No. I've had the wedding I wanted. Now you can have whatever you want."

She bent to kiss him, her eyes shining brightly.

The next day Ross walked outside the cabin for the first time. Being able to see the sky, trees, and river and breath the fresh spring air seemed to double his strength. Marlette was gone most of the time, coming back to the cabin only to fix their meals. She said little but she glowed with such happiness, the Ross knew she was planning her wedding on a larger scale than he would feel comfortable with, but he said nothing. Jacques, too, seemed secretive and he wondered what the fun-loving Frenchman might be planning.

Two days wasn't long to wait and Ross awoke somewhat apprehensively on his wedding day. Marlette made breakfast for him and prepared to leave.

"I won't be back for lunch. Will you be at the church by two?"

He nodded.

She bent to kiss him and he pulled her down on his lap. She struggled a little as he kissed her too long and too well.

"Ross! Please! I've got such a lot to do."

Jacques came in with a bucket of water and grinned. "Already it begins, my friend. Already she has to much to do to make a little love."

Reluctantly, Ross released her. He wanted to share her joy and she had been so busy that he was beginning to feel left out.

She must have seen the hurt in his eyes and turned to Jacques, pleading, "Jacques, tell him. Surely you should know it is bad luck to see a bride on her wedding day before the wedding?"

Jacques shrugged his shoulders. "I'm afraid she is right."

She hurried off with a happy smile and left the two men alone. Ross said thoughtfully, "You know, Jacques, I'm beginning to understand how you civilized people feel. I think the Indian way of marriage is much better."

Jacques laughed. "You are right, my friend. That's why Jacques never marry. But of course a French wedding is even more difficult than the one you will have."

"I think she is worth it, otherwise I wouldn't do it."

Jacques nodded. "She is even worth a Catholic wedding, mon ami."

A few minutes before two o'clock, Jacques and Ross entered the side door of the small white church which overlooked the river. To Ross's surprise the church was filled with people. He even recognized the Tuckers as Nathaniel waved to him from the center of the crowd.

He stopped just inside the door and whispered to Jacques, "Did you know about this?"

Jacques nodded, grinning broadly, and led Ross past the curious onlookers toward the first bench in front of the pulpit. He needed the rest after the unaccustomed exercise, but found himself tightening up in a way he had never before experienced. Jacques gripped his arm reassuringly.

Opposite them, facing the congregation, a woman sat behind a small organ. She began to play while Ross tried unsuccessfully to relax. The side door opened and a black-robed minister appeared.

He walked directly toward Ross and smiled patronizingly. "Mr. Chesnut? I need your signature, or your *X,* on this paper. It will legalize your marriage."

Ross took the paper, commenting, "I can read and write." He glanced at the paper, found its contents satisfactory, and signed the document. He smiled faintly as he returned it to the minister, feeling that the most important paper of his life had just been signed.

The minister smiled benevolently at him and said, "If you'll come stand beside me now, gentlemen, we'll get on with the wedding."

Ross walked toward the pulpit and turned to face the congregation at the minister's direction. The organ music built up to a crescendo and all eyes turned expectantly toward the rear.

The doors suddenly swung open and Marlette appeared in a pale blue and white gingham gown, carrying a bouquet of white flowers. She looked so beautiful that Ross's heart thumped painfully at the sight of her. She walked slowly toward him, her full skirt swaying to the rhythm of the music, and there was a strange, tremulous smile on her otherwise serene face. A rush of emotion overwhelmed him when she looked into his eyes with love and joy, and he stared at her raptly, oblivious to the minister's words, until Jacques nudged him.

The minister repeated the question and Marlette's lips formed the words, "I do," as she nodded slightly at him. He heard his own voice, husky with emotion, repeat the words after her.

He realized then that he had better pay attention to the minister and the vows were repeated without falter until the minister asked for the ring. He suddenly realized with alarm that he had forgotten about a ring. Marlette was whispering something, when he remembered that he had a ring he could use.

Quickly he spoke up. "Wait. I have a ring." He pulled his medicine bag from under his shirt and untied the leather string fastening its top. His finger caught a metal object inside and withdrew it. The minister nodded in approval and said, "Take her left hand and repeat these words after me as you put the ring on her third finger."

He looked at Marlette's radiant face as he took her hand and slid the golden circlet over her finger repeating the minister's words, "With this ring I thee wed."

The minister smiled triumphantly and said, "I now pronounce you man and wife."

The organ resumed joyfully and Ross knew it was over but he wasn't sure what to do next. He looked at Marlette in bewilderment and she slipped her hand over his, leading him gently down the aisle. He walked between the smiling, curious faces feeling both relieved and tired.

Jacques followed them to the porch of their cabin to say good-bye. "Well, my friend, I will leave you now. I go to Vancouver but I will be back in a day or two."

Marlette took the big Frenchman's hand. "Thank you, Jacques, for everything."

He nodded, smiling broadly and winked at Ross. "Don't overdo, mon cher."

"Don't worry about me." Ross grinned back.

Jacques patted him on the shoulder and strode down the path. Marlette entered the cabin and Ross followed, closing the door and leaning against it tiredly. Marlette stood expectantly with her back to him but when he didn't come to her she turned around. Her face immediately filled with concern.

"Oh, Ross, forgive me. You must be tired."

She came to his side, ready to help him. He smiled at her weakly and walked to the bed relieved to lie down at last.

Smiling up at Marlette, he took her hand and said, "Sit down."

She sat, the new material of the dress rustling softly. The gold ring on her finger gleamed and she raised their locked hands to see it better. He didn't have to look at it to see the delicate carving of entwined orange blossoms, hearts, and hands.

"Was it your mother's?"

"Yes."

She released his hand and slipped the ring to the end of her finger. She saw the engraving on the inside and asked, "And her name was Abigail?"

"Yes." He raised his hand to her hair and stroked its pale sleekness. A ghost of a smile touched her wide mouth and her lips parted slightly as she turned toward him. He felt the violent wrenching of his heart as desire filled him and he pulled her close in a prolonged embrace.

A sudden pounding on the door startled them both. Instantly he was her protector again and all passion was swept away in his instinctive reaction to keep her safe. He jumped to his feet, his exhaustion gone, and he grabbed his rifle resting against the wall.

Someone pounded again and a voice yelled, "The boat from the fort's come."

Marlette answered immediately, "I'll be there as soon as I can."

A knowing chuckle came from the other side of the door, "It'll be about twenty minutes before they leave, ma'am."

The footsteps receded from the door and Ross let the rifle slide back to the floor. She put her arms around him, hiding her tear-filled eyes against his shoulder. He held her for several minutes, attempting to conceal his growing frustration. Finally he raised her head and looked searchingly at her sorrowful face. "Marlette, it's time to go."

"Yes," she breathed, controlling her tears.

He kissed her lightly and dropped his hands. Her magnificent jaw squared as she wiped the tears from her cheeks and turned to gather up the few things she had to take.

"I have to stop by the minister's to get my other clothes."

"You'd better take one of these blankets."

She nodded and folded a blanket into her bag. She turned to him and smiled wistfully. "I guess this is good-bye."

"Not yet. I'm going with you."

Her lips parted in protest, but she apparently thought better of it and said nothing although she looked concerned. He gathered up the gun and powder horn and started for the door. As he swung it open, Jacques came thundering up the path. He took one leap onto the porch and stopped, breathing heavily.

"I pass the bateau on the way downriver. I paddle like hell to get back."

Ross leaned against the door with a welcome smile. He knew he was hardly up to taking her, no matter how much he wanted to be with her. Marlette came through the door, a look of relief on her face.

"You are ready, mademoiselle?" He grinned, and corrected, "Madame?"

Marlette nodded hesitantly, glancing at Ross. Jacques caught the look.

"You have not said adieu yet? You have a little time. But hurry, eh?"

Ross held out his hand and drew Marlette back into the cabin, closing the door. She came into his arms, holding him so tightly he could feel the pounding of her heart.

He whispered against her hair, "My heart will be without joy until you return."

She raised her head to see his face and her eyes were filled with tears. "Oh, Ross, my darling."

He kissed her then, with a fierceness that made her gasp for breath. He released her and she took a backward step, her breast rising sharply as she breathed deeply after his crushing embrace. He remained motionless and the tenderness in his eyes was slowly replaced by the usual impenetrable expression he presented to the world. She reached for the door and opened it.

Jacques turned from his vigil of the river and looked into Ross's grim face. "I guard her with my life, mon ami."

Marlette stepped from the porch and hurried down the path without a backward glance. Jacques shouldered his gun and strode after her.

Ross watched them leave, feeling completely drained of strength. He saw Marlette hurry up the path to the minister's cabin and return shortly dressed in her old clothes. Clusters of people gathered on the landing as the Frenchmen from the fort loaded the boat. Jacques and Marlette were the last to get in and the heavy craft slowly swung from the bank.

Vancouver Revisited

MARLETTE DID NOT LOOK toward the cabin again until the bateau had swung about and started downriver. She saw Ross's figure still in the doorway and she raised her hand in a final gesture of farewell, then brought her hand down quickly, pressing a knuckle against her lips as tears gathered in her eyes. Jacques gripped her arm gently in a gesture of comfort as she watched the cabin doorway until the timbered bank hid the settlement from sight. She felt a great emptiness and gazed blankly at the water with tear-filled eyes as the boat made its way downstream.

Late that afternoon they entered the Columbia and the Frenchmen had to pull mightily to turn the cumbersome boat toward Fort Vancouver. As the sun descended over the distant hills, they neared the north bank of the Columbia and Fort Vancouver.

The bateau bumped against the dock and the Frenchmen shouted exuberantly as they began unloading the boat. Marlette was helped onto the dock by Jacques's strong hand and he led her up the wide road toward the fort. Her heart twisted as she remembered her first walk up this road when she had seen Ross standing with Dr. Barclay's wife in the distance.

McLoughlin was waiting at the gate to greet them, his tall, white-haired figure standing out easily amid the men around him. He strode forward with an outstretched hand and a warm smile as Marlette reached the gate.

"Welcome! Welcome back." He took Marlette's hand and pressed it warmly.

Marlette smiled distantly, feeling momentarily suspended from reality. She had already forced herself into a kind of emotional exile, to spare herself any more pain and to keep her thoughts private. She presented an impassive mask to the world, hiding her inner turmoil.

She was taken to McLoughlin's house where Madame McLoughlin greeted her with words of warm welcome and motherly sympathy. Burris was called and sent to prepare her something to eat. Jacques relinquished her into Dr. McLoughlin's custody and headed eagerly for the bachelors' hall and the visit he had started on earlier.

When Marlette saw the tray of roast beef, fresh bread, milk, and coffee she realized she hadn't eaten since early morning. Dr. McLoughlin waited patiently behind his desk while she ate. As she ate she relaxed, once again in touch with reality and confident she was in control. McLoughlin smiled benevolently and she returned the smile.

"Thank you, Doctor. It's the first time I've eaten since morning."

"You look a little tired, perhaps we should wait and talk tomorrow, after you've rested?"

"No. I'm fine now. I appreciate you sending the money I needed."

"Tut, tut, my dear. After what you've been through, I feel it was the least I could do. How is Chesnut?"

His name brought a painful wrench to her heart and she had to drop her eyes momentarily. "I think he'll be all right now. He's much stronger."

"Good, good. He was pretty bad, I hear."

"I really don't understand why he didn't die, Doctor."

McLoughlin shrugged. "Some of these men have a desire for life far beyond our wildest imagination." He paused and looked at her thoughtfully, trying to measure the depth of her endurance. "I can't tell you how upsetting it was to learn of what happened to your expedition. You were very fortunate to have lived through it. I can't help but feel responsible for that tragedy and I will see to it that those responsible will be brought to justice, especially those involved in your kidnapping at Champoeg. If it isn't asking too much, I'd like you to tell me the whole story?"

Marlette told the story, using the same words Ross had used in telling the men at Champoeg, enlarging upon them only when McLoughlin interrupted and asked for more details. There was a long silence after she finished while McLoughlin thought about what she had told him.

"Then you feel Chesnut did everything possible to avert this tragedy?"

"I'm sure he did. Why?"

"The lives of seven men is the reason. If you have any suspicion of him I would investigate it to the fullest."

Marlette shook her head. The thought of what might happen to Ross if McLoughlin felt he had betrayed them frightened her. "Surely, Doctor, the very fact I'm alive should attest to his innocence?"

"Not necessarily. Your father offered him a great deal of money to make sure he protected you. I wasn't to give him the money unless you were as sure as I was that he was without blame." He rose abruptly. "Now I think it is time we considered this money."

He kneeled before his safe and unlocked it, returning with the bags of silver coins her father had left for their return journey. They counted each bag until only the bag for Ross was left. The doctor dumped it out and, incredibly, it contained twice as much as she remembered they had agreed upon.

"I don't understand. I thought Father was to pay Mr. Chesnut only one thousand dollars. Where did he get this money?" As she asked she counted the bags and found one missing.

"Ah, then, your father never told you? You remember how adamant Chesnut was about not taking you in the first place? Your father had to agree to certain conditions before Chesnut would even consider it. Besides the conditions, your father decided to pay him the extra money to make certain that Chesnut brought you out alive. A sort of double insurance, so to speak."

"But this money was his passage home."

"Oh, well, you see he planned on using the refund on the horses for his passage home."

Marlette looked at the pale, gleaming pile of silver, and a slow, unbelieving sense of shock settled over her. "And what if I hadn't returned?"

"Then this money was to be the reward for Chesnut's life."

Marlette's face grew pale and taut.

"Miss Brightwood, is there anything wrong?"

She closed her eyes, fighting to subdue the confusion she was feeling. "No, no, Doctor. I've just had a long day."

"And I have kept you far too long. Forgive me. What do you want me to do with this money for Chesnut?"

"Give it to him, of course. But I'd like to write a note with it, if I may?"

"Of course." He got paper, pen, and ink for her and stood solicitously by.

"If you don't mind, Doctor, I'd like to be alone for a while?"

"As you wish, my dear. Come into the sitting room when you are finished."

"Thank you."

She sat stiffly, waiting until the door closed and then the tears she had fought off all afternoon came rushing to her eyes in torrents. Doubts and fears suddenly flooded her mind. Had she made a mistake after all? Was it his life and his freedom, freedom he himself had admitted was so dear, that he had been concerned about all the time? And the money? He had denied needing money but now that he and Jacques could no longer make a living in furs, the money, undoubtedly, would make his freedom easier. Certainly the fact that McLoughlin was to decide his fate would make it necessary to have a witness in his favor. Was this, then, the reason he had made love to her, had even gone so far as to marry her? She heard her anguished voice whisper in the quiet room, "It can't be, it can't be!"

She sobbed bitterly until she could cry no more. Then anger replaced doubt and she caught sight of the ring on her finger and yanked it off, violently ramming its golden innocence out of her sight into the bottom of the leather bag. She furiously gathered up the silver, piling it on top of the ring.

After a few minutes of struggle to compose herself, she left the room.

McLoughlin rose as she came into the sitting room. "Miss Brightwood! You've been crying. Is there something wrong?"

"Yes, Doctor. But there is nothing you can do. Things are just catching up with me."

"Then, by all means it's time for you to be in bed. I've had the trunks brought to your room. I assumed you would want to take them with you but we can take care of that in the morning."

"Yes, I'll want to take them and if you'll help me carry in the money bags, I think it best to put each one with its owner's belongings."

"Of course, I'll help, but it can wait until morning."

"I know, but I'll rest better if everything's done now."

He nodded understandingly and led the way back to the office. They packed the money into the trunks and then he left her alone. She went through her own trunk and selected the dress she would wear for her departure. She folded the blue and white gingham dress into the bottom of her trunk as tears destroyed her momentary composure.

When she finally went to bed she could not sleep. Whether her eyes were open or closed she saw Ross's face before her, from the dark chestnut hair to the full mouth that was just short of being sensual. She remembered vividly the stray lock of hair that invariably fell across his forehead, and his unforgettable deep, dark brown eyes that could be piercing or tender, cold or sparkling, depending on his mood. She saw clearly the handsome, nearly perfect nose, the wide strong jaw, and the captivating dimples when he smiled. She turned her face into the pillow in agony.

It was impossible to erase his face or forget the touch of his hand or the feel of his body. Tears of anger, followed by tears of sorrow racked her body until she finally slept from exhaustion in the hour before dawn, only to be awakened by the clanging of the yard bell shortly thereafter. She was reluctant to rise and when she finally did the mirror above the chest showed the ravages of the night.

She endured breakfast and the polite conversation of Madame McLoughlin, excusing herself as soon as possible, and she was ready to leave when Dr. McLoughlin knocked on her door. She preceded him into the dining hall and found Jacques, a little the worse for wear after his night of carousing, and a lanky, weathered man in seaman's clothes.

"Miss Brightwood, this is Captain Weatherbee."

"How do, miss. I understand you need passage on my ship?"

"Yes, Captain. I have the money right here."

He smiled. "Dr. McLoughlin assures me you have more than enough so I'll not worry with it until later. Are you ready?"

"Yes."

"Well, then, let's be going."

She turned to Madame McLoughlin who was standing in the doorway and said, "Good-bye, madame, and thank you for all you've done."

Madame McLoughlin took her outstretched hand and patted it fondly, saying, "Bon voyage."

They followed the servants with her trunks down the steps. When they reached the gate McLoughlin stopped and turned to her.

"I will say good-bye here, my dear. I will pray for your safe journey."

A sudden lump rose in Marlette's throat as she blinked back tears. "Thank you, Doctor. I will never forget your help and your many kindnesses."

In a gentlemanly show of respect, he bent to kiss her gloved fingertips. "God be with you, my child."

Marlette turned away and Jacques fell in beside her. She could think of nothing to say, at least nothing that would not be upsetting to both of them. The captain strode ahead of them and took charge of loading her luggage into the longboat.

She and Jacques stopped at the edge of the wooden moorage and she turned to him, placing her hand on his arm. "Good-bye, Jacques, and thank you." Her voice sounded strange as she tried to quiet her conflicting emotions.

She thought she saw a glimmer of wetness in the emotional Frenchman's eyes as he softly bid her "Au revoir," and raised her hand to his lips.

The Boston captain came toward them. "All set, miss."

Jacques turned to the captain and said with a deadly seriousness she had never before heard in his voice, "Let nothing happen to her, Capitaine."

The keen blue eyes of the captain narrowed as he understood the threat in Jacques' voice and nodded his head curtly. Marlette's heart wrenched as she thought of Ross and wondered, achingly, how he was. The captain helped her into the boat and they were soon being rowed toward the ship. She turned back for one last look and saw Jacques standing quietly on the shore.

The Long Voyage Home

A WOODEN LADDER descended from the side of the ship and, with a little help, Marlette was soon aboard. The captain stood ready to introduce her to the other passengers.

"Miss Brightwood, these are your shipmates, Mrs. Caldwell and Mr. and Mrs. Grant."

Mrs. Caldwell nodded shortly. Marlette knew the woman from Willamette Falls. Hers was a heartbreaking tale. She had been with the White wagon train and had lost her entire family during the long journey west. She had spent the winter working at whatever she could to buy passage home. Her gaunt, bitter face and her thin body clearly marked the depth of her tragedy.

The Grants were more pleasant but their story was equally tragic. They were members of the Lee mission and, like most mission people, they had contracted the intermittent fever. They were emaciated and hollow-eyed from their fight against the fever but the disease had conquered them and they were returning home, unable to be of service to their cause any more.

The captain ordered her trunks placed in her cabin. He turned to the first mate and asked, "Is everything ready to get under way, Hawkins?"

"Yes, sir, Captain."

"Good. Raise anchor and set sail." He turned to Marlette as the first mate shouted out the orders and the ship came alive with action. "I'll show you to your cabin, Miss Brightwood."

Marlette followed him below, absently noting that this ship was larger than the barque they had come to the Oregon Country on. Her cabin was roomier and more comfortable.

"I hope it meets with your approval? Meals are served at seven, twelve, and six. You'll dine with the officers."

"Thank you, Captain. The cabin is fine."

"I understand from Dr. McLoughlin you have had quite an adventure. I'd like to hear the story some time, if you feel like telling it."

"I will gladly tell you, Captain, and anyone who will listen. I will spend the rest of my life telling it and if I can dissuade just one person from making the journey here I will feel all that has happened to me has been worthwhile."

"I take it you don't figure this to be the promised land?"

She smiled bitterly, "It is the promised land, Captain, but the promises it keeps are death, violence, despair, and hardship. The Grants and Mrs. Caldwell are lucky, they're going home. There are many more who can never go home, who are doomed to die in this cruel land."

He looked at her keenly, unsure how to react to her bitter vehemence.

"I must get to my ship. If you need anything, let me know." He retreated quickly.

Marlette closed the door and leaned against it, suddenly very tired. She went to the bunk and in a few minutes she was asleep.

She was awakened later by a loud knock on her door. Groggily she called, "Who is it?"

"Captain sent me to call you for lunch, ma'am."

"Thank you. I'll be there in a minute."

She got up, hurriedly straightened her dress and splashed water into her heavy eyes. As she walked down the passageway she brushed her hair back into the old familiar bun at her neck. She stepped through the doorway into the small dining room and all eyes turned to her as she smiled a little self-consciously and apologized, "I'm sorry I'm late. I fell asleep."

The captain gave a curt nod of forgiveness and passed her the kettle of potato soup as she took her seat on his right. There was little conversation and as soon as the crew was finished, they hurried off to relieve those still on duty.

After lunch, Marlette climbed the steps to the deck and walked toward the aft rail. She leaned against the rail, watching the water and the vast, shadowed forest that loomed along the shore.

The intense emotions of the past twenty-four hours had left her emotionally exhausted and she thought it strange that she felt only a vague sense of relief at being alive and able to escape this wilderness. She knew all too well the only reason she was alive, regardless of his motives, was because of Ross Chesnut. Stranger still, the thought of him didn't fill her with hate or anger, only a faint sense of loss—loss of something so beautiful it now seemed unreal.

Idly she wondered how many days had passed since they had come down that other, wilder river and as she counted she felt a twinge of anxiety. Was it possible she carried his child within her? She closed her eyes, feeling a little faint. How was it possible he could have been so gentle, so considerate if he hadn't cared for her? But she remembered the first impression she had had of him. Had her suspicions been correct after all, that he had a way with women?

All the more tragic was her realization that she would do it again because she still loved him; she even regretted now that she had not surrendered earlier. She wished now she could have talked to him— given him the chance to explain about the money and the conditions for earning it. But it was too late. She looked at the finger that had held his ring. She had felt such overwhelming joy when she walked down the aisle to become his wife. And such angry despair when she thought he had, after all, only needed her to save his own life. But she would never know and maybe it was just as well. It would be less painful for her this way. It had been foolish to think of coming back and now there was no need to. She felt a different sense of relief, the relief of a mind at last restored to peace.

Now she could look at the river mirroring the blue sky, the fluffy white clouds, and the deep green tranquillity of the forest, and find beauty there. And as she watched, the river changed direction and familiar snow-capped mountains disappeared from view. Sadly, she whispered, "Good-bye, my love."

She threw herself determinedly into the rewriting of the lost journals. Oddly, she felt a strange lack of emotion as she wrote about the first days of the expedition with Ross.

A few days later, she had proof that she wasn't carrying his child and she felt strangely sad. Subconsciously she had hoped to have something of him to cherish forever. She knew, however, that it was for the best.

She kept to herself except for meals. She wasn't ready to be questioned and she didn't want Mrs. Caldwell to ask about her marriage. If she happened to be on the deck with the other passengers, she was politely aloof. So far they had respected her privacy.

The days passed and she worked on the journals. She found she had no trouble remembering every detail vividly, although recalling it all only made her more aware of the danger they had been in and their total reliance on Ross. She was thoroughly convinced that without him they would have had no chance at all. He had done everything humanly possible to save them. If he had been any less of a man, she wouldn't have lived to rewrite their story.

She found herself pausing for long minutes to relive little details of their relationship. She was still hurt that he hadn't told her about the money. Surely he couldn't have forgotten about it? She found it hard to believe money was really so unimportant to him. However, she had made up her mind it was over and settled and that she would never go back.

During one such reverie she was interrupted by the captain.

"Haven't seen much of you, Miss Brightwood. Thought maybe you'd like to come on deck for a spell. It's a fine day."

She smiled. "Thank you, Captain. I've been so involved in my work, I haven't been getting enough fresh air."

She pulled her shawl from its hook and followed the captain up the stairs. It was a lovely day. The sea was calm, the sun was warm, and the air was fresh with the tang of salt. She breathed deeply and moved her shoulders to rid them of the hunched feeling.

The captain smiled with pleasure. "Got to get back to my duties, miss. Enjoy the air."

"Thank you, Captain, I will."

She walked toward the afterdeck and noticed the Grants seated against the rail. She paused indecisively for a moment, then straightened her shoulders and cast off her reluctance. Sooner or later she would have to face people again. She walked toward them and noted their pleased surprise at her visit.

"Lovely day. How are you feeling?"

Mrs. Grant smiled warmly. "We are much improved, thank you. We have been wondering if you were ill?"

She smiled at them reassuringly. "I'm quite well, thank you."

Turning away, she leaned over the rail to watch the frothing water as it curled away from the ship. She felt their eyes watching her curiously and was aware of an uncomfortable twinge. Had Mrs. Caldwell told them that she was married? Surprised at her somewhat guilty feeling, she wondered why their knowledge of the marriage should bother her. She had nothing to feel guilty or ashamed about and her affairs were none of their business. She moved away from them to the other side of the ship, but the nagging feeling persisted.

She was beginning to regain her peace of mind when Mrs. Caldwell came up the stairway. Marlette turned to greet her, wanting to be friendly but she found no answering warmth in the cold eyes that met hers. Nonetheless, Marlette gave the older woman a pleasant smile and said, "Good afternoon, Mrs. Caldwell."

Mrs. Caldwell returned the greeting curtly and looked reproachfully at Marlette.

The uncomfortable feeling returned heightened by a strange restlessness and she went down the steps with quick, frustrated strides. She circled the deck of the ship endlessly, resolving to develop strength. She realized how Ross must have felt under her unreasoning dislike. Unlike Ross, she wouldn't wait until Mrs. Caldwell was ready to accept her, she would talk with her at the first possible opportunity.

She returned to her cabin, feeling too disturbed to settle down to work. Her watch told her it was nearly time for supper.

She felt much better when she entered the officers' dining room. The Grants looked up simultaneously as she came in but Mrs. Caldwell gave her no more than a fleeting glance.

The captain seemed to sense a change in her mood for he asked, "How are you coming with your work?"

"Quite well."

"I'd like to read your journals, if you don't mind?"

She smiled. "No, I don't mind. I'm writing them to be read. I hope I can get them published to warn everyone of the dangers of coming to the Oregon Country."

The whole table was watching her now with interest. The Grants nodded mutely, their bodies living sacrifices to the cruelty of the land.

Mrs. Caldwell remained silent.

"Well, there'll be more to join those already there. I heard talk last winter in Boston about starting a wagon train in the spring. They should be well on their way by now."

Marlette noticed Mrs. Caldwell shake her head with dismay at the news. The captain also saw the movement and said, "It looks like you have more than one who'll back up your claim. Only thing is, I doubt you'll change many minds. The only solution is to wipe out the Indians."

Mr. Grant stirred restlessly and his wife looked at the captain with vaguely sad eyes. Neither spoke. Only Mrs. Caldwell glanced approvingly at the captain. Marlette felt she had to say something, regardless of their personal opinions.

"Captain, I know you think I should be the first to agree with you, but somehow I can't be so cold-blooded as to sentence all the Indians to death because of the few who are willing to fight for what they feel is rightfully theirs."

Mrs. Caldwell laid down her fork with a disapproving clank and got up, leaving the cabin without a word as the others watched.

Mr. Grant rose to follow her but Marlette intervened. "Please, let me speak to her. I think I know what is bothering her."

Marlette hurried after the woman and saw her disappear inside her cabin. She knocked on the door.

"Mrs. Caldwell, I'd like to talk with you."

"Got nothin' to say to Indian lovers."

"Please, Mrs. Caldwell, you're wrong about that. Will you give me a chance to talk to you?"

There was a long moment of hostile silence, then the door slowly swung open. "What you got to say?"

"I want to know why you are angry with me? I have suffered at the hands of the Indians as much as you."

"You married one of those heathen savages. I want no truck with the like of you." She started to slam the door.

Marlette quickly wedged her body into the opening. "Mrs. Caldwell, I married a white man whose family was also destroyed by the Indians. It is true he was raised as an Indian, but he is white."

Uncertainty clouded the bitter woman's eyes and for a moment she relaxed the pressure against the door that held Marlette prisoner.

Her eyes hardened again. "Don't explain you bein' on their side."

"Yes, it does. My husband made me realize that Indians feel just as threatened by the white man as we do by them. They're not all to blame. They're victims of our greed just as we are."

The older woman turned away, her shoulders suddenly sagging. "I 'spose you're right." She was silent for a moment, then turned toward Marlette with questioning eyes. "Why'd you leave him? Why ain't you usin' his name?"

Marlette faltered, "I have to take care of my father's business. I'm not sure I will return."

Mrs. Caldwell's shrewd eyes appraised her and a light of understanding began to flicker. "Guess we're all entitled to one mistake."

Marlette smiled uncertainly. "Thank you for hearing me out. Good night."

She walked to her own cabin a few feet away and entered its sanctuary, feeling empty and drained. Sleep was a welcome friend that night.

The weeks passed slowly as the ship made its way toward the southern straits. Her relationship with the others was more amiable but somehow she couldn't find comfort in their friendship and kept to herself more often than not. By the time they reached the southern passage she had finished her journals. The captain read them and received requests from his crew to read them. Even the Grants and Mrs. Caldwell read them and made the appropriate dismayed remarks about the trip.

Her journals became the distraction they needed to endure the long voyage. However, even the brisk discussions about the Indian problem couldn't last forever and only delayed the inevitable return of boredom and restlessness.

With nothing to occupy her mind and hands, Marlette became increasingly aware of her loneliness. She tried to join the other passengers but their company didn't help. She finally had to admit to herself that she wanted Ross, wanted him desperately. At night she would awaken with such a terrible longing for him she would cry. His voice, his face, his touch haunted her dreams. Her appetite waned and so did her desire for companionship with the others.

Home

WHEN THE SHIP finally docked in snowy New York in late December of 1843, Marlette was as thin as she had ever been. Now she was truly alone and for the first time in her life, she knew she needed someone and that someone was a vast continent away. She repressed the feeling, summoning her determination and pride, and fought to erase what she felt was a foolish woman's weakness.

It was already dark when she entered the hotel. The smell of dinner and long-denied foods sharpened her appetite and she looked forward to eating for the first time in months. She took time to change and refresh herself with a warm bath, relishing the thought of fresh meat and vegetables. She ate alone, savoring each bite and her loneliness faded for a short time in the crowded dining room of the hotel.

After dinner she arranged for the trip to Philadelphia and was filled with excitement at the thought of home and familiar surroundings. She went to sleep recalling every detail and knickknack in her home and awoke early the next morning with uncontrolled anxiety and a stack of trunks that dismayed the coachman.

The trip to Philadelphia was long and tiring, taking two days through a cold, snowy countryside. The lights of Philadelphia were a heartwarming sight and some of her exhaustion disappeared. She hired a carriage at the hotel, where the coach stopped, to take her home.

It was quite late when the carriage stopped before her home. One feeble light showed in the otherwise dark and desolate house and she cried uncontrollably as she scrambled from the carriage before the driver could help her. She opened the gate and ran up the slush-covered brick walk to pound on the door. After what seemed like an eternity a light finally appeared and a familiar voice, harsh with irritation, asked, "Who's there? What do you want this time of night?"

Marlette sobbed, "Martha, it's me. It's Marlette."

There was an answering gasp and sob on the other side of the door as it was flung open. The light from the lamp blinded Marlette for a few moments, but as Martha recognized her, the lamp was hastily set on the table and the two weeping women fell into each other's arms.

The cabby interrupted their reunion as he carried up the trunks. Marlette paid him and they were soon settled in the warm kitchen, each trying to ask questions.

Finally, holding on to each other's hands, they sat silently, just looking at each other. Marlette was struck by how much the older woman had aged. Her hair was completely gray and there were dark circles of anxiety under the once fiery eyes. She had lost none of her stoutness and it helped disguise her aging face, keeping it deceptively plump and unlined.

Martha regained her aplomb and asked, "All right now, child, where have you been? Where's Mr. Brightwood? I've been waiting for word so long I figured I'd never hear."

"Martha, they're all dead. I'm the only one to come back."

Martha gasped in dismay. "Oh, no! I was so afraid something had happened—." Tears rolled down her flushed cheeks and she lifted her apron to wipe them away, while Marlette patted her arm comfortingly. "You poor child. What a terrible thing you must have been through. How did it happen?"

Marlette took a long swallow of the hot tea. She settled back and told Martha briefly of their terrifying experience, saying little about Ross. Finally her exhaustion caught up with her and she rose to go to bed. It brought Martha out of her dazed shock and, once more the efficient housekeeper, she soon had Marlette in bed.

The big double bed welcomed her like a long lost friend and she at last felt safe and secure under the feather comforter with a fire crackling pleasantly in the fireplace. As tired as she was she didn't fall asleep immediately. As she snuggled into the familiar coziness of her own bed, she thought of Ross and her hand drowsily sought his warm body between the cool clean sheets. She felt nothing but cold bedding and closed her eyes regretfully.

Martha entered her room the next morning to put more wood on the fire and Marlette was awakened by the noise. She stirred sluggishly, only half-awake and called out dreamily for Ross. She heard footsteps approach as she murmured the name that filled her with joy. She opened her eyes expectantly but her smile faded when she saw Martha standing over her.

"Is there something wrong, child?"

"No. I'm fine. I slept so soundly."

Martha looked relieved. "What would you like for breakfast?"

Marlette brightened at the thought of all the foods she had missed for so long. "Eggs, and fresh bread and the biggest glass of fresh milk and I'm dying for a piece of apple pie."

Martha gave a pleased chuckle. "You get dressed. I'll see what I can find."

Marlette lay quietly for a few minutes after Martha left, letting her eyes roam over the familiar room. How wonderful it was to be home. Only one thing could make her happiness complete and she tried to imagine Ross holding her in his arms here in her own bed. Her heart twisted with the thought and tears welled in her eyes.

She threw aside the covers and got out of bed, forbidding herself to cry. She opened the closet door and the strong smell of moth repellent assailed her as she looked for something to wear. She chose a warm woolen gown with a wide white collar and hung it to air while she washed. She brushed her hair and looked closely at her gaunt face in the mirror. Her mouth was pinched and her cheeks were hollow. She brushed her hair down around her face as Ross had liked it and her features softened. Gazing at herself, she wondered how she could have been naive enough to think any man could desire that reflection in the mirror. She sighed deeply and quickly swept her hair into a bun, scolding herself silently for her indulgence in fantasy.

Martha served her breakfast and sat silently while she ate. Marlette became increasingly aware that Martha was deeply distressed. She finished her meal and quietly asked, "All right, Martha, what is it? You're worried about something."

Martha's thin lips moved nervously and tears sprang to her troubled eyes. "Miss Marlette, I almost wish you hadn't come home, 'cause I don't know how to tell you, but Thomas lost your father's business."

Marlette sat in stunned silence while Martha sobbed bitterly. She finally got up and turned to the fireplace, filled with cold despair as she leaned her forehead against the mantle. When Martha's sobbing stopped she asked calmly, "How did it happen?"

Martha wiped her eyes and nose. "Oh, Miss Marlette, I'm so sorry. So ashamed. I couldn't stop him. He got so high and mighty. He was so proud at first that your father left him in charge of the business. Then it must've started going to his head. He saw his chance to get rich while you were gone. He took on more and more work. The men got tired of working seven days a week and fourteen hours a day and one by one they quit.

"Pretty soon no one would work for him and he had all this lumber and hardware ordered and instead of paying what he owed when he saw things were going bad he took all the money and left." Another dreadful sob escaped her and the tears streamed down her cheeks again.

Marlette put her hand gently on the other woman's shoulder. "Don't cry, Martha. We'll work it out."

She left the room and walked rigidly upstairs to her bedroom. After a long moment of total disbelief that everything she had had was gone, she threw herself on her bed and cried. Not all her tears were for the business. She had been a foolish woman in more ways than one. Finally her crying ceased and she squared her shoulders with determination. She had only herself to rely on now.

She went to the window and looked out across the familiar yard surrounded by the now grayish white picket fence. If she had come home in the daylight she would have seen the house was falling into disrepair. She dropped the curtain and warmed her numbed body by the fire. The first thing she had to do was to find out how bad things were. She went to the closet and got out her warmest cape.

Martha was standing in the kitchen doorway when she came downstairs. "Martha, I'm going to the lawyer's. I'll try to be back by dinner. Is there still a buggy in the stable and a horse to pull it?"

Martha nodded. "I had to take other housekeeping jobs to earn money so I kept the buggy to get around."

Marlette smiled. "Can I drop you off any place?"

Martha answered her smile, a spark of determination returning to her eyes. "I'll be ready in a minute."

Marlette entered the lawyer's office. The balding head was bent over a sheaf of papers as he mumbled a request for patience and Marlette waited patiently until he was finished. When he finally looked up, he jumped out of his chair in startled recognition.

"Marlette Brightwood! Is it really you?"

Marlette smiled and extended her hand as he hurried around the desk to greet her. "How are you, Mr. Finlayson?"

"Fine, fine. But I didn't have hopes of seeing you again. For heaven's sake! Where's Joshua?"

Marlette sobered. "Father and the rest were killed by the Indians in the Oregon Country."

His face went pale with shock. "My God! I'm terribly sorry, Marlette. Your father and I were old friends and I will miss him deeply." He paused and saw the quiet resignation in her eyes. "I guess Martha told you about Tom?"

"Yes. How bad is it, John?"

He held a chair out for her and returned to his desk, sitting down with a sigh. "It's bad. I'm not certain myself how things could've gotten so out of control. I blame myself. Josh told me to let Tom make the decisions. He wanted him to have full control. When I heard he had taken the books back from the accountant I went to talk to him. Everything was, or at least seemed to be, in order so I didn't worry about it.

"A month later Elridge came to me and said Tom wasn't paying the men. I went to see Tom again and you wouldn't believe the amount of material he had on hand. He showed me twice as many orders for wagons than I felt he should have accepted. He seemed honestly concerned about completing his orders and professed bad judgment in taking on so much work under deadlines. He asked me if I would loan the business enough money to pay the men and cover the costs of some of the material until he got his orders out and his money back. Naturally, I agreed.

"The next thing I knew, I had a man here who claimed he had bought the business from Tom. He had a bill of sale and Tom had

his money and the man came to me for the papers. Tom had told him
I'd take care of the whole thing." Finlayson shook his head sorrow-
fully.

Marlette sat silently, momentarily speechless. At last she
breathed, "I'm sorry, John. Perhaps it's better Father isn't here. What
will have to be done to clear up these debts?"

Finlayson's rounded shoulders drooped even more. "I'm afraid
you'll have to sell the house as well as the shop in order to pay the
men their back wages, pay off the supply bills, and return the money
the man from New York is suing for."

"And what about your loan?"

"On the basis of our friendship I can't hold you responsible for
it. It was my mistake for being so gullible."

"I can't ask for any dearer a friend than that, but I intend to pay
you, too, if I possibly can."

"Marlette, you are a courageous woman. How can you be so calm
in the face of such misfortune?"

She smiled, her serious expression relaxing momentarily. "I have
been close to death so many times in the last two years and lost things
that are so much more important than money, that I'm afraid this
seems quite an anticlimax."

He rose and came around the desk, shaking his head in admiration. "Come," he said with a warm smile, "let's get the constable to
open the shop for you."

Going through the gloomy, silent building gave Marlette a
strange, unreal feeling. Her heart ached at the sight of the familiar
tools lying in disarray and covered with dust. John Finlayson held
her arm and swept aside the festooning cobwebs as they walked across
the hard, earthern floor.

They reached the office and John unlocked the door and lit the
lamp. In a few seconds the room came to life and Marlette had to
wipe away tears when she saw her father's desk and the table she had
worked on for so many years keeping the books. They looked through
all the drawers and cubbyholes but found nothing of importance.
Marlette carefully stuffed everything into some empty folders and
with a last sad look, she bid good-bye to all that remained.

Afterward she picked up Martha and they drove home in silence.

Martha cared for the horse while Marlette went into the cold, dark house, quickly lighting the fire to ward off the somber atmosphere and her deep depression.

Martha came in and their gazes met and locked. "How bad is it?"

Marlette sat down heavily before the fire. "It looks like I'll have to sell everything to pay the debts."

Martha hid her face in her hands and Marlette let her cry. She didn't have the strength left to comfort anyone at the moment.

Martha pulled herself together and turned around to face Marlette. "I'm so ashamed. I have prayed and prayed Tom would come to his senses and return. I have nothing to offer you except myself for as long as I can work."

Martha's loyalty brought Marlette out of her daze and she rose silently and encircled Martha's stout body, holding her close. Tears were the only way to express the deep emotions they felt.

At last Marlette said, "I would like you to stay with me, Martha. I won't be able to pay you, but we're not licked yet. I have rewritten all the journals of our trip and I plan to sell them. I can get a job and maybe together we can live comfortably in some small place of our own."

Martha straightened, inspired once more by Marlette's determination. She smiled through her sniffles. "We can do it, Miss Marlette."

Marlette smiled in return. "Yes, we can do it. No more tears, and no more looking back. All right?"

Martha's smile broadened confidently. "All right. Now let's have dinner. You must be starved."

The next couple of weeks were busy for Marlette. The ordeal of settling her father's estate and preparing for the various sales was an exhausting job.

The process of moving was also extremely painful to Marlette. She and Martha rented a small cottage and Marlette found she had to sell many of the furnishings she had. There were difficult decisions, but at last everything was sold and they moved.

Now she had the time to take care of other matters. She still had the trunks and money belonging to the members of the expedition. She wrote letters to the families of the men briefly explaining what had happened and expressing the desire to see them when it was convenient.

She received a reply from Andrew's wife almost immediately, requesting the return of his things. Marlette took them personally since she had known Mrs. Proctor's family for many years. She also knew that any meeting with Mrs. Proctor would be difficult because she felt Andrew Proctor could have been a far better man than his wife had let him be.

She was ushered into the stiff and obviously expensive parlor. Hester Proctor stood waiting, dressed in black, a handkerchief conspicuously dangling from her slender hand. She was a brittle woman, imperious and critical, with a sharp face. The sadness Marlette felt was for Andrew, not for his wife.

"I'm sorry to have to be the one to bring you the bad news."

Hester's face crumpled and she sat down, dabbing at her eyes with the lace-edged handkerchief. "Tell me, how did it happen?"

Marlette repeated the story. Hester listened with widening eyes as Marlette recounted every fearful incident.

When she was finished, Hester stood up and paced the floor. "I just can't believe he'd ever do a thing like that. I never believed he'd go through with it." She paused and her lips curled in a sarcastic smile. "I thoroughly expected him to come home with that whipped-dog look after a couple of weeks at sea."

Marlette wanted to say something in Andrew's defense but knew it was useless. Instead she said, "You'll find the thousand dollars that was to be used for his return passage in his trunk."

Mrs. Proctor's eyes brightened. "Thank you for all your trouble. It must have been very difficult for you, too?"

Marlette nodded stiffly. "Well, I have another appointment, Mrs. Proctor, so I won't keep you."

Hester accompanied Marlette to the door, but there was nothing left to say and Marlette departed with a sense of relief.

A few days later there was a knock at her door and Marlette opened the door to a young man and woman, both short, plump, and fair-skinned. She knew who they were before they said a word.

"Miss Brightwood?"

"Yes. You must be Mr. von Hout's family?"

"Ja. Ve got your letter."

"Come in." She stepped aside and they entered, obviously disturbed and nervous. Marlette closed the door and said, "Please sit down."

"Ve come only for Papa's tings."

Marlette shrugged. She went to her bedroom and opened the door. "His trunk is in here. All his things are there and the thousand dollars for his return passage."

Surprised glances passed between the two. Papa Hout's son hurriedly picked up the trunk and followed his sister to the door. The sister turned in the doorway and said curtly, "Tank you, miss," before following her brother to their wagon.

Marlette closed the door angrily. Not even their father's death had tempered their greed. She didn't know if they felt guilt or not but she hoped, passionately, that they did.

The next day she decided to deliver the trunk she held for the Long family. It had been two weeks since she had notified them and she had heard nothing. Their shop was across town and she went there after delivering Martha to her work. Even in the chilly weather of February the doors of the blacksmith shop were open, the heat from the forge pouring into the street.

A tall, big-boned woman dressed in man's clothes and a leather apron looked up from her work.

"Mrs. Long?"

"Yes, ma'am."

"I'm Miss Brightwood. I wrote you a letter about Mr. Long."

Her bony face stiffened perceptibly and there was a sudden silence as a man hammering on the anvil in the back of the shop stopped. He came forward and Marlette saw he was not much more than a boy. He was tall and rangy like his mother.

"We don't need his things." The boy had his father's surliness.

"Hush, Ethan. Let's hear what she's got to say."

"He said it all, Maw, when he walked out and left us with nothin'."

She looked reproachfully at him and said sharply, "That's enough, Ethan."

The boy muttered an oath and stormed out of the shop. Mrs. Long watched him go sadly and said, "I'm sorry. He can't forgive Evan for leavin' us. I would've answered your letter except the boy would have none of it. His things ain't of any use to us."

"Mrs. Long, there is one thousand dollars in that trunk. I think you can use that."

Her eyes widened in surprise. "How in the world—?"

"It was the money for his return passage."

She nodded and tears sprang into her tired eyes. "Thank you, Miss Brightwood, thank you."

Marlette reached out and placed a sympathetic hand on the woman's muscled forearm. "If you ever want to come and visit me, you're always welcome."

The woman nodded silently and Marlette gave her the trunk.

There was a letter for her from Mr. Ashton in New York, one of Isaac Thompson's associates when she returned home. It was an invitation to visit his office in New York and bring her journals. It came at an opportune time since she had already received answers from Gaylord Taylor's father and Isaac Thompson's wife, both of whom lived in New York. Mr. Taylor had expressed a desire to see her but couldn't get away at the time and Mrs. Thompson was ill and unable to travel.

She decided quickly to make the trip to New York and returned to town to make travel arrangements. This time she decided to go by train. Although it was more expensive, the shorter length of traveling time more than compensated the difference.

Next morning she had Martha take her to the station. It was a day-long trip and she arrived in New York late at night and worn out. Her head ached from the rattle and throb of the train and she rejoiced in the quiet of her hotel room away from the constant chug of the engine. She half-expected the bed to sway when she climbed into it and was relieved when it did not.

Early the next morning she dressed for her visit with Mr. Ashton. When she arrived at the office she was pleasantly greeted and ushered into his private office immediately.

Mr. Ashton rose to welcome her with the vigor of youth, but his black hair had a touch of gray at the temples. He came around the desk with positive strides, and his black eyes appraised her so shrewdly that she grew uncomfortable and defensive.

"Ah, Miss Brightwood, so we meet at last."

His handshake was strong and sincere and his friendly smile put her at ease. She remembered another man who had affected her in this way, only he had been cold and aloof whereas this man was warm and affable.

He held a chair for her. "Please sit down. I have been anxious to hear about the expedition ever since I got your letter. I must say we were all shocked to learn that none of the rest of the party came back. But with your help, maybe we can still learn what we were interested in."

"I have brought the journals and I will tell you everything I can. However, as I pointed out in my letter, I can't afford not to sell these journals if possible."

He smiled genially. "We understand, and if the information you have is useful to us we will make arrangements to have them published at a fair price. Do you understand what we are interested in and for what party?"

"Yes."

He smiled again. "Good. Then in your honest opinion do you think the Oregon Country should be annexed by the United States, regardless of the cost?"

"My honest opinion is, no. But it isn't a question of opinion now. The people already there want and need the protection of the United States. Just before I left, the settlers in the valley voted to set up a provisional government. If people continue to immigrate to Oregon the United States will eventually have to make a decision on the Oregon Country."

His eyes sparkled with enthusiasm. "Yes. That is why we must move decisively in this election year to elect a man who will protect the interests of the Americans already there and those who are on their way. Would you be willing to speak in support of our cause?"

"I can't honestly encourage the settlement of that country. I do not believe it is worth the risks the people or the government will have to take. It is my desire to discourage people from going. I have been there and I have seen the hardships and violence of the land. The country is divided by a range of mountains. Everything to the east, and that is the biggest percentage of the land, is too arid for farming. The relatively small valley where the Lee mission is located is indeed a virtual Eden, but if the settlers don't have enough food to last through the winter, or the tools and seed to plant when the weather permits, then it is not Eden but Hell."

He looked at her thoughtfully. "What about the Indians?"

"Most are hostile."

"Then we would need Army protection?"

"Yes."

"Do you advocate wiping out the Indians in a massive extermination effort?"

Marlette looked distressed. "No. There are some who would probably accept the white man, but there are many who would not. These are the Indians who will make it necessary to provide protection."

He shook his head and laughed shortly. "You speak in contradictions, Miss Brightwood. We must either be for or against the Indians, and for or against the settlement and annexation of Oregon. Which cause will you support?"

"I support the cause of the people, Mr. Ashton. I don't want to be involved in anything where politics are more important than peoples' lives. If you want to use any part of my journal I must stipulate that you use it all. Unless I can have your assurance of that we have nothing further to discuss."

He sobered as she spoke and his eyes appraised her admiringly. "Then your solution would be to bring back all the Americans who are there and refuse to let any more go?"

"Yes."

"You realize how unrealistic that is?"

"Yes."

"Then you must agree that we need a president who essentially shares your views about the people."

"Yes."

"Regardless of the cost?"

Marlette had to smile. "Yes."

"Then you will help us find such a man?"

"Do you have anyone in mind?"

He smiled tentatively. "We are not sure just yet. One thing is sure, it is not Van Buren."

"What about President Tyler? He's in favor of annexing Texas."

"That's true, but he cannot possibly win with either party now. He is a political orphan." He stood up signaling the end of their meeting. "Will you be in New York at least for tomorrow?"

"Yes."

"I would like to have a chance to go through these journals and let my associates see them so that we may formulate some plans. Could you come back to see me tomorrow afternoon? We may possibly have a direction by then."

"Of course."

He showed her to the door and his handshake was warmer than before.

It was afternoon before she reached the Taylor Bank. The coachman followed her inside with Gay's trunk. George Taylor looked up from his desk and rose as she entered his office.

"Miss Brightwood! I didn't expect to see you so soon. Come in and sit down. Is this my son's trunk?"

"Yes." The coachman set it down and George Taylor quickly pulled a silver dollar from his pocket and gave it to the man who smiled broadly.

Gay's father closed the door of his office and sat down. He was a well-built, distinguished man with a full head of hair, although it was steel gray, and a flowing mustache. Marlette wondered if Gay would have looked as well at that age.

"I'm sorry I wasn't able to come immediately to Philadelphia. I hope this didn't cause you any trouble?"

"Not at all. I had to come to New York on other business."

"Good. Now I want to hear how my son died, if you can bear to tell the story one more time?"

Marlette told him and then added something she knew he wanted to hear, although he hadn't asked. "I think you would have been proud of Gay, Mr. Taylor."

The gray eyes sparkled with unshed tears. "Thank you for that. I think you know how much I wanted to hear it, but please don't say it if it isn't true."

"It is true, Mr. Taylor. For a long time I didn't think it would be, but one day Gay shot a rattlesnake that was about to strike me. From that day on he changed. I think he realized life wasn't a game and I think he would have come home and done something useful with his life."

"Then he really straightened himself out?"

"Yes. It was a hard way to grow up, but I think he made it."

There was glow of pride in the man's tears and an even greater sadness. "It doesn't mean much now though, does it?"

Marlette could say nothing.

Finally he sighed, "Well, it does no good to regret it now. Is there something I can do for you?"

"No. Thank you. You'll find the money that was to be used for Gay's passage home in the trunk."

He stood up abruptly. "I'm sorry about your father. He was a good man and a fine craftsman. What will you do with the business now?"

"There is no business. The man we left in charge sold it and left the country."

He frowned in shock. "Were you able to salvage anything?"

"No."

"Why didn't you let me know? Surely I could have done something for you."

She smiled gratefully. "It is all worked out now."

He came to her and took her hand. "You're just as independent as your father. In the future if you need help, I hope you won't forget who your friends are."

"I may have to hold you to that, Mr. Taylor."

He smiled benevolently. "Anytime, my dear."

Marlette rose and he released her hand. "It is getting late and I'm keeping you from your work."

He nodded. "Yes. I suppose there's no point in knowing more?"

She shook her head.

"Thank you for coming. And don't forget me if you need help."

She smiled, nodding gratefully. "Good-bye, Mr. Taylor."

The next day she called on Mrs. Thompson and found the Thompson home a depressing imitation of grandeur. It was a gloomy and had the same sickly pall that Isaac Thompson had had. Marlette was shown into a parlor furnished in lavish bad taste. In a few minutes Mrs. Thompson entered and it was obvious she had been ill. Her clothes hung on her thin, birdlike body and her face was starkly pale.

She extended her hand timidly. "How do you do, Miss Brightwood. Please sit down. I'm sorry I had to put you to this trouble. I'd offer to pay you but—." Her voice trailed off weakly and she looked ready to cry.

"I understand, Mrs. Thompson. I had to come to New York on other business so it was no trouble."

"I just don't know what I'm going to do. We weren't wealthy people and Isaac—Mr. Thompson—left me very little to get by on while he was away on this trip."

Marlette smiled encouragingly. "Well, then, I have some good news for you. There is one thousand dollars in silver in his trunk. It was for his return passage."

The tears so near the surface suddenly spilled over and Marlette waited patiently until the woman was in control again. "Thank you, Miss Brightwood. Would you do me one small favor?"

"If it's possible."

"This may seem like a ridiculous thing to you, but to Mr. Thompson this expedition was his crusade. It would've meant recognition and perhaps position had he been able to further the good of his party and his country." She paused to delicately blow her nose and wipe her eyes.

Marlette nodded. "I understand."

"I hope you do. I'm sure it would please Mr. Thompson to know he would be remembered."

Marlette stood up. "I will do what I can, Mrs. Thompson. Now I think it's best if I leave before you get overtired. Good luck and good-bye."

The woman smiled appreciatively and Marlette hurried from the oppressively ugly house.

That afternoon she was welcomed back into Mr. Ashton's office warmly. "Good afternoon, Miss Brightwood. I'm glad you were able to come back. I have some good news for you. Please, sit down."

Marlette sat down with a faint smile on her lips.

"We have gone over your journals and found them very interesting and informative. We think they should be published. Not only to help the people who are thinking of moving west but to inform the general public. We've got to get some public reaction going to arouse some interest in the coming election. So far, neither Van Buren nor Clay have expressed any sentiments about this annexation thing, either for Texas or Oregon. If we can get the people to take a stand we have a much better chance of showing how little is being done to protect the interests of those Americans already in the territories.

"We are going to run your journals as a daily column in all the partisan newspapers. We will give you an initial payment of two hundred and fifty dollars and if we have estimated the power of this thing correctly, you will no doubt get invitations to speak to people all over the country on this subject. You will in effect be working for the party and we are prepared to pay your expenses and a little extra for each lecture you give supporting our candidate."

"Who is your candidate, Mr. Ashton?"

He smiled broadly. "I'm not at liberty to divulge that information just yet, but you will be the first to hear when we have made our decison."

"May I ask who, exactly, you are working for or with?"

"I am not at liberty to tell you. The man behind this has many enemies and it is best not to let it be known prematurely that we are not behind Van Buren until we have a candidate to give the people."

Marlette nodded. "All right. But you must understand, I will not say or do anything that I think will influence people wrongly."

He smiled benignly. "We only want you to be honest."

"I intend to be nothing less than honest."

"We can ask for nothing more than that. Then we are agreed?"

Marlette stood up. "Yes."

"Good! How do you want your first payment?"

"In silver."

He laughed. "You are a hard woman to do business with. I will have to go to the bank for that. Will you come with me?"

"Of course."

Marlette returned home the next day. She was bubbling with excitement, yet tired from the long train ride and she threw her arms around Martha in relief.

"I take it you had success?" Martha's eyes glowed expectantly.

"Yes. Mr. Thompson's backers want to run the journal in the party newspapers and they paid me and if I get any invitations to talk to people, they will pay me for that, too."

Martha gave her an excited squeeze. "Oh, I am glad! And I have some good news for you, too. Mr. Mabley wants you to work part time as a bookkeeper at his store."

"Oh, Martha," she hugged the older woman in return, "I think things are going to be all right now."

The Gallighers

DURING THE next several weeks, she began to receive letters from groups interested in hearing of her experiences firsthand. Some of these groups included people who were preparing to head west and join the wagon trains to Oregon in the spring. They didn't have time to wait for anything but return mail since they were ready to leave. It was a long trip just to reach the Mississippi River by April. She felt she could do little to help these people. They had undoubtedly sold everything they had and would not be dissuaded at this point.

The actual speaking engagements were more successful, especially if there were women in the audience. She would never know how many she was able to convince, but there was satisfaction in giving them a full and fair warning. Her satisfaction increased as the newspapers began following her speaking trail and Mr. Ashton and his associates had her journals published in book form.

She now felt she had some weight to back up her convictions and decided to approach the Mission Board with her plea to recall the Whitmans. She hoped it wasn't too late. In the days before she had left Oregon she had learned of several disturbing events that occurred after they had left the Whitman mission. The very night they had left someone entered Narcissa's bedroom. She had screamed loudly enough to awaken someone else staying in the house and the intruder had been frightened away. It had upset Narcissa so badly she left the mission the next day for the fort at Wallula. Later she went to another mission located at The Dalles on the Columbia, and spent the winter there, critically ill.

Marlette also learned that Dr. White, leader of the first immigration to the valley, had been appointed by the United States government to manage the Indian affairs in the Oregon Country. At the time of Marlette's kidnapping at Champoeg he had been in the vicinity of the Whitman mission to settle trouble with the Indians there.

Marlette added this news to her own observations—opinions formed from Ross's knowledge—in the letter she wrote to the Mission Board. She could not bring herself to charge that the Whitmans were not suited to the work they had chosen but she did emphasize their lack of progress with the Indians and pleaded for their immediate recall. She mailed the letter along with a copy of her book in which she marked all information that would bear out her fear that the Whitmans were in danger. She hoped it was enough.

As Mr. Ashton predicted, interest in Texas and Oregon was snowballing. Marlette was increasingly aware, after every new speaking engagement, that people were becoming concerned about the delay of their elected legislators to create protection for Americans moving westward. This concern soon crystallized into a clamor for statements by the presidential candidates on the annexation of Texas and Oregon.

In April of 1844, James Knox Polk, in an attempt to become Van Buren's vice-presidential running mate, came out in favor of reannexation of Texas and also advocated the annexation of the Oregon Country. Clay and Van Buren both issued statements opposing the annexation of Texas and Oregon.

Shortly after this Marlette was summoned to New York by Mr. Ashton. When she entered his office she immediately knew he had some news by the suppressed excitement of his manner.

"You have been quite a busy woman. I want to compliment you on the job you are doing but I have much more important news. I can now tell you we have a candidate to back. Have you heard of James Knox Polk?"

Marlette remained expressionless, trying not to show any emotion. "Yes, I have heard of him. He favors annexation."

"That's right. He has been picked by our people to run for the presidency. How do you feel about backing him?"

Marlette frowned. "I'm not sure. Then Jackson is the man behind this?"

"Yes."

She thought for a long moment. Jackson and Polk were men she had often had reservations about. The Whigs had been especially hard on Polk when he was Speaker of the House. His personality had been so maligned that Marlette, knowing a good deal of slander was nothing more than politics, still wondered just how much was true. And ex-president Jackson would never be free of scandal. Yet Van Buren's and Clay's lack of motivation was discouraging.

"Well, Miss Brightwood. Are you still with us?"

"I'm afraid I do not know Mr. Polk well enough to decide whether I can support him or not. If I can continue in the same manner —above party lines—I will. If not—." She shrugged.

"I had hoped you would be a little more enthusiastic, however, if neutrality is what you want, you have it. You have done too much for us to stop you now. I think if you were to meet Mr. Polk you might change your mind."

"That is likely. However, I can't imagine I am that important."

He laughed. "Then you don't know Mr. Polk very well. Entering the race this late as a dark horse, forces him to consider everything important."

"Then perhaps you'd better find out if Mr. Polk approves of me, and not vice versa."

Again he laughed. "That's fair enough. We are having a party tonight to celebrate. Would you care to join us?"

"Thank you, but if I am to remain neutral, I had better not come."

"That is true, but I had hoped we could win your support." He smiled, a little disappointed. "Well, I'm afraid I have another appointment, if you will excuse me."

Marlette stood. "Of course."

He escorted her to the door and she extended her hand. He took it and held it firmly. " 'Til we meet again."

Spring turned into summer and the political fires waged hot. Marlette found it hard to remain neutral as each speaking engagement turned into a near riot.

It was on one such trip into the farming communities of upper New York that she saw a man in the audience who looked strikingly familiar. As she answered questions about Oregon, her eyes were attracted to a middle-aged man who sat silently, watching her intently.

His eyes reminded her of Ross and as she glanced frequently at the man, she became increasingly excited, recognizing other familiar characteristics. His hair was the same dark chestnut color, just beginning to gray, with the same slight wave. And when he turned his head to speak to the man next to him, she saw Ross's own profile.

After the meeting she tried to get to the man but she was cornered by a group of eager men who wanted more information. When she was free at last, the man was gone.

Although it was foolish, Marlette stayed in town the next morning to try and find the man. She even asked to see the town marriage records for the year that had been on Ross's mother's ring. She found nothing. She asked some of the local officials who had been at the meeting, but none of them could identify her man. She hated to give up. Now that a clue to Ross's identity was so close, she realized how much she had been looking for just such a revelation. She knew she should leave on the next stage, but she just couldn't, not until she had exhausted every means of finding that man.

After lunch she decided to visit the town stores. Possibly one of them would recognize the man from her description. She walked to the stores nearest her hotel and found no help. She started down the street to a somewhat run-down store at the edge of town. As she neared the store the man she was looking for came out with a sack of flour over his shoulder and laid it in a wagon already loaded with supplies.

Marlette picked up her skirts and ran toward him. He was climbing into the wagon seat and she had to call, "Please, sir. Wait a moment."

He turned in his seat and looked at her as she came running up beside the wagon. "Are you callin' me, miss?"

"Yes," she panted breathlessly.

"Well now, what is it you'd be wantin' with me?" He eyed her warily, his manner defensive.

She smiled reassuringly. "I wanted to ask you something. I think I may know a relative of yours. Was there anyone in your family named Ross who married a girl named Abigail over thirty years ago?"

His eyes studied her without reflecting any sign of recognition. "All me family which is not in Ireland, is right here." He lifted the reins but Marlette stepped into the street beside the wagon, taking hold of the horse.

"Please. It's very important to me. Is there someone in your family who could tell me?"

"And what makes you think this person is related to me?"

"You have the same hair and eyes and the shape of your head is the same." Marlette glanced over him, looking for something else. Her eyes caught his hands on the reins. They were Ross's hands, big hands with long, strong fingers. She shuddered visibly. "Your hands are like his. Please, won't you tell me?"

"And why should I now? It means nothing to me. All me family is right here."

"I had imagined there might be someone, a mother, father, or brother who might like to know what happened to their kin."

He looked at her thoughtfully for a moment and slowly lowered the reins. "Can you be comin' with me for awhile?"

Marlette smiled with relief and hurried around the wagon. They traveled for several miles in almost unfriendly silence. She understood now why so many of the people here were interested in the Oregon Country. The farms here were run-down and the crops already growing in the lusty spring looked thin and unhealthy.

The depression in the late thirties had hit everyone but it had been hardest on the farmers. Their ground was worn out and few had enough money to buy new land. Many were near starving. It was no wonder they wanted to risk what little they had on a new start in the so-called promised land.

The horses turned into a farmstead that looked just a shade better than the rest. The house was two-storied and at one time had been painted, but the paint was almost gone now. The outbuildings were in good shape and the yard was uncluttered. A woman was hanging clothes on a line at the side of the house and several children played near her. A boy of about sixteen came out of the barn toward them. He, too, looked strikingly familiar.

The man jumped down from the wagon. "You can unload the wagon, Cam, but leave off unhitchin'. We'll be takin' the lady back to town presently."

The boy nodded and looked at her with Ross's eyes. The man came around to help Marlette down and she followed him into the house. He pointed her into a parlor room and she stopped in the doorway while he went down the hall. He returned in a few minutes with an older woman.

"What is it now, Timothy?" She caught sight of Marlette. "Sure now, I've told you not to bring company without warnin' us."

"She's not company, Mother. She's the woman I heard at the meetin' last night. She wants a word with you."

The woman's eyes narrowed suspiciously and she came toward Marlette.

She smiled suddenly, a winning Irish smile. "Well, now, I don't know what you be wantin' with the likes of us, but come in and state your business."

"I'm Marlette Brightwood. I'm sorry, but I don't know your name?"

"Ah, Timothy, have you forgotten your manners? I'm Mrs. Galligher and this is my son, Timothy."

Marlette smiled. "I'm very glad to meet you, Mrs. Galligher and I did want to talk with you, but if I've come at a bad time I'd be happy to come back later, if you like."

"If Timothy brought you now there must have been a good reason, so let's be hearin' it." Her eyes were questioning and reserved.

"I think I may know a relative of yours. Was there someone in your family named Ross who married a girl named Abigail?"

The woman stiffened and glanced darkly at her son. "And why would you be wantin' to know that?"

"I met a man in the Oregon Country. He had a ring belonging to his mother with the names Ross and Abigail engraved on the inside."

"Did he tell you now, what his last name was?"

"The name he uses is not his real name. He doesn't know what his real name is."

Again there was a surreptitious glance between mother and son. "Then what makes you be thinkin' he's kin of ours?"

"He bears a striking resemblance to your son. His eyes and hair, the shape of his head, his whole physical appearance is very much like your son's."

"Well, now, a man's looks is not much proof. Can you tell us why it's so important to you to find his kin?"

"I thought there might be someone, somewhere, who would like to know what happened to their family."

She smiled negatively. "Well, you be wastin' your time, Miss. We don't have any kin but what's right here. Timothy'll see you get back to town."

Marlette realized it was hopeless. She didn't understand why, but these people didn't want to hear about the man she felt certain was their relative. "I'm sorry I bothered you, Mrs. Galligher."

Timothy showed her out of the house. The boy was seated in the wagon and Timothy helped her in, giving his son a warning scowl. "You be comin' straight back, now, Cam."

"Yes, sir."

The boy lifted the reins, wheeled the horses around and headed out of the yard. Marlette was deeply disappointed.

They were away from the house and out of earshot before the boy spoke.

"Are you a Whitteker?" There was little of the Irish accent in his speech.

"No. Why do you ask?"

"Oh, nothing."

Marlette's curiosity was aroused. "What about the Whittekers, Cam?"

"Mrs. Whitteker died this past winter. I heard Father and Grandmother talking about it one night. I thought maybe you might be one of them."

"What did they say about her?"

"Oh, I guess she was related to us somehow, but they never told me nothin' about it and I didn't ask 'cause it was something they didn't want talked about."

Marlette was beginning to see a glimmer in the darkness. "Cam, do you know if your grandmother had a brother named Ross?"

"They mentioned that name. But I think it was my grandfather's brother. He's the one they mentioned when they were talking about the Whittekers. What do you know about it?"

"I met a man in the Oregon Country who looks enough like you to be your brother. His father's name was Ross. His mother's name was Abigail."

The boy turned to her eagerly. "That was the other name they mentioned. Abigail. She was Mrs. Whitteker's daughter."

Marlette smiled. "That's why I came to see your grandmother. I saw your father at the meeting last night and he reminded me so much of Ross, I wanted to find out if they were related. Your grandmother wouldn't tell me but now I'm sure you are. Do you know why they wouldn't tell me?"

His face clouded. "I'm not sure I should tell you. They don't know I know. Why is it so important?"

She placed her hand on the boy's arm and he looked into her eyes. "I married this man whose name is Ross. He knew nothing of his family. His father was killed by an Indian before he was born. His mother was taken captive by the Indian and he was rasied as an Indian. I thought maybe somewhere there were people who might want to know what had happened to his mother and father."

His eyes, so much like Ross's, were wide with excitement. "Boy! I'd sure like to meet him. What's he like?"

Marlette smiled. "He is a very strong, capable man. He was to be chief of his Indian village but he felt he didn't deserve it because he wasn't an Indian. He left the tribe and went west with the fur traders and has lived at a place called Vancouver for several years, trapping in the mountains during the winter."

His eyes sparkled. "Are you going back there?"

Marlette hesitated, "No, Cam. At least not in the near future."

His face fell. "Then why do you want to know about him if you're not going back to him?"

A lump rose in Marlette's throat and her eyes clouded with tears. "Because I still love him very much."

After a few minutes he said, "All right, I'll tell you. But please don't ever let my father know."

Marlette promised.

"My grandfather's brother, Ross, ran off with the Whitteker girl. Her folks didn't want her marrying him because we were poor farmers and they owned the bank. And we are Catholic. I guess they went to another county and got married but, anyway, when they got back her folks locked her up and our family wanted to get the marriage annulled since they weren't married in the church.

"I'm not sure how long they kept them from seeing each other, but it must have been quite awhile. Then, one day they just disappeared and nobody ever heard from them again."

"But why wouldn't they admit he was related to them?"

"There was a lot of hard feelings between the families. The Whittekers accused Great-Uncle Ross of takin' her against her will and went to court but they couldn't prove it. For awhile there was a reward out for them. I heard Grandmother say something about them livin' in sin and being excommunicated. I'm not sure I understand it all. Do you?"

"Yes, Cam, I think I do." And she understood too, why Abigail had told her son he could never go back to his own people.

"Where did you say he lives?"

"At Fort Vancouver in the Oregon Country."

He smiled dreamily. "I'd sure like to go out there. Do you think he'd mind if I showed up out there some day?"

She smiled. "No. I don't think he would. I think he'd be glad to see you."

He straightened up in the wagon seat. "Some day I'm going."

"Cam, have you read anything about my trip to the Oregon Country?"

"No. Just heard Father talk about going to the meeting."

"When we get back to town I'll give you my book. You'll learn a lot about Ross Chesnut from it. He was out guide."

"Chesnut? Is that what his name is?"

"Yes."

He smiled, his eyes glowing at the thought of adventure.

They arrived in town and she hurried up the hotel stairs to her room. She opened her small trunk, removed a copy of her book and returned to Cam.

With trembling hands, identical to the hands that had been so familiar to her, he took the book. "Thank you very much."

She smiled a little wistfully. "Thank you, Cam, and good luck."

They looked into each other's eyes and then he lifted the reins and the horses took off at a brisk trot. She watched him disappear down the street. It was like watching Ross leave her and her heart twisted.

She spent a sleepless night fighting half-forgotten memories that her recent discovery had stirred up. It was early in the morning before she dozed, only to be awakened by the desk clerk calling her for breakfast so that she could catch the stage to Albany.

When she finally reached home she was worn out and depressed.

Martha was worried about her and it was difficult to reassure her, but she passed it off as hard work and that satisfied Martha for the present.

The summer dragged on and the campaign to elect a president of the United States began to overshadow every other interest. Her speaking tours dwindled except for local interest and she found time increasingly heavy on her hands.

One day when she returned home from work, there was a letter awaiting her, written in a feminine hand. She opened it curiously. She knew of no one who would write to her, especially from Baltimore. It was from a woman she didn't know, but who apparently knew her, for she was coming to see Marlette in two weeks. She said nothing more in her letter but did include her return address. Marlette replied that she would be available to speak with the woman. Curiosity wouldn't let her do otherwise.

When the woman arrived at her door in two weeks, Marlette was somewhat perplexed. The woman was a few years older than Marlette, and obviously not a woman of respectable means. Her dress was daringly flamboyant and her face was heavily made up.

"Miss Brightwood?"

"Yes. Are you Miss Damion?"

"Yes. Can I come in?"

Marlette stepped aside and the other woman swept in, her figure provocative in its tightly corseted dress.

"Sit down, please, Miss Damion, and tell me why you have come to see me? Do I know you?"

She laughed throatily. "No. Ladies like you don't know women like me. I was a friend of Major Holliway's. I read your story in the paper and found out you were looking for someone who knew him or was related to him. Have you found anyone?"

"No. No one has contacted me about him."

She smiled. "Then if no one else wants his things, I'll take them."

"Why? They're only his clothes."

"I know. But he was a friend. I would like a keepsake."

Marlette appraised the other woman. "I see."

"Do you, Miss Brightwood?"

Marlette smiled slightly. "Perhaps more than you realize, Miss

Damion. Did he promise to marry you when he returned from the Oregon Country?"

She looked startled and then laughed. "Say, you're all right, Miss Brightwood. I didn't figure a lady like you would even think of such things."

"I have a few secrets of my own."

"Well, well! You make me feel at home. Yes, Sam was going to marry me when he got back. He was stubborn and difficult but I really cared for him. I'm getting past the age of working for a living, if you know what I mean, and I thought there was a chance to make it with him. He wasn't shocked by my past and didn't care what people said." She paused and Marlette could see tears sparkling in her eyes.

"I'm sorry, Miss Damion."

She waved off the sympathy. "It doesn't matter now. It's over with and being sorry ain't going to bring him back. Can I have his things?"

"Yes. And there is something in his trunk I think you'll be able to use. Be sure you go through everything very carefully searching for that keepsake."

"I will. Thank you, Miss Brightwood." She rose, looking at Marlette thoughtfully, and said, "You've been so nice to me I'd like to give you something."

Marlette protested, "That isn't necessary."

"Nonsense. I want to." She opened her bag and pulled out a small golden vial. "Here. I'd like you to take this."

"Thank you, but I couldn't."

"I won't take no for an answer. It was a gift to me but it doesn't suit me. It's expensive stuff and I think it will suit you just fine."

Marlette accepted the vial because she didn't want to hurt the woman's feelings by saying she never used perfume. "Thank you, Miss Damion." She raised it to her face and caught the delicate flower scent with a trace of something she couldn't identify. "It's lovely."

Miss Damion gave a pleased smile. "I'll call my driver now."

She went to the door and motioned to the coachman and Marlette showed him the trunk. As they drove away the woman turned to wave and Marlette waved back.

At last everything had been taken care of and she felt a sort of wistful emptiness that only increased her depression.

Martha immediately knew that something had happened when she returned home. "That woman came today, didn't she?"

"Yes, she did."

"Well, for heaven's sake tell me all about it."

Marlette smiled. "You're as incorrigibly curious as I am. It seems Major Holliway had a lady friend. He promised to marry her when he got back from Oregon."

"Did you let her have his things?"

"Yes. Any woman who could love Holliway deserved to have his money."

Martha snorted. "Love! I bet she was just a good actress."

"No. I don't think so."

"Well, I wish I'd 'a' been here. I could've told whether she was acting or not."

Marlette snapped, "What difference does it make? It's over and done with."

Martha's lips pressed together tightly and she looked hurt.

"I'm sorry, Martha. I didn't mean to be so cross," Marlette immediately apologized.

"It's all right. I still think of you as a little girl, not able to judge things. But you're a lot different than when you went away. Like right now, you've got something bothering you and you won't tell me. You used to tell me everything."

Marlette smiled. "You're too observant."

"I'm concerned about you. Your trouble is my trouble. If I can help, I want to know what it is."

Marlette shook her head. "There is nothing to help, Martha. I would have told you if there was."

Martha looked at her keenly. "Sometimes just talking about it helps."

Marlette stood up and said firmly, "No. Now let's go get some supper."

James Knox Polk

THE NEXT DAY she received a letter from Mr. Ashton advising her that James K. Polk was going to be in Philadelphia in two days and wanted to meet her. Arrangements had been made for him to stay at a hotel and she was requested to meet him there after his campaign speech.

Marlette was excited and nervous. She had been following the campaign closely. She had also been doing some research of her own into his background. He seemed a man of great capability. He had handled his job as Speaker of the House with an ability that few men before, or since, had. In addition to his annexation policy, he was vowing not to run for re-election, an unheard-of promise in political circles. He even wanted to pass a law to that effect.

Naturally the opposition had nothing good to say about him. But as she read and compared, she found that their accusations were not faults but virtues. They accused him of being entirely unemotional, a cold, machine-like Jacksonite, during his Speaker days. She interpreted his lack of emotion as unbelievable self-control and unswerving loyalty to the cause he had sworn to serve. She still did not agree with his Oregon policy, but she did feel he was the right man for the presidency.

On the day she was to meet him she took great care with her appearance. She allowed herself the luxury of a new dress and felt guilty about it afterward, reprimanding herself for spending her hard-earned money on a dress instead of her debts. She took great pains to look as attractive as possible—a vanity she usually ignored—but she couldn't bring herself to wear her hair down although she did curl if so it waved softly around her face and formed a chignon of curls.

After all, she reasoned, this man might be the next president of the United States and he had requested to see her.

She was in the crowd in front of the speaker's stand at two o'clock that afternoon eagerly waiting to hear his speech. She was further impressed by his integrity, ability, and concern for his country after his speech. She was also struck by his slightness of frame, although the summer sun had disguised his pale skin with a healthy tan.

After the speeches were over the men returned to the hotel. Marlette followed in her buggy and waited nervously in the sitting room while her summons was verified.

She heard footsteps approaching and stood up, anxiously smoothing her skirt, as Mr. Ashton opened the door. The man entering was even slighter of figure than she had imagined. Here was a man whose ability and courage far outweighed his physical endurance.

Ashton closed the door and said, "Miss Brightwood, this is Mr. Polk."

Marlette curtsied deeply and murmured, "I am honored, Mr. Polk."

"The honor is all mine, Miss Brightwood."

Marlette met his eyes and noted a glimmer of suppressed humor which put her immediately at ease. Bravely she added, "Not entirely dubious, I hope, sir."

He laughed good-naturedly. "I'm glad you brought that up, Miss Brightwood. It was my intention to ask you how you can campaign so actively for me and yet oppose my policy on the Oregon Country?"

There was no anger in his question, only gentle chastisement and Marlette smiled. "I find increasingly that I am a majority of one."

"Ah. Then you are ready to change your opinion?"

She answered frankly, "No, only my method of informing people."

He glanced at her admiringly and she knew he respected her. "May I ask how you are going to inform them now?"

"I have come to the conclusion that people are not interested in hearing the truth about the Oregon Country. They are determined to go, so it becomes a matter of how well prepared they are for the trip. I will still advise against it, but I will make sure they understand fully what they will need if they do decide to go."

His smile held genuine admiration. "You are a woman after my own heart. I am indeed fortunate you are not on the other side. But let us sit down. I have read your journals and there are a few questions I wish to ask you, if you don't mind."

He indicated a chair for her and settled across from her. Ashton remained standing by the door.

"In your journal you intimate that the British will not press their claim to the Oregon Country, at least the southern part. I'd like to know more about this."

"That is true. From what I was able to learn, they are not making money on the fur trade there. They have had orders to relocate north of Fort Vancouver and close that post down."

"In your opinion is the fur trade really finished there?"

"I can only tell you what I observed from the men I spent the winter with. They apparently did not take as many furs as they normally do and were quite serious about moving out."

"You are sure they were not trying to mislead you?"

She hesitated momentarily before she answered, "No. I don't think so."

His keen eyes caught her uncertainty and he leaned forward, "You hesitate. Why?"

"I'm sorry. It has nothing to do with what I said."

Sternly he advised, "Everything may have bearing on this matter. If you can't be completely certain, at least tell me so I can make the decision."

Marlette swallowed hard. "Can this be between only the two of us?"

He smiled in understanding and turned to Ashton who nodded and left the room. Polk then turned back to Marlette.

"If you read my journal, you know I spent the winter with the man who was our guide." She stood up and walked tensely around the room while Polk sat patiently. "No one knows this and you will understand my hesitation to tell even you. An hour before the boat came to take me to Fort Vancouver, I married this man."

His face broke into a smile and he leaned back. "I can find nothing improper in that. There is more?"

"Yes. When I reached Vancouver I learned from Dr. McLoughlin that my father had paid Mr. Chesnut twice as much money as agreed upon to insure my protection. I didn't know Dr. McLoughlin wasn't to release the money until he had my approval and Mr. Chesnut never told me about this. Since he was incapable of accompanying me to the fort, I wasn't able to question him about it before I left. For this reason alone I hesitate to profess absolute certainty that everything he told me was true."

"Then you feel he compromised you?"

"Yes."

"Did you have any other doubts about this man?"

"Yes. I doubted him from the first moment I saw him but not because of anything he said or did in our presence. I doubted him because I thought he was an Indian and therefore untrustworthy. When I learned he was not an Indian I abandoned my prejudice and I believed him. In fact, much of my knowledge of the Oregon Country is basically his but when this money thing came up, all by doubts returned."

"Knowing his motive for marrying you, would you do it again?"

Marlette's cheeks reddened and she had to look away from his penetrating gaze. Softly she murmured, "Yes."

A silence followed her admission and she glanced up. He was still studying her, weighing and measuring the importance of her personal feelings.

Quickly she blurted, "But that is a ridiculous thing on which to base such a decision."

He smiled slightly. "I think I understand. But I would like to have seen the original journals."

The surprise showed in her face. "Why?"

He laughed. "Because then I could tell just how much you doubted this man. I think in your rewriting, because of your highly conflicting feelings for him, you suppressed those doubts in an attempt to be fair to him. I'm inclined to think you gave this man a bad time."

Marlette felt her face grow warm and knew she was blushing again. "I'm afraid I did."

He placed his hand on his chair decisively. "I think I am going to overlook that doubt. But now I am curious. Is he coming here or are you going back there?" There was a twinkle in his dark eyes.

"Neither."

The twinkle faded. "I'm sorry. Well, Miss Brightwood, they are waiting for me. I've enjoyed our talk and I thank you for your help, however illusive."

Marlette rose and held out her hand. "I think I can be less illusive now, Mr. Polk. Thank you for wanting to meet me. It is an honor I won't soon forget."

He smiled and raised her hand to his lips in a brief but sincere gesture of esteem. When he was gone she sat down, feeling as if it had all been a dream.

She returned home to find Martha waiting with supper. She withheld her curiosity until they sat down with their coffee.

"Well, what did you think of him?"

"I liked him, Martha. I think he is a good man."

Martha smiled in agreement. "I like him, too. I can't understand why you don't agree with him about Oregon."

"You would have to see it to understand. It isn't the country itself. I think there is much of value there. But the price these people are paying in lives and hardship is just too high."

Martha sighed. "Well, if you say so. I guess I'm just like all the rest and don't want to hear the truth about it."

"It's only human nature to want to hear only the good things and overlook the rest."

Captain McNeal

ELECTION DAY arrived and James Knox Polk was elected president. Before the end of the year she received a thank-you note written personally to her. It was a nice gesture and a fitting end to a busy year. But now that the excitement was over, Marlette grew increasingly depressed. Her job did not suffice to break up the lonely monotony she felt.

Martha accepted her silence grudgingly, afraid to question her. They spent evenings before the fire in silence with Martha sewing and Marlette reading or answering infrequent letters about Oregon.

It was on one such cold, gloomy evening that she had a surprise visitor. Martha was in the kitchen preparing supper and Marlette went to answer the knock. A familiar figure in a dark seaman's coat with a frosted brown beard smiled at her.

"Good evening, lass. Do ye remember an old sea dog?"

"Captain McNeal! What a surprise! For heaven sake, do come in."

She stepped aside for the stocky figure and he came in bringing with him a vitality that seemed to crush her despair and she felt alive for the first time in months. Martha came through the kitchen door suspiciously to see what was going on.

"Martha, this is Captain McNeal. He was the captain of the ship that took us to Oregon."

Martha nodded curtly and hovered about Marlette protectively.

"Have you eaten, Captain?" Marlette inquired. "We just got in and would be glad to have you join us."

"I've already dined but I'd be happy to share a cup o' coffee with ye."

Dinner passed pleasantly as the captain told stories about his travels. After dinner Marlette and the captain went back into the small parlor, leaving a dubious Martha in the kitchen. The captain built a fire to warm the chilly room and came to sit beside her on the settee. Impulsively he took both of her hands in his.

"Aye, lass, it is good to see ye again. But now I've done all the talkin'. Tell me when did ye get back and where is your father?"

The happy smile left Marlette's face as she told him, "I've been back a year. Father and the others were killed in the Oregon Country."

"Oh, no, lass! What a sad thing to happen. I have nae been back to Vancouver since I left ye there and I had nae heard what tragedy befell ye. I'm sorry to hear it. How did it happen? How did ye manage to escape?"

"We were on our way back from the Whitman mission. The day after we left an Indian intercepted us while we were stopped for lunch. He offered us safe passage down the Columbia in exchange for our horses and guns. Our guide, a man called Chesnut, advised us against it and we voted to stay with Mr. Chesnut. We were attacked the next morning but we were able to fight them off without serious injury.

"During the night they fired the plain on us but fortunately, Mr. Chesnut was able to save us from that, too.

"They didn't bother us for the next two days and we thought we had escaped them but as we were preparing to cross the Deschutes River they attacked us again and caught us totally off guard. Some of the men were off their horses and they didn't have a chance. Mr. Chesnut and I had not dismounted and we were able to escape." She looked down at his hands, vivid memories of that tragic day flooding her.

The captain's hands tightened on hers. "Great God! And that is nae all of it, I ken. Ye said ye'd been home a year. Where were ye that winter if ye were nae on your way home?"

"Mr. Chesnut and I had to spend the winter in the mountains. Some Indians caught up with us in the mountains but Mr. Chesnut knew them and they let us live although they took our horses, guns, and food. I didn't realize it then but they knew and Chesnut knew, that it was going to snow. They didn't think we could make it out alive. If it hadn't been for Chesnut we wouldn't have. He knew those mountains and he and a friend had a cabin near where we had been stranded. He managed to get us there despite the snow."

The captain dropped her hands and rose, a look of distress in his eyes. "Is nae wonder my conscience has bothered me for letting you off my ship. I can't say I didn't have hopes as to what ye might have become to me if ye'd come with me but to have been taken like that!" He slammed one fist against the palm of his other hand in anger.

She was not as surprised by his words as she was by the depth of his feeling. She spoke quickly to ease his anger. "Captain, please. You judge too quickly. I was not mistreated in any way."

Relief flooded his face. "Thank God! They must've been saints."

Marlette looked down at her tightly clasped hands, sighing as memories engulfed her.

The captain returned to her side, urgently trying to erase the past from her mind. "Enough of the past, lass. What are your plans now? Do ye have any permanent ties?"

Marlette faced him and smiled, shaking off the ghosts of the past. "No plans, Captain, other than to work and pay my debts."

"Aye then, there's nae a man in your life?"

She blushed in confusion and he apologized before she could answer.

"I've been too blunt. Forgive an ill-mannered old salt, will ye, lass?"

She nodded, feeling the attraction she had once had for this man returning. "There's nothing to forgive."

He smiled hopefully. "Then ye are nae angry with me?"

"No, Captain."

His smile broadened. "I'm glad and I'll promise to behave if ye'll put up with me?"

She returned his smile, aware that she needed his companionship. "Are you planning to leave soon, Captain, or are you in port for a while?"

He sobered. "I have but a couple of days to spend while they scrape the ship, then it's off to sea again. But tell me, how are ye fixed with your father gone?"

"To be honest with you, Captain, not very well. We lost everything while we were gone. I had to sell the shop and our home."

His eyes darkened with dismay. "Aye, that was a harsh blow. Do ye have any means now?"

"Yes. I sold the journals I kept of the trip and I have a bookkeeping job. We've been managing fairly well."

"Aye, that's good, but I hate to think of ye bucking the world all alone. Is there anything I can do to help ye?"

She smiled in appreciation. "Thank you, but I can't accept your help. This is something I must do on my own."

He nodded in understanding. "You're a determined lass. But if ye should change your mind—?" He didn't finish but his eyes told her all she needed to know.

She smiled and shook her head. The clock struck ten and he looked up and sighed. "How the time flies. I'd best be shovin' off but if ye have nae other plans for tomorrow, I'd like to take ye to dinner, if ye'll have me?"

She stood and placed her hand on his arm. "I'd like that very much, Captain."

"What time can ye be ready?"

"I think by six."

"Fine." His eyes glowed warmly and she felt an answering warmth.

She was beginning to feel reckless so she said quickly, "I'd better get your coat. Thank you for coming, Captain. I'll look forward to seeing you tomorrow."

His smile was tender. "Nae half as much as I, lass. Good night to ye."

When he left Martha immediately came in frowning at the happy glow on Marlette's face. "Never fall for a sailin' man. You'll spend a lonely life."

Marlette laughed. "And what makes you think I'm falling for him?"

"First time I've ever seen that look in your eyes."

Marlette sobered. "Martha, sometimes a little happiness is better than none at all. Good night."

She left Martha staring at her curiously and went to her bedroom. She thought of Ross and had to bite her lip to hold back the tears.

Once in bed she couldn't sleep. If only Ross were here, there would be no question of what to do. But he was not and never would be and she couldn't remain faithful to a memory. She would take whatever happiness the captain could offer. If he felt the way she thought he did, she would not hesitate to obtain a divorce. She had to be practical.

The next morning she took Martha to work but she decided to take the day off herself. She was determined to have a pleasant evening with the captain and she felt the need to make herself as attractive as she knew how.

She spent the day remodeling and freshening her nicest dress, bathing, and washing her hair. She sat before her mirror combing her hair in a dozen different ways to find the most flattering style, but there was only one way it looked best.

Late in the afternoon she went to pick up Martha. Her excitement was ill-concealed and Martha pursed her lips in disapproval. Marlette patted her hand reassuringly.

"Don't you think I deserve a little diversion?"

"I think you deserve a lot of diversion, but not from a grizzled old seaman like him."

"He happens to be the only man available who is interested in me and he is not that old."

Martha sighed. "Well, don't say I didn't warn you."

Marlette laughed. "Don't worry. The captain leaves in the morning."

Martha grimaced. "A lot can happen in one night."

Marlette felt a sudden twinge in her heart. "I know, Martha, I know."

Martha looked at her piercingly. "Just what do you mean by that?"

Marlette slapped the reins against the horse and he broke into a trot. She grinned recklessly at Martha. "Just that I'm not the same naive little girl that left here three years ago."

Martha didn't question her again but her eyes were frankly curious and her forehead wrinkled with concern.

Once home, Marlette happily and painstakingly dressed for her evening out, ignoring Martha's patent lack of enthusiasm. She looked at her almost beautiful reflection in the mirror and noticed for the first time that she had gained enough weight to diminish the bold lines of her face. Her pale, silvery hair fell softly around her face and enhanced the illusion and she smiled with approval at the lovely woman in the mirror. With reckless abandon she picked up the golden vial of perfume and cautiously dabbed its exotic fragrance on her skin.

Martha came into the room and stared at her. Marlette turned around slowly. "Do I look all right?"

A slow smile of approval spread over Martha's face. "You look lovely. Too lovely for the likes of him." She sniffed and her eyes widened with alarm. "And wearing perfume, too!"

Marlette laughed and picked up her heavy cape while Martha went to answer the captain's knock at the door. Marlette entered the parlor with slow dignity and the captain's eyes widened as she approached. She held out her hand and he took it eagerly.

"Ye look lovely, lass. A feast for a starvin' man."

Marlette laughed lightly. "Thank you, Captain."

He helped her into her cape and his hands lingered on her shoulders until Martha cleared her throat in warning. The captain winked and opened the door.

He had hired a closed carriage and it was cozy and warm despite the chilly, snowy night. He held her hand tightly in his as they sat close in the carriage and Marlette smiled with pleasure.

The captain noticed her smile and asked, "A penny for your thoughts?"

"I'm just being a foolish woman."

"Ye! I find that hard to imagine. Ye are the most practical woman I've ever met."

She laughed softly. "Maybe that's why I enjoy acting foolishly for a change. I shouldn't confess this to you but I've never been taken out by a man before."

"Well, then, it is high time, is it nae? We'll do the town in grand style." The captain inhaled deeply, "Ahhh, ye smell good, lass. What is that perfume your wearing?"

She smiled, "I don't know. It was given to me."

"Well, who ever gave it to ye did a good job. I could nae picked better for ye myself." There was a moment of silence before he asked curiously, "Was it a man?"

Marlette laughed, "You'll never believe this, captain, but it was a woman."

Incredulously he said, "A woman?"

"And even more surprising," added Marlette, "it was Major Holliway's woman."

"Ye can't be serious, lass. That man had heart for nae but himself."

"I thought so, too, but one day I got a letter from this woman and she wanted to see me. It turned out that Major Holliway had promised to marry her when he returned. I let her have his things and she gave this perfume to me."

The captain slapped his knee. "Well, I'll be damned. I'd never ha' guessed it." He laughed heartily and Marlette laughed with him feeling the contentment of a shared emotion.

They arrived at the restaurant the captain had chosen. It was the best in Philadelphia. The captain took charge, clearly at home in fine restaurants.

When they were seated he asked, "Do ye have a preference, lass?"

"No, Captain. I'll let you decide. I'm sure you're much better at this than I am."

He smiled. "Please, lass, I wish ye'd use my given name, 'tis Duncan."

She returned his smile. The waiter came and he ordered wines and the most elegant of dinners. The first bottle of wine was brought shortly and the captain sampled it. He approved and the waiter poured. The wine went immediately to Marlette's head and she felt giddy.

"You seem to have had quite a bit of experience at this. Tell me about some the places you have been."

He laughed. "I've been every place my lady of the sea can take me. What else is there for a lonely seaman to do but find the best places to eat? Ye are well aware of how limited a diet can be on a long voyage."

She retorted teasingly, "And with a pretty girl in every port, too?"

He smiled. "Ye be wantin' to know all my secrets? Well, lass, I'll tell ye, there are none I'd rather be with than ye."

Marlette took another sip of the wine and felt her cheeks flame. "You flatter me, Duncan, but it is nice to hear."

Their meal came and they stopped talking long enough to sample the various dishes the captain had ordered. Marlette was enjoying herself immensely.

As they sat over coffee, too full but very content, the captain asked, "Now where would ye like to go?"

"I really don't know where else to go." She smiled wryly, "I've really led a very sheltered life 'til now."

"Well, we can't take ye home so early. I'll find someplace to go."

He helped her with her cape and they hurried out to his waiting carriage.

"I know just the place," he informed her, as the carriage rocked over the cobblestones.

After a short ride to the outskirts of town, they came to an old inn. Marlette instantly recognized the place. It had a scandalous past.

"Duncan, do you think we ought to go in here? I've heard about this place."

He laughed. "Where's your spirit of adventure, lass?"

She clutched his arm and said recklessly, "All right, but will you leave if I want to?"

"Aye."

Marlette soon discovered she enjoyed the gay roadhouse and was not at all shocked or embarrassed. The inn featured saucy dancing girls, entertaining singers and musicians, and a clever storyteller. She found it all delightful, if not in the best of taste. After the entertainment there was dancing. There were, she discovered, quite a few ladies out tonight and they all seemed to be enjoying themselves as much as she. They danced to the fashionable waltz music, considered slightly indecent by some standards, and Marlette felt more than one memory pang as she danced with the captain. She forced herself to concentrate on the captain and found he was an accomplished dancer and she whirled around the room gaily, lightheaded from the wine.

It was the captain who finally suggested that they should leave and she regretfully agreed. Cinderellas always had to return to the ashes. The ride back to town was all too short and they rode in rapt silence, Marlette contentedly snuggled close to the captain encircled by his comforting arm.

When they reached her home the captain told the carriage to wait while he saw her to the door. Wanting to prolong the evening Marlette asked, "Won't you stay for a nightcap, Duncan? I think I can find some of father's peach brandy."

He stepped toward her and placed his broad hands on her arms. "I'd like to, lass, but it is late, and I must be up early in the morning."

"I'm sorry. I've so enjoyed the evening. Will I see you again?"

"Aye, lass, if ye want to?"

"A year is a long time. I wish you weren't leaving so soon."

His eyes were dark and intense. "If I had known for sure I was going to find ye I would've planned otherwise. When I return I will see ye again. In the meantime I want ye to know I have been thinking a lot about ye ever since that night on the deck of my ship. I was a damn fool to know nae then how much I cared for ye. Ye are a woman a man could love as much as the sea."

She laughed teasingly, "And you think I wouldn't be jealous?"

He grinned broadly. "I think ye are practical enough to know a man can nae be held if he does nae want to be held. I think ye would understand and be contented to wait. Would ye nae?"

"I don't know, Duncan. I would have to do a lot of thinking about it. Certainly it wouldn't be much different from what I have now."

He laughed. "Well, ye'll have a whole year to think, lass. And now that I know ye are here I'll do some serious thinking, too. God knows I would miss ye as much as the sea."

He pulled her close and his face blurred in front of her eyes. He pressed his lips against hers and she felt the soft bristle of his mustache and breard against her face. Although she had thought she wanted his kiss, it only served to remind her of Ross's kisses with his week's growth of beard. And stranger still, she felt no answering passion although his kiss was ardent.

He released her and stepped back, a little bewildered by her lack of response. "I've been too forward again. I'm sorry I've misjudged ye and gone too far."

She shook her head realizing she had hurt him, and abandoning propriety she placed her hands upon the lapels of his heavy coat and moved closer to him. "Duncan, forgive me. It was my fault not yours. If there were more time I would explain it to you. If you still want to come back, I will tell you then."

He looked at her thoughtfully and his hands covered hers. "If I were a wise man I would shove off and nae return." He took a deep breath. "But like the poor dumb beasties of the sea, ye have harpooned me."

She laughed softly and slipped her hands around his neck, willing herself to respond to something she didn't honestly feel. She pulled his head down and his arms went around her, his lips devouring hers. She became aware of the heat of his body, the intensity of his kiss, and realized the dangerous game she was playing.

There was a light rapping on the door and the passion of the moment was broken. Hoarsely the captain demanded, "Who is it?"

"The coachman, sir."

Duncan opened the door. "Good-bye, lass. I'll be back."

Then he was gone and Marlette, in a daze, stared at the closed door for a long moment. Martha's bedroom door opened and she appeared with a scowl on her face.

"This is no decent hour for a young lady to be getting in."

Marlette laughed with a touch of hysteria. "Martha, I'm almost thirty years old. I am not young and I am not really concerned about being a lady at this moment."

Martha harrumphed with disapproval. Marlette came to her and impulsively hugged her. "I had a wonderful time, but it is over, so don't spoil it."

"You've been tasting the spirits!"

Marlette laughed gayly. "Yes. And now I'm going to bed. Good night."

She walked briskly to the warm security of her bedroom and was immediately sober. She felt guilty and ashamed because she hadn't been honest with the captain nor with herself. Ross was still in her mind and heart. She cried herself to sleep.

During the next few days her depression returned with deepening severity. She fought stubbornly to put Ross out of her mind, aware that her love for him was futile and his memory was destroying her life. It was difficult at first, but she had unexpected help. Now that the election was over, people were becoming restless again and with a president in favor of annexation, people once again wanted information about Oregon.

She accepted speaking invitations gladly but she had to finance her own trips now and she found she couldn't afford the expense. When she explained her situation many were willing to take up collections for her and usually there was enough to cover her expenses.

Her job at the store became full time and by working steadily she was able to afford more trips, though at times she had to take extra days off. But by working weekends and evenings she made up the difference. It was a brutal pace but she kept it willingly, feeling a growing sense of duty to answer every request. It filled the time and left her too exhausted for any other thoughts.

The Unexpected Gift

BETWEEN HER WORK and her traveling, Marlette managed to make it through the summer. The cold, rainy fall weather slackened her interest in travel. It had been enjoyable, but with the early darkness of approaching winter she was content and somewhat relieved to stay at home.

The government had not acted on the Oregon situation during the year and a war between Texas and Mexico seemed imminent, but Marlette was no longer concerned with these problems. Rest and relaxation were of primary importance. She actually felt she had regained her peace of mind and was filled with an illusionary contentment. Even Martha felt the change and they talked more than they had in a long time.

Late in January she received a note from Captain McNeal. He was in Boston and he would come as soon as he could get away. In less than a week he was knocking at her door. She greeted him happily as he swept her into his arms and kissed her soundly. She responded more out of happiness at seeing him than anything else.

"Let me look at ye, lass." He studied her face and his eyes eagerly took in every inch of her.

She laughed delightedly and he hugged her again. "Aye, I've missed ye." She raised her lips for another kiss aware of how much she needed someone. He kissed her again and asked seriously, "Ye have missed me, too, I ken?"

She smiled happily. "Just a little."

Martha made her presence known with a loud cough and the captain released Marlette. "I see ye still have this good woman to keep an eye on ye."

Martha scowled at him. "Your flattery will get you nowhere with me, Captain."

He laughed heartily and unbuttoned his coat. Marlette took it and almost dropped it, it was so unexpectedly heavy. "What are you carrying in your coat, Duncan? It's so heavy."

"Och now! I almost forgot about that with the fine greetin' ye gave me." He reached into the pocket and pulled out a leather bag.

Marlette's eyes widened as she recognized it. With a catch in her voice she asked, "Where did you get that?"

"Ah, now that's a story, lass, I can only tell over a hot cup o' tea."

Marlette turned to Martha and she grudgingly went to get the tea. The captain took her hand and led her to the settee, placing the heavy leather bag between them. Marlette wanted to touch it and open it. Her heart pounded and she felt a little shaky. Martha came in with the tea and the captain smiled at her, but when he turned around and saw the anxiety on Marlette's face he sobered immediately.

"Is there something wrong, lass?"

In a strained voice she pleaded, "Please, Duncan, tell me where you got this bag?"

"I did nae think it would upset ye so. I met a man at Fort Vancouver when I was there. He asked if I knew ye and I told him I did. He said ye had told him about me and he thought he could trust me to deliver something to ye. I told ye were the first person I intended on seeing when I got back. He gave me this and said to bring it to ye."

He lifted the bag and moved it closer toward her. With trembling fingers she loosened the drawstring and the leather opened, revealing the dull sheen of silver coins. Tears sprang to Marlette's eyes. The captain didn't see them for he was emptying the bag of coins on the settee between them. He gave the bag a last shake and a round golden object fell with a tinkle onto the coins.

"What's this?" The captain picked up the ring. "Why 'tis a wedding ring." Her self-control suddenly crumbled and the tears streamed down her cheeks. He pushed the coins aside and put his arm around her. "What is it, lass? What is it?" She buried her head against his chest and cried harder.

Martha heard the sobbing and rushed into the room. "What's going on? Are you hurting her, Captain?"

"Quiet woman. She's upset about that." He jerked his head toward the coins.

Marlette heard Martha's astonished gasp. "Where did that come from?"

"She'll tell ye when she's able. Now get back to your kitchen, woman."

Martha snorted angrily, but she left. The captain was not one to be disobeyed. Marlette wiped her eyes and tried to control herself. She had to find out more about Ross.

"I'm sorry, Duncan. I didn't expect this. Tell me, what did the man who gave you this look like?"

"Ah, he was a fine-looking man, lass. Dark hair, a chestnut brown it was, and dark brown eyes. He was dressed in buckskin. Do ye know him?"

"Yes. Ross Chesnut. He was the guide who led us."

"Aye. That's who he said he was. Did he steal this money from ye?"

"No. It was his pay for guiding us. Please tell me exactly what happened, what he said, how he acted, what you said to him?"

The captain looked at her keenly and she knew her voice and eyes betrayed the excitement and confusion she felt. He leaned back and began to talk.

"I reached the fort before noon and we unloaded supplies for McLoughlin and the settlers. McLoughlin had some furs to trade but there was nae enough for full payment and we were settlin' up in his office. When he opened the safe he suddenly yelled for one of his servants and asked if I could stay a while since there was a man that wanted to see me. I said I would if it was important, and he said it concerned ye. So, naturally I stayed. They sent to the valley for this man and he arrived late that night and woke us up. McLoughlin took us to his office and this man, Chesnut, asked if I knew ye and I said I did. I told him I had seen ye and would see ye again as soon as I returned. Then he told me ye had spoken of me and asked if I would bring this bag to ye and of course I said I would."

Frowning, Marlette asked, "Is that all? Didn't he say anything else, give you a note or anything? Did he seem strained, as if McLoughlin was forcing him to do this?"

"No. He appeared at ease and certainly I did nae gather that

McLoughlin intimidated him in any way."

"Didn't he ask how I was or how I was getting along?"

"No, nothing. Just would I bring this bag of money to ye. What's it all about? I can't see a man giving up money like that. I do nae understand."

She got up and went to stare into the fire, only half-aware of the captain's questions. She had been wrong about the money all this time. And it was no wonder Ross hadn't questioned the captain about her. The captain had given Ross information merely from what he had said. How like him not to send any message. He didn't want to influence her in any way. What she did would have to be her own decision. He was telling her again that she had to want him as much as he wanted her or it would have little meaning for either of them.

She sat down again and looked into the captain's eyes. "Do you remember when you left I said I had something I wanted to tell you?"

"Aye. I remember. It has to do with this man and this money, does it nae?" A flicker of understanding dawned in his eyes.

She nodded. "Before I left Oregon I married Ross Chesnut." She paused in anticipation of some reaction but all she noticed was a slight narrowing of his eyes. "He wasn't able to go to Fort Vancouver with me because he was still recovering from injuries he had received trying to save me from being kidnapped. When I got to Vancouver, Dr. McLoughlin and I went through our things and I learned that Father had paid Ross twice as much money as agreed upon for guiding us. It was to insure that he would bring me out alive. McLoughlin was asked to keep the money and not to give it to Ross unless he was satisfied that Ross had done his job. Otherwise, the money was to be the reward for his life.

"Ross hadn't told me about the money and I suddenly found myself wondering if he had married me to save his own life as well as for the money. I didn't know, and there was no time to find out. But that doesn't matter now. The doubt was there and when I got on that ship I didn't think I would ever return. That is why I didn't tell you before. I honestly wanted to fall in love with you, Duncan. I could have very easily once. You know that. But I'm still in love with Ross Chesnut and I can't love you until I can stop loving him."

McNeal stood up and turned away. "I'm sorry, too, lass." He was silent for a few minutes, then he turned back to her. "I was ready to give up the sea for ye. Maybe 'tis just as well. I would nae been happy bein' a landlubber."

"Then you can forgive me?"

He smiled sadly. "Aye. The ship is my home and the sea is my mistress. She would nae let me go anymore than your love for this man would let ye go."

She rose and they held each other for a moment in gentle understanding.

Finally Duncan whispered, "I best be leavin' ye now, lass. Goodbye, and good luck to ye."

She stepped away from him and smiled tremulously. "Thank you, Duncan, for what could have been."

He smiled briefly and went for his coat. She watched him leave and turned back to the pile of coins glimmering on the settee.

Martha cautiously opened the door from the kitchen. "Is he gone?"

Marlette looked up and smiled, suddenly relaxed, and miraculously freed from the depression that had enveloped her for so many months. "Yes. He's gone."

"For good?"

Marlette nodded, her eyes returning to the pile of coins. Martha came to the settee and looked down on the small fortune scattered so carelessly.

"Are you going to tell me about it now?"

Marlette picked up the ring that lay among the silver and slipped it on her finger. "The man who sent me this money is my husband. I married him before I left Oregon. When I left I thought he had deceived me because he didn't tell me Father had paid him double to bring me out alive. Nor did he tell me his life depended on my verification that he had not betrayed us. I didn't tell you about it because I thought it was over."

"But it isn't over, is it?"

"No, Martha. I still love him. This money only proves how stupid I have been." She began to cry again as she thought of all the unhappiness she had brought upon herself. Stupid was not strong enough to describe her act. All this time she had been ashamed and now she knew why. She was not ashamed of Ross; she realized now she would be proud to introduce him to anyone she knew. He was more of a man than any man she had ever known. The irony of it! She had been ashamed of having given herself to him before marriage, and because she knew she wouldn't have changed what had happened between them for anything. What a hypocrite she had been! She had carried on like a martyr, feeding on her self-pity, forgiving him for wronging her and loving him still. How wise he had been. He had known how frail the slender thread of her love was. He had told her specifically that no matter what happened he would always love her. How quickly she had forgotten and doubted and she understood now why he had gone through the ordeal of a church wedding. He had known it was she who needed to be reminded that they were bound for life, for better or for worse. She wasn't worthy of his love.

Martha interrupted her thoughts. "Are you going back to him?"

Marlette wiped away her tears. "I don't know if I could stand going there again."

Martha sat down beside her and slipped a comforting arm around her. "You haven't been happy since you came back. I only know what I read in your journal about him but I don't think you will ever be happy unless you are with him."

"It's a long, hard, and dangerous trip. Would you want to risk it?"

"Are you asking my opinion or inviting me to go with you?"

Marlette smiled with pleasure at the idea. "I don't want to go alone, but the decision is yours to make."

"I already told you I would stay with you for as long as I could be of use to you. Maybe I can even find that scoundrel son of mine and tan his hide."

Marlette's face fell. "Oh, Martha. It's an impossible undertaking. It's foolish to even consider it."

Martha looked at her sternly. "I didn't think I'd see the day you'd say anything was impossible. You must not love this man very much if you'd give up so easy."

"I love him enough to know he'd probably be better off without me."

Martha snorted. "You're feelin' sorry for yourself. He didn't send you all that money because he felt he'd be better off without you."

Marlette felt the tears starting again. She got up and said in a trembling voice, "I'm very tired. I'm going to bed."

Martha didn't stop her and she fled into her room, letting the tears flow freely. How she wanted him and needed him. She ached at the thought of him, his touch, his smile, his voice. Regardless of the cost, she knew she had to go to him. She finally fell into an exhausted sleep.

It was late when she awoke in the morning. Her first thought was of Ross, but it was no longer a disturbing thought. She had made her decision and now she would act on it.

She fairly leaped out of bed. If they were to reach the Missouri by April, there was much to be done. She dressed hurriedly, anxious now to be on her way. Her spirits were soaring when she entered the kitchen.

Martha looked up and smiled approvingly. "I see you have decided."

"Is it so obvious?"

Martha shook her head in self-reproach. "I don't know how I failed to figure out what was eatin' you before."

Marlette put an arm around her and kissed her smooth cheek. "Do you want to go with me?"

"You don't need to ask, do you?"

Marlette smiled knowingly. "Do you have any idea what you are letting yourself in for?"

"No. And maybe it's just as well I don't, because I'm not sure I haven't lost my feeble mind."

Marlette laughed and hugged her again. "I'll start looking for a wagon today. I suppose it would be wise to find some people to travel with and maybe hire someone to drive our wagon." She paused, thoughtfully. "I wonder—?" But didn't finish.

"Wonder what?"

Marlette sat down at the table seeing Cam Galligher's face in her mind. If she had read those eyes correctly and the intent behind his words, he would be foolish enough to try to make it to the Oregon Country on his own.

"Do you remember when I got back from that trip to upper New York before the election?"

Martha laughed sharply. "I can't forget that. I never had seen you quite so depressed before."

"While I was there I saw a man who looked like he was related to Ross. I was able to get him to take me to see his mother. They wouldn't tell me anything. However, this man had a son of about sixteen who drove me back to town. He was able to tell me enough so that I am sure they are related. The boy, Cam, was very interested in Ross and in Oregon. If I wrote and told him I was going, I believe he would come, too."

Martha frowned. "That wouldn't be right."

"I know it isn't right. It wasn't right for them to deny Ross, but they did. Cam knows about him now and I feel sure, with or without me, he will eventually leave home to find Ross."

Martha shrugged her shoulders noncommittally. "Suit yourself. But I don't approve."

"Will it make a difference in your going?"

Martha looked sharply at Marlette's inquiring face and answered slowly, "No. I'd worry if I wasn't with you. I won't let it stand between us."

A Promise Kept

MARLETTE WROTE a letter to Cam Galligher immediately. She felt guilty knowing she was going to cause the boy to make a decision. She was careful not to invite him or mention when she was leaving. If he wanted to come badly enough, the decision had to be entirely his without any urging from her.

The next couple of weeks were busy ones. She had to buy supplies, horses, and a wagon, and she planned to take a crate of chickens, a cow, and a calf. She knew the value of fresh eggs and milk and if necessary, the animals themselves could be eaten. There was no need to take up wagon space with anything but the bare essentials; she now had the money to ship some of her furniture to her new home. She would yet feel Ross beside her in her own bed and the thought excited her. With a forced lack of sentimentality she discarded everything that wasn't absolutely necessary. It was a painful process but a necessary one. Even Martha felt she was being too efficient when it came to the smallest of keepsakes. At last in compromise they filled a trunk with things they decided they could not part with and arranged to send it with the furniture and a beautiful new stove.

Marlette also set aside enough money to repay John Finlayson for his losses on the business. She had been trying to save the money she owed him but it had been a slow process and less than half had been accumulated. It was just one more load off her mind when she arranged for the money to be delivered to him after she left. He would be amazed that she had found out what she owed him and she smiled with satisfaction.

She also wrote a letter to James Knox Polk. She had to tell him he had been right to overlook her doubts about Ross and that she was going west to join her husband. Husband! She fairly trembled at the thought and she felt bursting with love for him. She wished the president well and invited him to visit them in Oregon.

Two days before they were ready to leave Cam Galligher knocked on their door. Marlette welcomed him with a happy smile. "Cam! You're just in time."

He stared at her curiously. "You knew I'd come?"

She laughed. "That's why I wrote you."

He looked at her with boyish admiration. "How did you know I was thinking of it?"

"I saw it in your eyes. I thought it was better if you went with me than by yourself."

His smile broadened. "How soon do we leave?"

"Now that you're here, we can start tomorrow."

Martha came through the door, a look of disapproval on her face. "Is this the boy?"

"Yes. Cam, this is Martha. She is going with us."

"Glad to meet you, ma'am."

Martha nodded curtly.

"Don't mind her, Cam. She thinks I was wrong in writing to you."

"I would've gone anyway. After I read your book I made up my mind to go."

"See, Martha. I told you it would make no difference."

Martha stared silently at Cam. "Is this what your man looks like?"

Marlette turned back to Cam and appraised him. He had grown since she last saw him and was now as tall as Ross. The boyishness was turning into assuredness and he carried himself with the same certainty that Ross had. He still needed to fill out but that would come in time. He had the same chestnut hair and dark eyes but he would never have the captivating dimples and his nose was not as finely shaped, nor his mouth quite as full. These traits must have come from Abigail. "I'd say he looks enough like him to be his brother rather than a distant cousin."

Cam flashed a pleased smile and the similarity was even more apparent.

Martha's lips quivered a little as her face softened. "Well, he must be a fine-looking man then."

They stood looking at each other, their smiles broadening until they laughed together in mutual understanding.

That night, sleeping for the last time in her own bed, Marlette began to have second thoughts about Cam. She wondered if he realized how deeply this break with his family might become. It was one thing for a married man to run off to the wilderness with his bride but Cam was still a boy. She couldn't sleep and finally she got up and tiptoed to his door. Quietly she opened it and saw him stir restlessly. Softly she whispered, "Cam, are you awake?"

"Yes."

She came across the floor and sat down at the foot of his bed. "I've been thinking about the trip and I was wondering if you realized how this might affect your relationship with your family?"

"I'm not worried about their reaction anymore."

"Do you realize they may disown you as they did Ross's father? And what about your church? We will have little contact with your religion until we reach Oregon. Will it bother you?"

"I've thought about it a lot since you were at our place. The more I thought about it the more I felt they were wrong. Ever since I was little they preached about love, understanding, and forgiveness for sinners. But as I got older I realized what a lie it all was. They never forgave anybody and they certainly never tried to love or forgive Great-Uncle Ross. Maybe he did sin, I don't know. But we were also taught that children are innocent and if that is true, then your Ross is innocent and should be welcomed into the family, but he never was and never will be. Maybe I'm too young to understand but I know only one way to find out if I'm right."

Marlette smiled at his serious face. It was the type of reasoning another Galligher would have used in the same circumstances. It reassured her that she had done the right thing.

He mistook her silence for disapproval. "Do you think I'm wrong?"

"No, Cam. I was just thinking how much like Ross you sound."

He smiled. "Do I?"

"Yes. But don't think I won't tell you when you don't sound like him."

He chuckled softly. "Yes, ma'am."

She placed a hand on his arm. "Good night, Cam."

In the morning they ate their last breakfast in Philadelphia. The wagon had been loaded the day before with Cam's help and they were all ready to leave. John Finlayson came to take care of the things that were to be shipped and they exchanged sincere but not entirely sad good-byes. They finally climbed into the wagon, bundled against the uncertain chill of late February. It would be a long, cold trip to Pittsburgh over the mountains, more than three hundred miles away.

At Pittsburgh they met up with other travelers heading west and joined forces with a family named Jessup. The Jessup's had three sons and a young daughter, and Cam struck up an instant friendship with their middle son. Marlette also found a friend in Mrs. Jessup and the traveling became more pleasant. The Jessups had intended to hire a flatboat and drift down the Ohio to Evansville and then proceed across country again to St. Louis. It sounded like a good plan to Marlette and she readily joined them. They welcomed the additional money since their own finances were barely enough to hire a decent boat. With five strong men to help the captain of the boat, they didn't need to hire additional help.

The river was high and muddy the morning they started out. They drifted along at a fast pace but it was a constant challenge to avoid snags, drift, and bars that were hidden in the dirty brown water. Fortunately the captain knew the river well and they avoided most of the trouble spots. The captain decided it was wise for them to join other boats along the way for mutual protection and assistance. The Indian threat was not as formidable as it once had been, but there were still unscrupulous white men who would use any devious means to obtain their supplies and livestock. The company of half a dozen clumsy flatboats propelled by well-armed men must have been too formidable a challenge for the river pirates, because they had no trouble. Marlette thrived on the excitement of the voyage, so vastly different from her other two trips.

As the days slipped by she grew increasingly anxious. Had they started soon enough? Would they be able to make it in time to join a wagon train or would they be stranded on the frontier? The thought that they might not get there at all never crossed her mind.

The captain of the flatboat convinced them that they would save time by continuing on to the Mississippi by boat rather than overland to St. Louis. They agreed they made better time by boat with less wear and tear on the equipment and animals.

By the middle of April they reached Cairo, on the Mississippi. Marlette, worried about the time, felt they should try to find passage on a steamboat going upriver. It would be much faster and they were running out of time. The Jessups, however, couldn't afford the fare and Marlette didn't want to leave them behind. If it hadn't been for the Jessups they would not have made it down the Ohio. She decided to pay their way, although it meant a dent in her precious savings.

On the steamboat they had a real vacation, free from worry about losing the boat in a rapids or ramming into snags, although snags were still a menace this time of year on the Mississippi. But it was no longer their personal problem. After the first few days she never regretted paying the passage for the Jessups. The happiness and rest it gave them all was more than enough compensation.

There were many people on the boat to join the wagon train west. The captain of the steamboat advised them that people had been coming in for more than a month and supplies were dwindling as people bought up everything available. There was now a waiting list for incoming supplies. Marlette discovered the captain was bringing supplies to the merchants at Independence and she asked him to sell her what they needed. She was afraid their late arrival would leave them no recourse for obtaining much-needed supplies. At first the captain refused, but she wouldn't take no for an answer. She shadowed him night and day, never allowing him a moment's peace until he finally agreed to sell her what she wanted at one and a half times their original cost. She knew even at that price they were a bargain, because the demand was so great out there they would probably be twice or three times the original cost.

They reached Independence, Missouri near the first of May. The city was teeming with people and wagons. They couldn't have rented a place to stay even if they had wanted to. They camped outside of town on the edge of the prairie which would be their highway and home for many weeks to come. Their first business was to find the wagon train leader and they decided to send Marlette since she had bargained so successfully with the captain. They also realized someone had to stay with the wagons at all times to guard their precious store of supplies.

With Cam leading the way to break trail in the crowded town they went in search of the train leader. Wagons and buckboards stirred up the dust in the road and the streets, such as they were, were alive with hurrying, sweating, and shoving people. Marlette, following closely behind Cam, looked away for a moment as they came to the edge of the walk, and bumped into him. He had stopped abruptly and was staring intently across the street.

"What is it, Cam?"

With a strange tremor in his voice he asked, "Didn't you say I looked like him?"

Marlette heard the excitement in his voice and followed his gaze across the street to the elevated porch of a store. She let out a gasp as she saw a familiar figure standing against the porch post in an attitude of watchful bewilderment. She pushed around Cam and ran into the street, oblivious to a buckboard coming briskly toward her. The driver hauled in on the team so sharply they reared and he yelled at her in surprised profanity but she heard nothing beyond the pounding of her heart.

The commotion caught the attention of the man on the porch and he looked toward Marlette and straightened as he recognized her. At that moment a large conestoga came wheeling around the corner and blocked Ross from her sight for a few timeless seconds. When the wagon finally passed he was in front of her, hugging her tightly with a look of indescribable joy on his face. Their lips touched and clung and Marlette forgot everything around her. She heard nothing and saw nothing and was aware only of her overwhelming happiness.

When their lips finally parted, she opened her eyes and heard the cheers and laughter around her. She looked about in embarrassment and saw wagons halted and people grinning. Ross lifted her in his arms and carried her to the porch, setting her on her feet. She clung to him.

Eagerly they asked one another, "Were you coming—?" and laughed happily as they answered in unison, "Yes."

The crowd moved on and they were completely alone, wrapped in their own cocoon of love, feasting on one another's face, until tears blurred Marlette's vision and she hid her face against his chest. She felt him tense against her and she looked up to see what was wrong. He was staring intently over the top of her head and she wiped away her tears and looked around. Cam was standing behind her.

"Who is this?"

Marlette saw the confusion of recognition and disbelief widen his dark eyes. She laughed gaily. "Do you recognize him?"

"It's like looking in a mirror."

"Ross, this is Cam Galligher, the son of your cousin."

Slowly his face broke into a smile of surprised pleasure, and his hand went out to take the slightly smaller copy that came eagerly forward.

"Is that what my name is, Galligher?"

Cam answered, "Yes, sir."

Ross shook his head and looked at Marlette, still holding Cam's hand. "Is he going home with us?"

Marlette nodded her head, too happy to speak.

"Well, then, let's get started."

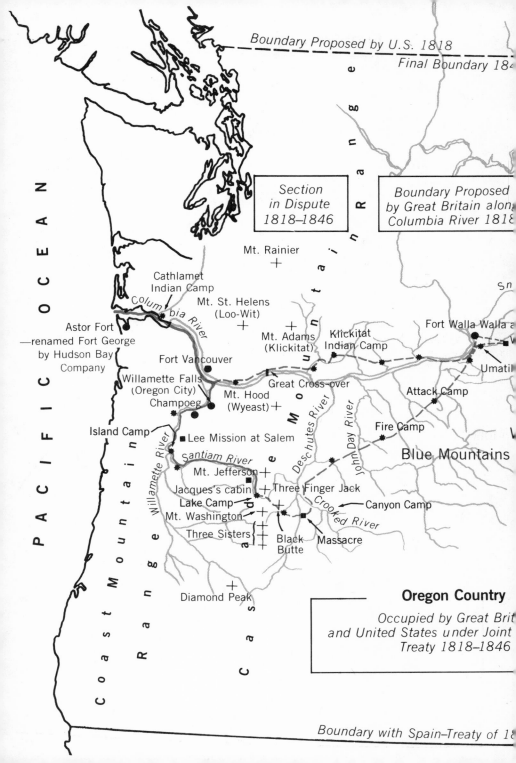

Boundary Proposed by U.S. 1818

Final Boundary 184

Section in Dispute 1818–1846

Boundary Proposed by Great Britain alon Columbia River 1818

PACIFIC OCEAN

R   a   n   g   e

M   o   u   n   t   a   i   n

Mt. Rainier
+

Cathlamet Indian Camp

Columbia River

Mt. St. Helens (Loo-Wit)
+

Astor Fort —renamed Fort George by Hudson Bay Company

Fort Vancouver

Mt. Adams (Klickitat)
+

Klickitat Indian Camp

Fort Walla Walla

Umati

Willamette Falls (Oregon City)

Great Cross-over

Champoeg

Mt. Hood (Wyeast)
+

Attack Camp

Island Camp

Lee Mission at Salem

Santiam River

Deschutes River

John Day River

Fire Camp

C   a   s   c   a   d   e

Willamette River

Mt. Jefferson
+

Jacques's cabin

Three Finger Jack

Lake Camp

Mt. Washington
+

Canyon Camp

Crooked River

Blue Mountains

Three Sisters
+ + +

Black Butte

Massacre

Diamond Peak
+

Coast   Mountain   Range

Oregon Country

Occupied by Great Brit and United States under Joint Treaty 1818–1846

Boundary with Spain–Treaty of 18